The
Island
We Left
Behind

The
Island
We Left
Behind

Kate Hewitt

bookouture

Published by Bookouture in 2021

An imprint of Storyfire Ltd.
Carmelite House
50 Victoria Embankment
London EC4Y 0DZ

www.bookouture.com

ISBN: 978-1-80019-896-8
eBook ISBN: 978-1-80019-895-1

To my own Ellen—have you changed your mind about Lucas yet? And to Caroline, who always knew. And to my dear Mom, who is a true 'island girl'.

CHAPTER ONE

NEW YORK CITY, JANUARY 1929

The cry echoed through the upstairs of the house, followed by the terrible, rattling coughing that sent Ellen's heart racing, panic clenching her insides.

She started from the chair in her son Jamie's bedroom where she'd briefly succumbed to sleep, after waiting hours for him to settle, praying that he finally would.

"Jamie... Jamie, darling." She dropped to her knees by his bed as she touched his flushed forehead. His pain-glazed eyes were full of misery as he looked at her, each breath drawn from his frail chest a painful rasp.

"Mama..." he gasped out. "When will it stop hurting?"

"Soon, I promise. Soon." She pressed one hand to his chest and felt the telltale rattle that had plagued him repeatedly since his birth just over five years ago. "I'll get a poultice," she promised him, doing her best to keep her voice from catching. "It will help."

As she rose from the bed, she saw Rosie, her seven-year-old daughter, standing in the doorway, looking far too wise for her years, with her large hazel eyes unblinking. "Will he ever get better?" she asked softly.

"Yes, of course he will." Ellen forced a reassuring smile she didn't really feel. "You know how he gets in winter. It will pass, I promise. I'm sorry he woke you."

While Rosie watched from the doorway, Ellen went down to the kitchen, reaching for the ingredients she knew so well in the dark—mustard powder, flour, a square of cotton muslin. She mixed the flour and mustard into a paste with a bit of warm water and spread it on the cloth. Jamie hated the smell, but sometimes it was the only thing that helped ease the dreadful rattling in his chest.

Back upstairs, her poor, wee boy was tossing and turning in his twisted sheets, his face flushed and feverish as that hacking cough seemed like it might tear his slight frame to pieces. He'd been fine that evening, she thought with a now-familiar mix of fear and guilt. Perfectly fine, save for a little tickle in the throat that always made her worry. Still, if she'd suspected he might get as bad as this, she would have moved him into the bed she'd set up in her dressing room several years ago, so she could be near him in the night. As it was, she'd sent him to bed with a hot-water bottle and a kiss on the forehead—a forehead that was now burning with fever. Would it ever end?

She glanced back at Rosie. "Go back to bed, darling. I'll be with you in a little while, after Jamie is settled again."

Rosie hesitated, looking reluctant, and then she silently slipped away. Ellen heard the click of her bedroom door closing a few seconds later.

"Jamie... Jamie, darling." She smoothed his sweaty hair away from his forehead—the same sandy brown hair as his father's. Jamie was Lucas Lyman in miniature, Ellen had often thought, with identical blue eyes too, his studious manner and quiet kindness, albeit also with the impish fearlessness of a five-year-old. Unlike Lucas, who had always had a robust constitution, Jamie had, after a long and difficult premature birth, been born frail and prone to sickness.

"He's likely always to have weak lungs, if he survives," the doctor had told her with brutal matter-of-factness as Ellen cradled her newborn son in her arms, almost as if she could shield him from the news. "Infants born so early often do."

"What will that mean for him?" she'd asked anxiously. "What can we do? There must be something—"

"Not very much, I'm afraid." The doctor had been kindly but dismissive. "Don't let him exert himself too much or become too breathless. And be careful with even the common cold—it could so easily develop into pneumonia, which is, as I'm sure you know, so often fatal." He'd glanced at the scrap of an infant, so beloved, so small. "But try not to wrap him in cotton wool. That wouldn't be good for him, either."

When Ellen and Lucas had taken him home, Ellen had been terrified to leave him for so much as a moment. She'd spent hours looming over his cradle, watching him breathe, willing him to be strong, his life all the more precious because the doctor had told her, with the same matter-of-factness he'd delivered his other painful prognosis, that due to the difficult delivery she was unlikely to have any more children.

With two-year-old Rosie to care for as well, she hadn't been able to indulge her concern for her small son as she might have wished, and in any case, Lucas had always been insistent that they give Jamie as normal a life as possible. Five years on, Ellen still struggled with how much to let him do, torn between longing to keep him safe and wanting him to have the fun any little boy would long for.

She had enough experience with weak lungs and sickbeds; her own mother had died from a similar condition, but she'd lived in the sooty rail yards of Springburn, back in Glasgow where Ellen had been born. Little Jamie had had the advantage of the clean air of the countryside outside Toronto, at least as a baby. Now, living in New York, the air was not as fresh, but it certainly wasn't anything like what Ellen had experienced growing up—clothes on the line coated with coal dust, the vegetables in the market stall covered with a layer of grime, every breath clogging in your lungs.

Springburn felt a very long way from Manhattan, Ellen

reflected as she gazed down tenderly at her young son. As she smoothed his sweat-dampened hair from his brow, she recalled the journey that had taken her across the ocean so many years ago.

When she'd been only thirteen, Ellen had emigrated to Seaton, Vermont, with her father Douglas. They'd sailed past the elegant, blank-eyed Lady of Liberty and Ellen had only just dodged being sent back for looking scrawny, terrified she'd be separated from her father forever—a fear which didn't come true then, but soon after. They'd had plans to live with family in Vermont. But after just a few weeks, Ellen's father had grown restless with life in a small town, and he'd set out for the rail yards of New Mexico, leaving Ellen with an aunt and uncle she'd barely known. But then she'd spent a summer on Amherst Island in Lake Ontario, with Douglas's warm-hearted sister Rose and her husband Dyle and their noisy, lovable brood of five children—and she had found a home at last.

For several years, Ellen had traveled between her beloved island in Ontario and Vermont, before starting nursing school in Kingston, a practical job for a girl who had spent her childhood tending her mam in a sickroom.

That brief period seemed a long time ago, too; after just a year in nursing school, an illness and what she'd thought was a broken heart had forced her to change her plans, and she'd returned to Glasgow to attend its prestigious School of Art, until the Great War had broken out and she'd nursed on the Front for four years, before returning to her beloved island—and realizing she'd been in love with her childhood friend all along.

She and Lucas had been married now for over eight happy years, and Ellen thanked God every day for the life she enjoyed, determined never to take its blessings for granted.

Another cough shook Jamie's chest and he glanced up at her with glazed eyes. "Sorry... Mama..." he managed to get out.

"You never need be sorry, darling," Ellen returned, her tone both gentle and fierce as she touched his hot cheek. "Do you want to sleep in my dressing room again?"

He nodded, looking even younger than his five years, and Ellen scooped up his slight frame as easily as she had when he'd been a baby.

Within a few minutes, she had him settled on the cot in the dressing room adjoining her and Lucas's bedroom. Her son smiled at her weakly as the cough rattled through his lungs, and then, after a few more minutes, he finally, thankfully, settled back into sleep, his breath still rasping but without the terrible coughs that tore at his body—and Ellen's heart.

After a few more minutes of simply watching him sleep, satisfied he was finally settled, she tiptoed to Rosie's room to say goodnight, but as she peeked around the door, she saw her daughter had already fallen back asleep, curled on her side, knees tucked up to her chest, her chestnut hair spread across her pillow. Ellen's heart ached as she gazed at her little girl, who was so often stoic and silent in light of her brother's ailments—never complaining, but also choosing to keep her own counsel in a way that made Ellen worry. Surely a seven-year-old girl shouldn't have to be so serious? Yet she knew she'd once been the same.

Ellen closed the door again and then went quietly downstairs, where a light still burned in Lucas's study, even though it was after midnight. They had moved to New York City four years ago, when Lucas had been offered a position with a large, well-regarded law firm, managing the accounts of several prestigious corporations. Ellen had been reluctant to leave their cozy home on the outskirts of Toronto—her cousin Peter, the oldest of Rose and Dyle's children, lived in the city, an affable bachelor at twenty-nine and working as a clerk for The Dominion Bank, and her Aunt Rose and cousin Sarah were not too far away, living in Gananoque. Sarah was married now, with a young son, and Rose lived with the little family. Ellen and Lucas had often had Peter to dinner, and it wasn't so far to travel to Gananoque to see Aunt Rose and Sarah.

They'd even rented a house on Amherst Island for several summers, which had been bittersweet; her beloved island didn't quite feel like home anymore, and yet it still was the place Ellen loved most in the world. Her cousin Caro, the oldest McCafferty daughter, and her husband and war veteran, Jack Fleming, had held on to their little farm, and they now had two children of their own, in addition to the three little ones they'd adopted after their mother had died of the Spanish flu right after the war.

Since moving to New York City, visits up north had become all too infrequent, and Ellen hadn't seen any of the McCaffertys in over a year, save for Gracie, who had moved to the city two years ago but had been too busy lately to keep in touch. Ellen hadn't seen her in six months, at least, and she'd never known her as well as her older cousins; she'd been a little girl when Ellen had left for Glasgow, to take up her place at the city's School of Art.

Her and Lucas's most recent summers were now spent exchanging the city's heat for the breezy cool of the Hamptons, the playground of the city's bored and wealthy. As Lucas's career had risen, so had his ambitions, although he remained as mild and cheerful as ever, the man who had captured Ellen's heart without her even realizing.

She pushed open the door to the study and regarded her husband with a tender, rueful smile. Hard at work as always, his sandy head was bent beneath the green shade of a brass banker's lamp that cast a pool of golden light across the floor. Unaware of her presence, he continued working while Ellen watched him, caught between exasperation and a deep, abiding love. Eight years on and she loved Lucas more than ever—their strong friendship had grown into an abiding love as well as a surprising passion, and while their marriage had held its share of sorrows as well as joys— the impossibility of any more children had grieved them both sorely—she knew she had no regrets. She was so very thankful not just for Lucas, but Rosie and Jamie, as well. She had finally found her heart's home, and it wasn't on her beloved island, after all. It was with the people she loved.

Finally, after a few minutes, Lucas looked up, a smile creasing his face and crinkling his hazel eyes. "How long have you been standing there?"

"Not too long."

"Long enough." He glanced wryly at the mantel clock ticking the hour. "I should have been in bed an hour ago, I know."

"At least." Ellen crossed the room to put her arms around him as she dropped a kiss on the top of his head. "You work too hard, Lucas."

"I know." He gave her a wry, apologetic grimace and squeezed her hand before turning back to his work and, with a tiny sigh, she straightened and moved to the window, pulling the heavy velvet drape across the glass to keep out the January draught. It had been a cold winter this year; some people had thought the East River might freeze. Ellen had made sure to wrap Jamie up warmly and keep him inside as much as possible, yet he'd still developed this cough. As she moved away, Lucas picked up his pen again.

If she had any reservations or worries about her marriage, Ellen reflected, they were lodged in that seemingly insignificant act— Lucas picking up his pen at half past twelve in the morning. Since their move to Manhattan, he'd become increasingly driven and ambitious, working until the small hours more nights than Ellen would ever wish. He tried to kiss the children goodnight every evening, and most days he managed it, brief as it was. He doted on them on the weekends, and Ellen had never doubted his love for her or the children, not even for a moment. But she had become all too used to spending the evenings alone, stirring sleepily to find her husband slipping in next to her hours after she'd gone to bed, pulling her toward him with a sleepy kiss and a murmured apology.

"Jamie was coughing again," she told him as she turned from the window. "And he seems feverish, as well. I'm worried it could become pneumonia."

"I thought he seemed a little quiet earlier." Lucas frowned. "I suppose the cold weather doesn't help his chest, and this month has been one of the coldest on record."

Ellen nodded soberly. "The snow started falling on the first of January and it still hasn't let up three weeks later."

"Should he see the doctor?" Lucas asked. "Dr. Thornton is always willing to listen to his chest."

"Little good that it ever seems to do." Visits to the doctor meant more of the same advice—stay inside, wrap up warmly, mustard poultices and prayer. There was little else that could be done.

"Still, it can't hurt." He reached out a hand, catching her fingers in his own. "And if it keeps you from worrying..."

"I don't think anything will keep me from worrying."

"I know, darling." Lucas pulled her gently towards him, and with a small smile, Ellen let him ease her onto his lap, his arms around her. "I'm sorry."

"It's just so miserable for him," Ellen said as she leaned her head against his chest. "I want him to have fun, to run and jump and play like any other little boy..."

"But you also want him to be well. It's forever been the dilemma, hasn't it? I'll call Dr. Thornton in the morning. Perhaps he'll have some better advice than to keep poor Jamie wrapped up. I'll feel better talking to him, anyway."

"But if it develops into pneumonia..." Ellen couldn't keep the fear from her voice.

Lucas's arms tightened around her. "It won't. We'll make sure of it."

She nodded, her head still against his chest, even though she knew, of course, he could promise no such thing.

"He's sleeping now?" he asked.

"Yes... I moved him into the dressing room though, just in case he wakes." She fell silent as they both listened for the familiar tortured rasp of their son's coughing, but the house was quiet, the only sound the settling of the dying embers in the grate. Ellen twisted in his arms to look up at his face, so familiar and dear. "Come to bed, Lucas."

He smiled, and Ellen knew it was an apology. "In a little while, I promise."

"What is so important you have to work on it at this hour?" She glanced at the papers on his desk, but the columns of figures were indecipherable to her. She knew Lucas handled the legal research for several important corporate cases, and advised on their investments as well. But other men didn't work so far into the night, surely.

"I won't be long."

Ellen chose not to press the matter. They'd had this conversation too many times before; in the past, Lucas had given way good-naturedly, but more recently Ellen had sometimes picked up an unusual and increasing tension from him that she tried not to let hurt.

"And Jamie?" she asked.

"I'll call the doctor in the morning, I promise."

"But will you come to the appointment?"

Lucas hesitated, and then nodded. "Yes, of course I will."

Restlessly, she rose from his lap and prowled about the room while Lucas watched her, his eyebrows knitted together in concern. "I can't bear it if Dr. Thornton says the same thing yet again," she said. "I won't just stand by and watch Jamie struggle. There must be something more we can do to help him."

He nodded soberly. "I know how hard it is for you."

"Isn't it hard for you?" she asked in reply, and he sat back, surprised, a look of hurt flashing across his face.

"Of course it is. You know that, surely. I only meant that mothers feel these matters even more sorely."

"Perhaps they do, when fathers work so hard," Ellen returned before she could keep herself from it, and Lucas sighed.

"I'll come up soon, I promise."

Ellen bit her lip, doing her best to keep from saying something else she would regret. She and Lucas never fought; he was far too even-tempered for that, even when she felt querulous, which over the years had been rare indeed. How could she be cross with a man who was so gentle, wry, loving and warm? Lately, however, she'd sometimes wished he'd raise his voice, show his ire the way she wanted to, but he never did. It was one of the things she loved about him, and yet at moments like this she almost wanted a proper, blazing row, or at least something close to it, rather than this new, insidious, unspoken tension that coiled its invisible tendrils around them both.

Lucas, she saw, had already returned to his work, absorbed once again in his columns of figures. She slipped out of the room without him noticing.

A year ago, they'd moved from their apartment on the Upper West Side—three bedrooms, a living room, dining room, and kitchen—to this tall and elegant brownstone by Central Park, just two blocks from where the great Andrew Carnegie had built his magnificent residence, and where his wife Louise still lived. The neighborhood, from Madison Avenue to the park and Eighty-Sixth Street up to Ninety-Third had come to be known as Carnegie Hill, after the industrialist's grand mansion, and it was home to many wealthy bankers and businessmen, most of whom Ellen had never had the occasion to meet, although Lucas rubbed elbows with enough of them through work.

Compared to the Carnegie mansion or the Italian-style palazzo across the street, their own narrow brownstone was suitably modest, and yet it still was the grandest house Ellen had ever lived in, with its servants' quarters in the attic, five bedrooms below and a gracious drawing and dining room on the main floor, the kitchen in the basement beneath. Ellen's favorite part was the garden, a narrow rectangle of green bordered with flowers that reminded her just a little of her dear island.

A year on, however, she still felt a little uncomfortable with the level of luxury they now enjoyed—a live-out cook, Maisy, as well as Eva, live-in maid; a chauffeured car Lucas took to work; dinner parties on the weekends, stuffy affairs Ellen and Lucas laughed about after, for all the pretensions of their newfound company. Sometimes Ellen could hardly believe this was her life—she, the tangle-haired lass from Springburn with coal smuts on her cheek! And yet she would trade it all for a son who was healthy and whole, and both her and Lucas to finally be free of these fears for Jamie.

She rested one hand on the bannister of carved wood, gazing unseeingly around the marble-floored foyer, the table and hatstand now cloaked in shadows, the tall grandfather clock marking out the hours, before she slowly walked upstairs to return to bed alone.

"That rattle in his chest does worry me."

Ellen stared at Dr. Thornton in alarm as he pressed the cold metal stethoscope to Jamie's scrawny chest. It was the day after she'd woken up to his coughing, and although his fever had broken, Jamie still looked flushed and miserable, coughing every few minutes, although he tried to stop it, pressing his lips together in brave yet futile effort. Rosie had gone happily to school that morning, through drifts of new snow; she had started at The Nightingale-Bamford School, located only a block away from their house, that September.

Lucas had accompanied them to the appointment, and now he leaned forward, his brows knitted together. "Worries you?" he repeated. "Do you mean more than usual?"

Dr. Thornton was silent for a moment, looking so serious that Ellen clenched her hands together in her lap, trying not to show her panic. "He hasn't had a clear chest all winter," he finally replied as he put his stethoscope away. He patted Jamie's shoulder kindly. "Put your shirt on, lad. Don't want you going blue with cold."

Ellen leaned over to help Jamie button his shirt, but with a frustrated glance, he pushed her hand away, wanting to do it himself. She sat back, chastened. Lucas was always telling her Jamie needed more independence, more freedom, and yet she couldn't seem to give it to him, as much as he wanted it.

"So what do you recommend?" Lucas asked, and again the doctor hesitated before speaking.

"Jamie, why don't you go out into the waiting room for a minute, while I speak with your parents? There should be some peppermint drops my secretary can give you."

Jamie glanced uncertainly at his parents before Lucas gave him an encouraging smile. "Go on then, son."

As soon as the door had closed behind him, Dr. Thornton turned to them both with a sober look. "It's been a miserable winter already," he said, "and it looks only to get worse. They're saying the snow won't stop until April." A pause while Ellen and Lucas both waited, silent and anxious. "I don't think with his current constitution Jamie can withstand such a winter."

"You're worried he'll get pneumonia?" Lucas said gravely, and the doctor turned to him, his face set in grim lines as he gave them both a frank look.

"I'm worried he won't survive."

Ellen drew her breath in sharply, one fist pressed to her mouth. It was what she had always dreaded, and yet to hear the doctor voice her darkest fears out loud was so much worse than to battle them in the quiet of her own mind.

Dr. Thornton held up a placating hand. "Now, I don't want to frighten you. If you kept him inside all winter wrapped up in blankets and never seeing anyone, then perhaps he'd manage. But that's no life for a little boy, and in truth the inactivity could make him weaker. No, what he needs is a change of scene, a change of climate. A chance to strengthen his lungs along with his legs, to grow a little stronger, a little taller. If he could have a winter, or even a whole year, in a warmer, drier climate, without succumbing to these coughs and fevers, he'd have a chance of growing up into a reasonably healthy adult, or really, growing up at all." The smile he gave them was full of sympathy, touched by sorrow. "I'm sorry to recommend so drastic a remedy, but at this point I really think it's his best chance."

"A warmer, drier climate," Lucas repeated. "What exactly are you suggesting?"

"If you were willing, I'd suggest relocating for three months to Arizona or California. Better yet, six months, at least until summer."

Ellen's mouth dropped open in amazement. She thought of the

hot compresses, mustard poultices, and foul-smelling liniments Dr. Thornton had suggested over the years, all to little avail. She'd never considered a solution as drastic as this, and yet she knew she'd do anything to ensure Jamie's health. His survival.

"Six months..." she repeated slowly, her mind reeling.

"Or at least three. Such a climate could do wonders for his lungs as well as his constitution, and more time might mean a permanent change for the better. Obviously, such a solution is not possible for everyone, but I thought I should suggest it. Otherwise, I'm afraid it's the usual remedies—wrap up warmly, stay inside..."

More or less a prison sentence for a small boy who wanted to run and play, as Lucas often told her. "When I was his age," Lucas had stated more than once, "I was tearing through the woods, getting into all sorts of scrapes. I know we live in the city, but I want that sort of freedom for Jamie."

"As I recall," Ellen had returned wryly, "when you were a boy, you were often curled up in a windowsill, reading a book or sketching plants."

Lucas had simply smiled, shaking his head. "That may be so, but I still had my fair share of excitement. Jed wasn't the only one who liked to explore the wood." Although he had spoken lightly enough, his voice had held the very slightest undercurrent of resentment, or perhaps just memory; although they never spoke of it and it hardly mattered, Ellen knew neither of them could forget that she'd fallen in love with his brother Jed first, or at least thought she had. For several years, she'd nursed a broken heart, an indulgence she now regarded ruefully. It had been puppy love, no more than girlish infatuation, forgotten in the light of the deep love she felt for Lucas.

Jed and his wife Louisa, a childhood friend and erstwhile enemy of Ellen's, had been living in Seaton, Vermont, since after the war. Jed, a farmer born and bred, had become a banker for his wife's sake. After the loss of their little son from influenza, their marriage had almost broken apart. Louisa had never been cut out to be a farmer's wife, and Jed hadn't liked the thought of town living. And yet, for the sake of their marriage, they'd compromised and, Ellen knew, found happiness in Vermont; Jed took to working in a bank with more ease and enthusiasm than anyone had expected, and Louisa was now the proud mother of two children— Violet, a daughter the same age as Rosie, and another little girl, Imogen, who was a year younger than Jamie.

Her thoughts moved back to the matter at hand... *California.* Could they really go there? She'd been to New Mexico once, a long time ago, to visit her father, but never all the way to the west coast. Yet for Jamie she would do anything. But would Lucas? Could he give up work, the hectic buzz of the city?

"California," Lucas said, and his tone was firm. "That's an excellent suggestion, Dr. Thornton. Thank you."

CHAPTER TWO

"I think it's a capital idea."

Ellen stared at Lucas in wary surprise, her glass half-raised to her lips. They'd had no time to discuss the doctor's suggestion of spending the winter out west, as Lucas had had to rush off to work after Jamie's appointment. It wasn't until that evening, when the children were in bed and they were eating a quiet dinner alone, that they were able to discuss the notion properly.

"You... do?" she asked as their maid Eva cleared away the first course. Even though Lucas had sounded approving of the idea in Dr. Thornton's office, she still couldn't credit that he'd be willing to leave the city for so long.

"Yes, of course, if it makes a difference to Jamie, and it sounds like it will. Really, we haven't any choice in the matter, do we? If Jamie's health, even his survival, is at stake."

"No, I don't suppose we do," Ellen agreed shakily. She'd been trying not to think of Dr. Thornton's grim prognosis if they didn't make the change, and yet it had been tormenting her all day. "I'm glad you are so amenable."

Lucas gave a little shrug. "We can afford it, and California is beautiful, or so I've heard. I've always wanted to visit, see the orange trees, the movie stars." He spread his hands, making it all seem so simple, while Ellen stared at him in wonder and dawning hope from across the mahogany expanse of their dining room table.

"But we'd be gone for three months at least."

"Three months isn't forever."

"No, indeed not, but still, it's a long time to be away from the city." She felt she had to warn him, for she could hardly believe he would be willing to give up work so easily. It caused her an almost painful flare of hope; perhaps Lucas wasn't becoming as obsessed with ambition as she sometimes worried. Perhaps a trip to California could be the remaking of them...

He gave her a teasing smile as he picked up his own glass. "Somehow I don't think you'll mind being away from the city for a time."

No, Ellen reflected, she wouldn't. While she still enjoyed the hustle and bustle of New York, she also found it exhausting. Seven years on and she still missed the green fields of Amherst Island, the sparkling jewel tones of Lake Ontario. The winding dirt roads, the yellow leaves of the birches fringing the pond between the McCafferty and Lyman farms... except they weren't the McCafferty and Lyman farms, not anymore. They'd been sold to a rich islander to make one large holding, and the McCaffertys and Lymans had been scattered to the winds like a handful of chaff.

Although that was, Ellen acknowledged, a touch fanciful. Thinking of the island as it was now always made her feel a bit melancholy, with so many of her loved ones gone from it. Even so, they were not truly scattered to the four winds—merely to Toronto, Gananoque, Vermont and now New York. Not as far as all that, and yet sometimes it felt like she and Lucas were a world apart, especially in their stately home just off Fifth Avenue, eating dinner alone, served by a maid in a black dress and lace-edged apron.

As quietly as a shadow, Eva came back into the room and set their main course—roast duck with a cranberry-orange sauce—in front of them. Ellen murmured her thanks.

"I thought you might mind it," she resumed as she gazed at Lucas, her head cocked. "It is a long time to be away."

He gave a grimacing sort of nod. "I will mind, of course. I'll miss you and the children dearly."

Ellen stilled, an icy sensation of deep disappointment trickling through her veins, turning her cold, even as she realized she'd known his easy acquiescence was too good to be true. "Miss us," she repeated slowly. "So you mean you wouldn't be coming?"

She caught the flash of guilt that crossed her husband's face for no more than a second before he smiled in heartfelt apology. "Oh Ellen, my dear, as much as I would love to accompany you all... surely you realize I can't be away from the office for that long?"

Yes, she had realized it, or at least suspected, which is why she'd been so surprised, so *pleased*, by his enthusiasm for the idea. She swallowed a mouthful of lemonade that now tasted like vinegar in her mouth, sour and old. "Perhaps not for that long, but you could come for part of the time, at least?" she asked, trying not to let her voice waver.

"Yes, yes, that's a grand idea." Lucas latched onto her suggestion with eager alacrity, which helped soothe Ellen's wounded soul a little. "Perhaps in March, when things are less busy."

"Could you not travel out with us at the start, see us settled?" Ellen hated how she sounded, pleading for her husband's attention. Perhaps she was being unreasonable, expecting so much.

Lucas shook his head with a regretful sigh. "I'm afraid I couldn't take the time off at such short notice, and in any case I think it's best that you go at once, for Jamie's sake, don't you? But I will travel out to join you later. I will be counting the days until I can." He reached over to touch her hand. "It will be such an adventure for you."

Ellen managed a stiff nod. Why did he have to sound so *equable*, she wondered with an uncharacteristic spurt of bitterness. It almost sounded as if he wanted them gone. No one to nag him for keeping late hours, his only company a sheet of figures and a tumbler of medicinal brandy, allowed by prescription, since alcohol had been banned nine years ago, although most people still found ways to indulge, either with the wine stored in their cellars

or the bathtub gin offered by plenty of establishments. New York
state had been particularly reluctant to crack down on the illegality
of selling the stuff.

"I don't know if I can manage the journey on my own," she said
after a moment, struggling not to sound as hurt as she felt. "All the
way to California. It will take four or five days, at least. And what
about Rosie's schooling?"

"An adventure in California is better than any fusty, dusty
school!" Lucas exclaimed with a laugh. "And in any case, surely
she can attend school there... there must be some decent schools.
Eldon West, one of the law partners, lived in Los Angeles for a
time. I believe he still has a house there. Perhaps you could rent it
for the duration. I can ask him—"

"I'm sure it will be too grand for me," Ellen returned. She felt
both impressed and intimidated by how easy Lucas made it all
seem—as if a trip across the country with two children in tow, and
then setting up in a strange city, was a simple matter. Of course,
she reminded herself, she'd done as much before. When she'd been
but twelve years old, she'd moved from Scotland to Seaton and
then onto Amherst Island, before returning to Glasgow to attend
art school. From there, she'd gone to nurse by the battlefields of
France before returning once more to Ontario. All things considered, she'd moved around a great deal. Why should she tremble at
the prospect of another adventure? And yet it was one without
Lucas, and two children in tow...

"And of course I wouldn't want you to have to manage on your
own," he continued. "But that is easily remedied. Why not hire a
nurse or a governess to accompany you?"

Ellen hesitated. She did not particularly want to make the
journey with a stranger, entrusting her children to hired help she
barely knew, something she hadn't done in her seven years of
motherhood so far. Besides, it would be expensive, and no matter
how extravagant Lucas's largesse, at heart Ellen was still a Springburn lass who counted her pennies.

"Or better yet," Lucas continued, clearly sensing her dislike of that suggestion, "what about family? Hasn't Gracie been kicking her heels as of late?"

"I wouldn't really know." Gracie McCafferty, the second youngest of her island cousins, had moved to Brooklyn two years ago. Ellen had been delighted to have family so close by, but over the last few years, she'd seen Gracie only a handful of times; her young cousin, always having possessed a streak of impish wildness, ran with a faster, younger set than Ellen and Lucas did. She'd been working in an office for a while, and she'd been engaged to some young lad about town, but both seemed to have come to nothing, as far as Ellen knew. She'd telephoned Gracie a few months ago, asking her to visit, but Gracie, more flippant than usual, had replied she was far too busy. Ellen had been stung.

"Well, you could find out," Lucas coaxed. "It might be good for Gracie. I've been worried about her. She seems to have fallen in with a fast crowd, which is easily done in the city. But she's a country girl at heart."

"I always thought so, but she hasn't seemed to mind the company she keeps," Ellen replied.

Lucas smiled. "I think she could use your influence."

"Perhaps." She knew she was being deliberately querulous, and all to hide the hurt she still felt that Lucas wouldn't be going to California with her... *if* she went to California, yet she already knew she would, of course she would, for Jamie's sake.

"Shall we invite her to dinner at the weekend and put the idea to her then?" Lucas suggested. "I'll look into train tickets, and I'll ask Eldon West about his house, and what the best neighborhoods near Los Angeles are. If you are settled on Los Angeles? I'd rather you were near a proper city, with good transport and schools."

"I suppose Los Angeles is as good as anywhere," Ellen replied. "Although I'm not sure I want the best neighborhood. I'd much prefer something homelier."

"Then I'll ask about that," Lucas promised. "You could be away this time next week, perhaps even before we suffer another snowstorm. Wouldn't that be good for Jamie?"

"Yes," Ellen murmured, knowing it would be very good for Jamie, and yet wishing her husband didn't sound quite so pleased about it all. It was almost as if he couldn't wait for her to go.

As if he could read her thoughts, he leaned over the table and captured her hand in his own. "Ellen, darling, you know I'd rather go with you?" He gazed at her, his blue eyes so earnest that Ellen felt her hurt ebbing, her ire melting away.

"I know you would."

"You have every right to be annoyed with me for working too hard," he told her with a wry grimace. "And I know you are so, so don't bother to pretend."

Ellen couldn't help but smile. "All right," she said, managing a laugh, "I won't."

He squeezed her hand. "It won't be forever, I promise you."

"I should hope not!"

He laughed, and twined her fingers with his own. "Indeed, indeed. What I really meant was, it should only be for a season. While things are pressed—"

"But how long will that be?" Ellen asked quietly. "It's been months already."

"And only months more, I'm sure. It's an exciting time to invest. You'd curse me if I didn't take advantage of it, both for our client and ourselves."

"I could never curse you," Ellen protested, and he rose from the table, tugging on her hand so she came to him with a tender smile.

"I've very glad to hear it," he murmured against her lips, and then he kissed her.

Three days later, Gracie McCafferty sailed into the Lymans' house, discarding a spangled wrap with careless ease as she looked around the marble-tiled entrance hall.

"Goodness, you *have* moved up in the world!" she laughed as she kissed both Ellen and Lucas on both cheeks like a European.

Ellen breathed in the vanilla and bergamot scents of the new fragrance Shalimar, and wondered where Gracie had got the money for such an expensive perfume. It smelled far more glamorous than her own sensible and rather staid lavender water.

"You should have visited sooner," Ellen told her cousin with a smile. "We've missed you, Gracie."

"And I've missed you! I'm sorry—I'm the pits at letters and telephone calls. But I'm here now!" She gave them all a bright smile as she patted her hair. She was wearing a sleeveless dress of purple silk that barely skimmed her knees, and her dark hair was cut in the latest shingled bob, her mouth a livid scar of carmine lipstick. Rosie goggled at her glamorous cousin, and Ellen struggled not to feel dowdy in her navy-blue drop-waist dress, three years old at least, its hem brushing her ankles.

"Look at you!" Gracie exclaimed as she hugged Rosie and Jamie in turn. "So grown up. I should have come sooner to see you. I'm kicking myself now, honestly. What are you two bubs up to these days?"

"I'm in school," Rosie offered, blushing and shy.

"School!" Gracie raised her eyebrows, impressed. "Well, you'll have to tell me all about that! I always liked a bit of book learning, myself."

"Gracie came first in her year at university," Ellen told the children.

"Beat out all the boys," Gracie agreed with a wink for Rosie, who grinned.

Ellen felt herself warming towards her young, irrepressible cousin; Gracie was vibrant and laughing, full of life—wasn't that what the children needed, never mind a bit of lipstick and a daring hemline?

"So, how have tricks been, then?" Gracie asked as they went into the drawing room for drinks before dinner. Eva handed around a tray of lemonade; Ellen didn't miss her cousin's slight grimace as she took her glass. No doubt Gracie had had her fair share of speakeasies and bathtub gin, but besides Lucas's so-called medicinal brandy, there was no alcohol in the Lyman house. They'd drank the last of the wine in their cellar years ago.

"Things have been well," Lucas replied as he took his own glass. "Although I'm sure Ellen will say I've been working too hard. And she'd be right."

Gracie let out a laugh while Ellen met Lucas's wry gaze with a small smile. "I'm afraid this cold weather hasn't been good for Jamie's chest," she remarked, which caused a rather sulky look from her son, who hated any reminder of his frailty. Ellen gave him a quick, sympathetic smile in return. "I've never seen such snow, not even in Canada."

"It's been a hoot, hasn't it?" Gracie agreed as she sprawled in a chair, long slender legs stretched out in front of her. Ellen could see her lacy garters peeking from beneath the hem of her dress. "Have you gone sledding in Central Park, Rosie?" She turned to the young girl, who was still looking wide-eyed.

"Yes, once or twice, but Jamie can't go out."

"I can, too," Jamie piped up, scuffing his foot along the floor, and Rosie gave him an exasperated look. They both knew Ellen and Lucas had forbidden him from sledding, and with just cause. A single outing in the snow back in December had given him a wracking cough for weeks.

"Poor sport," Gracie said with a shake of her head. "It's hard when you're not feeling up to much, isn't it? I wasn't well for a bit recently, and it was tough, for sure." She smiled at him in sympathy, and Jamie grinned back.

"You weren't well?" Lucas repeated, eyebrows raised. "I hope it wasn't anything serious."

"Oh no, not really. Just a touch of the flu. Got over it quick enough." She wagged a finger at Jamie. "But I had to rest up, let me tell you! No gadding about when you've got a cough rattling through your lungs like a freight train. Wait till you're better and then you can have all sorts of adventures."

"But what if I'm never better?" Jamie asked seriously, clearly hanging on Gracie's every word. There was something mesmerizing about her, Ellen had to acknowledge, with her dark hair and bright lips and eyes, the lithesome way she moved, the energy that crackled around her like a charismatic force field.

"Oh, you will be," Gracie assured him and Jamie nodded, satisfied, while Ellen smiled faintly. Perhaps Gracie's air of careless confidence was just what they all needed. She was evidently charming both Rosie and Jamie, regaling them now with stories of skating on The Lake in Central Park and doing the charleston in Greenwich Village—clearly editing out a few of her more questionable activities, which was thoughtful, at least.

"What's hooch, Gracie?" Rosie asked at one point, while Ellen pressed her lips together.

"Never you mind, lamb," Gracie returned with a wink, patting Rosie on the cheek. "Never you mind."

"There's nothing wrong with being a little high-spirited at her age," Lucas murmured mildly to Ellen when Gracie was in the middle of another rousing story and couldn't hear them. "You don't need to look quite so disapproving, my love."

"I don't look disapproving," Ellen protested, keeping her voice low as she gave him a wry smile. She'd been trying her hardest to look amused by her cousin's antics, but obviously not hard enough —as she was starting to wonder if Gracie's spirits were just a little too high for the likes of her and her children, and the quiet life she hoped to live in California.

"I can still tell," Lucas told her with a smile. "I see it in your eyes, and that little wrinkle between your eyebrows, as well. Don't be annoyed with me because I know you so well."

Ellen gave a soft laugh of acknowledgement. "Very well," she said, still low-voiced, "I might be a *tiny* bit disapproving, and I'm probably just being stuffy. In fact, I know I am. But, Lucas, do you really think she's the right role model for the children?"

"She'd be going as your companion, not their role model. They have you for that, my girl." He brushed her fingers with his own and Ellen smiled, glad that Lucas could still make her heart flutter. "In any case, I hardly think she'll lead them astray with a bit of lipstick and bathtub gin," he continued. "We are in the Roaring Twenties, you know. It's the spirit of the age, Ellen—you can't escape it, I'm afraid."

No, she couldn't, although sometimes she wanted to. She'd felt this way before, Ellen recalled—this tangled sense of nostalgia and loss, longing and sorrow. When she'd sat with her Uncle Hamish over twenty years ago, and lamented the end of the era of the general store, with the advent of the bright and shiny Sears Roebuck catalogue where you could pick out whatever you wanted. She'd felt it at the end of the war, when the optimism of a generation had trickled away, soaking into the bloody battlefields of France. And she felt it now, when Gracie talked so laughingly of speakeasies and moving pictures and Ellen felt as if the world were rushing by while she was left behind, wondering whether she even wanted to keep up.

Perhaps she was destined to always feel at sea, she reflected, before she gave herself a good mental shake. There was no need to feel *quite* so melancholy—she was thirty-seven, not eighty! She had a lot of life left, no matter how the world turned and changed around her. Gracie might be more high-spirited than she'd ever been, but that didn't mean she had to be quite such a stick-in-the-mud. She vowed to be more engaging during dinner.

"Time for bed, I think," she told Rosie and Jamie, who both gave her long faces, while Gracie laughed.

"I'll come back, sweet peas, I promise," she told them, and Ellen was gratified by her cousin's interest in the children. Perhaps their suggestion to have her accompany them to California would be welcome, although she still didn't know how to feel about it all, and she had no idea what Gracie's response would be.

"Gracie is *fun*," Rosie told Ellen earnestly when she headed upstairs with her and Jamie. She sat in bed, her hair in plaits, her hands laced around her knees as she gave Ellen a serious look. "I like her," she pronounced. "I like her very much."

"Do you, darling? I'm glad." Perhaps fun was what both her children needed, not someone staid and matronly and frankly dull, which would have been Ellen's instinctive preference. Rosie was so serious, and Jamie's life so restrained already. Perhaps Gracie could liven them up in a way Ellen knew she couldn't. And yet her cousin's wild streak still concerned her. She didn't want to have to worry about Gracie as well as her own children while travelling across the country. But like Lucas said, a little lipstick and gin was hardly the epitome of wildness, especially these days.

"Will we see her again?" Jamie asked when she went to his room to tuck him in. "Soon?"

"Yes, I should think so." Ellen hadn't yet told the children about their plans to go to California, although Lucas had already looked into train tickets and a place to stay. If Gracie agreed, they could be leaving for California this time next week. It seemed a strange thought, and one that was exciting but not entirely welcome. Did she really want to be separated from Lucas for so long, and in a strange place, no less?

"It's clear you brought me here for a purpose," Gracie declared when Ellen returned to the dining room. Eva had already brought in the first course, salmon mousse cups resting delicately on lettuce leaves. "And I hope it's not to scold me for not seeing you sooner, because you know I can't bear scolding." She gave a funny little pout, while Lucas looked on, amused.

"Scold you?" he repeated with a laugh. "Certainly not, Gracie. We're just pleased to see you."

"Well, I'm pleased to see you," Gracie returned with a sudden and surprisingly earnest look. "Truly. You're family. I know I should have visited sooner, and part of me wanted to, but if I'm honest, I went a bit blue after Fred and I ended things." She toyed with a forkful of mousse, her gaze lowered. "It was a tough time, to tell you the truth."

"I'm sorry," Ellen murmured sincerely. She'd never even met Gracie's fiancé, Fred Baker, but she knew he was a man about town and Lucas had called him a bright spark on the stock exchange. It had been a whirlwind romance, lasting only a few months, but even whirlwinds could leave broken hearts.

"Well, I'm on the mend now," Gracie declared, lifting her head to give them both a bright, glittering look. "No more moping about for me, I can promise you that."

"I'm glad you're feeling better," Ellen replied, "and I hope you might feel better still. You're right, we have asked you here for a purpose, an important one, and I hope you might be amenable to it."

"Oh?" Gracie raised her perfectly penciled eyebrows. "Now I'm dying with curiosity!"

"Well, we'll put you out of your misery, then," Lucas said, and he quickly explained the situation with Jamie's health, the proposed trip to California—renting a house, staying until spring.

"All the way to California?" Gracie marveled when Lucas had finished. "That would be the bee's knees! I've never been out west. What an adventure. I could meet a movie star."

"You should know it will be a lot of hard work," Ellen felt compelled to warn her. It would not be all cocktail parties and moving pictures, not at all, if that was what Gracie was imagining. "Children can be demanding, lovely as they are—"

"Oh, I know all about children," Gracie assured her. "I grew up as one of five, remember, Ellen! I'm not the glamor gal you seem to think me."

"Perhaps not, but you were one of the youngest," Ellen reminded her. "You didn't have the care of them—"

"I rocked Andrew to sleep nearly every night!" Gracie exclaimed. "And changed his diapers."

"Did you?" Ellen couldn't help but feel a bit dubious of this claim. She didn't recall Gracie doing any such thing; she was only three years older than Andrew, after all, and Ellen remembered her as something of a tearaway, even at a young age, full of the same snapping humor and good fun she was now.

"Honestly, I'll be as good as gold," Gracie promised, her laughing tone suddenly turning serious again, the change of her moods like streaks of lightning. "I can be, Ellen, you know that. I worked hard at Queen's, do you remember?"

"Yes, of course I do," Ellen replied, unbending a little. "I told the children you came first, remember." She knew Gracie had always been whip-smart as well as charming. "But what about your life here? I know things have ended with Fred, but you might still have colleagues, commitments..."

"I quit my job a few months ago," Gracie replied with an airiness that gave Ellen pause. She'd known Gracie had left her work, but she seemed rather insouciant about the fact. "Office work was awfully dull," she continued. "I've been doing temp work to keep afloat, but this will suit me right down to the ground, I promise you. As for friends..." She shrugged and for a second her laughing young face hardened, a flinty look in her eyes. "Easy come, easy go, eh?"

"I suppose," Ellen replied after a moment. She felt there had to be quite a bit Gracie wasn't saying, but she had no idea what it was, and she didn't feel she could ask.

"And your kiddies are sweet—I adore them already," Gracie continued. She leaned forward, her eyes alight, her smile wide. "What do you say? You and me and the kiddos on the adventure of our lives?"

"We intend to live quietly," Ellen reminded her. "For Jamie's sake. I don't know how much of an adventure it will be, Gracie, honestly."

"The travel, at least," Gracie replied as she sat back and scooped out the last of her salmon mousse. "And the orange trees and the movie stars! That's enough for me."

"I doubt we'll see any movie stars—"

"Oh come on, Ellen," Lucas interjected with a laugh, "you're sure to see one or two, especially if you're living so near Hollywood."

"I thought you said Pasadena was ten miles from Los Angeles," Ellen protested. Lucas had arranged for them to rent a bungalow in the resort city on the recommendation of Eldon West.

"Yes, but only ten miles," he replied. He smiled at Gracie and she grinned back.

Looking at them both, Ellen realized how stuffy she sounded. Gracie was right, it *was* an adventure, even if Lucas wouldn't be sharing it as she still wanted. She didn't have to keep pouring cold water over every idea. And the children clearly adored Gracie.

"Well, if you're sure," she said, and Gracie let out a delighted whoop.

"Hollywood, here we come!"

CHAPTER THREE

The 20th *Century Limited* was considered the most famous train in the world, at least according to its advertisements. It waited on the tracks at Grand Central Station, made of gleaming, streamlined steel, its interior decorated with a distinctive crimson carpet and fluorescent lamps, velveteen sofas and leather club chairs. It was the epitome of elegant travel, aimed at the wealthy; a ticket to Chicago cost the princely sum of thirty dollars, and a berth in one of the Pullman cars was even more.

Lucas had, in his typically generous way, splurged on two adjoining private compartments of their own for the twenty-hour trip to Chicago; the train left in the late afternoon, so they could enjoy a three-course dinner in the dining car before retiring for the night, pulling into Chicago by nine o'clock in the morning as they breakfasted on eggs and bacon. From there, they'd take *The Chief* to Pasadena—a deluxe express train that had been introduced only a few years ago and boasted the 'extra-fast' travel time of just sixty-three hours.

Ellen's head spun as she clung to Jamie and Rosie's hands on the crowded platform where well-dressed passengers and officious-looking conductors swarmed busily. Pullman porters with their distinctive uniform and dark green caps were heaving trunks, and in the distance a whistle blew.

"I'll see you settled in your compartment," Lucas told them, "before the train departs. I want to get a gander at the Pullman car!"

Ellen had taken long train journeys before; she'd been out to Santa Fe nearly twenty years ago to see her father, and she'd taken the train all the way from Glasgow to Dover to cross over to France, but she'd never been on a train like this. Her eyes were as wide as Rosie's as a Pullman porter escorted them past the open section of the train to their two private compartments, with their wide velvet seats that could be transformed into sleeping berths. There was even a basin and toilet, and a movable divider that separated her and Gracie's compartment from Jamie and Rosie's.

"Wowee," Gracie exclaimed unabashedly as the porter showed them the compartment's conveniences. "This is some luxury."

"You shouldn't have," Ellen told Lucas with gentle reproof, but he just laughed.

"Would you really have wanted to sleep in the open section with everyone else snoring around you? This way you can be well rested when you arrive in California. *The Chief* is even more luxurious, I've heard—the train has its own beauty salon and barber!"

"What nonsense," Ellen replied, but she was smiling. The lingering sense of sorrow she'd felt at being separated from Lucas for so long was giving way to a heady, tingling excitement. This really was an adventure.

"Look at all the people," Jamie exclaimed as he pressed his face against the window. "And so fancy!" Everyone had dressed up to travel on the famous train—women in fur coats and designer dresses, men in double-breasted, pinstriped suits and sharp-brimmed fedoras.

Gracie scanned the guest list that had been printed for every passenger. "Would you look at this—Babe Ruth is traveling on this train!"

"Babe Ruth?" Jamie repeated excitedly, whirling away from the window. "Where?"

"In his own private drawing room, I'm sure, but maybe we'll get a glimpse of him on the way to the club car."

Ellen shook her head, laughing, and Lucas chucked Jamie under the chin. "Get his autograph for me, would you, scamp?"

All too soon it was time for Lucas to go; porters were knocking on doors calling for anyone who wasn't a passenger to exit the train, and despite the excitement she'd been feeling, Ellen's heart lurched.

"So soon..." she murmured, and Lucas gave her a tender smile.

"You'll be having too much fun to miss me," he assured her. "Although I will miss you every day." He ruffled Jamie's hair. "I wish I was going on this fancy train, let me tell you!"

"So do I," Ellen murmured. She watched, fighting a sudden, sweeping sense of homesickness, as Lucas gave Rosie and Jamie tight hugs and then kissed Gracie's cheek. Ellen walked with him down the narrow corridor to say her goodbye in private, or at least as much privacy as could be had when a dozen similar farewells were happening up and down the train.

"You'll write?" she asked, not for the first time, as Lucas settled his hat on his head.

"I'll write and I'll telephone!" he promised. "As often as I can. You know there are three transcontinental telephone lines now?"

"Are there?" Ellen replied a bit shakily. She'd never made a transcontinental telephone call before, and wasn't even sure how to do it. "Well, be sure to use it, then, as well as good old-fashioned pen and paper."

Lucas folded her up in his arms, heedless of the other passengers nearby who were saying their own goodbyes. "I will miss you, you know," he murmured against her hair, his chin knocking her hat askew. "Even if you're afraid that I won't, that I'll be too busy with work. I won't be, I promise you. The house will feel empty, and I'll be counting the days till you return. Every single one."

"Do you mean that?" Ellen asked, her arms around him as she breathed in the scent of his 4711 eau de cologne. "Do you really?"

"Of course I do, my girl." Lucas leaned back to look at her seriously. "You know how much I love you, don't you? Because I do, tremendously, and have done for as long as I can remember. I'd be lost without you, Ellen."

"And I'm lost without you." She could never doubt Lucas's love for her. He had loved her since she'd been little more than a girl, shy and dreamy-eyed, sketching under a maple tree. He'd loved her and he'd waited so patiently for her to come to the realization that she loved him as well. It had taken her far too long, over ten years, and yet he'd waited all the while, her greatest and truest friend and stalwart supporter. She could never, ever doubt that he loved her.

And yet... she hated the thought of being apart from him, hated the tension that had sprung up between them so recently, because of his work, and now might even increase because of the distance. Three months suddenly seemed like forever.

"I love you," Lucas told her seriously, all laughing lightness gone from his face. "And I always will."

"I love you, too," Ellen whispered back.

She tried to smile as he kissed her and then stepped down from the train, doffing his hat. The train whistle blew, a breathless screech in Ellen's ears, and with a great heave and a sound caught between a hiss and a sigh, the 20th Century Limited began to move off. Ellen took her lace-edged handkerchief from her sleeve and, like so many other women on the train, waved it at Lucas as he waved his hat in return, his lanky form becoming smaller and smaller until he was no more than a speck, and then he was nothing at all.

She felt a pang of loss so sharp it could have sent her to her knees before she took a steadying breath and turned back to the compartment where the rest of her family waited.

Gracie had, to her credit, settled both Jamie and Rosie in their seats and unpacked their travelling cases in the drawers provided.

Dressed in a modest, ankle-skimming skirt of navy blue with a middy blouse, her bobbed black curls neatly pinned back and not a speck of lipstick in sight, she looked like the most dutiful of governesses.

She gave Ellen a sympathetic look as she came into the compartment. "So it's goodbye for three months at least."

"Yes, till May, I should think," Ellen answered as she tidied her hair in the small mirror by the door. She tried to keep her voice bright, but she felt the threat of tears behind her lids. "Although Lucas said he might visit a bit earlier." He certainly hadn't made any promises, though. Ellen turned to the window. "Goodness, look how fast we're going! The world is positively blurring by. They do say the 20th Century Limited is just about the fastest train there is."

"Can we go to the club car?" Rosie asked eagerly. "Gracie told me they serve banana splits!"

"Do they?" Ellen returned, giving Gracie a questioning look, and she laughed as she tossed her head, black curls bouncing.

"Well, we have to have some fun, don't we?"

"I suppose we do," Ellen agreed. She was determined to shake off her gloomy homesickness, knowing it was ridiculous when they'd barely started their journey. Gracie was right; this was an adventure, and they were going to have *fun*. That was all part of going to California, surely. "It's an early dinner for you two," she told her children, "with the biggest banana splits for dessert and then straight to bed after." That was as much fun as she was willing to entertain, at least for the moment. Too much excitement had made Jamie feverish in the past, but the prospect of ice cream was too irresistible, and she wanted this to be a journey they could all remember.

Looking as angelic as they possibly could, eyes wide and earnest, both Jamie and Rosie gave her dutiful nods, and Ellen couldn't keep from bursting out laughing. She felt lighter suddenly, caught up in the fizzy excitement that Gracie had generated.

"Very well, let's find this club car and see if they really do have banana splits."

Two hours later, replete with a lovely supper, as well as banana splits complete with cherries on top, Jamie and Rosie were tucked into their sleeping berths, their Pullman porter promising to keep an eye on them as Gracie and Ellen headed to the dining car for their own more elegant meal.

Gracie had exchanged her governess' outfit for a knee-length sack dress in crimson silk which made Ellen struggle not to feel a bit dowdy in her far more modest gown in dark green crepe, although she did her best not to succumb to such feelings. She was a matron, after all, thirty-seven years old with two children, not a young woman like Gracie, with so much still ahead of her.

"That green brings out your eyes," Gracie told her as she slipped a gauzy wrap around her shoulders. "You look like a real smasher, Ellen!"

"I don't know if I've ever been called that before," Ellen replied, but she felt mollified, the slight wound to her pride healed over in an instant. "You look gorgeous," she said frankly, and Gracie preened.

"In this old thing?"

Ellen couldn't keep from laughing. "This old thing, indeed! As if you don't know how fabulous you look."

Gracie grinned then, making Ellen smile in return. "Well, how often does a girl get to ride a train like this? I want to make the most of it."

"I'm sure you do," Ellen agreed with a little laugh. She thought Gracie probably made the most of many things in life, which she supposed was to her credit.

The dining car was as impressive as every other car on the train, as well appointed as a proper restaurant, with tables adorned with white linen and silver serving dishes, menus at every place setting, full of well-dressed passengers dining on lobster and caviar.

"Russian caviar and filet mignon, oh la la," Gracie remarked, eyes dancing, as she perused the offerings once they'd been seated by one of the waiters. "If only we could have champagne as well!" She glanced around the crowded car, a speculative gleam in her eye. "There must be a way... Babe Ruth will be having champagne, I'm sure of it. A bucketful in his private dining car, no doubt. Perhaps a quiet word in the steward's ear..."

"Babe Ruth might be, but we will not," Ellen returned, softening her firm words with a smile. She had no intention of getting involved in procuring bootleg liquor, although she knew plenty of people did, and she suspected Gracie was right—a quiet word and a slipped five-dollar bill would no doubt see them both drinking champagne easily enough.

Gracie gave a little pout before she shrugged and laughed. "Oh, very well," she said. "No fizz, more's the pity." Then, with casual aplomb, she took a pack of cigarettes from her handbag and fitted one into a long, slender holder.

"Gracie..." Ellen began, unable to keep from sounding at least a little censorious. She knew plenty of women smoked these days, including several women in her own circle, but it still seemed like a fast habit to her.

Gracie merely raised her eyebrows, a smile dancing about her lips. "Don't look so horrified, Ellen. Everyone smokes these days."

Before Ellen could reply, a young gentleman at the table across from them, dapper and distinguished in a three-piece pinstriped suit, leaned forward, a silver lighter in hand, his eyes gleaming appreciatively as he glanced at Gracie. "May I?"

Gracie fluttered her eyelashes at him, while Ellen watched, lips pursed. "Why, thank you," she said, and he clicked the lighter while she inhaled, a smile still lurking about her mouth.

"My pleasure, ma'am." The man's gaze flicked from Gracie to Ellen and then back again with rather insulting speed. "Where are you ladies heading to?"

"All the way to Los Angeles, of course—"

"Actually, Pasadena," Ellen interjected, for Lucas had arranged for them to rent a bungalow near Westridge School, where Rosie would attend for the few months of their stay. She tried to sound polite but dismissive. She had no intention of encouraging a conversation with a strange gentleman on a train.

"How marvelous," he enthused, undeterred. He had the scrubbed, blond looks of a schoolboy but was dressed like a well-heeled gangster. "I'm headed to Hollywood myself, staying at the Beverly Hills Hotel. Have you heard of it?"

"Why, yes, of course," Gracie purred, while Ellen bit her lip to keep from saying something sharp. Her cousin was flirting rather shamelessly, eyelashes fluttering over the haze of her cigarette smoke, carmine mouth curved beguilingly, while Ellen simply sat there, trying not to fidget or fume. Was she being priggish, disapproving of Gracie's behavior? She had a feeling she was, and yet she could not keep herself from it.

"Perhaps you'd like to meet me there for a drink when you've settled in?" Smoothly, the man withdrew a business card from his billfold. "Emmett Hughes, Hollywood producer, or about to be." He gave a grin Ellen suspected was meant to be disarming. "At your service."

"Charmed," Gracie practically cooed as she plucked the card from the man's fingers. "My name's Gracie McCafferty."

"So very pleased to meet you, Miss McCafferty." The man's smile seemed far too familiar. *Hollywood producer...!* Ellen thought with some scornful doubt. He couldn't be more than twenty-five, and was likely to be some spoiled heir intent on lavish living. There were plenty of them these days—gadabouts who were both charming and louche, spending their money as quickly and recklessly as they could.

"I think we should order," Ellen stated pointedly, and with another eyelash flutter for the young Mr. Hughes, Gracie turned her attention to the menu.

"I believe I shall have the caviar, the filet mignon, and the deviled lobster," she announced with a flourish and Ellen only just kept from reminding her that the steak cost sixty cents extra. They could certainly afford it, and now was the time to enjoy such plea-sures, surely.

A waiter, black-jacketed with a white cloth over one arm, took their orders and then melted away. At the table across from them, Emmett Hughes was drinking and talking loudly with his compan-ion, another dapper gentleman, and Ellen took the moment to lean forward and say with gentle firmness, "Gracie, I can appreciate the excitement of such a journey has given you excessively high spirits, but I'm afraid I must insist you behave more sensibly and modestly."

"Sensibly and modestly," Gracie repeated on a yawn. Her mischievous glance slid toward Emmett Hughes and back again. "How utterly tedious."

Ellen opened her mouth and shut it again. She hadn't expected this, although perhaps she should have. Gracie had always been high-spirited as well as a bit mischievous. "You are here as my *companion*—" she reminded her, a slight edge entering her voice.

"And so what if I smoke?" Gracie challenged, her eyes now possessing a dangerous glitter as she leaned forward to hiss at her from across the table. "What if I flirt?" For a moment, she looked almost wild. "What does any of it matter?"

The question hung in the air between them and Ellen watched, feeling disconcerted, as Gracie stubbed her cigarette out in the heavy crystal ashtray.

She leaned forward to address Mr. Hughes, her voice a purr. "Thank you *so* much for the light."

"Gracie," Ellen said in a low voice once her cousin's attention had returned to their table, "please. You must realize it's—it's not seemly—"

"*Seemly.*" Gracie threw her head back and let out a throaty laugh that had half the diners and all the men looking at them. "Oh, Ellen, you sound as if you're about a hundred years old. You were always such a serious one, but really? It's 1929, not the eigh-teen hundreds. Don't be such a fuddy-duddy, for heaven's sake. I'm just having a little fun. There's no harm."

Ellen prickled, stung by Gracie's laughing contempt. Was she that ridiculously old-fashioned? "I hardly think—"

"Do you know who else is on this train?" Gracie demanded, her voice hardening. Her mercurial changes of mood had Ellen's head spinning. "Jane Addams. Do you know who she is?"

"No, I don't."

"She's a world-famous suffragette and reformer. She co-founded the ACLU—do you know what *that* is?"

"The American Civil Liberties Union," Ellen replied. Gracie didn't need to treat her quite so much as if she were an idiot. The ACLU had been founded nine years ago, and was a champion of both civil rights and free speech. Several well-regarded attorneys had foregone their private practices to work for the organization free of charge. "What does Jane Addams have to do with you flirting with a stranger?" she asked levelly.

"She campaigned for women to have the same rights as men," Grace replied, her voice throbbing with a passion that reminded Ellen of when her cousin had been young, arguing about beating the boys and desperate to come first in her year, which she had. "Equal opportunities, equal pay... can you even imagine?"

"I still fail to see how this relates to your behavior." Ellen knew she sounded like a stern schoolmarm, and she wished she didn't, but she couldn't help it. She'd brought Gracie along to help her with her children, not smoke and flirt her way across America. Did that make her a fuddy-duddy? If so, then she'd have to be one. Wouldn't she?

"Look around you," Gracie said, flinging an arm out in dramatic fashion. "Every gentleman in this dining car, or near enough, is smoking."

Ellen's gaze moved around the dining car, realizing uncomfortably that it was true; most men had a cigarette or cigar clamped between their teeth or carelessly held between their fingers. A blue haze of smoke hovered in the air.

"What of it?" she asked eventually, although she was already starting to see Gracie's point.

"No one calls them fast," Gracie stated with some heat. "No one says they aren't being *seemly*. Why should a woman be judged in such a way?"

"I can see what you mean, Gracie, but that doesn't change the way things are now." Exasperated, Ellen shook her head. "I'm simply saying that there is a certain standard of behavior—"

"And what if I flirt a little?" Gracie challenged, dropping her voice so the object of her flirtation, chatting expansively to his companion, couldn't hear. "So what? Men do it all the time, and no one thinks the worse of them. Why shouldn't I? It's a new world out there, Ellen. Can't you see it? Women don't have to hide their ankles or speak modestly or apologize for who they are. Isn't that good news?" Her voice rang out with both determination and pride, her face aglow with the zeal of an evangelist, or perhaps a prophetess.

A waiter glided forward to give them their first course—caviar for Gracie, and a more modest fruit cup for Ellen. She glanced down at the tinned pineapple swimming in its own juice and heaved a sigh.

"You may have a point, Gracie," she conceded, "but so do I. I asked you to come along to help me with the children. That should be your focus, not..." She paused, and then continued determinedly, "Seeking your own amusements."

A flash of hurt crossed Gracie's face like a streak of lightning, making Ellen's insides curdle with guilt. Was she being too harsh? Gracie was young, after all, and this was an adventure. A bit of flirting, even a bit of smoking, wasn't all *that* bad, especially when the children were in bed...

"Point taken," Gracie replied shortly, and turned back to her caviar, her expression shuttered.

As the train rattled west, the sun setting over the Hudson, Ellen couldn't help but feel her young cousin had got the better of the conversation.

CHAPTER FOUR

PASADENA, CALIFORNIA, FEBRUARY 1929

"Welcome to California!"

Ellen smiled and murmured her greeting as Maria and Eduardo, the couple who managed the bungalow Lucas had arranged for them to rent, threw open its front door. Since arriving in Pasadena an hour ago, her mind had been spinning from all the new sights and sounds. The weather was pleasantly balmy without being too hot, with blue skies and a dry heat that seemed to penetrate into her bones—and her young son's lungs.

After taking a poorly turn in Chicago, where the bitter, freezing winds had funneled down the platform as they'd exchanged the 20th Century Limited for the elegant and luxurious *The Chief,* Jamie was finally looking a bit more alert and interested, and the cough that had been rattling through him in recent days—and worrying Ellen to no end—had subsided to no more than a tickle, much to her relief.

Both Rosie and Jamie's noses had been pressed to the window as a taxi had taken them from the train station in the center of picturesque Pasadena, known as a resort town for the last fifty years, to this charming bungalow on its outskirts just ten miles from Los Angeles. Set in Bungalow Heaven, a neighborhood of similar cozy cottages with their second stories tucked under the eaves, Ellen was charmed by it all—the craftsmen-built houses with their wide verandas and brightly painted shutters, the manicured green lawns, the palm trees that lined the pleasant, wide boulevards.

"How was your journey?" Maria, a smiling, round-cheeked woman, asked as she ushered them into the bungalow's main sitting room, its French windows open to a wide patio out back, and beyond that a swimming pool. "You must be tired!"

"Actually, I feel quite refreshed," Gracie said as she prowled around the airy sitting room, inspecting everything with an avid curiosity.

Ellen sank onto a sofa, unwilling to admit just how exhausted she was. Jamie's cough had kept her up at night, both from its dreadful, wheezing sound as well as the worry that always accompanied one of his bouts, although at least this one hadn't been as serious as many of his others. Gracie, however, had seemed to sleep like a log.

She glanced at her cousin, who, after two and a half days on a train, looked as fresh as if she'd just come out of a bandbox, thanks to a visit to *The Chief's* beauty parlor that morning before the train had pulled into Los Angeles. Her bobbed curls were perfectly shingled, and her drop-waist dress with its sailor collar looked as fresh as if she'd put it on but a moment ago. In comparison, Ellen felt as if she were wilting a bit; her skirt was crumpled from where Jamie had pressed against it, and her waist-length hair was starting to fall from its pins.

"Look at the swimming pool," Gracie exclaimed as she reached for Rosie and Jamie's hands. "Who's going to have a dip first?"

Ellen couldn't help but smile as Gracie took the children out onto the patio while they squealed in excitement and Maria beamed in approval. Eduardo was already shouldering their trunks and cases inside, and a gusty sigh escaped her without her meaning to. They were finally here. Surely things would start to improve now.

The tension between her and Gracie for the rest of the journey had been palpable but unacknowledged, as they'd moved rather stiffly around each other in their small compartment. Gracie had taken the children out to explore the new train, and thankfully she hadn't flirted with anyone else, although they'd seen Emmett Hughes boarding *The Chief*, and he'd once again insisted Gracie meet him for a drink when they reached California.

"So what if I do?" she'd flung at Ellen with a pert, challenging look. Ellen had bitten her tongue rather than offer another unwelcome lecture on modest behavior. There was only so much she could say, and Gracie was a grown woman, after all. "Didn't you once meet a strange gentleman in Chicago, Ellen?" she'd continued, her eyebrows raised in challenging query. "As I recall, that's how you came to be at that art school in Glasgow!"

And what could Ellen say to that? It was true; she'd met Henry McAvoy on the train to Chicago just as Gracie had met Mr. Hughes. He'd invited her to dinner—a scandalous invitation nearly twenty years ago now—and Ellen had even more scandalously accepted, something Gracie had yet to do. Yet it had all felt oddly proper compared to everyone's frenetic determination to have fun that Ellen felt all around her now. Perhaps she really was an old stick-in-the-mud, just as Gracie had accused her of being.

"You're right, I did meet Mr. McAvoy on a train," she'd told Gracie, "and I even had dinner with him. So I suppose I can't fault you for speaking to Mr. Hughes."

In typical Gracie style, her mood had changed and she'd wrapped her arms around Ellen. "You are a dear. I know I can be a bit much to take—Mum was always telling me so, wasn't she? But I don't mean anything by it. You know that, don't you, Ellen?"

She'd looked so anxious that Ellen had patted her cheek and smiled. "Yes, I think I do know that," she'd admitted. Things had eased a bit between them after that, although Ellen still felt a little tense, or perhaps just weary.

"Would you like a drink, madam?" Maria asked, and Ellen smiled at her gratefully.

"Yes, and please do call me Ellen." She glanced again outside;

Gracie had taken off her stockings and shoes and was sitting on the edge of the pool, splashing her feet in the water. Jamie had followed suit, tossing his socks and shoes aside with unbridled glee. A warning caught in Ellen's throat and she swallowed it down. This was why they were here, she reminded herself. So a five-year-old boy could enjoy the things five-year-old boys were meant to enjoy. She didn't need to fuss. She didn't need to fear.

And yet, a little voice inside her whispered, *what if the water was too cold? What if Jamie caught a chill?*

Laughing, her head thrown back, Gracie skimmed a toe along the water, deliberately splashing Jamie a little, causing him to shriek delightedly as he wiped the droplets from his face. Ellen bit her lip.

A tug at her hand caused her to start, and she looked down to see Rosie had moved silently to her side, her hazel eyes as serious as always. "May I put my feet in the water too, Mama, please?"

"Yes, of course, darling, if it's not too cold." It was typical of Rosie to ask while Jamie went gamboling ahead. Ellen sometimes wished her daughter would share her younger's brother desperate zest for life. Jamie was the one who needed to be careful, but Rosie was the more cautious of the pair.

Maria came back into the room, holding a tray of frosted glasses filled with lemonade, decorated with mint leaves and lemon slices.

"Oh, Maria, that looks wonderful," Ellen said as she gratefully took a glass. "Thank you so much." She took a sip of the drink, both tart and sweet.

"Mama, come in," Rosie called. She'd taken off her shoes and socks and was sitting on the edge of the pool, barely touching her toes to the water.

"Is it cold?" Ellen called, and Gracie threw her a laughing look. "It's refreshing."

"Come in, Mama," Jamie entreated, and Ellen wondered why she was hesitating. There was something about Gracie's gleeful recklessness, she realized, that turned her into the female equivalent of a shriveled prune—all pursed lips and sanctimonious silences. She hated it about herself, and yet she couldn't seem to stop, but at least she could try, starting now. She could have, if not as much fun as Gracie, then near enough.

"Such happy *bambinas*," Maria murmured, smiling indulgently, and with a spurt of determination, Ellen put down her glass.

"All right, I'm coming," she called, and Jamie let out a whoop.

Outside, the sun beamed down over the terrace and garden, and the pool sparkled under its crystalline light. At the back of the lawn, Ellen glimpsed a small grove of orange and lemon trees, as well as a smaller bungalow that she knew belonged to Maria and Eduardo. It all looked so perfectly peaceful, and the sun was so warm and healing, that she felt something stir in her soul, a mixture of joy and relief. They were finally here, and it was going to be good. It was going to be *wonderful*. She would make sure of it.

Carefully, she removed her shoes—sensible lace-ups as opposed to Gracie's delicate pumps—and then rolled down her stockings, conscious of her children's avid stares as they waited for her to join them at the poolside. Gracie had dipped her legs in right up to the knee, her dress rucked about her thighs as she tilted her face to the sun, her hands braced behind her. Ellen sat down gingerly on the other edge of the pool and dipped her toe in, not quite feigning a shiver.

"It *is* cold!" She couldn't keep from giving Jamie an anxious look. "Perhaps I should fetch your sweater..."

"I'm *fine*," he told her with a twitchy shrug and, with a suppressed sigh, Ellen let it go, putting both feet in the water, up to her calves. It was decidedly cool, and yet she had to keep reminding herself not to fuss. Hopefully she would not need the reminder after a few weeks under the healing sun, enjoying a leisurely pace.

"Isn't it lovely, Mama?" Rosie asked. She still only had her toes in the water, but she was smiling shyly, her eyes sparkling with delight. "And do you see the orange and lemon trees?"

"I do," Ellen told her, resting one hand on her sun-warmed hair. "They're lovely. It's all so lovely." Again, she felt that stirring inside, a sense of expansion, of possibility. They could pick the lemons from the tree and make lemonade. They could sit by the pool and explore the neighborhood and Jamie could run and jump and play. Perhaps she would even get him a bicycle, or roller skates...

"*Oh!*" The shocked syllable exploded out of her as water splashed over her from head to foot, drenching her dress. She blinked through the droplets to see Gracie grinning at her, one foot flexed for another splash.

"Got you," she said lazily.

"Oh..." Ellen spluttered as she plucked her wet dress away from her skin. "*Oh...*"

"She got you, Mama!" Jamie exclaimed gleefully. "She *got* you!"

"She certainly did." Ellen scrambled up from the pool edge, struggling not to feel furious, or worse, hurt by Gracie's splashing. She was absolutely soaked, but perhaps Gracie hadn't meant to make her so wet. On second thought, Ellen thought as she caught sight of her cousin's rather sly smile, perhaps she did. "I need to change," she said stiffly.

"Oh, your dress will dry, Mama—" Rosie began, but Ellen just shook her head. She was far too wet—and too sensible—to sit about while her dress dripped onto the ground.

Sparing a smile for her children, she walked stiffly into the house. From behind her, she heard Gracie say something, and both children laughed.

Upstairs Eduardo had left her trunk in the master bedroom, a neat, airy room with a wide, wooden bed covered in a colorful embroidered quilt, and a dormer window overlooking the orange trees.

Don't be cross, Ellen told herself as she riffled through her packed belongings, looking for something to wear. *She just meant it in fun, and it delighted the children. There's no point picking a fight over something so silly.*

Taking a deep breath, she unbuttoned her dress and changed out of her slip and underthings, hanging them over the railing by the wardrobe. Then she pulled on a day dress of navy crepe with a dropped waist and bell sleeves. Tidying her hair as best as she could, she returned downstairs to find Gracie had brought the children back inside, and they were dried off, socks and shoes back on, seated at the table with glasses of lemonade and a plate of sugar cookies, crisp and golden.

"Mama, you got so wet!" Jamie chortled, and Gracie caught Ellen's eye, looking cheerfully abashed.

"Did I get you terribly wet?" she asked, lowering her gaze demurely.

"You did, actually," she replied, keeping her tone mild as she ruffled Jamie's hair. She was determined to take Gracie in her stride, now that they were in California. She would not let herself get riled by her playful antics. "But I was happy enough to get out of my traveling clothes, so I didn't mind. I expect they needed a good wash, anyway."

Gracie glanced up again, a gleam in her eyes that Ellen couldn't quite discern. But she decided she'd expended enough energy worrying about what Gracie was up to, and so she turned to her children instead.

"When you've finished your cookies and lemonade, shall we explore the garden?"

"The oranges are ready to be picked," Maria said, as she came in from the kitchen. "If you pick them, I will make juice."

"Juice!" Jamie exclaimed wonderingly. "You mean from the oranges?"

"Why, yes, that is how it is done." Maria smiled at Ellen over Jamie's head. "You squeeze the oranges and out comes the juice!"

"That sounds marvelous, Maria, thank you." She felt heartened by the presence of the friendly couple; Maria would cook and clean for them, and Eduardo would tend to the garden and act as chauffeur when they needed to use the car that came with the house. It all seemed most satisfactory, and some small, mean part of her wondered at the necessity of having Gracie there at all.

As if sensing her thoughts, Gracie rose from the table in one brisk movement. "While you take the children outside, shall I see to the children's cases? I can unpack all their things and put them away."

"Thank you, Gracie, that would be most kind." Once again, Ellen had to suppress a sense of guilty unease when it came to her cousin. Just when Gracie seemed to be at her most reckless and irresponsible, she did something perfectly helpful and pleasant. But it had occurred to Ellen, as they'd crossed the country by train, that she didn't really know Gracie that well anymore, if she ever really knew her at all.

She remembered the cheerful, impish girl with eyes like buttons and a head full of curls from her days on Amherst Island, but she'd left the island for Glasgow when Gracie had been only ten years old, and when she'd returned Gracie had been twenty, a young woman at university, with a head full of plans. In the years since marrying Lucas and leaving the island once again, she'd only seen Gracie a handful of times, even after she'd moved to New York. Could she really say she knew her at all?

But that was one of the benefits of this time away, she reminded herself as she took Jamie and Rosie by the hand and led them outside. She could get to know Gracie properly. She could be a good influence on her, the way Lucas had said, although at the moment, Ellen thought that prospect unlikely.

CHAPTER FIVE

The next day passed so pleasantly Ellen was glad to let all her apprehensions about Gracie drop away. They picked oranges from the garden, and Maria made freshly squeezed juice that they had with their breakfast the next day, and Rosie and Jamie both exclaimed over how sweet it was. They explored the neighborhood of neat bungalows with their wide verandahs and dormer windows, each one slightly different from any other, and introduced themselves to their neighbors—a former silent movie actress on one side, now living alone with her huge, fluffy Persian cat, and a young couple with a baby on the other. Both were friendly, welcoming them to Pasadena and telling them the sights they should take in—including the newly built Pasadena Playhouse, Central Library, and City Hall, as well as the more unusual ostrich farm on the south side of the city, the first in the country.

"You can even ride the ostriches," Helena, the former silent movie star, told Ellen, "although I'm not sure I'd want to."

The afternoon after they arrived, Ellen used the telephone to call Lucas, which seemed to her an incredible thing.

"For heaven's sake," Gracie laughed, "haven't you made a telephone call before?"

"Of course I have," Ellen replied with some spirit, for she'd had a telephone in the house her whole married life, "but all the way to New York?"

"It doesn't matter how far away it is," Gracie replied, rolling her eyes teasingly. "It's the same no matter what. I bet good old Lucas will sound as if he's right next door."

Amazingly, he did. It took several minutes of speaking to a telephone operator, or "hello girl," and a few crackling connections, but then his voice came on the line, and Ellen would have sworn he could have been in the next room.

"Lucas!" she exclaimed in astonishment while Gracie grinned and shook her head. "*Lucas.*" She was so very glad to hear his voice.

Lucas seemed less astonished by the technology, although just as pleased to hear her voice as she was to hear his. "You've arrived at last!" he cried. "How was your trip? How is California?"

"We had orange juice for breakfast, Daddy," Jamie cried, scrambling onto Ellen's knee as he reached for the telephone receiver. "From oranges we picked in the garden!"

"How wonderful," Lucas replied warmly. "It sounds as if you're exactly where you need to be."

"Yes, I think we are," Ellen replied, but the words came out a bit shakily, for hearing Lucas's warm, wry voice caused a shaft of longing to pierce her right through. It had been less than a week, but she missed him desperately. Did he miss her the same way? He didn't sound it, she couldn't help but think, and then forced herself to banish the thought. "How are you? How is work?"

"Busy," Lucas replied. "But good. Booming, really. The city has been absolutely bustling since Hoover was elected." He sounded both enthused and purposeful, and Ellen wasn't exactly sure about what. He hardly ever spoke about the details of his work, except to laughingly say how dull it could be and Ellen wouldn't want to hear about it.

"Bustling...?" she ventured.

"Oh, you know, business, that's all. Stocks and bonds are going through the roof at the moment. Railroads and steel, radios and telephones—it's an exciting time to be alive. Some of our clients' stocks are absolutely *soaring*—but let me hear about you. Have you been in the swimming pool yet?"

"We have, Daddy, we have!" Ellen let out an *oof* as Jamie fidgeted in her lap, digging one bony elbow into her middle. "And Gracie splashed—"

"The pool's lovely," Ellen interjected. "The children are in heaven, having it right in our backyard."

"Capital. That's capital," Lucas approved. "Things are going well on both sides of our great country, it seems!" A pause and then he added, a little too quickly, "Except I'm missing you, of course. Terribly."

Ellen tried not to mind that he'd said that last, almost as an afterthought. He hadn't meant it that way, she told herself. She knew he hadn't. "I'm glad you're doing so well," she said after a pause. "And Eva and Maisy are taking good care of you, I suppose?"

"Excellent care. I had a three-course dinner last night all to myself, which admittedly was rather lonely! But tell me more about California. Have you seen any movie stars?"

"Our neighbor is a movie star," Jamie said, reaching once more for the telephone, "but she doesn't look like one. She's very wrinkly and *old*."

"Oh Jamie," Ellen protested, but then, with a laugh, she handed the receiver to her son and let him jabber to Lucas all he wanted.

Gracie gave her a shrewd look as she took a few steps away from the telephone and Jamie's chatter. "He does miss you, you know."

"Yes, I know that," Ellen replied, determined to sound sensible, and Gracie gave her a smile of sympathy.

"You do, but you don't always feel it, I can tell. Lucas is a busy, successful man these days. But he still adores you. It shines out of him every time he looks at you." There was a note of something almost like envy in Gracie's voice that gave Ellen pause.

"What... what happened between you and Fred, Gracie?" she asked suddenly. "Why did you end things?"

Gracie's face crumpled for a split second, so briefly that Ellen wondered if she'd imagined it, and then she gave one of her usual insouciant shrugs. "Oh, you know. Matrimony is considered so dull these days, isn't it? Very passé."

"Is it?" Ellen replied, trying for wry, although she was startled by Gracie's dismissive attitude.

Her cousin moved past her to Jamie, putting a hand on his shoulder. "Now give your poor sister a turn, toots," she teased, "before your dear old dad's ear falls off from all your yammering." Ruffling his hair, she took the telephone receiver and handed it to Rosie, who smiled shyly.

It had been foolish and insensitive to ask Gracie about Fred, Ellen realized, in the middle of such a scene—Lucas on the telephone, the children about, Maria humming in the kitchen. Yet she hadn't realized until just that moment how much she wanted to know, to be able to understand her enigmatic cousin, and what, if anything, she hid beneath her devil-may-care exterior.

She was not about to discover it then, and Gracie made sure she had no opportunity for a serious conversation over the next few days. After their telephone conversation with Lucas, they went to explore the downtown of Pasadena's resort community, admiring the newly constructed Playhouse on South El Molino Avenue. It was currently performing the world premiere of *Lazarus Laughed* by Eugene O'Neill, and Gracie sallied up to the box office to ask if they had tickets.

"There's seats still available for tomorrow night," she told Ellen. "And only a dollar fifty each! Shall we go?"

"Go to the theater?" Ellen was startled. She might have lived in New York for the last four years, but she couldn't remember the last time she'd seen a play or a musical. She'd been so busy with the children, and when she and Lucas went out, it was usually to a dinner party with his work colleagues.

"Yes, the theater! Maria can keep an eye on Rosie and Jamie. It's only a short walk away. What do you say?"

Why am I hesitating? Ellen wondered. Why did Gracie's reckless confidence make her feel like a tortoise slipping back into her shell, even over something as small as this? Yet she'd always been this way—cautious, wary, hesitant. Perhaps it had been bred in her bones, or perhaps it had been learned in her mother's sickroom during her childhood, but she was suddenly irritated by her own milksoppish nature.

Rosie tugged on her hand. "I don't mind if you go, Mama," she said. "Will you bring back the program?"

"Of course we will, sweet pea," Gracie promised. "And you can look at it all you want."

"Very well, then," Ellen said, almost defiantly, and went to the box office to purchase the tickets for the following evening, while Rosie grinned and Jamie clapped his hands.

The night air blowing in from her bedroom's open windows was cool and silky as Ellen dressed for the theater. Rosie sat on her bed, trying on a long string of pearls and a pair of gloves.

"You look beautiful, Mama," she said while Ellen made a silly face at her reflection in the mirror.

"Thank you, darling," she said, although she feared she looked a bit stodgy. Her dress was several years old—she had never seen the point of going about in new gowns every year, although Lucas always encouraged her to buy things for herself—and, she now suspected, she appeared rather dreary in the dress of dark gray silk with a drop-waist and a discreet bow on the side, and no other embellishment. Well, Ellen reminded herself, she was a matron of thirty-seven with two children to care for. Fancy frocks were for the lighthearted likes of Gracie, not her.

She'd just roped her pearls twice around her neck when Gracie came into her bedroom, humming under her breath.

"Ta-da," she announced, holding her arms up for inspection. "How do I look?"

She looked, Ellen thought, like a vivid, burning flame, in a bright orange dress with a loose cowl neckline. The front hem only touched her knees but the back brushed the floor, and when she twirled around, Ellen saw the back of the dress was cut down nearly to her tailbone, revealing a smooth, bare expanse of skin.

"You look beautiful, Gracie," Rosie exclaimed. "Like a movie star!"

"Thanks, pet." Gracie ruffled her hair before turning to Ellen with a frown. "You can't wear that. You look like you're going to a funeral."

"I don't," Ellen replied, glancing at herself again, and then realizing Gracie had a point. The dress *was* dour, especially compared to her cousin's daring ensemble.

"Borrow something of mine," Gracie suggested. "Something bright to bring out your eyes. You're a beautiful woman, Ellen, you don't need to look like a housekeeper!"

"There's nothing wrong with looking like a housekeeper—"

Gracie rolled her eyes. "No, not if you are one. But you're not, and you're going to the theater, not a wake. Come on." Tugging her hand, her eyes as bright as a child's, she drew Ellen to her bedroom. With a giggle, Rosie followed, and even Jamie poked his head out of his bedroom, only to give a snort of disgust when he realized all the excitement was about nothing more than dresses. "Now let's see what we've got..." Gracie mused, going into officious mode while Ellen stood in the doorway, uncertain.

"Do you ever clean your room, Gracie?" Rosie asked seriously, and Gracie just laughed.

"Only when I have to."

The room was a colorful disaster of spilled dresses, kicked-off shoes and stockings, necklaces and earrings in a jumble on top of the bureau, and a powder puff tossed carelessly aside, along with a silken spill of powder. A stack of movie magazines was piled next to the bed—*Motion Picture Magazine, Screenland, PhotoPlay.*

Ellen glanced at the glossy illustration of screen actress Madge Bellamy looking playful, with the caption "Screen Kisses—Are They Hot or Cold?" beneath her coy, red-lipped smile.

"How about this?" Gracie suggested, and held up a dress in lavender chiffon, with a row of diamantés sewn on both the hem and wide neckline.

"I'd be showing my knees," Ellen exclaimed, knowing how prim she sounded and yet unable to keep herself from it, but Gracie just laughed.

"Exactly. Haven't you worn a swimming costume before?"

"Not to the theater!"

"Try it on, at least," Gracie coaxed, and Ellen stole another glance at her reflection. Did she really look like a housekeeper?

"Oh, very well," she said, and let Gracie unbutton the back of her dress, before she slipped on the chiffon concoction over her slip, the material as light as air as it floated around her.

"Oh, *Mama*," Rosie said breathlessly, her hands clasped to her chest.

"You're a stunner," Gracie pronounced in satisfaction. "I knew you would be."

Ellen felt as if she were nearly naked. "Let me look..." She turned to the mirror, but Gracie whirled her away from the glass, her hands on her elbows.

"Not yet, missus! We need to do your face first."

"My *face*..."

"Warpaint," Gracie stated succinctly as she reached for a lipstick. "Can't be without it."

"I don't think..." Ellen began, trailing off when Gracie began to paint her mouth in carmine red. She'd never worn makeup in her life. She knew many women did, even the grand ladies of Carnegie Hill, but she'd never seen the point of bothering, and she feared it might make her look something like a clown. Now she felt her stomach clench with nerves as Gracie finished with her mouth and moved on to eyeshadow. "Nothing too dramatic, please, Gracie," she implored nervously. "I don't want to look ridiculous."

"You won't," Gracie promised. "You'll look stunning, believe me. Won't she, Rosie?" She winked at the girl, who beamed back.

"Oh, yes, Gracie, she will."

"Right, that's your eyes done, and now something a *leetle* more interesting than your standard string of pearls." She whisked off the pearls Lucas had given Ellen for her thirtieth birthday with one swift jerk. "Shame you never had your ears pierced. I could do it quick as a wink with a needle and an ice cube..."

"No, thank you," Ellen replied firmly, and Gracie just laughed as she fastened a diamond and jet pin to the bosom of her dress.

"Right, I don't suppose you'd bob your hair either, would you? One chop of the scissors, that's all it would take..."

Horrified, Ellen held a hand up to her thick chestnut hair, curled into its usual modest coil at the nape of her neck. "Never!"

"It must be so very hot," Gracie wheedled mischievously, her hands on her hips, "with all that hair on your neck in this climate."

"It's fine, I assure you."

"All right, all right, keep your hair on," she soothed, winking at Rosie again. "Literally, I mean. Now, let's have a quick dusting of powder and then we're off!"

Ellen tried not to sneeze as Gracie brushed the powder puff all over her face and then stepped back.

"There she is, the Queen of Pasadena! Come and have a gander at your beauty, m'lady."

Smiling and yet full of trepidation, Ellen turned to the mirror. And blinked. Stared silently, while Rosie stood behind her, eager and apprehensive, and Gracie just watched, her head cocked, a faint smile to her lips.

"Well?" Rosie finally asked eagerly. "Don't you like it?"

"I..." Ellen shook her head slowly. "I don't know what to think," she said honestly. The truth was, she hardly recognized herself. She looked younger and yet more worldly; the eyeshadow made her hazel eyes appear larger and greener, reminding Ellen of a cat. Her mouth was so lush and red... and as she gazed at herself it curved into a secretive, knowing smile.

"She likes it!" Rosie exclaimed. "Mama, you're smiling!"

"I knew she would. Now all we need is a wrap," Gracie hunted through the mess of clothes before she found a gauzy, spangled wrap that would do very little to ward off the chill, but as she draped it about her bare arms, Ellen decided it finished the outfit very well. Still she couldn't help but hesitate.

"I don't know..."

"Too late," Gracie replied breezily. "No time to change or we'll miss the curtain." She gave Rosie a smacking kiss on her cheek. "Be a good girl, lambchop," she said. "And as for you, Ellen... the finishing touch!" Before Ellen knew what she was doing, she found herself drenched in a cloud of exotic-smelling Shalimar. "Off we go," Gracie sang, linking her arm with Ellen's, and together they sashayed down the stairs and out the door, with Rosie and Jamie both grinning as Maria stood behind them, smiling placidly and waving them off.

Ellen felt the whisper of the breeze against her bare knees, the stickiness of the lipstick on her lips, and a sudden shudder of apprehension went through her as she yanked her arm from Gracie's. "I can't..."

"You can and you are," Gracie said firmly, reaching for her arm again. "I mean it, Ellen Lyman. No ifs, buts, or ands. You look marvelous and not a bit scandalous, if that's what you're worried about. Look." She nodded toward a couple who were also walking towards the theater on South El Molino Street. "She's showing her knees."

Ellen glanced dubiously at the woman who walked a bit ahead of them. She looked to be about thirty or so, with bright blonde hair in a sleek bob. She was dressed in a knee-skimming dress of vivid green with a matching feather boa. Ellen thought she looked like a showgirl.

"I don't know..." she said nervously. She smoothed her hand down the front of the dress, her fingernails snagging on the diamantés.

"What are you so scared of?" Gracie demanded, stopping right there in the street, her hands planted on her hips as she gave Ellen a challenging look. "Of showing your knees? Or having some dowdy matron thinking you're a bit fast? Or is it just change itself? The fact that it's not the same as it was?"

Ellen hesitated, and then said honestly, "I suppose the last, really. I've never liked change."

"Why not?" The question, asked with such matter-of-factness, startled Ellen, and for a second she couldn't reply. "Because you've certainly seen enough of it," Gracie continued frankly. "Emigrating from Scotland, coming to Amherst Island, nursing, moving to New York... your life has been all change, Ellen, and you've managed all right so far. Why worry about a single dress or a lick of face paint?" Her expression hardened briefly as she tilted her chin. "Life's too short for those kinds of fears, trust me."

"I can't help the way I am," Ellen protested, and Gracie rolled her eyes.

"That's why you've got me," she told her, and grabbing her arm, she started propelling her down the street. "Now let's hurry up before we miss the show."

CHAPTER SIX

The play was like nothing Ellen had ever seen, and at first she feared it might be considered blasphemous. With a cast of over one hundred masked actors like in a Greek tragedy, the story centered around Lazarus from the Bible, and how after he'd risen from the dead, he'd laughed and laughed, and his laughter somehow made him both younger and stronger, and turned his wife Miriam weaker and older. Gracie seemed utterly absorbed in the drama, but Ellen feared the message went over her own head.

"What do you think of it?" Gracie asked as they went into the lobby in the intermission, where everyone was mingling and ordering drinks.

"I'm not sure," Ellen admitted. "It's quite... strange."

"It is, isn't it?" Gracie agreed. "But typical that the man gets younger and stronger while the wife turns into an old frump!"

Before Ellen could reply, a waiter came up to them with a little bow. "May I offer you ladies some refreshment?"

"You surely can," Gracie answered pertly before Ellen could say anything, and she slipped him a one-dollar bill with a wink. "We're *awfully* thirsty, if you've got anything with fizz."

The waiter nodded, blank-faced. "Very good, madam."

"Gracie!" Ellen was as impressed as she was scandalized. "What was all that about?"

"This place serves booze for sure. Why shouldn't we have some of it?"

Ellen let out a choked laugh, shaking her head. She knew she should be disapproving, but she'd been so primly disapproving for so long. She was tired of it, of herself, and something about the play had resonated deep inside her, even without her really understanding it. Why shouldn't she have fun? Why should she stay dowdy and dull just because? She kept telling herself she was going to have fun, but then when it came to it she held back, out of nervousness or fear. Well, no longer.

When the waiter returned with two glasses of champagne, Ellen took hers defiantly, clinking with Gracie's glass before she tossed back a mouthful—and then nearly choked. She hadn't had champagne in so long, the bubbles tickled her nose and caught at her throat.

"That's the spirit!" Gracie exclaimed as she patted her on the back.

Ellen swallowed the mouthful, her eyes watering, and then determinedly took another sip.

"Gracie," she asked once she'd swallowed again, "what did you mean about it being typical that the wife turns old and frumpy?"

"Well, she does, doesn't she? Poor old Miriam goes from bad to worse while Lazarus just bumbles along, giggling away." The hard note in her voice surprised Ellen, along with Gracie's shrewdly narrowed gaze. "That's how it always is between men and women."

"Is that why you broke off things with Fred?" Ellen asked. The champagne had certainly loosened her tongue. "Because you didn't want to be constrained by marriage?"

"Actually, he broke things off with me," Gracie replied, her tone almost nonchalant. She tossed back the rest of the champagne and then riffled in her purse. "I'm dying for a gasper."

Ellen didn't even purse her lips as Gracie took out a cigarette and fitted it into her holder. "Why did he? Break things off, I mean?"

Gracie shrugged, her tone turning slightly brittle. "Why does any man? This looks like a well-heeled crowd, doesn't it?" she remarked as she gazed around at the other audience members in their daring gowns and smart suits, natty hats and glamorous stoles and furs. "Do you suppose we'll see a movie star?"

"I wouldn't recognize one if we did," Ellen replied. She wanted to ask more about Fred, but just as before, she knew it wasn't the right time.

Sure enough, a few minutes later the bell rang, and they trooped back into the theater to watch Lazarus gallivant through life with increasing hilarity while his wife was poisoned by the emperor Tiberius and died, and then Lazarus himself was burned at the stake, laughing the whole while.

"I really don't know what that was all about," Ellen confessed wryly as they walked back to Bungalow Heaven in a silky, cool darkness. The play had engaged and baffled her in turns, although judging from the standing ovation, most people had thought it magnificent. She couldn't quite see how.

"Laughing till the end," Gracie mused, her head tilted to the sky that was scattered with stars as if a giant had flung a handful of diamonds across an expanse of black velvet. "Maybe that's the way to do it."

"You want to be like Lazarus?" Ellen asked dubiously. She had not been particularly impressed by his carefree manner, which had seemed to her, by the end, to border on cruel indifference.

"Why not? He enjoyed himself, didn't he?"

"While his entire family suffered and died!"

"So?" Gracie shrugged her shoulders. "It didn't bother him much."

"Gracie..." Ellen wasn't sure what was going on, but from the dark undercurrent in Gracie's voice it was clear they weren't really talking about the play.

"Oh, don't get all in a lather. I'm just joking." Gracie let out a laugh that didn't sound quite right to Ellen. "I'm not completely without a soul, even if you think I'm scandalous."

"I don't think you're scandalous—"

"Oh, you do." Gracie gave her a cheeky smile. "I don't mind. I quite like being scandalous, actually. Perhaps I'll be a bit *more* scandalous. Now that would be fun."

"I'm not sure—" Ellen began, alarmed even though she knew, or at least hoped, Gracie was teasing her.

Gracie laughed again, the sound heartier this time. "Oh, don't worry, I really am just joking. It wouldn't do to corrupt the young minds of your kiddies, would it?"

"No, but it's not them I'm worried about," Ellen replied, gentling her voice. "Gracie, are you sure—"

"Look, we're home." Lightly, Gracie ran the last few yards to the bungalow; Maria had left a lamp on in the window. "I'm completely wrung out. Time to hit the hay, I think." She ran up the steps and slipped through the front door before Ellen could say anything else.

Maria slipped off to her own bungalow in the back of the garden as soon as they came in, and Gracie went right up to her bedroom, making Ellen feel a bit unsettled. What was really going on beneath her cousin's insouciance? She sensed something hard and dark and brittle, and it worried her. She feared Gracie would never give her an honest answer, just slip on yet another mask. Or was she being fanciful about it all?

With a sigh, Ellen slipped into Jamie's room, smoothing his hair away from his forehead as she watched him sleep. Already he looked a little browner and sturdier than he had in New York. His cheeks were filling out and his chest had been sounding clearer than it had been in months. That alone made Ellen thankful they'd made the journey, even if this new world still felt rather alien and strange. Her son was finally thriving.

Rosie was asleep when she went to check on her, but her eyes fluttered opened when Ellen bent over her to kiss her goodnight.

"Mama..." she breathed, a sleepy smile curving her mouth. "Did you have a lovely time?"

"Yes, we did."

"And the play? It was good?"

"It was enjoyable, if a bit strange," Ellen admitted with a soft laugh. She tucked a tendril of hair behind Rosie's ear. "I brought you the program, you can look at it at breakfast. Go back to sleep, darling. It's late."

"I will." Rosie's eyes fluttered closed. "You look so beautiful, Mama."

"Thank you, darling." But Rosie had already fallen back asleep.

In her bedroom, Ellen glanced at the letter she'd been composing for Lucas, left on her desk. She'd told him about the orange groves and the swimming pool, the sightseeing they'd done, and how welcoming Maria and Eduardo had been. She glanced up at her reflection; although she'd bitten off most of the lipstick, there were traces of dark red on the corners of her mouth, and she still smelled spicily of Shalimar. Would she tell Lucas about her evening at the theater? Would she write of how she'd borrowed Gracie's dress and worn her lipstick and felt like a different person for a few hours, and that hadn't actually been a bad thing?

She could already picture Lucas's smiling bemusement at reading such things; she could hear his steady voice assuring her that no matter what she wore or did, she would always be his Ellen.

Abruptly, Ellen took the pins from her hair and shook it out, watching the chestnut waves tumble all the way to her waist. She'd always loved her hair, but now she wondered if it looked old-fashioned, or worse, like a woman clinging to girlishness. Was that a gray hair, she wondered, stepping closer to the mirror to examine a few glinting strands by the light of the lamp. It was, and more than one.

With a sigh, Ellen turned away from the mirror. Who was she fooling? And what was she trying to prove? She was no Gracie, to gallivant about with cigarettes and champagne, short dress and high heels. She knew that, and yet for the first time in many years she found herself wondering who she really was.

She'd felt the same way as a child, caught between an old world and new, and then between her life in Vermont and the one she enjoyed on Amherst Island. Later, it had been a struggle between nursing and drawing, and later still between a modest life on her island and a far more glamorous one in New York. Always a struggle, always a choice to be made...

She'd found her heart's home with Lucas and the family they'd made together, but he seemed very far away, and not, she knew, simply because of the continent currently yawning between them. How long had he been spending so much time in his study and at work? When had he begun to look so preoccupied, and sometimes even impatient or irritated, as if the life they'd made together had started to bore him, just a little bit?

Or was she being fanciful again, even paranoid, because he wasn't here to reassure her, catch her up in his arms and tease her before kissing her soundly? In any case, she realized, this wasn't really about Lucas. It was about *her,* and the knowledge, shameful as it felt, that despite her disapproval she was just a little bit envious of Gracie's carefree independence. She didn't regret any of the choices she'd made, or begrudge Lucas or her children the life she now led, not even for an instant, but the world *was* changing, and she was only thirty-seven, with children who were growing up every day. What could the future hold for her?

Briefly she thought of the sketching she'd done as a child, the years she'd spent at the Glasgow School of Art. Her fingers flexed instinctively; she'd continued with her sketching during her marriage, but only as a hobby, a pleasant pastime, nothing more, of the children playing, or the flowers in the garden. Once, her painting *Starlit Sea* had hung in the Metropolitan Museum of Art; her charcoal sketches had been shown in a gallery in the city. That all felt very far away, and yet...

Could she have it again? Or some part of it? Did she even want that? Or did she simply want to wear a bit of makeup, drink some champagne, and *live* a little?

Such thoughts felt traitorous to who she was, the life she'd built and enjoyed with Lucas, with Rosie and Jamie. And yet. *And yet—*

A sudden sound had her turning from the mirror. She froze, straining, and then she heard it again—the hacking cough she knew so well, and yet hadn't heard since their first day in California.

With her heart thudding, Ellen hurried from the room to her son's. Jamie remained asleep as the cough tore at his chest, practically lifting him off the bed.

Ellen dropped to her knees beside the bed and touched his forehead, but it was thankfully cool. He coughed again, and she sat back on her heels, struggling not to feel anxious and even guilty, for having gone out at all. Had he seemed tired at dinner? Why couldn't she remember? She'd been so preoccupied with her evening at the theater, she might have missed some telltale warning sign.

Another cough, his thin body twisting beneath the sheets, and she decided to stay by his bedside until the episode fully subsided. She shouldn't have gone out, she thought wretchedly. If he'd had a warm bath and gone to bed early, perhaps this could have been avoided. Perhaps he'd been spending too much time in the pool... yesterday he hadn't dried his hair properly afterwards, and she'd let him run off into the garden anyway.

The thoughts rushed through her mind as they always did, as she raced to think of what she could have done differently or better, to keep her son safe and well. Would she ever be free of that fear? That guilt?

Another few minutes passed, enough for Ellen to hope he'd settled, and then he coughed again, and she waited once more for blessed silence, her head drooping toward her chest, her hand resting on Jamie's arm. Just a few more minutes and she'd go to her own bed...

· · ·

"Ellen, for heaven's sake!"

Ellen stirred from her place on the floor, every muscle aching as she blinked the sunlit-filled room into focus. Jamie was asleep, his breathing wonderfully steady and even; she'd fallen asleep on the floor next to him, still in her evening dress, her head resting on the side of the bed.

Gracie bustled toward her, her expression caught between exasperation and concern. "Have you been here all night?" she exclaimed.

"He was coughing..."

Gracie pressed her hand to Jamie's forehead as she shook her head. "He's not feverish."

"I know, but the cough—"

"Was just a cough. Children do have them. Come on." She reached a hand down to help Ellen up from the ground.

Ellen winced as she rose. She was too old to spend the night crouched on the floor, and yet she knew she'd do it again for either of her children in a heartbeat.

"I'm running you a bath," Gracie said firmly. "And then you can go to bed for the rest of the day, while I occupy Master and Miss Lyman."

"What are we going to do, Gracie?" Jamie asked from behind them as he rubbed the sleep from his eyes. He did not sound as if he'd had a moment's bad health, Ellen thought ruefully. Had she been overprotective as Lucas seemed to think she was? And yet that cough...

"Wait and see, mister," Gracie replied smartly. "Now hop downstairs and get yourself some breakfast. Maria has made the most delicious *huevos rancheros*. As for you." She gave Ellen a pertly bossy look. "To the bath. Goodness, that dress is crumpled!"

"I'm sorry—" Ellen began helplessly, too tired to offer any more resistance.

"I'm just teasing! Come on."

Too tired to resist, Ellen let Gracie lead her to the bath. She gave herself a good wash and then nearly fell asleep up to her chin in warm water, before Gracie rapped on the door and insisted she get out.

"Now to bed," Gracie stated, and Ellen tried to protest. She *was* tired, but she was used to spending many a night by Jamie's bedside, and she didn't want to miss the whole day with them. They'd been planning to visit the library to check out some books, and then head to the park.

"What did you bring me along for, if not for days like this?" Gracie asked, pragmatic but also a little bit exasperated. "Unless it was to worry you sick with all my silly antics?" Ellen smiled at that, while Gracie shook a finger in her face. "To bed! I promise I won't dunk Jamie underwater *too* many times."

Ellen held her tongue, because she knew Gracie was teasing, but she still felt apprehensive about leaving her cousin in charge. She hadn't given the care of her children to Gracie— or anyone— for a whole day since they'd been born. But then Gracie was turning back her covers and drawing the curtains, shutting out the bright sunlight, and somehow Ellen let herself be tucked up in bed like a child, and before Gracie had closed the door, she was already gladly succumbing to sleep.

When she woke, the light slanting in from the chink in the curtains was hazy and muted, and as Ellen stretched luxuriously and blinked the world back into focus, she saw, to her surprise, it was already four o'clock in the afternoon. She'd slept the whole day away, and she could hardly believe it. It seemed like a waste, and yet she couldn't remember the last time she'd felt so well rested, her muscles loose and relaxed. Years of sitting by Jamie's bedside, watching him toss and turn, had clearly taken their toll.

She rose from bed, hurrying into a day dress and tidying her hair as she threw off the last of her grogginess. The house seemed utterly silent and still, and a sudden, nameless anxiety gripped her. Where were her children?

Downstairs, all was peaceful and quiet, and yet Ellen couldn't keep from feeling just a little bit unnerved. If Gracie had taken them out, why hadn't she left a note? And where were Maria and Eduardo?

"Ah, Mrs. Lyman!" Maria came in from the kitchen's back door with a broad smile. "I was wondering when you would wake up. May I bring you some lemonade? Or coffee?"

"Oh yes, please, Maria, to lemonade." She'd stopped insisting the housekeeper call her Ellen, for she had continued to insist on formalities. "Where are the others?"

"Miss McCafferty took them to the park. They were going to fly a kite, I think. Such happy children!"

"Oh, how lovely." Ellen gave a little laugh, feeling completely silly at how worried she'd been feeling just a moment ago. With a murmured thanks, she accepted a glass of lemonade from Maria and took it out to the patio. She'd only had a few sips before she heard the front door open, and then Jamie was barreling toward her, with Rosie not far behind.

"Mama, we flew a kite!"

"It went so high, it looked like a bird!" Rosie chimed in. "Or even an airplane."

"My goodness." Laughing, Ellen hugged them both before gazing over their heads to Gracie, who had come onto the patio behind them, holding a kite and looking fresh and pretty in a white dress with navy piping and a sailor collar, her curls pinned back. "Thank you for taking them out, Gracie. It sounds as if they've had an absolutely marvelous time."

"Oh, we had heaps of fun, didn't we, darlings?" Gracie replied, giving Rosie and Jamie conspiratorial grins. "Heaps and heaps. The library, the pool, the park...! But I must fly now—Eduardo's driving me into the city in half an hour."

"Into the city! You mean Los Angeles?" Ellen stared at her in surprise. "Whatever for?"

The look Gracie gave her was arch. "To have a drink with Mr. Hughes at the Beverly Hills Hotel. You hadn't forgotten his invitation, had you?"

"I didn't think you'd actually take him up on it," Ellen replied, startled, and yet at the same time not altogether surprised. "Never mind that you'd set a date."

"Oh, don't *scold*. It's just a drink, Ellen." Gracie rolled her eyes at Rosie and Jamie. "Isn't your mama silly?"

They looked at her uncertainly, and Ellen did her best to dismiss her unease, as well as her annoyance at Gracie's manner. "You'd best get ready, then," she said. "Rosie, Jamie, shall we pick some oranges?" Taking them each by one hand, Ellen marched off to the small grove of lemon and orange trees at the back of the garden while, with a laugh and a shrug, Gracie headed indoors.

The late-afternoon sunlight slanted through the trees and made patterns on the grass as Ellen twisted an orange from its stem with a smooth, hard jerk. Next to her, Rosie reached for another of the bright, round fruit.

"Why are you cross with Gracie, Mama?" she asked as she plucked the orange from tree.

"I'm not cross."

"You sounded cross."

Ellen sighed, doing her best to let go of the irritation she didn't fully understand. Gracie had been a marvel today, seeing her to bed and then taking care of the children. And yet Ellen's head spun from her cousin's changes of mood—from doting governess to gadabout flapper in the space of a few seconds! It made her wonder, not for the first time, if she knew Gracie at all. Why hadn't she told her about having made plans with Emmett Hughes? She hadn't mentioned him once since they'd disembarked from *The Chief*. Ellen had assumed, with relief, that she'd forgotten about him.

"Should she not meet Mr. Hughes?" Rosie asked, sounding anxious.

"You know about Mr. Hughes?"

"Gracie said he worked in the movies and was really nice."

Ellen bit her lip. The last thing she wanted was for her children to come into the middle of this futile argument. Gracie was a grown woman, and she would do what she liked, no matter what Ellen thought about it. She needed to stop fussing so much. She knew that, she really did, and yet she couldn't keep from feeling a deep-seated unease at Gracie's seemingly forced gaiety, her utter determination to be reckless, that glitter in her eye that to Ellen seemed somehow almost dangerous.

"I'm sure he's very nice," she told Rosie. "I'm not cross. I'm just sorry I missed flying the kite with you in the park."

Rosie regarded her with her wide, hazel eyes unblinking, and Ellen knew she hadn't fooled her daughter at all. As she reached for Jamie's hand to head back to the bungalow, she heard the trill of Gracie's laughter and then, in the distance, the slam of a car door.

Regardless of how she felt about the matter, Gracie had already gone.

CHAPTER SEVEN

Ellen had been determined to wait up for Gracie's return, but she found herself, despite her day-long nap, curled up on the sofa and nodding to sleep in the small hours of the morning without any sign of Gracie. Eduardo had come back with the car soon after he'd dropped her off, informing Ellen that Gracie had insisted he return, as Mr. Hughes would be driving her home. Ellen had not liked that bit of news at all, and Eduardo, looking anxious, had asked her if he should have waited anyway.

"No, no," Ellen had hurried to appease him, "you did the right thing. I'm sorry for the long trip, Eduardo." It took half an hour to drive into Los Angeles from Pasadena.

The noise of a car door slamming had her blinking awake groggily. Light footsteps, and then Gracie opened the front door, while Ellen half-staggered from the sofa.

"Oh, Ellen!" Gracie let out a breathy little gasp as she theatrically put one hand to her heart. "You startled me."

"It's three in the morning, Gracie." Ellen sounded weary rather than accusing. Gracie's face was flushed, her lipstick smudged, and her dress, a black sheath with a wide collar, was askew enough to reveal the strap of her brassiere. Deliberately Ellen averted her eyes. "What on earth have you been doing?"

"Emmett was showing me the sights," Gracie replied carelessly. "Hollywood is *so* much fun! We went to Café La Boheme—they had dancing and I saw Douglas Fairbanks *and* Alla Nazimova! Of course, she's completely past it—she never made it in talkies—but she *is* glamorous."

"Till three in the morning?" Ellen asked, although it was obvious.

"And what of it? Most movie stars stay out until dawn!"

"You're not a movie star, Gracie," Ellen returned a bit sharply, and her cousin raised her eyebrows as she gave her a smug little smile.

"I may not be yet, but Emmett has offered me a part in his new movie. It's why he came to California. They start filming next week. Can you even believe it?"

"What!" Ellen stared at her in disbelief. "You're going to be an *actress?*"

"It's just a walk-on role, it won't take long to film." Gracie shrugged, careless, defiant. "It's a wonderful opportunity. I'd be crazy not to take it." She gave Ellen a look of cool challenge, while she struggled to organize her thoughts.

"We'll talk about this in the morning," she finally said.

"There's nothing to talk about!"

"Gracie..." Ellen shook her head helplessly. She was too tired, and her mind too muzzy, to have this discussion now. "In the morning," she repeated, and then she headed upstairs to bed, her heart heavy, her mind spinning. Gracie in a *movie...*

By morning, after a few hours' rather dismal sleep, Ellen felt no clearer on the subject. She breakfasted on scrambled eggs and coffee while Jamie and Rosie played in the garden, her eyes narrowed against the hard glint of sunlight as she considered the matter.

She could not, she realized, be responsible for Gracie. She didn't want to be, and in any case, she *wasn't*. Gracie was twenty-eight years old, a grown woman fully capable of making her own decisions, even if Ellen regarded some of those decisions as unwise. She could be as censorious as she chose, but she couldn't control Gracie, and she should stop trying. In fact, Ellen reflected, it might be easier if Gracie were away filming for a few days, or weeks—give her a little space to enjoy her children without worrying what Gracie was up to, or trying, futilely and perhaps unnecessarily, to regulate her behavior.

And really, why should she be so bothered whether Gracie starred in a movie or stayed out till dawn? Admittedly, Jamie and Rosie in particular turned a bit goggle-eyed when they watched their young, glamorous cousin, but Gracie wasn't too shocking around them. Ellen supposed it was hard to let go of the sense of responsibility she'd had when Gracie was young, a mop-topped three-year-old with eyes that sparkled, but even so, she didn't need to be so priggish. And so, she determined, she wouldn't be. It was as simple as that.

As if summoned by her thoughts, Gracie strolled onto the patio, wearing a loosely belted silk wrapper with, Ellen suspected, nothing underneath.

"Goodness, I'm pooped," she declared as she sprawled across from Ellen, running a hand through her wild curls. "What a night." She yawned hugely and then gestured to the coffee pot. "Any chance I can have a cup of that?"

"Of course," Ellen replied, and despite her best intentions, she could not keep from sounding a little stiff. She rose to fetch another cup and saucer from the kitchen, and then poured Gracie a cup and pushed it over to her.

"You have a mouth like a prune," Gracie told her as she dumped two full spoonfuls of sugar into her cup and stirred. "Go on and say it, whatever it is. I can tell you're dying to." She looked amused more than anything else, but there was a hard set to her mouth.

Ellen took a sip of her own coffee and replaced her cup to its saucer before replying. "Tell me about this movie," she said, managing to injecting a light friendliness to her tone. "What sort of picture is it?"

Gracie's eyebrows rose, but then she sat back, her cup cradled in her hands, her legs sprawled in front of her. "It's a gangster movie, called *The Lady and The Brute*. I'm one of the gangster's molls. I've only got a few lines, but I'll be on camera a bit." She finished with a shrug, while Ellen swallowed down any number of remarks she could have made.

"I see," she said after a moment.

Gracie let out a hoot of laughter. "You're horrified, I can tell! Gangster films are all the rage now, Ellen, really." She cocked her finger like a pistol as she took on a gruff voice, eyes dancing. "Give me the cabbage or it's a Chicago overcoat for you, bub!"

"I have no idea what that means," Ellen replied with a forced laugh.

"Give me the money or it's a coffin for you," Gracie translated blithely. "Your face, Ellen! What a picture!"

Ellen tried to school her features into a more bland expression. "I admit, this has all taken me by surprise. I had no idea you had any interest in acting." Although she supposed she could have guessed, and in truth she thought Gracie's pale skin and dark hair, her sense of vitality and mischief, would translate superbly on screen. But a role as a gangster's moll in a movie called *The Lady and the Brute*?

"I don't know if I like acting or not," Gracie replied with a shrug. "I've never tried it."

"Well, then," Ellen said as lightly as she could, "I suppose you'll find out."

They both fell silent then, sipping their coffee, while Rosie and Jamie ran through the orange trees.

"Yesterday Jamie ran with the kite," Gracie said after a moment. "All the way down the hill at the park, and he didn't even get breathless." She gave Ellen a smile that seemed genuine, kindly, not one of her cheeky grins or a sly devil-may-care curving of her lips. "This climate agrees with him. You and

Lucas were right to bring him here. He's getting stronger every day."

"It seems so," Ellen agreed, her voice a little shaky as she watched Jamie's slight form disappear behind the trees. Gracie was right; he *was* getting stronger. "I hope a few months here will make him stronger still." She paused and then admitted, "It's so hard to stop worrying, though. I try, and I find I can't. I keep fussing even when it annoys him—it feels like the only way to keep him safe."

"There's nothing like a mother's love," Gracie replied, and while it could have been one of her usual blithe quips, it didn't quite sound like one. It sounded heartfelt, almost wistful, and Gracie looked away before Ellen could meet her eye. "I forgot to tell you," she said after a pause where Ellen struggled to think of something to say. She wanted to ask Gracie something of how she was feeling underneath that bright, hard gloss, but she couldn't find the words.

"Forgot to tell me...?"

"Emmett is taking us all out for the day, to show us the sights. He's got the most amazing bucket—it really is the cat's meow."

"The what?" Ellen asked, baffled again by Gracie's easy slang.

"His car, silly! It's a Rolls-Royce Phantom, the absolute bee's knees. Wait until you see it."

"But... what do you mean he's taking us all out?"

"For the day! He's promised to show us the Hollywood Bowl and the Chinese Theatre and the La Brea tar pits."

"Tar pits!" Ellen had never heard of such a thing.

"Yes, apparently they're something." Gracie wrinkled her nose. "I'd rather see the Chinese Theatre than a bunch of dinosaur bones, though. He's promised us lunch at his swanky hotel. He should be here in half an hour."

"Half an hour!" Ellen stared at her in complete dismay. "But you didn't even tell me, Gracie! You could have asked—"

"There wasn't any time, and why should you say no?" Gracie countered. "It will be a wonderful day for the children. Rosie!

Jamie!" she called over to them, clapping her hands. "Guess what we're doing today?"

Once again Ellen had to hold her tongue as Gracie whipped the children into a near-frenzy of excitement about all the enticements of the day, none of which she was very sure about.

"You'd better go get dressed," Ellen said briskly once she'd finished and they were both leaping up and down. "Jamie, wash behind your ears! Rosie, I think your pink dress." She turned back to Gracie, who was watching her with that catlike expression of speculative amusement that Ellen was learning not to trust. "I will have to thank Mr. Hughes for his generosity."

Gracie let out a cackle of laughter. "I'm sure you will," she said as she rose from the table, pulling her wrapper more tightly around her. "And now I'd better get dressed, as well! Can't have Emmett seeing me half-naked!" With another laugh, she hurried upstairs while Ellen cleared the breakfast things, her mind now in a ferment.

She changed into her smartest day dress, in light green organdy with a low, belted waist and a straw hat with a deep brim and a matching ribbon in green. If she was going to go about Los Angles in a fancy motorcar, she wanted be suitably appareled.

"Mama, do you think we'll see a movie star today?" Rosie asked as they waited downstairs for Emmett Hughes to arrive in his much-talked-about Phantom.

"I hope not," Ellen said tartly. "I wouldn't know what to say to one."

Rosie slipped her hand in hers. "You could just say hello," she offered seriously, and Ellen gave a little laugh.

"You're right, my love. That's what I should do."

They didn't say anything more, for Gracie was tripping down the stairs in a lovely lavender ensemble, and the most stupendous car Ellen had ever seen had pulled up in front of the bungalow and Jamie let out a squeal of delight.

CHAPTER EIGHT

In the end, despite Ellen's initial misgivings, they all had a rather marvelous day. Emmett Hughes was a charming and gracious host and tour guide, speaking knowledgeably of the tar pits in La Brea—discovered nearly thirty years ago, although the pits and surrounding park had been donated to Los Angeles County just five years earlier by George Hancock of the Rancho La Brea Oil Company.

"And animals got stuck in that muck forever?" Rosie asked, sounding troubled, as she gazed down at one of the hundred or more pits that scored the park, the thick, dark tar bubbling up ominously from deep within the earth.

"Yes, they wouldn't be able to move because it's so sticky," Emmett replied. "It's very sad, but it happened a long time ago and gave us the most fascinating fossils." He smiled at her kindly, and Rosie looked nominally comforted.

"I think it looks like molasses," Jamie said, hanging off the railing that guarded visitors from getting too close to the bubbling black pits.

"Careful," Emmett replied, pulling him back a little with a friendly hand, "or you'll get stuck in the tar yourself. Glug—glug—

glug!" He held his nose as he mimed sinking beneath the thick, gooey substance.

"The brochure said it took months for animals to sink," Jamie scoffed, but he stepped back all the same.

"You know so much about the city," Ellen remarked as they walked through the newly made Hancock Park with its palm trees and stretches of verdant grass, watered from the Los Angeles Aqueduct that piped water in from Owens Valley, over two hundred miles away, much to the contention of the farmers of that area.

Emmett had already taken them through the park's little museum, and they had toured some of the many tar pits. Next they would be going to Grauman's Chinese Theatre, to see the handprints that now decorated the sidewalk outside; Douglas Fairbanks and Mary Pickford had done the first ones, less than two years ago.

"I've always loved the idea of Hollywood," Emmett told her with a rather bashful shrug. "I'm just glad to have finally made it here."

Ellen had learned, over the course of their morning, that Emmett was from a wealthy banking family in New York; he'd been expected to follow in his father's footsteps, but had been given eighteen months to make or break a career in Hollywood. *The Lady and the Brute* was his first attempt at producing, the position arranged by a friend of his father's. She'd been surprised at how charming he was, without the hard gloss of Hollywood, just a boy in a fancy suit. She liked him more for it.

"I hope your movie is a big hit," she said, meaning it for his sake, although she still felt more than a little dubious about Gracie's role as a moll in a gangster film.

"Ellen is afraid you'll corrupt me," Gracie told Emmett conspiratorially, while he blushed and Ellen, trying not to sound annoyed, stammered out her denial.

"I'm... I'm afraid of no such thing, Gracie! Really—!"

"You do like to stir the pot," Emmett told Gracie with an affectionate look; she blew him a kiss in return. He was half in love with her already, Ellen suspected, and why wouldn't he be? Gracie was so lovely and light and fun. She also suspected Gracie wasn't in love with Emmett even one bit, although she clearly enjoyed the attention. Emmett, as kind a host as he'd been, had eyes for no one but her pert and pretty cousin. Ellen hoped it wouldn't end in heartbreak, for either Emmett or Gracie, whose moods continued to be so mercurial.

They took the Phantom, with Jamie scrambling all over the backseat trying to get a good view, to Grauman's Chinese Theatre on Hollywood Boulevard, glimpsing the now-famous Hollywood-land sign perched on the hills high above them, its large white letters stark against the rocky hillside.

"It was just an advert for a housing development," Emmett told them, "but everybody recognizes it now. I wonder if they'll ever take it down."

Grauman's Chinese Theatre was every bit as grand as Rosie and Jamie could have hoped, and they marveled over the imposing pagoda, the Chinese murals on the walls inside, and the fact that the theater was, Emmett told them, the first to offer air conditioning. It also had a 17-rank Wurlitzer organ, although with the advent of talking pictures that was, he informed them, less of a draw.

They were most fascinated, however, by the handprints in the forecourt outside. Gracie walked up and down, slowly examining the prints and the accompanying signatures scrawled in concrete. "Norma Shearer... Gloria Swanson..." she murmured as if reciting poetry.

"Tom Mix and Tony the Wonder Horse!" Jamie exclaimed as he pointed out the hoofprints of the horse that had starred in so many Westerns. "I would have liked to have seen them."

Gracie looked up from her perusal of Norma Talmadge's handprints. "Maybe I'll have my prints here one day," she told Emmett saucily.

He smiled back easily, his thumbs hooked through his belt loops. "I certainly hope so."

"Perhaps your film will be the start of a great and glorious career," Ellen remarked lightly. She realized she could imagine Gracie as a film star easily enough, although she didn't particularly like to think of it. She didn't know much about movie stars, but what she'd read and heard about had not assuaged her fears. It seemed a wild and reckless world of glitz, glamor, gambling, drink and drugs, with stories of movie stars falling out of the public eye and into disrepute and despair. More than one scandal had rocked Hollywood in recent years, so much so that there was talk of disciplinary measures, or at least a code to keep the films from being as disreputable as their stars.

"Mama, may we see a movie here?" Rosie asked, nodding to the sign in the window of theater's box office that announced *The Broadway Melody*, Hollywood's first talking musical with scenes in Technicolor, had premiered last week. "There's a matinee this afternoon."

Ellen glanced skeptically at the movie's rather lurid poster of an embracing couple. "I don't think so, darling. We have plans for lunch."

"I'll take you another day, Rosie," Gracie promised.

Rosie looked thrilled and Ellen determined to have a talk with Gracie about what a seven-year-old could and could not watch. A movie about what looked like a turbulent love affair between actors hardly seemed appropriate.

They ate lunch by the pool at the Beverly Hills Hotel on Sunset Boulevard, with its vista of rocky mountains stretching above them to a hard blue sky. Even in New York Ellen had never dined so fancily—Oysters Rockefeller, deviled eggs, smoked salmon, and strawberry-lemon cheesecake for dessert, all washed down with a bucketload of illicit yet available champagne, and lemonade for Rosie and Jamie.

Throughout the course of the meal, several glamorous-looking people stopped by their table to say hello to Emmett, who already seemed to know everyone, thanks, Ellen suspected, to his family connections and money. They also gazed speculatively at Gracie, while Ellen watched, bemused and invisible.

"That was Mary Astor!" Gracie hissed after an elegant blond woman, her hair in perfectly glossy marcelled waves, had sauntered past. "She's starring in *The Lady and the Brute*. She was in *Dry Martini* last year. It was fabulous."

"Was it?" Ellen murmured. She hadn't seen many movies at all, just a few silent pictures years ago, when she and Lucas had marveled at the quick, jerky movements of the actors on the screen, the blur of motion, the close-ups of expressive faces. It had seemed both exciting and alarming, and yet Ellen knew the movie industry had already progressed far past those—why, to think you could hear the actors talk now, and some scenes were even in color!

"Many of the silent film stars didn't have the voices to transition to talkies," Emmett explained as he poured them all more champagne. "They're all having to do sound tests, and if they don't pass, that's it. Curtains." Melodramatically, he drew a finger across his throat. "No more film career. Mary Astor was one of the lucky ones."

"Why wouldn't they pass?" Ellen asked, curious now. She felt slightly and pleasantly muddle-headed from the champagne, and Rosie and Jamie were busy attacking the knickerbocker glories that had been brought for them specially.

Emmett shrugged. "Their voices might be too reedy, too weak, or, for a woman, too deep." He gave Ellen a thoughtful glance. "You have a pleasant voice, Mrs. Lyman. I could imagine you in a talkie well enough."

"Ellen in a talkie?" Gracie exclaimed, a hint of teasing disbelief in her voice. "What a laugh! I can't think of anything she'd detest more." Gracie propped her chin in her hand as she gazed at Ellen with that mixture of mischief and defiance that now made Ellen instinctively tense. "Why, she doesn't even want *me* in your film, dearest Emmett."

"What?" Poor Emmett blushed again, looking alarmed. "I didn't realize—"

"Gracie is talking nonsense," Ellen said with a quelling look for her cousin that she completely and blithely ignored. "I was startled to hear she'd got a role in a movie, it's true, but I'm sure she'll have a marvelous time." She couldn't bear to be seen as rude to Emmett, who had been so kind to them all day, and who, despite his Hollywood aspirations, seemed quite young and naïve to Ellen, adopting a slick manner like an overcoat he put on that didn't quite fit. Underneath, he was nothing but a shyly eager, chubby-cheeked boy; he'd admitted he was only twenty-five.

"Oh, I always talk nonsense," Gracie returned, stretching slender arms high above her head, her body as sinuous as a cat's beneath her drop-waisted dress. "If that's what you want to call it." She turned to Emmett with another sly smile as she leaned forward to splash more champagne into her glass. "I shock Ellen at least three times daily, without even meaning to." She glanced at Ellen, and Ellen thought she saw a spark of something almost malicious in Gracie's dark eyes. "Of course, I wouldn't if she wasn't such a Mrs. Grundy." Ellen had no idea what a Mrs. Grundy was, but she knew it was nothing complimentary. "She blushed when I came downstairs in my dressing gown, of all things," Gracie continued, giving Emmett another arch look as she downed her champagne. "Of course I wasn't wearing anything at all underneath."

"Oh, er, well now," Emmett said, tugging at his collar in embarrassment.

Rosie and Jamie had stopped eating their ice cream and were watching the exchange with wide eyes.

Ellen reached for her purse and gloves. "This has been such a lovely lunch, Mr. Hughes, but I'm afraid we must return home. Jamie can't spend too much time in the sun."

"I can, Mama—"

Ellen gave him such a stern look, he thankfully fell silent. She was practically shaking with anger, and worse, hurt; Gracie had ruined a perfectly pleasant time with her provocative comments— and why had she made such mean-spirited digs at Ellen? Yes, she was a middle-aged matron. What of it? Gracie was, Ellen realized, quite drunk. She'd had more champagne than her and Emmett put together, and when she tried to refill her glass yet again, the fizz slopped onto the table.

Emmett, looking unhappy, rose as Ellen did. "Let me drive you—"

"I couldn't possibly inconvenience you in such a way," Ellen returned. "You have been so kind already. We'll take a taxi. It's no trouble." It would cost a fortune, but she could afford it, and right now Ellen's only desire was to escape such an embarrassing, awful scene—and get Gracie home in one piece. She helped Rosie and Jamie from the table before turning to Gracie, who was still lounging back in her seat. "Gracie?"

"I'm not ready to go quite yet," Gracie replied lazily. "Emmett, darling? What shall we do tonight? Café La Boheme again? I've always wanted to try the Trocadero."

"Oh, er..." Emmett looked even more miserable. "The thing is, kid, I've got to work this afternoon. If we're to start filming next week, I'll need a lot of dough." He gave Ellen an unhappy, apologetic smile.

Gracie remained where she was, sprawled in her seat, her eyes narrowed, for several taut seconds before she uncoiled herself with another lazy smile. "Oh all right, then. If you've got to go and be a bore." She gave his cheek a lingering kiss, while relief flashed through Emmett's eyes that there wasn't going to be more of a scene.

Ellen had taken Jamie and Rosie by the hand and, after thanking Emmett again for their day out, she turned and walked through the sea of tables, back through the hotel, and out onto the circular drive, where a bellhop whistled for a taxi. Gracie strolled slowly behind her, and Ellen was tempted to leave her behind so she could make her own way back, after her theatrics. Silly antics, indeed! Gracie had behaved atrociously, and yet Ellen knew she could never leave her here to find her way home alone, because underneath the anger she felt at Gracie's behavior was a far more pressing concern. Why did her cousin behave so wildly, so suddenly swinging from light, teasing fun to something dangerous and tinted with malice? Ellen didn't understand it at all.

Gracie was quiet as she slid into the taxicab next to Ellen, and they rode in tense silence the full half-hour back to Pasadena, where Ellen paid the driver an exorbitant sum for the fare before trailing the children into the bungalow.

"I really am pooped," Gracie announced with a yawn as Rosie and Jamie ran into the kitchen to tell a smiling Maria of their adventures.

Ellen took off her hat and placed it on the hall table before she tidied her hair in front of the small mirror.

Gracie watched her with a cat-eyed smile, half-slumped against the stair bannister. "You might as well go ahead and give me a scolding," she remarked on another yawn. "And then I can go have a nap."

"I'm not going to *scold* you, Gracie. You're a grown woman."

"I'm glad you've finally realized it."

"But I don't understand you," Ellen stated frankly. The journey from Beverly Hills to Pasadena had given time for her temper to cool, and now she just felt weary and rather sad. "Why did you cause such a scene?"

"Oh, Ellen, don't be such a bluenose. It was hardly a *scene*."

"A bluenose? I suppose that's on par with a Mrs. Grundy."

"Just about," Gracie tossed back with a laugh that held an edge.

Ellen stared at her with something approaching despair. "There are times," she said slowly, "when I feel as if you... you almost hate me." The words fell into the stillness of the hall.

Gracie straightened, looking away, and Jamie's boyish laughter floated out from the kitchen.

"I don't hate you," Gracie said finally in a low voice.

"I don't know why you would," Ellen returned, determined to remain honest. "I admit, I can be priggish sometimes and perhaps I am a bluenose, whatever that is. I can guess well enough." She sighed. "I'm trying not to be. But you don't make it easy for me, Gracie."

"Oh, I don't?" Gracie's voice flared. "*So* sorry."

"I didn't mean it like that." Except Ellen wasn't sure how she meant it, and she could sense this conversation would go nowhere good with the mood Gracie was in, as well as still being somewhat sozzled. "Go have a rest," she said wearily. "We can talk about this later, I suppose."

"I can hardly wait," Gracie retorted, and then flounced upstairs.

Ellen closed her eyes briefly before turning toward the kitchen to give Maria a welcoming smile.

"Have they talked your ear off with their adventures? It was quite a day." Out of habit, she put the back of her hand to Jamie's forehead, and he jerked away, scowling. "Sorry, love," she murmured.

"It sounds like it was very good," Maria replied, smiling at both children. "Very fun."

"It was." Rosie slid her mother a searching a look. "You're not cross with Gracie again, are you, Mama?"

"No, of course not," Ellen answered automatically. She caught Maria's eyes and saw the glimmer of sympathy there that both heartened and saddened her. Was Gracie's misbehavior obvious to the housekeeper as well? She suspected it was. "Why don't we call Daddy?" she suggested. "And tell him all about today?"

"Yes, yes!" they chorused, and with another smile for Maria, Ellen went back into the hall with Rosie and Jamie both in tow.

But when she managed to get an operator to make the connection to New York, Lucas's telephone simply rang and rang. Ellen glanced at the clock in the hall, and mentally did the arithmetic. It was past seven o'clock on the east coast; late enough for Lucas to be home, but he obviously wasn't. Was he working—or doing something else?

Finally, just when she feared the operator would tell her no one was answering, someone picked up, but it wasn't Lucas—it was Eva, their housemaid, who never liked answering the telephone, which was why it had probably rung for so long. "Butterfield

0355," she said cautiously, giving the name of the exchange and number.

Ellen heard the click of the operator hanging up and said brightly, "Eva! It's Mrs. Lyman ringing from California—"

"All the way from California!" Eva exclaimed, sounding almost horrified.

"Yes, indeed, isn't it amazing? Is Mr. Lyman available?"

"I'm sorry, he's gone out, Mrs. Lyman."

"Oh, has he?" Ellen tried to fight a sweeping sense of disappointment that was surely an overreaction to this somewhat predictable news.

"He's been very busy since you've gone," Eva confided. "He's gone out most evenings, for dinner as well. Maisy hasn't made a proper supper in over a week."

"Is that right?" Ellen gave a light laugh. "Well, I'm glad she's having something of a holiday. As should you. Do tell him I rang, won't you, Eva?"

"Of course, Mrs. Lyman."

"Thank you, Eva. Goodbye." Slowly, Ellen replaced the receiver in the cradle. "Never mind," she told the children as she turned to them with as bright a smile as she could manage. "We'll call him another time, shall we?"

"Where is Daddy?" Jamie asked, frowning. "Why isn't he home?"

Ellen ruffled his hair. "You know how busy he is with work."

"Do you know what Gracie calls the telephone?" Rosie said, her tone solemn even though a grin lurked about her mouth.

"No, I don't." Some more new-fangled slang that would make Ellen feel old-fashioned, no doubt. "What does she call it, Rosie?"

"The horn." Rosie's grin became full-fledged. "Instead of calling someone, she says you have to get on the horn. Isn't that funny?"

"Yes, it is." Some of Gracie's ways were simple, silly antics, Ellen reflected, just good-natured fun, and nothing malicious about it at all. It was important to remember that. "We'll get on the horn to Daddy tomorrow, perhaps," she added, making her daughter giggle.

The children went back into the kitchen with Maria, and feeling restless, Ellen took the opportunity to slip out. The late-afternoon air was already starting to cool, the sun beginning its descent towards the jagged, rocky horizon. A few people were about, strolling along or walking their dogs, and Ellen set out towards the center of town without really knowing where she was going or why. She felt the need to clear her head, but her mind felt both blank and full, her thoughts circling so fast she couldn't grab hold of any of them.

Was she right to be angry at Gracie? She didn't know; she didn't know if she even *was* angry, or just worried. And *why* was she worried? Simply because she'd noticed a gleam in Gracie's eyes, a certain recklessness to her actions? That was hardly enough to kick up a fuss about, as Gracie would tell her herself.

And what if you're just envious? a sly voice whispered inside her. *You're feeling old and tired and dull. Lucas was happy enough to send you off, and he doesn't seem to miss you very much. Out every evening and not one letter since you arrived! What if this bluenose prudishness Gracie accuses you of is simply because you feel so washed up, as dull as ditchwater at only thirty-seven?*

Ellen let out a sigh that was more like a groan. She truly didn't know what to think, but she more than half-wished she hadn't brought Gracie to California, hadn't opened up this Pandora's box of emotions inside her, never mind having to deal with her cousin's antics on a daily basis. And they'd only been here a little more than a week!

She walked towards Pasadena's downtown, passing the Play-house where she and Gracie had watched *Lazarus Laughed*. She passed the huge Mediterranean-style Civic Center, and then turned down Raymond Avenue, past the public library and opera house. As Ellen kept walking, she realized she had come onto the California Institute of Technology's new campus, past Grant Park and the magnificent Throop Hall. She hesitated, watching as undergraduates walked briskly along, many of them in deep discussion, waving their hands, bending their heads to listen. She was the only woman, she could see; like many other universities and colleges, Caltech did not, Ellen knew, accept female students.

Feeling conspicuous, she started to turn back, and wondered whether she'd even be able to find her way back to Bungalow Heaven. She'd been so lost in thought while she'd been walking, she hadn't paid attention to where she was going.

Frowning, Ellen scanned the college buildings in the attractive Spanish Mission style. She should be able to trace her steps, surely...

Then she froze as she heard a sudden indrawn breath from behind her and a deep male voice exclaim in disbelief,

"Ellen? Ellen Copley?"

CHAPTER NINE

Slowly, Ellen turned around at the sound of the familiar voice, shocked right down to her toes to see, of all people, Will Turner standing there. William Hancock Turner the Third, to be precise, an old acquaintance from her days in New York back in 1920, when she'd been the guest of the wealthy Frampton family and had briefly considered moving to the city as a young single woman to take up a position as mistress of art for the Spence School for Girls—a life not lived, one she'd deliberately turned away from, to choose something—and someone—better.

"Will..." she said faintly, still hardly able to believe her eyes. There he stood, looking exactly the same—thick blond hair, light blue eyes, that roguishly wry smile. He was dressed in a double-breasted suit of pinstriped poplin, holding his straw boater in his hands as his gaze scanned her face.

"Of course, it's not Ellen Copley now, is it?" he remarked, an impish glint entering his eyes. "It's Mrs. Ellen Lyman, as I recall from our mutual friends, the Framptons. They told me about your wedding."

"Yes, it is Mrs. Lyman." She shook her head slowly, wondering and incredulous at the sight of him. "What on earth are you doing here?"

"That's a question I should really be asking you. The last time I saw you, you were determined to return to your poky little island." He grinned good-naturedly to take any sting from the words. "What brings you all the way to the Golden State?"

Ellen hesitated, and then said, "It's a long story."

Will glanced at his watch. "I have half an hour before I have to be somewhere terribly boring. How about we grab a cup of coffee?" His eyes creased in good humor. "For old times' sake?"

"All right," Ellen answered after a second's hesitation. She was so flummoxed at seeing Will Turner again that she felt as if she could barely string two words together. The last time she'd seen him he'd been giving her that same wry smile, and Ellen hadn't been able to escape the feeling that she might have almost broken his heart. Or perhaps he'd almost broken hers...

But no, she was being fanciful and far too nostalgic. They'd been friends, that was all. Good friends, who had briefly found in each other a solace and a kindred spirit in the shattered aftermath of the war.

"Shall we?" Will asked, holding out his arm, and Ellen slipped her own into it, unable to escape a sense of unreality that this was happening at all as Will escorted her to a nearby coffee shop on Colorado Boulevard.

"So," he said once they were both settled in a deep booth with cups of coffee in front of them. "How have you been?" He shook his head in amazement. "It's been nine years since I last saw you. Feels like a million years ago and yesterday all at the same time."

"I know what you mean." Ellen lowered her gaze as she took a sip of her coffee. She'd met Will when she'd been staying in New York, and they'd grown closer during a week-long stay in the Hamptons, the city's playground for the rich, that summer. Before she'd left, Will had hinted that he harbored feelings for her, but he'd never declared them properly and Ellen had told herself she'd only seen Will as a friend. She *had*, but it still felt odd to see him now, looking so much the same as he had nine years ago.

"You haven't changed a bit, you know," Will said, as if he'd read her thoughts, and Ellen let out an uneven laugh as one hand, seemingly of its own accord, flew to her hair as she recalled those glinting gray strands she'd seen the other night. "Oh, I have."

"No," Will assured her, his gaze steady and warm. "You haven't."

Ellen willed herself not to blush as she took another sip of coffee to hide her expression, which she didn't trust. *I could have fallen in love with you, you know.* That had been one of the last things Will had said to her, back in New York, before she had left. *It was a close-run thing.*

She had no business recalling such sentiments now. She hadn't thought of Will—or at least thought of him properly—in years. She'd written to him briefly to let him know of her engagement, but they'd lost touch after he'd moved to California. Ellen had occasionally felt a pang of nostalgia for him, for their old, brief friendship, and nothing more.

"You're the one who hasn't changed," she remarked as she put down her coffee cup and gave him a bright look. "Not a bit, Will!"

"Alas, I think you're right." The darker twist to the familiar wry smile gave Ellen pause. Of course, she'd known Will had something of a darker side. He'd flown in the war, been shot down and kept as a prisoner of war for a year. He never spoke of it, deliberately made a joke of everything, but the pain was there, running right through him like a deep, dark ribbon no one could see. At least it had been. Was it still?

"You wanted to change?" Ellen asked as lightly as she could.

Will shrugged. "What did Confucius say? Or perhaps Lao Tzu, if I recall my ancient Chinese philosophy aright." He paused to summon the quotation, his eyes cast to the ceiling. "'If you do not change direction, you may end up where you are heading.' Perish the thought, of course."

"That would be such a bad thing?"

Another shrug, this time dismissive. "Let's not bore ourselves with stodgy philosophy. You still haven't told me what you're doing here in California."

"I came for the sunshine. Well, the climate, really." She paused. "For my son Jamie. He's had poorly lungs since he was born. The doctor said a dry, hot climate for the winter could help."

"I'm sorry to hear he's been unwell," Will replied gravely. "Has the climate helped as you hoped?"

Ellen thought of Jamie's rounder, browner face, but then the cough that had kept her up the other night. "I think it has," she answered, "but it's hard not to worry."

"I'm sure it is. I always thought mothers *should* worry. It would be strange if they didn't." His whimsical, understanding smile was a balm to Ellen's doubting soul. Unlike Lucas, he didn't make her feel silly for hovering, almost as if she were doing something wrong. But no, Lucas didn't make her feel silly. She felt treacherous for so much as thinking such a thing. He just wanted to keep her from coddling their son too much, which was understandable.

"What about you, Will?" she asked. "You're not at Stanford anymore, I take it?" She'd known he'd studied there, and had his first professorship, but clearly he'd moved on.

"No, I took a research position at Caltech three years ago, under Dr. Millikan." He gave a rueful smile. "You probably haven't heard of him, but he happens to be quite an eminent physicist."

"I'm impressed, of course, or I would be, if I'd heard of him. I'll take your word for it, though." He inclined his head, and after a second's hesitation, she asked lightly, "Any other changes in your life?"

"Do you mean a wife or family?" Will returned, astute as ever, an ironic twist to his lips. "I'm afraid it's a resounding no to both of those. I never managed to find a lovely lady who wished to share my life, more's the pity. I wasn't as lucky as you in love, Ellen, but then I never expected to be." He shook his head, his eyes glinting humorously, but again Ellen sensed that darkness that ran deeply through him.

She reached for her coffee cup again. She had no idea how to reply.

"Tell me," Will asked after a moment, his tone turning jocular, "have you seen many of the sights here in Pasadena, or even further afield? If you can, it's worth it to take a trip up north to see the sequoias. They're the most magnificent trees, utterly enormous. Gives you a sense of perspective, really. Humbling." Another pause, only slight. "I'm sure your husband would enjoy seeing them."

"Oh—Lucas didn't accompany me," Ellen replied a bit stiltedly. She felt as if she should have mentioned it before. "He stayed in New York—his work, you see. He's in law, corporate law—it's been very busy. I've travelled with my cousin Gracie. She's helping me with the children." Somewhat, at least, but she was hardly going to explain to Will about all that.

"I see." Will gave her an appraising look. "Too bad. I was looking forward to meeting the man who stole your heart."

She did her best not to blush. "Well, perhaps he'll come out for a visit. I don't know."

Will raised his eyebrows. "He hasn't said?"

"He's very busy."

"I see." And Ellen was afraid he saw too much. "Well, perhaps then you would grace me with your presence again? I'm afraid I have to rush to a meeting right now, but if Providence has had our paths cross in such a way, it seems prudent to make the most of it, don't you think?"

His whimsical smile, with a hint of challenge in it, both unnerved and charmed her. "I suppose so," she agreed hesitantly.

"Perhaps you would have dinner with me? The Raymond Hotel has a marvelous menu, as well as its own rose garden and a host of other delights. It's the nicest hotel in all of Pasadena, now that Castle Green has been turned into private apartments. That place was amazing, back in the day—it had its own Bridge of Sighs, admittedly across the less lovely Raymond Avenue. The Rio di Palazzo is a prettier sight by far. But Moorish towers, Victorian verandahs, Spanish balconies... I think they've contrived to put every architectural indulgence in a single edifice. But that's Hollywood for you. Even more of a playground for the rich than the Hamptons were. Do you remember?"

"When we were in the Hamptons together? Yes, of course."

"You were quite scathing about all the wealthy wastrels there, myself included."

"You weren't a wastrel, Will," Ellen said quietly. "You never have been."

"Just giving a good impression of one, then," he returned with a laugh.

She let out an unsteady laugh. "You know, I've been to the Hamptons several times since then, now that Lucas and I live in New York. I sometimes wondered if I'd see you there."

"You've become part of that set?" Will remarked, his eyebrows raised, a small smile quirking his mouth.

"Not really—"

"I've stayed mainly on the west coast." He glanced away as he added, "There isn't much left for me back in New York."

"Your parents—"

"They're desperate to see me settled. It gets tiresome. Anyway." He turned back to her, his tone deliberately light again. "How about it? Dinner at the Raymond?"

Ellen hesitated, considering her response. Would it be wrong to have dinner with Will Turner? He was an old friend, nothing more; nothing romantic had ever actually *happened* between them, not a breath of scandal or a hint of impropriety. And yet... *I could have fallen in love with you.* But that had been years and years ago, and in point of fact he hadn't. Ellen knew her heart belonged to Lucas and always would, even if he'd seemed distant recently. A dinner with an old friend would never, ever change that. And to refuse, she reasoned, would be both nonsensical and embarrassing, making it seem as if something had happened back then when it hadn't.

"Yes, that would be lovely," Ellen said as firmly as she could. It would be lovely... and of course perfectly innocent.

"Next weekend, then?"

So soon! "If that suits."

He withdrew a card from the inside pocket of his jacket and scrawled a number on the back. "Here is my business card, and my telephone number on the back. Shall we meet at the Raymond Hotel at seven on Friday? You can give me a bell me if you have to make a change."

The swift way he'd seen to the arrangements startled Ellen, but she also felt gratified. "Thank you, Will. It was good seeing you again."

He tossed a couple of quarters on the table to pay for their coffees before taking her hand between his own. His skin was warm and dry as he pressed her palm between his. "It's been so good seeing you, Ellen. Why, it's made my day. My whole week, even." Another press before he stepped back. "I'll see you on Friday."

Ellen couldn't remember the walk back to Bungalow Heaven. She felt dazed, her mind reeling back through the years, drifting through a haze of memories. It was both pleasant and poignant to recall the girl she'd once been, her whole life in front of her, and yet hardly daring to dream. She'd been as cautious as she was now, and yet had she needed to be? What if she'd been brave enough to take the position at Spence? What if she'd stayed in New York and made a career for herself, as both artist and teacher? Her friend Elvira Frampton had been more than willing to help launch her artistic career. She'd died several years ago, but what if Ellen had stayed in the city all along? What if she'd stayed friends—or even more—with Will Turner?

And yet she hadn't wanted to, she'd known that, and still knew it. She'd chosen Lucas because she loved him, and he'd made her so very happy. Yet seeing Will again felt, bizarrely, like missing the last step in a staircase, leaving her just slightly off balance, and she didn't quite know why. The sensation, as well as the fact that she was experiencing it at all, was disconcerting. She wondered if she should call him and cancel their dinner, and yet what explanation could she possibly give? *I've been thinking about the life I could have lived, and even though I've been happy all along, thinking about it makes me feel sad.* He would think she was crazy... Except, somehow, Ellen thought Will would understand perfectly.

"Where have you been?" Gracie asked, her hands on her hips, as Ellen slipped inside the bungalow. "We've already had our supper."

"Have you?" Ellen started guiltily as she glanced at the clock; it was after six already. "I'm sorry. I went for a walk and I must have lost track of time."

"Did you get lost, Mama?" Rosie asked, her voice full of under-standing sympathy, and Ellen went to the table where she and Jamie were sitting, to hug and kiss them both. She felt suddenly and almost tearfully grateful for them—for the solidness of their little bodies, for the softness of their hair and the readiness of their smiles. She was an idiot, poring over the bygone years as if it made any difference. As if she would ever have made a different choice—would have *wanted* to make a different choice!

"I did get lost," she told them, "but only for a few minutes." She glanced up and saw Gracie eyeing her speculatively, her expression shrewd.

"Did you?" she remarked, sounding both dubious and assessing, and Ellen straightened.

"Yes, I walked all the way over to the Caltech campus, and all their buildings look the same—Spanish Mission, very grand." She was talking too fast, Ellen realized, and she strove to slow down. "I had a hard time finding my way back, but then I did."

"Quite a story," Gracie remarked, and Ellen raised her eyebrows. Why should Gracie not believe her? What on earth could she suspect?

"Did you sleep off your lunch, then?" she asked, and was ashamed of the sharp, almost shrewish note in her voice.

Gracie took it in her stride, laughing easily. "Oh, yes. Champagne at noon does make me sleepy. And of course I had hardly any sleep the night before," she added with a knowing wink.

"Gracie—"

"Come on, kiddos," she called gaily, turning away from Ellen before she could make more of a protest. "I said we could have a swim before bed, remember?"

"A *swim?*" Ellen glanced out at the darkening sky. "It's February, Gracie, even if we're in California, and there's a chill in the air."

"It will be bracing!"

"I don't think Jamie should have a swim when it's so late," Ellen stated firmly. "It's far too cold."

"Mama, I want to," Jamie said, his tone pitched between wheedling and tragic. "And Gracie said we could. Please?"

"No, I don't think so," Ellen replied, determined to establish her authority. She could not have the children listening to Gracie more than to her, and she wanted to guard the progress Jamie had already made. "Tomorrow morning, perhaps. The swimming pool isn't going anywhere, you know." She tried to inject a playful note into her voice, but Jamie only scowled.

"But Gracie said!" he complained, scuffing his foot, and Ellen gave him a quelling look.

"Upstairs to bath, please," she told him briskly. "You can pretend the tub is a swimming pool."

With a theatrical groan, Jamie stomped upstairs, followed far more quietly by Rosie.

Ellen took a deep breath and then turned to Gracie. "Please don't contradict me in front of the children."

"Oh la la, is that what I did?" To Ellen's irritation, Gracie only looked amused. "And here I thought I'd made a fun suggestion while you were nowhere to be found." She raised her eyebrows. "Where were you, anyway? You're looking like the cat who was too afraid to eat the cream, but feels guilty anyway."

Gracie's perceptiveness caused a blush to rise to Ellen's face, and she turned away quickly. "What nonsense."

"Is it?"

"Of course it is. I went for a walk, as I said." She had absolutely no reason to feel guilty, Ellen knew, and yet Gracie's laughing, speculative gaze made her feel so. She felt she could hardly admit to her dinner plans now, and yet why shouldn't she? It wasn't as if they were wrong.

"All right, then," Gracie said on a laugh. "Don't tell me your secret if you don't want to."

Ellen took a deep breath. "There's no secret, Gracie. The truth is, while I was on my walk I ran into an old friend. It surprised me, that's all. I hadn't seen him in many years."

"*Him*," she exclaimed triumphantly, and Ellen bit her lip, only to have Gracie dissolve into peals of laughter. "I'm only joking, Ellen! Goodness, your face." Still laughing, she put her arms around her, while Ellen stood stiffly, barely able to submit to the careless embrace. "I'm sorry. I'm terribly naughty, aren't I, teasing you this way? As if you could be accused of so much as a single speck of impropriety!" Her laugh became a full-throated chuckle. "Not in a million years."

And somehow this made Ellen feel as irritated as anything else Gracie could have said.

CHAPTER TEN

For the next week, Ellen debated whether to telephone Will and tell him she could not meet him at the Raymond Hotel for dinner on Friday, after all. It seemed the most sensible thing to do; a dinner alone with a handsome bachelor was, if not scandalous, then perhaps at least unwise. But just when she'd resolved to pick up the telephone and call, something would make her pause.

Gracie had started filming *The Lady and the Brute*, and was gone first thing in the morning to late in the evening. When she finally had a day off, she lazed around in her dressing gown, telling Rosie about all the movie stars she'd met, the stories she'd heard.

"Gloria Swanson has a bathtub made of solid gold," she said, her head tossed back as she reclined on the sofa. "And did you know a mysterious woman in black comes to Rudolph Valentino's crypt on the anniversary of his death? She holds a single rose. No one knows who she is, but, of course, nearly every woman in the country was in love with him!"

Ellen wasn't sure of the value of telling such wild stories to a seven-year-old girl, and she was relieved when, a week after they'd arrived in California, Rosie began at the Westridge School on the west side of Pasadena. Eduardo drove them both in the car, and Ellen was received by the school's founder and headmistress, Mary

Lowther Ranney, a kindly woman in her late fifties, and a reputable architect as well as teacher.

"I'm sure Rosie will be very happy at our school during her time here," she said as she served Ellen tea in her comfortable office. "We have several pupils from families who winter in Pasadena and therefore only attend for a few months, so she will not be alone in that regard. She will be well looked after."

"I'm sure she will," Ellen murmured, reassured.

Ellen returned to the house in Bungalow Heaven with a sense of both satisfaction and relief; she was impressed with the Westridge School, and was glad that Rosie had seemed excited to meet other girls her age.

Jamie, however, was not as pleased to be deprived of his playmate. Ellen did her best to amuse him, taking him swimming or flying kites in the park; to the library or Pasadena's new museum, but she knew instinctively—as well as from what Jamie muttered—that she did not possess Gracie's sense of fun, her infectious excitement.

Eduardo kindly took him in hand, showing him the inner workings of the car's engine, and then helping him to build a scooter out of a wooden orange crate and some wheels taken from an old pair of roller skates. Soon, Ellen was standing on the sidewalk outside of their bungalow, her heart in her mouth as Jamie raced down the street on his newly built scooter.

And meanwhile Friday came ever closer. Ellen had not informed Gracie of her plans, since her cousin was out most of the time now anyway, and Maria had already offered to watch Rosie and Jamie while she went out.

"You're going out to a fancy hotel?" Rosie asked as she lay on her stomach on Ellen's bed, her legs kicking up in the air, while she went through her rather paltry selection of dresses on Friday evening. Jamie was outside with Eduardo, tinkering with something or other, and Ellen could hear Maria humming in the kitchen. "Have we ever met Mr. Turner?"

"No, I knew him before you were born. Perhaps you'll meet

him one day, though." Ellen gave Rosie a quick smile. She'd been heartened to see how her daughter had taken to the Westridge School; after just a few days, she was already enthusiastic about both tennis and art, and had seemed to make friends with a few of the other wintering girls.

"Does Daddy know him?" Rosie asked artlessly, and Ellen hesitated for no more than a second.

"No, he's never met him, but if he visits he might."

"Do you think he *will* visit?" Rosie asked, a note of longing in her voice. They had tried to telephone Lucas again, to tell him about her first day of school, but once more Eva had answered, and once more he had been out. There had still been no letters, and it was over three weeks since they'd left New York. Ellen was trying not to let it worry her, but it felt like a loose thread she could not keep from tugging.

"I hope he will, darling. But he is very busy." Although why he needed to be quite so busy, why he seemed to *want* to, Ellen still didn't fully understand.

"I know he is." Rosie let out a sigh as her chin dropped into her hands. "What dress are you going to wear?"

"I don't know." Had her clothes always looked so fusty, so out of date? Everything was either dark blue or green, up to her neck and down to the ankles, with nothing light or frothy or fun.

"Why don't you borrow one of Gracie's dresses?" Rosie suggested. "You looked so pretty the last time."

"I don't think so." Gracie wasn't here to ask, and in any case, Ellen didn't want to show up at the Raymond Hotel looking like a dressed-up doll, as if she'd made too much of an effort. "I think I'll go with my green crepe," she said decisively. The dress had served her well for several years, although its tubular style, falling straight from her shoulders to her calves, was now decidedly out of date. Gracie's dresses had far more flounce and swing. Perhaps when Ellen returned to New York, she'd make an appointment at one of the department stores on Fifth Avenue—Franklin Simon or Saks—

and buy some new frocks. Nothing too outlandish, but a bit more fashionable and young.

As she slipped into the dress and brushed a bit of powder across her face, Ellen told herself she was dressed perfectly appropriately. She had a feeling Gracie would say the same thing. *You look every inch the staid matron.* Except, she realized, she didn't *want* to look like a staid matron, at least not entirely.

"Oh la la!" Gracie's voice floated musically from the hallway as she poked her head around Ellen's door, face flushed and eyes sparkling. "Maria said you were going out tonight! You surely aren't going to wear *that* old thing, are you?"

"It's perfectly appropriate—"

"And that's hardly what you want to look like!" Gracie scoffed. "Who on earth wants to look *appropriate*? Scandalous, maybe, or at *least* smashing." She shook her head, hands on hips. "You'll have to wear something of mine."

"No, Gracie," Ellen said as firmly as she could, even though part of her was longing to wear something sparkly and frothy and light. "I really don't think I should."

Gracie let out a theatrical sigh, conceding the point more easily than Ellen had expected. "Oh very well, if you're going to be boring. At least let me give you a little sparkle, or do something with your hair."

Ellen put one hand self-consciously to her hair. "What would you do with my hair?"

"Cut it all off," Gracie said promptly. "No one has hair as long as yours anymore, Ellen, not even the stuffiest of stuffy old matrons. You look like you're a ghost from the 1800s, or an extra on *The Pony Express*. That was one of George Bancroft's pictures, you know. I had a scene with him today—he's quite old, but I think he's still handsome."

"She doesn't look like that," Rosie protested loyally, while Ellen studied her reflection, her hair caught up in its usual simple roll. In the plain green dress, with her hair pulled back, she looked worse than boring, she realized. She looked positively frumpy.

"All right," she said suddenly. "Let's cut it all off."

Gracie's eyebrows rose as she grinned. "Now you're talking! Let me get the scissors."

"Mama, really?" Rosie asked excitedly and Ellen felt her heart thudding. She'd had her hair nearly down to her waist since she'd been a child.

"Yes," Ellen proclaimed, meeting her own tremulous gaze in the mirror. "I really should keep up with the times, at least a little bit."

Gracie returned, holding aloft a pair of wicked-looking scissors she'd taken from the kitchen. "Right, here we go!"

"Perhaps I should go to a salon—"

"No time," she said succinctly as she began to take the pins from her hair. "Don't worry, I've got a steady hand. And we'll use my curling irons anyway, to give it a bit of bounce."

"Oh Gracie, I don't know—" Ellen faltered, beginning to regret her moment of recklessness, and Gracie met her gaze in the mirror, the scissors held aloft.

"I won't do it if you really can't stand the thought," she said, and opened and closed the scissors for effect. "But I think you'd look lovely with a bob."

"Oh, Mama, I think you would, too," Rosie exclaimed. "You're always having to put your hair up, and you've complained about how heavy it is."

"Have I?" Ellen fingered a tendril of hair with apprehension.

"Well?" Gracie asked, her eyebrows raised.

Ellen met her gaze in the mirror and nodded, seized by a sudden, wonderful recklessness. "Yes, let's do it."

Despite her determination, she couldn't keep from giving a soft gasp of dismay as nearly a foot of hair fell to the ground, curling on the floor.

"*Mama!*" Rosie shrieked, and Ellen couldn't tell if her daughter sounded thrilled or horrified. Ellen didn't know how she felt either.

The metal scissors were cold against the nape of her neck as

Gracie continued to gleefully snip. Another lock of hair fell to the floor.

"You look so different," Rosie marveled, and Jamie came to the door to see what all the fuss was about.

"Your hair!" he exclaimed, and then ran to pick up handfuls of the stuff, tossing her chestnut locks into the air until, laughing a little, Ellen told him to stop.

A few more snips and it was done. "Don't look yet," Gracie ordered as she steered Ellen away from the mirror. "First a little pizzazz!"

Ellen submitted obediently to Gracie's ministrations—brushing and curling and crimping, and then a touch of lipstick and eyeshadow and a generous squirt of her Shalimar.

"There," Gracie said, her hands on her shoulders as she drew Ellen back to the mirror. "Have a look!"

Ellen took a deep breath as she opened her eyes and gazed at her reflection—as before, when she'd been primped and preened by Gracie, she didn't recognize herself—but this was at a much more fundamental level. This wasn't just a red lip or a frothy dress, it was her hair, her very *self*.

She lifted one hand to brush the bottom of her curls, which barely skimmed her jawline. She felt as if she could both laugh and burst into tears at the same time.

"I think you look very modern," Gracie stated firmly. "No one has long hair these days, you know."

"I know." Even Miss Ranney, the spinster school teacher, had had bobbed hair. Slowly, Ellen turned from side to side, amazed to feel the air on the back of her neck, the brush of her hair against her cheek.

Rosie came to her side and silently slipped her hand in hers.

"What do you think, Rosie?" she asked, with only a slight wobble in her voice. "Do you like it?"

"I do," Rosie said, and squeezed her hand, as if she knew how emotional Ellen was feeling. She felt different, as if she'd been changed from the inside out, and while that was a good feeling, heady and freeing, it was also more than a little scary.

It was only hair, she reminded herself. It would grow back. And yet she already knew she would never wear it long again. She let out a little laugh, and Gracie smiled.

"You're a stunner."

"I am," Ellen agreed with another laugh. "At least a little!"

"Right." Gracie clapped her hands. "Is Eduardo driving you? Where are you dining?"

"The Raymond Hotel."

"Oh la-di-da!" Gracie approved. "Emmett told me that was the finest hash house in all of Pasadena. It's the best place you can get some foot juice in this town. Well, you'd better get a wiggle on if you want to be on time!"

Ellen's stomach was fluttering with nerves as she kissed Jamie and Rosie goodbye, and Gracie practically marched her to the door.

"We'll be fine," she assured her. "Stay out as late as you like," she added with a wink, while Ellen couldn't help but bristle with outrage.

"Gracie—"

"Oh, keep your hair on—or at least what's left of it—you know I'm joking." She paused. "You look lovely, Ellen, truly. A modern woman, but not too modern, don't worry." Another wink, while Ellen managed an exasperated smile. At times like this, Gracie was lovable and charming, and she made Ellen wonder whether she'd been overreacting all along.

Soon enough, she was in the car for the short drive to the Raymond Hotel, an imposing edifice, which was every bit as impressive as Will had said, with its large gardens and red-roofed towers.

"You don't need to wait up," Ellen told Eduardo. "I'm sure Mr. Turner will be happy to escort me home, or I can get a taxi if I need to."

"As you wish, Mrs. Lyman," Eduardo replied, and Ellen

wondered if she was imagining the slight note of censure in his voice. Did he think she was having some scandalous *rendez-vous*? The thought was appalling.

"Mr. Turner is an old friend," she told the chauffeur. "When Mr. Lyman comes to visit, I know they will be eager to meet one another." Then she flushed, annoyed with herself for feeling the need to explain.

"Of course, Mrs. Lyman," Eduardo answered, and then he smiled, his round cheeks creasing. "Now you have a good time," he told her, and Ellen tried to relax. She must have been imagining the censure, simply because she felt it, just a little, in herself.

As soon as Eduardo had driven away, she headed into the main foyer of the hotel, already impressed and intimidated by all the grandeur—crystal chandeliers, everything made of marble or gilt, and well-heeled guests everywhere.

Ellen steeled her spine and lifted her chin as she approached the white-jacketed maître d' of the hotel's large, elegant restaurant.

"Madam?" he asked politely.

"I'm here to meet William Hancock Turner," she told him, and the man gave a swift nod.

"Of course, madam. He is waiting for you."

CHAPTER ELEVEN

Ellen's heart was beating hard and her hands felt clammy as she followed the maître d' to a table in the back of the restaurant, near a window overlooking the hotel's famed rose gardens.

Will stood up as she approached, dressed in a pinstriped suit of gray worsted, his blond hair brushed back from his tanned face.

"Ellen." He held both hands out and she took them as he leaned forward and kissed her cheek. "How lovely to see you again."

"And you, Will." Withdrawing her hands, she sat down in the chair opposite him, fussing with her heavy linen napkin in her nervousness. Why exactly was she here? And why was she so nervous?

"You've cut your hair," he remarked as he sat down.

"My cousin Gracie convinced me. She said no modern woman had hair the length of mine." Ellen spread the napkin in her lap, her gaze downcast.

"I liked your hair," Will remarked, and she blushed.

"You don't think the shorter length suits?"

"Oh, yes indeed! I think absolutely anything could suit you," Will said frankly. "But perhaps that's not the sort of compliment I should make to a married woman."

A silence stretched between them while Ellen struggled to know how to reply.

"I'm sorry. I didn't mean to sound improper." Will's voice was wry. "It's just good to see an old friend, Ellen, that's all."

"I know, and it is." She dared to look up and saw he looked rueful, his lips twisted in a grimace.

"Have I ruined our evening before it's begun?" he asked.

"No, not at all," Ellen said firmly. Somehow Will's compliment, which could have put her in even more of a tizzy, had calmed her. He really was an old friend, and nothing more. She knew that right down to her bones, and the way he gazed at her, with that frank wryness, made her realize he knew it as well. The realization brought relief.

"Champagne?" he asked as he gestured to the bottle that was resting in a bucket of ice next to the table. "Pasadena's dry, of course, but the hotel has a special license for guests."

"But we're not guests at the hotel?"

"They make exceptions." He hefted the bottle. "And I wanted to celebrate seeing you again." He poured them both glasses and then raised his in toast. "To old friends."

"To old friends," Ellen murmured back, and they clinked glasses and drank.

"So," Will said in a brisker voice, putting down his glass and giving her a direct look. "Tell me everything. You have a son..."

"And a daughter. Jamie is five and Rosie is seven."

"And does Rosie look like you?"

Ellen thought of Rosie's chestnut hair, her hazel eyes. "Yes, a bit. Quite a bit, I suppose."

"And is she as serious as you are?" Will asked, and Ellen let out a little laugh.

"Even more so, sometimes. I worry about her, because of Jamie's frailty—although you wouldn't think he was frail, seeing him throw himself into the pool or buzz down the street on his scooter. He's done marvelously here, but back in New York..."

Will had propped his chin in his hand as he regarded her with a level of focus she hadn't felt from anyone, she realized, in a long time. Not even Lucas. "You're worried that Rosie gets neglected, because of Jamie?"

"Yes, although not intentionally, of course."

"Is neglect ever intentional? Not," he added quickly, "that I think you are. You've always been so sensitive of others. And a very good judge of character."

"Do you really think so?" Ellen asked impulsively. Two sips of champagne had already gone to her head. "I didn't judge you very well at first."

"It didn't take you long to suss me out though," Will remarked, and Ellen dropped the laughing tone as she gave him an earnest look.

"How are you, Will? Really?"

Will toyed with the stem of his champagne glass, his gaze wandering away from hers. "How can anyone ever answer that?" he replied musingly. "I'm well, of course." He lifted laughing eyes to her. "What else can I say? You know, of course, I'm secretly a tortured soul."

She knew he was joking, saw the mocking lift of his lips, but underneath she sensed he wasn't, just as before, so many years ago. "Or not so secretly, if you're going to come out and say it," she replied lightly.

"True. The jig is up."

"You're not going to give me a straight answer, are you?"

"No," he replied agreeably, and she laughed and shook her head.

"Let's talk of something else, then. Tell me about your work."

"You really want to hear about physics?"

"Yes, I really do."

"All right, but before I bore you to death, I might as well give you your last meal." He gestured to the menu lying in front of her. "Let's order first, at least."

Ellen picked up the menu and scanned the usual elegant offerings—deviled eggs, Oysters Rockefeller, stuffed mushrooms, salmon mousse, lobster salad, steak, all washed down, of course, by endless bottles of champagne. For a few seconds, she let herself feel a pang of homesickness for the old-fashioned food of her childhood on Amherst Island—rich stews and nourishing soups, home-baked bread, raspberry pie...

"Anything take your fancy?" Will asked.

"It all looks delicious..."

"And a bit the same," he guessed. "Every fancy restaurant from here to Toledo serves the same hash. Steak, lobster, you name it, you can have it, even if all you want is a ham sandwich." He closed the menu with a smile.

"How did you know what I was thinking?" Ellen exclaimed with a laugh.

"Because it's usually the same thing I'm thinking. Why don't we be excessively dull and go with the salmon and steak? The waiter will try not to roll his eyes as he says 'very good, sir.'"

Ellen closed her menu and laid it on the table. "Very well," she said, and folded her hands.

Will let out a guffaw of laughter. "You look as prim as a schoolteacher! Tell me more about your life. You live in New York, after all?"

She heard the bittersweet note in his voice and felt it in herself. Back in 1920, when she'd left Will for the island and Lucas, she'd told him she couldn't move to the city, had no intention of living there, and yet just five years later that was exactly what she had done.

"Lucas took up a position with a law firm—corporate things, all to do with business I don't understand."

"I wouldn't bother understanding it. Sounds boring to me, full of flat tires and windbags."

"That's my husband you're talking about," Ellen reminded him, and he grinned.

"Barring the astute and charming Lucas Lyman, of course."

"I hope you meet him one day," Ellen remarked as Will summoned the waiter.

"I hope so, too," he replied smoothly, and the waiter came to take their order.

After he'd left, Ellen folded her hands in front of her and gave him a direct look. "So, physics. Tell me what you're researching—in layman's terms, if you can."

"The easiest way to describe it is we're realizing how much we don't know. At the turn of the century, many scientists thought we'd pretty much discovered everything. It was just a matter of understanding the information or manipulating the data. But now..." He shook his head slowly. "We're realizing a world exists that we barely understand. Twenty-odd years ago, all of physics was turned on its head with the evolution of something we call quantum theory—how energy and mass move at the smallest and most fundamental level. Essentially, we're realizing, at the subatomic level, something can be in two places at the same time."

"What!" Ellen exclaimed, laughing. "Surely not."

"It raises questions about the very nature of reality," Will said seriously. "Some, like Niels Bohr, have theorized that our subconscious can actually influence the movement of such particles. And there might be particles we don't even know about yet—Rutherford has put forth the theory of a neutron—a particle with no electrical charge—but he hasn't managed to prove it yet."

"You've lost me, I'm afraid," Ellen told him ruefully. "But what does this mean for you, Will? Are you researching—what is it —neutrons?"

"No, unfortunately not. I'd rather do that than what I'm doing." His face, so animated moments before, set into hard lines. "Our focus is more on how to manipulate these particles, to see what they can do."

"Do?" Ellen was struggling to keep up with the science.

Will reached for his champagne glass, rotating the stem around and around with his fingers. "Millikan, the president of Caltech, was Vice Chairman of the National Research Council during the war. He has a particular interest in harnessing our research for militaristic purposes."

"Militaristic?" Ellen, her glass half-raised to her lips, put it down again. "You mean defense?"

"Presumably."

The moody darkness in his voice made her pause. "Will, surely you're not thinking there... there will be another war?" The mere possibility, abstract as it was, had her mind swirling with both memory and fear. She'd been in France for four years; she'd nursed soldiers near the front lines, had cradled their limp, bloody bodies in her arms. She'd seen the futility of it all, millions of men lost over a few muddy feet in France, and she herself had fled from the oncoming German army, escaping the bombs with only seconds to spare. The thought of any of that happening again... well, it couldn't. It simply couldn't.

"I think there will almost certainly be another war. There always is," Will stated flatly. "It's just a matter of when. And it could be with Germany again."

"You can't be serious." Ellen shook her head, her reaction to his statement visceral and overwhelming, a clutch of terror at her chest, a clenching of her stomach. She thought of Rosie, of Jamie, their youth sacrificed to another pointless and futile cause. *No.*

"I've never been more serious," Will told her. "I wish I wasn't. But the terms of peace of the last war were atrocious. Have you read about the state of Germany in the papers?"

"Not really." She didn't read the newspapers, outside of the book reviews or perhaps the crossword in the fun section of the *New York World*. She didn't even want to *think* about Germany, after having lived in fear of their army for four years.

"Well, its economy is completely ballsed up. Their inflation has gone through the roof—I'm talking wheelbarrows of paper money for a loaf of bread. Things have gotten better since we—that is, the U.S.—helped them out with some loans, and I hear Berlin is a hell of town now."

"But?" Ellen prompted, for there clearly was more.

"But it won't last forever." He stretched an arm to gesture to the room, full of elegant diners, tables laden with linen and crystal, caviar and champagne. "None of this will."

"I don't suppose anything lasts forever," Ellen replied reasonably. She thought of her own resistance to change, her longing for the old days. Did Will have the same sentimentality? That ribbon of darkness that ran right through him seemed to be on more noticeable display, and it worried her.

"No, but I'm not talking Ecclesiastes here, with a time for everything under the sun," Will told her wryly, although there was still a grim look in his eyes and to the set of his mouth. "I'm not talking apocalyptic Revelation, either. I mean we have months. Maybe years, if the boom continues, but I doubt it."

The waiter came bearing several silver-domed dishes, and they fell silent as he put down their starters with a flourish—two perfect globes of pink salmon mousse resting on several crisp lettuce leaves.

"I feel as if you're talking in riddles," Ellen said as she picked up her fork. "First all this about physics and weapons and wars, and now a boom? What do you mean?" She dug into the salmon mousse.

"I mean we all have too far to fall. Everything's peachy right now, I know, even if you don't like some of the change." She opened her mouth to object, but he forestalled her with a swift shake of his head. "I know you, Ellen. I'm sure you've been dragged kicking and screaming into the Roaring Twenties with its loud jazz and short dresses, the radio and the telephone and the talkies. But everyone else loves it and they think it's just going to up and up and up, until we've reached the moon."

"Why shouldn't it?" Ellen asked as she took a bite of her mousse. "Surely no one wants to live through a war again."

"You'd be amazed at how short people's memories can be, and how long at the same time—which brings me back to Germany. They might be laughing it up in Berlin, with their cabarets and the modern art and wild living, but nearly two hundred thousand people are starving in that city alone. They remember the war, and they remember how little they had afterward. And now there's this new political party that's representing them, or says it is."

"So?" Ellen shrugged. "Surely that's a good thing, to have the poor represented?"

"It's a party that likes to beat people up in the streets. Some of their rhetoric is pretty ugly—and that's only what we read about all the way over here, which probably isn't much at all. National Socialists, they're called, and at the moment they're pretty unpopular. Something of a joke, really. They only gained one percent of the seats in the Reichstag last year."

"So why worry about them?" Ellen asked lightly. All this talk of war and politics was making her uneasy. She had an urge to run back home, to take Rosie and Jamie in her arms and hold them tightly to her. But surely this was just a lot of doom-mongering on Will's part, because he knew what war was like, and like her, he never wanted to see it again? Surely that's all this was?

"Because when this economic boom falls off a cliff," he stated flatly, "when the bubble bursts, a party like that could waltz—or march—right into power. People will be unemployed, angry, looking for someone to blame. They always are, when the pressure is on and they're behind the eight ball."

Ellen glanced down at the wilting lettuce leaves, all that was left of her salmon mousse. "But what if the bubble doesn't burst?"

Will shook his head. "Trust me, it will. Bubbles always do. It's just a matter of time. Already the Fed is trying to slow down stock prices, but it's too late. They're so inflated you couldn't possibly get the return that's being promised. It's absurd, it's the tallest tale ever told, and yet everyone wants to buy into it, speculating on stocks and bonds—"

Stocks and bonds are going through the roof. Ellen had barely taken in what Lucas had said on the telephone the other week, yet now she felt as if a chilly finger were trailing the length of her spine. "Stocks and bonds," she repeated neutrally.

"Yes, and the speculation. Believing you'll turn into a millionaire in a matter of months—and you might, but what happens when next year a million bucks only buys you a gallon of milk, or worse yet, that million bucks isn't worth the paper it's printed on?" Will raised his eyebrows in query as the waiter cleared their plates.

"Surely that won't happen," Ellen said once he'd gone. She didn't even like to think of it.

"That's what everyone is hoping," Will agreed, pouring them both more champagne. "And God knows, I'm hoping for it, too. Because if the economy crashes, and parties like the National Socialists get into power over in Europe, you can be sure as shooting, there'll be another war, and with the weapons we have now, the weapons we may have when it finally happens, if the theories physicists like me are dreaming up can be proved... it'll be nothing like the war you and I saw. It'll be much, much worse."

Ellen reached for her champagne and took a large sip. "Goodness, you're gloomy," she said as she swallowed, and Will let out a hard laugh before he hung his head.

"Sorry. Nature of the job—or perhaps the beast." He reached for his own glass. "I'm afraid of the future," he told her with such bleak honesty that Ellen felt like shivering. "And I don't like being afraid."

"And I thought I was the one who didn't like change," she said as lightly as she could. She glanced around the room again, with all of its complacent diners, enjoying their evening out. Nearby, a woman threw back her head and laughed, showing the long, white column of her throat, draped in iridescent pearls. Ellen had a sudden, surreal sensation of being entirely removed from what she saw, as if she had taken a step back, or perhaps forward, into the future. She pictured the diners vanished, the dining room empty and derelict, weeds poking through the floor, the ceiling open to the sky, and she shivered. She was being fanciful, fearful, and yet...

"Come on," Will said, almost roughly, reaching for her hand. "Our main course won't be here for a while. Let's dance."

Still feeling unsettled, Ellen let herself be led by the hand to where a large orchestra was playing a slow waltz as they took to the floor. Will's hand was warm on her waist, his other clasped with hers as they began the usual back-and-forth step.

"I'm sorry," he said in a low voice. "I've ruined our evening twice over now, with my gloominess."

"You haven't," Ellen assured him as they danced, both of them finding their rhythm. "But I am worried for you, Will. You... you don't seem happy."

Will was pensive for a moment as they moved around the floor. "I don't think I know how to be happy anymore," he said finally. "I've tried, God knows. When I first came out here, to Stanford, I think I was happy for a little while, or at least happy enough. I fell in love—I haven't told you about that. Her name was Charlotte."

"Oh?" Ellen asked as he swung her around. "What happened?"

"She met someone else who was a bit more fun. Can't say I blame her, really. Looking back, I think I was only playing at love, because it seemed like a good idea." He glanced down at her, his expression both wry and tender. "Do you despair of me, Ellen?"

"No," she replied slowly, "but I want to help you." She realized how much she meant it. The old, earnest longing to see Will happy had come back in full force.

"Help me how?"

"Why don't you come to dinner?" Ellen suggested. "I'd like you to meet Rosie and Jamie, and I'm sure they'd be pleased to meet you. Children have a way of making us look outside of ourselves. We can see the future in them, and it doesn't have to be bleak. Yours doesn't, Will." She looked at him earnestly and he smiled briefly before he looked away.

"Thank you for your invitation. I'll be glad to take you up on it." His hand squeezed hers before he nodded towards their table. "Now we should probably head back, because I believe our main courses are about to arrive."

CHAPTER TWELVE

"So how was it?" Gracie asked the next morning, as they spooned sectioned grapefruit while sitting on the patio when Jamie and Rosie had gone upstairs to get dressed.

Ellen eased a pink, glistening section of grapefruit onto her spoon before popping it into her mouth and giving a grimace; it really was awfully sour, although she was trying to get used to it. Apparently everyone in California ate the large, yellow-skinned fruit. "Not exactly what I expected," she answered as she swallowed. "Quite... bleak, really. In a strange way."

Gracie raised her eyebrows. "Bleak? Now that I wasn't expecting. The way you painted this fellow, I thought he was a good egg, a real swell fella."

"He is, but he's always been... a bit troubled, I suppose," Ellen said slowly. She still felt unsettled by the conversation she and Will had had, about weapons and war and looming disastrous economic crashes. She suspected all his doomsday prophecies revealed more about what he was feeling than what might actually happen. At least she hoped so. "He hides behind a façade of good humor and charm," she told Gracie, "but he has his own demons. He was shot down during the war."

"But that would have been over ten years ago," Gracie replied.

She'd only been eighteen when the war had ended, and she'd spent most of it at school. "And Peter recovered from his shell shock years ago. Surely this Will has got over it by now?"

"I don't know if he ever has. Can anyone get over something like that, really? Peter still has nightmares, doesn't he?" She paused in reflection, tapping her spoon absently against her plate. "Perhaps it's just who Will is—someone who sees the glass half-empty but downs it anyway."

"How poetic," Gracie teased. "Well, he sounds kinda interesting, if you ask me. Either that or a real flat tire. I can't decide which. I don't suppose I'll get the chance to meet him?"

"Actually, you will. He's coming to dinner here next week, so you'll meet him if you're not out late filming."

Gracie's face lit up. "I'll make sure not to be, then! I don't think I'm shooting a single scene next week," she added with a pout. "It's going to be just the big guns for a while now. I'll be bored to tears."

"How ever did you manage before you were a movie star?" Ellen teased. She'd found the best way of dealing with Gracie was lightly, lightly, even as she couldn't help but sometimes feel tense inside, as if her cousin was a delicate object that needed careful handling—either that, or she was a grenade who could explode in your face.

"I honestly don't know how I did," Gracie replied, and Ellen couldn't tell if she was joking or not. She so rarely could. "Anyway, I hope Mr. Turner isn't too much of a Gloomy Gus, because that would be really boring, let me tell you."

"I'm sure you can liven him up," Ellen replied with a smile.

"Oh, I intend to, I assure you!"

Rosie and Jamie came tumbling outside then, dressed in their bathing suits, even though the sun was only just starting to warm the earth.

"Swimming already?" Ellen exclaimed, unable to keep a note of anxiety from her voice. "The water will be so cold."

"I don't care," Jamie insisted. "It's plenty warm outside!"

Gracie lounged back in her chair. "No swimming at night, no swimming in the morning..." she murmured, eyes dancing.

"I didn't say they couldn't," Ellen protested before turning back to the children. "Very well, but the minute I see you start to shiver, Jamie, it's a towel for you!"

With a cry of glee, her son hurtled toward the water, while Rosie inched along, as careful as ever. Ellen watched them, her heart brimming with both love and fear. She thought of all that Will had said last night and another pang of apprehension assailed her. He couldn't be right. He just couldn't be.

"Gracie," she asked slowly as the children splashed in the water, "do you think there could be another war? Will said he thought there would be one."

Gracie's mouth dropped open with comic theatricality. "Another war! Why, that's baloney. Of course there can't be another war."

The ringing certainty in her voice filled Ellen with relief. "No, I don't think there could be," she agreed. "Not after the last one."

"Why on earth would he say such a thing?"

"I don't exactly know. Something about the economy and weapons and Germany—a new political party, I think." The details Will had so grimly told her last night remained thankfully hazy.

"Good gravy, he really is a Gloomy Gus!" Gracie burst out. "Another war? I've never heard such nonsense in my life. Absolute horse feathers. As if anyone on God's green earth wants another war. He needs seeing to, I think. He sounds screwy."

"No, he's just..." Ellen thought of the bleak look in Will's eyes, the grim set to his mouth. "He's just wary, I suppose."

"Well, I'll wary him," Gracie replied, balling up one fist as if she'd swing a punch. "When's he coming for dinner?"

"In a few weeks, I think. Things are busy with his work."

"Well, maybe by then he'll have his head on straight. If not, I'll straighten it for him."

"I'm sure you would, Gracie." Despite the tensions they'd been experiencing, Ellen couldn't help but feel a surge of affection for her exuberant cousin. If only she had that much vitality and emotion! She brushed her hand across her newly bobbed hair. Perhaps she was getting there, one small step at a time.

The rest of the day passed pleasantly enough, with the children in and out of the swimming pool before they finally dried off and walked to the Central Library, where Rosie picked out *The Magical Land of Noom* and *Doctor Dolittle*. Jamie was hard-pressed to find a book he liked; he much preferred being outside, in the pool or on his scooter. Finally, Ellen cajoled him into selecting *Milly-Molly-Mandy Stories*, although he complained it was a "girl book."

"Books are for everyone," Ellen admonished him with exasperation as he wriggled away from her and ran outside to play on the wide steps of the library that led to a courtyard studded with palm trees.

"Mama," Rosie asked, slipping her hand into Ellen's as they left the library with their books, "can we telephone Daddy again? We haven't spoken to him in ages, and he hasn't written any letters."

"You know he's busy," Ellen replied gently, even as a pang of sorrow twisted her insides, for Rosie's sake as well as her own. Why on earth had Lucas not written even once? They'd been in California for nearly a month already.

"I know he's busy," Rosie told her, "but I'd still like to call him."

"Of course, darling. We'll try when we get back. It's Saturday, after all. He should be home."

Back at the bungalow, Gracie was getting ready to go out for the afternoon, humming under her breath, the smell of Shalimar permeating even the downstairs with its expensive scents of bergamot, jasmine and sandalwood. No doubt she was going out again with the hapless and hopelessly smitten Emmett Hughes, Ellen thought with a sigh as she put the library books away. She had already resolved not to say anything more about that matter, but she worried both for Emmett—and for Gracie.

"Right, let's make that call," she told Rosie, and she sat down in the hall by the telephone table with Jamie on her lap and Rosie leaning into her side. She picked up the receiver and dialed the operator. "I'd like to call New York, Butterfield exchange, number 0355, please."

"Hold, please," the operator said briskly, and Ellen gave Rosie a reassuring smile.

"I'm sure we'll catch him this time," she whispered, although in truth, she wasn't sure of any such thing.

Then, a few crackling seconds later, Ellen heard a tinny ringing—once, twice, three times—and then, finally, thankfully, Lucas's familiar voice, kind and dear, came on the line. "Butterfield 0355."

"A call from California," the operator interjected. "Let me connect you, sir."

"Ellen?" Lucas said once the connection had gone through.

"And me, Daddy," Jamie yelled into Ellen's ear, making her wince even as she laughed.

"And me, too," Rosie whispered, standing on her tiptoes to get closer to the telephone receiver.

"We're all here," Ellen told him, a laugh caught in her throat along with a few tears. It was so very good to hear his voice.

"We've missed you, Daddy," Rosie said.

"And I've missed you, pumpkin! So much." Lucas's voice was full of warmth. "Tell me what you've been up to."

"I've been to school a whole week."

"Oh, excellent! Let me hear all about it."

Ellen kept one arm around a wriggling Jamie as Rosie hesitantly regaled Lucas with tales of school—the tennis, the art lessons, the other girls.

"And I've been on a scooter," Jamie, not to be outdone, shouted towards the receiver. "I built it myself."

"Did you, now?" Lucas exclaimed with a laugh, and yet Ellen

had the niggling sensation that he wasn't engaging the way he once would have done. He didn't ask how he'd built it, or what it looked like, or anything like that. Perhaps it was simply a matter of distance and time, she told herself; three thousand miles away, talking down a crackling phone line, wasn't the same as speaking in the same room, meeting her eyes over Jamie and Rosie as he gave her a tender smile.

No, it wasn't the same at all.

"They sound happy," Lucas remarked when Rosie and Jamie had finally exhausted all their news and run outside to pick oranges with Maria.

"They are." Ellen curled the telephone cord around her fingers, feeling suddenly shy. "You know we've been out here for nearly a month already."

"Has it been that long?" Lucas asked. "Goodness."

"Have you not been counting the days?" Ellen asked, meaning to tease, but it came out just a little sharp. She closed her eyes, summoned as much patience and understanding as she could. "We miss you," she stated more quietly. "I miss you."

"I miss you, too," Lucas replied in a low voice. "Truly."

Ellen longed to believe him, believe that throb of warmth in his voice. "When I telephoned the other day," she said hesitantly, "Eva said you'd been out most evenings. You must be very busy."

"I am. The city is booming, Ellen. There's so much to do." Lucas's voice brimmed with enthusiasm. "It's really quite an exciting time."

"Is it?" Ellen hesitated and then said, "I spoke to someone who said this... this boom will have to end someday. Collapse, really. He said the speculation over stocks and bonds couldn't go on, up and up, all the way to the moon. That the value of everything was inflated..." She trailed off, knowing she'd already betrayed her ignorance with her vague, hesitant statements.

"I suppose everything must come to an end," Lucas replied easily enough. "But at the moment there's no sign of the stock market even faltering, never mind an actual collapse. The Federal

Reserve warned of excessive speculation, but it's in hand now, thanks to the banks."

"Is it?" She felt a flicker of relief at Lucas's assured tone; surely he knew what he was talking about, even more than Will did. He looked into the legalities of it all for several large corporations, after all. Yet even so, she wondered if she simply wanted to have her fears assuaged, just as when Gracie had stated so firmly that there couldn't possibly be another war. It was all just Will's doom-mongering. *It had to be...*

"So who is this fount of wisdom you've been speaking to?" Lucas asked lightly. "It sounds as if you've made some friends in California, I'm glad to hear."

"It is an old friend, actually." This gave her relief, as well, to tell him about her dinner with Will. She didn't want it to be some sort of secret. "Will Turner. I met him in New York, before we were married. You remember when I visited the Framptons there?"

"Yes, of course I do. And I recall you mentioning Will Turner, as well." A pause, and then Lucas said, "As I recall, he was quite smitten with you."

"What!" Ellen shook her head, even though Lucas of course couldn't see her. "I never said any such thing."

"You didn't have to. Speaking as someone who was—and still is —very much smitten with you, I could tell."

"He's just an old friend, Lucas," Ellen said quietly.

"I know he is." Lucas gave a little sigh; Ellen thought he sounded tired. "And, truthfully, I'm glad you have a familiar face there, besides Gracie that is. How is she managing?"

"She's bagged a role in a motion picture, if you can believe it, but I suppose you've read about that in my letters." A slight, telling pause had Ellen stilling before she asked uneasily, "You have received my letters, haven't you?"

"Yes, of course," Lucas replied with ready cheerfulness. "The U.S. Mail Service is completely reliable, you know. A letter from California to New York only takes a few days."

Something in his tone compelled her to press. "But you've...

you've *read* them?" For he would have known about Gracie being in *The Lady and the Brute*. He would have asked about Jamie's scooter, Rosie's school. He would have heard about their trip into Los Angeles, visiting the La Brea tar pits and Grauman's Chinese Theatre... but he hadn't asked about any of that, almost as if he hadn't known. An awful, sinking sensation took hold of Ellen's stomach, growing only worse as Lucas did not respond. "Lucas?" she asked. "Have you?"

"I've been meaning to," he confessed in a low voice, the words an apology. "Honestly, I have. I've saved them all up—they're stacked on my bedside table, ready for when I have a spare moment—or really, an hour. You do write such lovely, long letters, and I can hardly wait to read them. Things have been so busy—I'm just waiting for the right time."

"We've been away for nearly a month," Ellen reminded him quietly. "And we've only had one phone call and no letters from you."

"Ellen—"

"Do you miss us at all?" she burst out. "Or are you just glad to have us out of the way?" It hurt her to say the words.

"Ellen, that's not fair," Lucas said, and now he sounded hurt. "You're the one reacquainting yourself with old friends, not me."

"*That's* not fair," Ellen shot back, hardly able to believe they were arguing. They *never* argued. Lucas was far too even-tempered for that. She loved him too much, and he loved her. She knew it, and yet...

"No, it isn't," he agreed with a sigh. "I'm sorry. I shouldn't have said it. I didn't mean it like that. It's just... I've been so very busy. Work has been crazy—"

"And all these investments?" Ellen asked. "The stocks and bonds? Railroad, steel?" She recalled his words. "What about them?"

"What are you asking?"

"I don't even know," Ellen admitted. Nameless fears were circling in her mind like a flock of buzzards, picking at the scraps of knowledge and supposition she'd been given. She felt as if she'd been infected with Will's gloom, although perhaps she'd always had it—this longing for the past, this fear of change. Perhaps that was why they'd become good friends; they really were kindred spirits in that regard.

"There's no need to worry, Ellen." Lucas's tone had turned soothing. "Yes, I'm very busy, it's true. While you and the children are gone, I want to make the most of the time, so I'll have more to spend with you when you return."

"We talked about you visiting us here, and it's nearly March," she reminded him.

"Yes, yes," Lucas replied after a second's pause. "Yes, of course. I'd love to see you all out there. Perhaps in April or May."

"We'll be going home in May, I should think," Ellen replied, trying not to let her tone betray her disappointment. "When the weather has turned warm."

"Before, then. Yes, that's an excellent idea. I'll look into tickets."

But Ellen had the feeling, leaden and certain, that he was only saying it to appease her. He didn't really mean it; he would be too busy then, too.

"Lucas..." she began, but then didn't know how to finish it. *Do you still love me?* was melodramatic and self-pitying; she already knew he did. *What is taking you away from me?* was unnecessary; the answer was, unfortunately, obvious. His work, his obsession with success, with status, with style. As much as she longed to, she could not find the words to bridge the chasm that had opened up between them.

"I'm sorry, Ellen." Lucas's tone was heartfelt. "I know I've been a disappointment to you lately, with how little I've been in touch, and I truly don't mean to be. It's just the days pass in such a hectic flurry... but I do miss you, you know. Terribly. You and the children."

Do you? Ellen forced the question down. She believed Lucas, of course she did, but missing someone and making the effort to keep in touch seemed to be two different things.

"I love you, you know," Lucas said in his old, wry tone. "So much. I always will."

"I love you too," Ellen managed back. She felt near tears.

A silence crackled on the line, and then Lucas spoke briskly. "I'm afraid I'm due at the office in an hour—"

"At the office on a Saturday morning?"

"Things really are busy. One of our clients got a tip and is about to make a serious investment, and they need legal advice immediately."

"I see."

"I'll telephone this week," Lucas promised. "And I'll read all your letters tonight."

Ellen bit her lip to keep from saying something sharp. *Don't read them if you don't want to.* The fact that Lucas had not been interested enough to open them right away stung more than a little. She recalled the days when she'd been in Vermont or Scotland, and they'd written letters to each other with wonderful regularity. They had been no more than friends, then, but Lucas had been a faithful writer—and reader. She'd loved his newsy missives, full of anecdotes and warmth. What had changed?

"Goodbye, then," she said dully, and after saying his own farewell, Lucas disconnected the call first, leaving Ellen sitting there, her heart leaden inside her, the telephone receiver lying limply in her hand.

CHAPTER THIRTEEN

"When is he coming? When is he coming?"

Jamie's nose was pressed to the window as he eagerly scanned the street for the first sighting of their guest.

"He's not due for another fifteen minutes, silly," Ellen told him with a ruffle of his hair. "You're going to be standing there for a long time, Jamie."

"I don't care."

Her children had worked themselves up into a fever of excitement over Will Turner coming to supper. It had been nearly three weeks since Ellen had dined with him at the Raymond Hotel; Will had been busy with work, and Gracie with filming. Ellen had occupied her days with taking Rosie to and from school and spending time with Jamie. She'd become used to a pleasant, easy rhythm of strolling in the sunshine while Jamie scooted along, or reading and lazing by the pool while he splashed and played, full of a new exuberance, thanks to the sun and dry air.

It was really rather amazing how quickly and easily the days slipped by, and she developed some sympathy for Lucas losing track of time and forgetting to telephone or write. Thankfully, he had written since their uneasy telephone call; a newsy letter each for Jamie and Rosie, as well as a long, tender missive for Ellen, which had done much to soothe her rankled soul. They'd spoken by telephone twice more, and she'd done her best to be cheerful and positive, refusing to give in to the needling temptation to ask him when he would visit, or if he was staying up too late working.

Things had thankfully seemed to settle down with Gracie too; she was so busy filming that she came home every evening to collapse into bed, only to rise early the next morning to head back to the studio. Eduardo gamely drove her to and fro, uncomplaining and proclaiming that he was lucky to know a movie star.

"Not a movie star quite yet," Gracie would laugh, "but I *am* getting there." She'd been given an extra scene with several speaking lines, which had thrilled her.

And now Will was about to arrive, which was making Ellen feel both pleased and slightly nervous, although she couldn't have quite said why. Gracie was still upstairs, getting ready, and Ellen was doing her best to keep Jamie and Rosie from becoming even more overexcited.

"Is that him?" Jamie asked, pressing his nose even harder against the glass. "Is it?"

Ellen came to the window and looked out. "No, darling, it's just a man walking his dog. I don't think Will is going to bring a pet with him, if he even has one."

Jamie sagged theatrically just as another man rounded the corner onto the sleepy street in Bungalow Heaven. He was wearing a light linen suit and a jaunty straw boater, and carrying a bouquet of calla lilies. When he caught sight of both Ellen and Jamie standing in the window, he gave a cheery wave.

"He's here!" Jamie squealed as Ellen went to the door. By the time she opened it, Will was already coming up the walk.

"There are some very excited children who can't wait to meet you," she told him with a smile, and Will handed her the bouquet. "Oh! You didn't need to—"

"I wanted to. Thank you for having me. Now, who's this?" He smiled down at Jamie, who, in a sudden bout of shyness, was standing behind Ellen and peeping out from behind her legs.

"This is Jamie," Ellen told him, putting one hand on her son's shoulder to steer him out from behind her. "And this is Rosie." She beckoned to her daughter who was lingering a few steps behind her. "Say hello to Mr. Turner."

"Hello," Rosie whispered, while Jamie blurted, "I have a scooter!"

"Do you?" Will's tone was grave. "Can you ride it?"

"Yes, I can!"

"That's swell. Perhaps you'll show me a little later?"

Jamie glanced eagerly at Ellen for permission, and she gave a small nod.

"Come in, Will," she told him. "We can't have you standing in the doorway like a peddler."

Will stepped across the threshold just as Gracie came to the top of the stairs. Ellen thought she must have timed her entrance perfectly; Will's eyes widened as she came down the stairs, one hand, with bright red lacquered nails, trailing the banister. She was overdressed for the occasion, but it suited her: a straight, sack-like dress in deep crimson to match her nails, with a deep V in the front trimmed with black satin. She'd straightened her hair with irons so her dark bob swung smartly against her cheek and her carmine-painted lips curved into a smile that was both knowing and coy.

"Well, well, well. We finally get to meet the enigmatic Mr. Turner."

"Enigmatic?" Will replied as he continued to appraise her. "Now that's something I haven't been described as before." He held out his hand, which Gracie took with the tips of her red-painted fingers. "May I have the pleasure...?"

"Hasn't Ellen told you about me?" Gracie slid Ellen a laughing look while she managed a smile. "I'm her cousin, Gracie McCafferty."

"Pleased to meet you, Miss McCafferty."

"Oh, now, now." Gracie gave a full-throated laugh as she glanced at Will from beneath her mascaraed lashes. "You must call me Gracie."

"Only if you'll call me Will."

"I certainly shall."

"Shall we sit down," Ellen suggested, trying her best not to sound stiff. She'd expected Gracie to flirt, but her overwhelming femme fatale routine seemed to Ellen both ridiculous and alarming. Will, she saw, only looked bemused.

Maria served everyone lemonade as they sat out on the patio, the pool shimmering under the setting sun. It was now the middle of March, and already the days were warmer, the nights longer. Ellen could hardly believe they'd been in California nearly two months already.

"Ellen hasn't told me a thing about you," Gracie pronounced as they sipped their drinks. The glance she gave Will seemed to Ellen to be both teasing and intimate. "She's kept you all to herself, the sly thing."

"I haven't—" Ellen began, flushing a little, and Gracie just laughed.

"I'm only teasing! But you really haven't said much about Mr. Turner at all."

"I thought it was Will," Will reminded her, and Gracie looked delighted.

"It is," she practically purred. "It *is*."

"I'm afraid there's not much to tell," Will said. "I'm an old stick, quite dull, really. Work and more work, that's me."

"I doubt that," Gracie murmured.

"I'd much rather hear about you," Will told Rosie and Jamie, angling slightly away from Gracie. "Tell me what you've been doing since coming to California."

Gracie lolled back in her seat while Rosie and Jamie regaled Will with stories of their time in Pasadena, and he listened attentively, interjecting encouraging remarks now and again. Ellen glanced at Gracie, trying not to fume—or worry. She really was acting rather shamelessly, with her innuendo-laced tone, her heavy-laden glances. If she didn't let up, Ellen vowed, she'd have a quiet word with her when Will couldn't hear.

After a few more minutes, Maria came to say dinner was almost ready, and Ellen took the opportunity to shepherd Rosie and Jamie upstairs for bed while Will and Gracie moved inside.

"I want to stay," Jamie complained, kicking his feet, and Ellen kept one hand on his shoulder as she steered him upstairs.

"You can come back down to say goodnight to Mr. Turner when you're in your pajamas and dressing gown," she promised. Upstairs, Rosie and Jamie went rather dejectedly to their rooms to change, while Ellen paused at the top of the stairs, straining to hear the conversation between Will and Gracie.

"How are you finding California?" Will asked politely.

"It's the absolute bee's knees. I've been filming a movie—has Ellen told you, or has she kept that a secret, too?"

"I don't think Ellen has too many secrets, but she didn't mention you'd been acting, no."

"Mama." Rosie tugged on Ellen's hand, startling her. "I can't find my slippers."

"Right, let's have a look." Somewhat reluctantly Ellen followed Rosie into her room, where she couldn't hear any more of the conversation downstairs.

A few minutes later, Rosie and Jamie were both changed, their faces washed and their teeth brushed, and Ellen brought them downstairs for a quick goodnight before they sat down to supper.

As they came into the living room, she saw, with a jolt, that Will was standing by the fireplace, and Gracie was standing very close to him, her elbow braced on the mantle, so she could whisper in his ear if she so chose. Was that what she had been doing? Ellen had only been gone for ten minutes or so, but she felt as if the mood had noticeably altered, become something separate and intimate, a secret she did not share.

"The children have come to say goodnight," she said, her voice a little too loud, while Gracie's eyes danced as she turned to give Ellen one of her knowing, catlike smiles.

"And I'm very pleased to say goodnight! Do you have trains on your pajamas, Jamie?" Will chatted to the children while Ellen gave Gracie a fulminating look, which her cousin predictably and blithely ignored.

Then it was back upstairs with the children while Gracie leaned in to Will to murmur something that Ellen couldn't hear.

She tried to untangle her feelings as she tucked Rosie and Jamie into bed; she wasn't jealous, even though she suspected Gracie would think she was. She was exasperated and annoyed at Gracie for doing her utmost to be the center of attention, and she was, Ellen realized, a bit embarrassed for her cousin's sake. Her obvious tactics were over the top and inappropriate, and they made Ellen worry.

Gracie had seemed to have finally found an even keel these last few weeks, so why had she plunged back into this daring, dangerous territory? Or was Ellen simply being a stick-in-the-mud, as Gracie would no doubt laughingly accuse? *He's a handsome man and I like to flirt. This is Hollywood, after all, Ellen, for heaven's sake!*

"I apologize for the interruptions," Ellen said once the three of them were seated at the dining-room table. "The children were so excited to meet you."

"And I was delighted to meet them. There's no apology needed."

"I trust Gracie was able to keep you entertained?" Ellen asked, and heard the slight edge to her voice. Gracie heard it too, and smiled.

"She was." Will gave Gracie a surprisingly warm look. "Your cousin is quite entertaining."

Ellen had no idea how to take that remark, and so she busied herself with the meal instead, murmuring her thanks as Maria served the first course, shrimp cocktail.

She continued to struggle as they began to eat; the mood around the table felt like a ship she could not steer, for Gracie was firmly at the rudder, amusing Will with anecdotes from the film set, throwing back her long, white neck as she laughed throatily, giving her knowing smiles whenever Ellen found herself looking censorious and feeling like a fusty schoolmarm.

By the time Maria served coffee and Ellen excused her for the evening, she found herself completely on edge, practically gritting her teeth as Gracie continued to flirt with a complete lack of shamelessness, and Will responded with an easy gallantry, reminding Ellen of how he used to be, when she'd known him so long ago—the effortless charm, the easy humor. Perhaps Gracie was more suited to him than she realized. He certainly seemed to be taking her flirtation in his stride.

"Ellen said you were a real Gloomy Gus," Gracie told Will over coffee, laying one hand on his arm, "but I don't think you are, at all."

"I said no such thing!" Ellen exclaimed, for it was Gracie herself who had said it, but her cousin just shrugged.

"Oh, you did, more or less," she dismissed. "You can't deny it, Ellen."

"Gracie—" Ellen knew there was nothing she could say to dissuade Gracie, or reassure Will.

"I daresay I am a bit gloomy," Will replied with a smile. "Ellen undoubtedly tired of my talk of war and economic downturns. It really is terribly boring stuff. You'd be asleep if you heard me go on about it, I'm sure."

"I think you need to have more fun," Gracie pronounced. "And I'm just the girl to give you a good time! We're wrapping up filming next week and there's a party—you should come, Will, as my guest."

Will looked surprised, but he inclined his head. "Thank you. That is a very kind invitation."

"And you can, too," Gracie told Ellen rather carelessly. "Emmett has invited you to the last day of the shoot—did I tell you? And Rosie and Jamie, as well. You can see what it's all about."

"That's very kind of him," Ellen managed. She felt furious, but she knew she couldn't show it or even explain why.

"Now let's end the evening with some giggle water," Gracie

said as she unfolded herself from the table in one languorous and fluid motion. "You can't leave without a nightcap, Will."

"We don't have any—" Ellen began, and Gracie's lips curved.

"Oh, but I do."

"Don't mind her so much," Will said quietly as Gracie went upstairs to fetch a bottle. "She's harmless, really."

"She's outrageous," Ellen replied. "But I suppose it is amusing to you."

"She's doing it on purpose. It's like a mask she puts on and off." He paused, his gaze distant, his eyes shuttered. "I know what that's like."

"So you and Gracie are kindred spirits?" Ellen replied a bit tartly, and then wished she'd bitten her tongue. She *did* sound jealous, and she wasn't. She absolutely wasn't.

"Of a kind, perhaps," Will replied, which only made her feel worse.

"Ta-da!" Gracie returned, brandishing a bottle of brandy. "This is the real jag juice." She fetched three tumblers from the cabinet and slopped in generous measures, while Ellen watched silently, struggling to control her temper—as well as her unease. "And we need some music, as well," Gracie insisted, and went to the large radio, housed in the corner cabinet in the living room, and began to fiddle with the dial.

After some crackling, the sound of a jazz orchestra came on, playing a low, swoony piece; Gracie held her tumbler aloft as she swayed to the music. "Isn't this peachy? I love jazz."

Ellen took a sip of her brandy, wincing as its medicinal taste scalded the back of her throat. Lucas had bought a radio for their house in New York a couple of years ago, but Ellen still hadn't gotten into the habit of listening to it, even though he'd told her there were now more than six hundred stations broadcasting throughout the country.

Will walked into the living room, cradling his tumbler in one hand, as Gracie continued to sway. Stiffly Ellen followed.

Gracie tossed back the rest of her brandy and held out her long, slender arms. "Dance with me, Will."

"Gracie—" Ellen began, but Will was already moving into Gracie's arms, taking one hand in his as he put the other on her hip. Ellen watched rigidly as they moved to the music, a basic box step, but with the lonely wail of the saxophone and the hushed, intimate atmosphere of the darkened room, it felt like something far more. Ellen almost felt like a voyeur. She stood stiffly in the doorway as Will and Gracie moved around the room, Gracie tilting back her head to smile at Will while he gazed seriously down at her. Ellen had the urge to turn off the radio, clear away the tumblers and brandy. This was not at all what she'd intended for this evening, and she felt hurt, embarrassed and angry all at once.

Finally the song ended and slowly, almost reluctantly, Will moved apart from Gracie. "I should go," he said, and Gracie let out a sound of protest as she sloshed more brandy into her glass.

"You can't go yet. The party's just starting."

"This is hardly a party, Gracie," Ellen interjected.

"Oh, Ellen, stop for one second, won't you?" Gracie tossed back another drink. "We're just having *fun*." She held out her arms, swaying even though the music had ended, her eyes glittering. "What's the problem?"

"You're embarrassing yourself," Ellen told her coldly, "and our guest."

Something flashed across Gracie's face before she lifted her chin in challenge, her arms still flung. "Am I embarrassing you, Will?"

"Not a bit," Will replied easily. "But it is getting late, and I should go. I'll see you at that party?"

Gracie dropped her arms as she smiled. "You betcha."

"I'll see you out," Ellen said, and walked with Will to the door, where he collected his hat. "I'm sorry," she said in a low voice. "I had no idea she'd behave in such a way."

"You don't have to apologize on Gracie's account," Will replied, and his voice sounded uncharacteristically sharp.

Ellen blinked, feeling chastised. "Are you angry with me?" she asked uncertainly. "For... for spoiling your fun?"

Will sighed. "No, of course not. You could never spoil anything for me, Ellen. But you shouldn't let Gracie's antics bother you. She's just a kid and—"

"She's twenty-eight—"

"And she's hurting," Will finished quietly. "Can't you see that? It's nothing more than bravado on her part, for whatever reason. I don't suppose she's told you why."

"No, not really," Ellen replied, both startled and chastened. "There was a breakup..."

He shrugged. "It's not my business. But remember that, when she's so clearly trying to get your goat."

"Does that mean I should just ignore her behavior?" she asked, unable to keep the hurt from her voice. She'd never expected Will to take her to task like this, and over Gracie.

Will ran a hand through his hair. "I don't know. Maybe just be a bit more understanding, I suppose."

"You seem to have got the measure of her rather quickly," Ellen retorted, and he gave her a long, even look as he opened the front door to the cool night air.

"Yes, I have. It takes one to know one, I suppose, when it comes to broken souls. Goodnight, Ellen."

Ellen nodded jerkily in return as Will placed his hat on his head and then started down the darkened walk. She felt both furious and hurt, as well as more than a little guilty; she'd been looking forward to this evening, and it had been a disaster—a disaster Will seemed to blame her for. Was he right to? Perhaps she was too harsh with Gracie. But even if she was, did that mean letting Gracie make a fool of herself?

With a dispirited sigh, Ellen closed the door and returned to the living room. Gracie, she saw, was curled up on the sofa, her hand tucked under her cheek, fast asleep.

CHAPTER FOURTEEN

"I'm sorry."

Ellen turned in surprise to see Gracie standing sheepishly in the doorway as she was having her coffee on the patio. Maria had taken both Rosie and Jamie out to accompany her shopping.

"It isn't too much trouble, is it?" Ellen had asked, and Maria had simply laughed and shaken her head.

"Too much trouble! Never. Jamie is a good little gentleman, carrying my shopping, and dear Rosie has a good eye for spotting the ripe fruit. Come, my *bambinas*." She'd shepherded the two children out, and Ellen had been glad for a few moments alone to collect her thoughts.

She'd barely slept last night, as she'd gone over the evening in all of its excruciating detail, wondering whether she should have been more accommodating, hating that Will seemed to think less of her. She hadn't come to any helpful conclusions, and she was in as much of a muddle now, at nine o'clock in the morning, as she'd been at midnight last night.

And now Gracie was here, her head hanging low, looking genuinely repentant.

"Sorry?" Ellen repeated, and Gracie let out a long sigh.

"Yes, I'm very sorry. I behaved badly last night. I shocked Will and scandalized you. I am sorry, Ellen, even if you don't believe me."

She came to sit down opposite Ellen, gazing at her with a puppyish earnestness.

"I don't know what to believe, Gracie," Ellen told her. "I never do."

"I am an enigma," Gracie replied with a little smile. "I don't mind that, but I went too far last night, I know."

"Why did you?" Ellen asked quietly, and Gracie shrugged, her gaze sliding away.

"I had too much to drink."

"Not until the end of the evening, and you were outrageous the whole night long."

Gracie gave her a playful look. "Not that outrageous."

"Outrageous enough."

"Will didn't seem to mind."

Ellen did her best to school her expression into something bland. "Perhaps not, but I must admit that I did. I know I seem severe to you, Gracie, but I am concerned for your wellbeing. You seem..." She paused. "Unhappy."

"Unhappy!" Gracie threw back her head and laughed. "Do I seem unhappy when I'm slow-dancing with the most gorgeous man I've ever laid eyes on? Because he is, you know. You kept *that* secret."

"Underneath, yes, you do," Ellen replied evenly, ignoring the remark about Will's looks. "And Will thinks so, too."

"Oh, does he?"

Ellen couldn't tell anything from Gracie's drawl, and she wondered if she should have admitted so much. Gracie fumbled in the pocket of her dressing gown and took out a packet of Marlboros, the "luxury cigarette" aimed at ladies "today—for a treat!"

"What's really going on?" Ellen pressed, trying to gentle her voice. "Is it to do with Fred, with your breakup?"

"Fred," Gracie repeated scornfully. She lit her cigarette and inhaled deeply.

"You said you'd taken the ending of your engagement badly. I can understand that—"

"Ellen," Gracie drawled, "ending things with Fred was an absolute relief."

Ellen stared at her, discomfited. "That's not what you said before—"

"It's not Fred I'm missing," Gracie replied, and now she sounded bitter.

Ellen shook her head, more confused than ever. "I don't understand—"

"You don't need to. All I wanted to say was, I am sorry. I shouldn't have flirted *quite* so much with dear Will, although he really is the duck's quack. I can't regret it entirely, even if I should. At least he found me entertaining, in a way. Anyway, I have to rush —Emmett is picking me up in half an hour."

Ellen stared at her unhappily, feeling as if she'd made no progress at all. "Gracie," she said as her cousin started towards the living room, "I'm worried about you."

Gracie stilled, and for a second, Ellen could see, in her pale, unlined face, what Will had meant. Even though she was twenty-eight, almost the same age Ellen had been when she'd had Rosie— Gracie still seemed like just a girl—a child, desperate and vulnerable, a *broken soul*.

Then Gracie's expression's hardened as she flicked the stub of her cigarette away. "Don't be," she said, and then she was gone.

Over the next few days Ellen did her best to obey Gracie's command not to worry. She focused on the children—with a spate of rain, Jamie's cough had returned, although not as badly as before, and he was right as rain within a day or two. Rosie was anxious about an arithmetic test, and Jamie suffered a bee sting. It almost felt like a relief, to involve herself in these small concerns, rather than worry about what her cousin was up to—or why.

Neither did Ellen let herself worry about Will, or his seemingly bruised opinion of her, although she couldn't help but go over their last, abbreviated conversation by the door with a wince. She told herself it didn't matter, but in her heart she knew it did. She valued his opinion, and she'd come to rely on and expect his good opinion of her, even after so short a reacquaintance.

Still, she did her best to push such worries to the corners of her mind, as she tried to keep Jamie from overtaxing himself, and Rosie sailed through her arithmetic test, thanks to practice the evening before.

As Ellen took her into school one day, the headmistress, Mary Lowther Ranney, stopped her at the gate.

"Rosie was telling me you used to be an artist," she said with a smile. "At the Glasgow School of Art?"

"Oh, well." Ellen blushed as she gave her daughter a gently reproving look. To talk about that, so many years ago...! "I suppose, yes, but it was a very long time ago." She felt embarrassed to think Rosie might have been talking up her modest achievements.

"Perhaps you would like to come into one of our art lessons and show your sketches? Our teacher of art would be most gratified if you did."

"Oh, I..." Ellen stared at her helplessly. She had brought her sketchbook to California, but she had not opened it once since she'd been here.

"Rosie mentioned you sketched, back in New York," Miss Ranney continued encouragingly.

"They're so good, Mama," Rosie chimed in. "I think you should show them."

"Well, I suppose I could," Ellen agreed after a moment, feeling she had no choice but to do so. "But they really aren't much at all."

"I'm sure the girls will be delighted."

Sure enough, the next day, Ellen brought her little book of

sketches to the art class, feeling embarrassed by the few pencil drawings. The girls, however, were fascinated by the little glimpses of life she'd captured on the pages—Jamie as a baby, playing with a ball; the boy on the corner who sold newspapers.

"Can you do a sketch of me?" one girl asked eagerly and, bemused, Ellen drew her likeness with a few quick lines. Soon, all the girls were asking for a drawing, while their art teacher looked on, both smiling and stern.

"You really do have a gift," she told Ellen when she had finally exhausted the girls' requests for sketches.

"Thank you, but I must admit I haven't drawn properly in ages," Ellen confessed. She'd enjoyed the day greatly, but she couldn't help but feel a bit like a fraud.

"Perhaps this will inspire you to take it up again."

"Perhaps," Ellen agreed, realizing the headmistress was right. There were scenes she'd like to sketch, she realized. Jamie splashing in the pool; Rosie picking oranges; Maria's smiling face and Eduardo in the automobile. Perhaps she would start again, after all.

As she was taking her leave of the school, Miss Ranney came up to her. "The lesson was a success?"

"Yes, I think so," Ellen replied. "Thank you for asking me."

"Of course." Miss Ranney's expression turned intent. "I mentioned your name to my former colleague, Eleanor Toll, and as it happens, she had heard of you," she said. "She used to be a teacher at Los Angeles High School, and is one of the trustees of the newly formed Scripps College, for women. Have you heard of it?"

"I haven't, I'm afraid."

"It's about thirty miles east of here, not too far if traveling by car or train. Well worth a visit. Eleanor would make you very welcome, I'm sure. She is hoping to arrange an exhibition of lady artists. Perhaps you would consider taking part."

"Oh, I couldn't," Ellen protested, while Miss Ranney merely

raised her eyebrows. "I have nothing to exhibit," she explained. "But thank you for the suggestion."

Miss Ramsey nodded, and with a smile of farewell, Ellen hurried away. Yet later, as she watched Jamie playing in the yard, the sunlight gilding his hair, she felt that old, familiar twitch of her fingers, the sudden desire to capture what she saw on paper and in pencil. Her sketchbook was lying right there on the table, and with a spurt of determination, Ellen reached for it, turning to a blank page, her brow furrowing as she glanced at her son and then began to draw.

It amazed her, how quickly she became lost in her sketching, the world falling away save for the scratch of her pencil on paper, her vision taking shape with each new line. She hadn't sketched anything since the children had been small, and while she hadn't missed it, not exactly, it felt good and right to be doing it again, like reclaiming some part of herself she hadn't even realized she'd lost.

Throughout the week, Gracie came and went, came and went, in a flurry of silk and satin, perfume and cigarette smoke, and Ellen held her tongue. Then, at the end of the week, Gracie reminded her that they'd all been invited to the film set for the last day of the shoot, and Ellen also to the party afterwards, once she'd taken the children home.

Ellen felt rather ambivalent about the whole affair; although she had a flicker of curiosity for what happened on a film set, she felt a far deeper unease at mingling with movie stars and other glamorous and sophisticated people. As for a party with them all... she suspected she would stick out like the bumpkin she still feared she was.

Sure enough, the day came, and Eduardo drove them into Los Angeles to meet Gracie, Jamie's nose pressed to the window as usual. Ellen had taken great care with her outfit, and she felt the drop-waisted dress in light green silk struck the right note between modest and fashionable. She'd straightened her hair and had even added some discreet mascara and lipstick.

"Mama, you look *bee-you-ti-ful*," Rosie had exclaimed, giving Ellen's rather fragile self-confidence a needed boost. Still, nerves fluttered in her tummy as they swept through the gates of Paramount Pictures' studio. After giving their names to a man in a peaked cap who ticked them off on his clipboard, they were escorted to one of a dozen long, low buildings.

"Quiet, in case they're filming," the man advised, and Ellen stepped into the dim building that reminded her of a large barn or shed, Rosie and Jamie jostling eagerly behind her. At the other end, a stage set had been assembled, with bright lights trained on a painted door and brick wall. It all looked ridiculously fake, and yet Ellen knew on film it would seem as real as the door they'd just stepped through. The air had a heavy, hot smell of greasepaint and something burning, most likely from the cameras, and a blue fug of cigarette smoke hung over the set, while actors milled around and cameramen fiddled with the large black movie cameras, looking like mechanical spiders on their long, spindly legs.

"May I help you?" a woman in a belted skirt suit, her hair a dark, sleek bob, asked officiously, but before Ellen could reply, she heard Gracie.

"Ellen! Darlings!" Gracie came towards them, arms outstretched. Ellen barely recognized her, with the white pancake makeup on her face, her stark, red lips, and more alarmingly, a purpling black eye.

"Gracie!" Ellen gasped. "What happened?"

Gracie let out a bright peal of laughter. "It's makeup, silly! I get a shiner in one scene—we've filmed it already, but we're doing another shortly, where I'm turned away." She pressed one hand dramatically to her forehead. "Oh, the despair!"

"Is it appropriate...?" Ellen asked, for she knew many of the moving pictures were considered somewhat scandalous. She recalled the talk of the studio ushering in a code of conduct for what could be shown on film, although it hadn't happened yet.

"Oh yes, quite," Gracie assured her, "but terribly sad. Come on."

She led them towards the set, where three folding chairs had been set up next to the director, Rowland V. Lee. Gracie introduced them all, kissed Mr. Lee's cheek, and then disappeared in a flurry of waves and blown kisses while Ellen told Rosie and Jamie to sit by her and watch.

"She's a star in the making," Rowland assured them with a smile. He was a dapper gentleman of about forty, his brown hair slicked back from a high forehead, and a scarf knotted loosely about his throat, underneath a white button-down shirt.

"Is she?" Ellen asked, and he nodded with surprising earnestness.

"Oh yes, she's got something, Gracie. A certain star power. She's put Mary Astor's nose out of joint because of it."

"Oh—"

"Gracie steals the scene without even trying," Rowland told her with a grin. "The camera loves her."

Soon enough, Ellen could see what he meant, when they started filming. She watched as in front of her eyes the laughing, light Gracie she knew was transformed into a tragic heroine, her heart-shaped face a perfect picture of desolation as she begged her brutish boyfriend not to send her away into the night.

Ellen found herself caught up in the story, a lump forming in her throat as Gracie clutched at the sleeve of the man whose face was as hard and unyielding as stone and he thrust her away. When she glanced at Rosie, she saw, to her shock, that her daughter was crying.

"It's just so *sad*," Rosie explained with a sniff, while Jamie kicked his heels against the rung of his chair.

"When will it be over?" he asked. "I wanna see Gracie."

"Soon, soon," Ellen promised him as she put her arms around Rosie. "Remember, darling, it's only a story."

"She's perfect!" someone exclaimed, and Ellen looked up in

surprise to see one of the actors offstage pointing to Rosie. "Rowland, there's your orphan!"

"Orphan?" Ellen repeated uncertainly, while Rowland leaned forward in his chair to peer assessingly at her daughter.

"She is pretty good," he admitted gruffly. "Can we get her into makeup?"

"Pardon?" Ellen asked. "I'm sorry, are you talking about my daughter?"

Quickly, Rowland explained they needed an orphan for the next scene; the little girl they'd already cast had taken sick. She was meant to offer Gracie an apple as she stumbled away, a heart-wrenching picture of the desperate woman's lot, from child to lady.

"I... I don't know," Ellen hedged, while Rosie gazed at her imploringly.

"Please, Mama, please, can I? Oh *please!*"

Ellen couldn't resist the look of pleading rapture on her daughter's face. Rosie so rarely asked for anything and shied away from any attention. To have this moment to herself... and if she was here the whole while watching, surely it couldn't be too dangerous? Perhaps it wasn't dangerous at all.

"Very well," she said as Rosie was whisked away to be given a costume and makeup.

"I don't want to be in any stupid old movie," Jamie said with a scowl, and Ellen patted his arm sympathetically. She was glad Rosie was getting a little bit of the limelight, she so rarely had it, and yet still Ellen couldn't help but be nervous. The situation was so surreal, so otherworldly, and more than a little shocking—as Rosie was having her makeup done, a woman in nothing but a feather boa and some spangled silk sashayed across the stage, a knowing pout to her made up lips. Ellen had to look away.

"Look at me, Mama!" Rosie exclaimed when she was brought back to the set for Ellen—and the director's—inspection.

Ellen let out a little gasp of surprise; her daughter looked both woebegone and exultant, dressed in little more than rags with smuts of dirt on her cheek and her hair in a tangle, but a radiant smile on her face.

"Now you're meant to look sad," Rowland instructed her, and Ellen had to stifle a laugh.

She found herself getting into the crazy, decadent spirit of the thing, her heart rate kicking up as the actors took their places, Rosie standing in a doorway with a basket of bruised apples, and the lights were turned on, washing everything in bright white.

"And action!"

Ellen held her breath as the scene unfolded: a gangster in an overcoat, hat brim pulled down low, and Gracie, looking heart-breakingly beautiful, even with a black eye, begging him to take her back. The camera cut to Rosie with her basket, watching the tragic scene with wide eyes; it was the same unblinking stare she often gave Ellen that tore at her heart.

Even Jamie forgot to sulk as the cameras continued to roll and the magic unspooled. And then, just as Ellen was falling into the dream, it ended with a sudden "Cut!" and the actors sagged visibly, shedding their personas like old snakeskin.

"She's a natural," Rowland told her, and Ellen didn't know whether to be proud or alarmed. Both, probably.

"Did you see me, Mama?" Rosie asked as she came running over.

"I certainly did." Instinctively, Ellen brushed at the smut on her daughter's cheek only to realize, of course, it wasn't dirt, it was greasepaint, oily on her fingers.

"Here." One of the many assistants circulating the set gave her a hand towel, which Ellen took with murmured thanks.

"You were amazing, darling. Truly amazing."

"She really is a natural," Gracie proclaimed as she sauntered toward them. "You'll have to stick with me, kid. We'll have both our names in lights."

"Wouldn't that be something," Ellen remarked with a little laugh. "You truly were incredible, Gracie. The director told me you've got star power, and I can see that you do."

Gracie glowed, and Ellen was glad she'd given the compliment. Here, amidst the greasepaint and glamor and lights, she could see how Gracie fit in—and shone. Her chameleon personality and lightning-quick changes of mood suited the camera and its endless shades. Perhaps she really would have her name in lights one day.

"Let me give you a tour of the set," Gracie said, "now that we're done filming. And then it'll be time for the party!" She ruffled Jamie's hair and smiled at Rosie. "But not for you two. Is Eduardo taking them back home?"

"Yes, I'll go with them. I want to tuck them into bed before coming back for the evening." Butterflies swarmed in Ellen's stomach as she considered that prospect. A party with Hollywood movie stars? She couldn't think of anything more daunting.

As Gracie showed them the set—the cameras, the bright lights, the pieces of scenery that looked so flimsy and fake and yet would show up wonderfully on screen—Ellen couldn't help but be wowed by an industry that made a fortune simply by play-acting. It truly was a brave new world.

Finally Jamie started to flag, and Ellen decided to take her brood back home. "What about you, Gracie?" she asked. "Do you want to come with us so you can change?"

"Oh no, I'm going back to Emmett's," Gracie answered carelessly. "He's got the most amazing digs—we'll start off with champagne and take a cake basket to the party. You know where it is? The Cocoanut Grove on Wilshire Boulevard? It's in the Ambassador Hotel."

Ellen nodded, determined not to offer unwelcome words of caution or judgment about such plans, even though she would have never dreamed of accompanying a single man back to his house to change clothes, of all things.

"What's a cake basket, Gracie?" Rosie asked.

"A limousine, my darling," Gracie answered. "We're going to arrive in style."

Ellen could not keep herself from feeling a sense of foreboding as Eduardo drove them back to Bungalow Heaven, Jamie and

Rosie tired but still chafing at being taken home rather than to the party. Fortunately Maria had their dinner ready, and Ellen was able to eat with the children before seeing to their bath and bed. She hoped Gracie wasn't being too wild, and yet she recognized there was absolutely nothing she could do about it. She wished Lucas was here to offer his sensible advice, his calm, competent manner always a reassurance. As she dressed for the party, she felt very alone.

Ellen had bought a new dress for the occasion on Gracie's insistence, although she thought it was still modest enough—made of peach silk and edged in darker peach satin, it hung straight from the shoulders to the hips, and then flared out in bright flounces. Ellen had liked it on the mannequin in the department store, but now she wondered if the color was too girlish and insipid. Well, she told herself, there was nothing for it now. She added a string of pearls and white satin gloves, a slick of lipstick and another of mascara, and then headed downstairs to wait for Will, who had offered to drive her back into Los Angeles, since he was also coming from Pasadena.

"Don't you look like the berries!" he exclaimed as she answered the door. Will was looking very dashing himself, his tuxedo and white dress shirt the perfect foil for his blond hair and blue eyes.

"I can't remember the last time I dressed like this," Ellen confessed as she accompanied him to his waiting car. "Even the theatre wasn't so fancy!"

"Don't you and Lucas hit the town back in New York?"

"Not really, although we go out to meet his clients for dinner sometimes."

"Not quite the same as a shindig like this one, eh?" he surmised, and Ellen nodded her agreement.

"We certainly don't rub elbows with movie stars," she said lightly, and Will gave a little grimace.

"They're not my favorite people, to tell you the truth. Stuck-up and overindulged, if you ask me. But there you are." He opened the passenger door and Ellen slipped in while he went around to the driver's side.

"Why are you going, then?"

"For Gracie," Will said simply. "She seems like she needs a friendly face in this crowd."

"I think she has a lot of friendly faces around her," Ellen couldn't keep from replying, and Will gave her a look that made her cringe inwardly. She'd wanted to start off on a better foot than last time, but already she felt the tension tautening the air between them.

"I mean a genuine friendly face," Will said as he pulled out into the road. "Hollywood is a cesspit of scandal—haven't you heard the stories?"

"Some of them, I suppose, but only vaguely."

"Well, they're not pretty. Girls flock here hoping to make their fortune—they sign with an agent and end up in a brothel."

"That won't happen to Gracie—" Ellen protested, alarmed at the very thought.

"No, but something else might. There's a man on every corner —and in every studio—just waiting to take advantage. Most starlets get used up and tossed aside within a year. There's always more who are eager to take their place."

Ellen drew her wrap more tightly around her shoulders. "It sounds completely horrible."

"It is," Will replied grimly. "And I don't want that for Gracie."

"You seem to have taken her under your wing," Ellen said a bit stiffly. "Considering you've only met her the once."

Will was silent for a moment and then he confessed, somewhat reluctantly, "We've seen each other a few times since we met at your place."

"You... have?" Ellen was flummoxed, as well as a little hurt. Why hadn't Gracie said? Why hadn't Will?

"Yes, we went out to dinner once, dancing another time." He glanced at her, his dark gaze inscrutable. "Gracie's good fun. I like her."

Ellen didn't reply, struggling with feelings she couldn't entirely pin down. "I hope you know I don't want anything bad to happen to her, either, Will," she finally said. "Anything I say is out of concern for her. I hope you believe that."

Will was silent for a long moment, making Ellen feel uneasy. "I think you believe that," he finally replied, and on that rather awful pronouncement, he turned onto Pasadena Avenue, the lights of Los Angeles glimmering ahead of them.

CHAPTER FIFTEEN

The party was in full swing when Ellen and Will arrived, with a band playing a jaunty jazz number and the champagne flowing freely. The place was packed shoulder to shoulder, with couples swaying to the music or guzzling champagne, a haze of cigarette smoke above a sea of gyrating bodies. The sound of laughter was raucous in Ellen's ears. She breathed in the smell of sweat and perfume, thick and cloying. Instinctively, she took a step closer to Will. It all felt even more overwhelming than she'd expected.

"Shall we find Gracie?" Will asked as he put his arm around her to shepherd her through the wild crowd. They'd barely spoken since their brief exchange in the car, which Ellen was doing her best not to feel stung by.

"If we can," she replied dubiously. In the dim lighting, she could barely make out the faces of the partygoers; it all passed by her in a surreal blur of noise and color.

"We will," Will told her firmly. "I'm not leaving Gracie alone in this nest of vipers."

Ellen wanted to ask when and how Will had developed such a sense of responsibility toward her cousin, but she couldn't think of a way to say it without sounding sharp, and in any case, the heaving music and loud, chattering conversation prevented her from making any remark at all, which was probably just as well.

Will shouldered his way through the crowd while Ellen clung to him. Finally, past the packed entrance to the club, the crowd cleared, and she was able to breathe—and take in her surroundings, the famous Cocoanut Grove club, fabled haunt of Hollywood stars. The sea of tables was studded with imitation palm trees that had, Gracie had told her earlier, been taken from the set of Rudolph Valentino's *The Sheik*. They were decorated with toy monkeys that gentlemen could purchase to give as favors to their ladies. On the far side was a painted moon and splashing waterfall, and the ceiling was a midnight-blue, studded with golden stars. Ellen had never seen anything like it before.

"Will!" Gracie's voice was practically a screech as she gestured them both over to her table on the side of the dance floor. She was sitting with Emmett Hughes and a few others Ellen didn't recognize, half-drunk coupes of champagne in front of everyone.

"Hello, Gracie." Will came forward and kissed Gracie's cheek, while Ellen stood there stiffly, feeling entirely out of place. She wished she hadn't come at all; she'd have much preferred to be tucked up in bed like Rosie and Jamie.

"Let me get you a chair," Emmett said graciously, and went to fetch two gilt chairs, drawing them up to the table.

"Have some fizz," Gracie insisted, and a waiter materialized with two extra glasses.

Emmett poured them both champagne while Ellen murmured her thanks. From the looks of it, Gracie had to be on her third or fourth glass already. She was lounging back in her chair, head thrown back, her mouth curved into a scarlet bow. She wore a black dress beaded with jet with a plunging neckline that made the most of her svelte figure. Next to her, Ellen felt like a fussy mutton dressed as lamb in her peach satin and silk, and she wished she'd worn something a bit more sophisticated.

"Isn't this place the bee's knees?" Gracie effused. "Emmett was telling me how Lionel Barrymore once released a whole load of real live monkeys into the crowd—he terrified everyone! What an absolute hoot."

"How... strange," Ellen murmured. She imagined dozens of monkeys running riot in the dining room, and slowly shook her head.

"You wouldn't believe some of the stories about this town," Emmett told her in agreement. "A real wild place! I think things are a little saner these days. We can't have Hollywood getting a bad rep, or my mother will never let me stay."

"Isn't he adorable?" Gracie patted Emmett's cheek. "His mother! He's only twenty-five, you know. A child."

"And you're only twenty-eight," Emmett replied, flushing a little. Ellen felt sorry for him. With his checked suit and baby face, he looked out of his element among this crowd, while Gracie, in her sophisticated black, seemed entirely at ease, or almost.

"Oh, I'm a world away from you, darling," Gracie told him. "A world wiser."

Ellen said nothing as she sipped her champagne, yet she wondered if Gracie could really be as experienced and jaded as she liked to seem. She'd grown up on the island, same as Ellen, although she'd most likely never admit it to this crowd. Ellen had seen her in a pinafore and muddy work boots, collecting eggs and weeding the garden. She'd seen her in her shirtwaist and serge skirt, heading to Glebe Collegiate in Kingston for high school— what a provincial town that was, compared to this! And Gracie had only been in New York City for two years before coming to California. Could she really be as sophisticated and worldly-wise as she claimed? Or was it all, as Will seemed to think, an act? A façade— but to cover up what? Gracie, she knew, would never say.

The band struck up another number, and Gracie sprang up from her seat, spilling a bit of her champagne as she grabbed Will's hand. "Let's dance," she said, and with a faint smile, Will followed her onto the dance floor while Ellen watched.

"She's something, isn't she?" Emmett remarked after a few moments, a note of something like sorrow tinging his voice.

"She is, at that." Ellen glanced at him, noticing the way he looked at Gracie, now swaying on the dance floor with Will, forlornly.

"She doesn't love me," he stated matter-of-factly. "I know that."

"Oh, Emmett..."

"I'm not even sure I love her. She thrills me, but she terrifies me at the same time, and that's not the right way to feel about a woman, is it?" He sighed and nodded to Will. "Do you suppose that fellow can handle her?"

Ellen glanced at Will, who was smiling down at Gracie as she talked earnestly to him, and she was surprised to feel a sudden clench of emotion—not jealousy, no, but rather fear. Would Gracie break Will's heart? She seemed perfectly capable of it—but maybe Will would break hers.

No, Ellen decided, as she watched him put his arms around her and draw her close. Will was too much of a gentleman for that —and Gracie was too cynical. And yet as she continued to watch them dance, she could not deny that there was something between them—a spark, a connection. She could sense it even from all the way over here, off the dance floor. Two broken souls, whole together.

Emmett must have seen something of it, too, for he let out a sigh as he drained the last of his champagne. "I'm not sure I'm cut out for this life," he told her morosely. "My parents want me to go back east after this movie, and I told them I wanted to stay, that I wasn't giving up yet, but now I'm not so sure."

"Because of Gracie?" Ellen asked, and he shrugged.

"Not just her. It's everything. I'm not tough enough for this world, or sophisticated." He hefted his empty coupe. "Tell you a secret—I've been drinking lemonade this whole evening. I can't stand the hard stuff. I tried to drink it because everyone else was, but it gives me a headache and makes my nose tickle."

This made Ellen smile, and she felt a sudden surge of almost maternal affection for him. "Perhaps you should go home, Emmett," she told him. "Not with your tail between your legs, but rather your head held high, because you turned your back on all this." She swept one arm out to encompass the club, the party, all of Hollywood. "Will told me that this city chews people up and spits them out, and I think he's probably right. Wouldn't it be better to live and work in a place that isn't so ruthless?"

"You'd think so," Emmett agreed, "but it isn't as if New York is much better. Did you see that picture, *The Wolf of Wall Street*? Rowland made it last year, it was Bancroft's first talkie. That painted a pretty bleak picture, lemme tell you. Stockbrokers who sold their friends and family down the river for the sake of some cabbage."

"Cabbage," Ellen repeated blankly, and he smiled wryly.

"Money. Filthy lucre. Cheddar, greenbacks, cold hard cash. Whatever you want to call it."

She nodded slowly. "I suppose one coast might be as bad as the other, when it comes to all this." The whole world seemed to be drunk on excess, she reflected as she gazed round at the partygoers. After the trauma of the war years, people wanted to have fun. Women wanted to cut their hair and show their legs and prove to the world they were as good as any man, for anything.

And why shouldn't they? She was the one who felt lost, Ellen thought with a pang of realization, not all the revelers around her.

She glanced again at the dance floor, and saw that Will and Gracie had disappeared.

The next hour passed slowly. Emmett continued to drink lemonade while Ellen sipped her champagne and the crowd whirled and blurred around them. A few times they made desultory conversation, but it never went far and after half an hour they stopped trying.

Ellen sat back in her seat and wondered how soon she could go home. She'd never been much of one for parties, she reflected wryly. She thought of her own surprise birthday party when she'd turned fourteen—she'd been so shocked by the crowd that had gathered, that she'd shut the door on them all! And then there was the ball Henry McAvoy had invited her to, back in Glasgow. She'd worn a borrowed dress and taken the snubs from the society matrons on the chin, even as they'd wounded her soul, and she'd left as soon as she'd been able. And then there were the parties at Royaumont, in France... spontaneous celebrations on the hospital wards, music and dancing and laughter edged with desperation... how many of those men had survived?

She shook her head, fighting off a rising tide of melancholy. It was pointless to think of those days; it was a different world now. A better world, or so people liked to think, but Ellen wondered.

Murmuring her excuses to Emmett, who was gazing blearily at the dance floor, she rose from the table and wound her way through the crowd, dodging a flung-out hand or jab from an elbow as people danced the charleston, arms out and heels kicked up.

Finally, with a sigh of relief, she slipped through the opulent lobby and then the front doors of the Ambassador Hotel and out into the blessedly cool air of the grand hotel's portico, facing Wilshire Boulevard. The night sky was dark, the only lights from a few cars sliding down the boulevard like black shadows.

Ellen leaned up against the wall of the Mediterranean-style building, its white stucco pressing into her back. She breathed in deeply, grateful for the fresh, cool, air and then turned to survey her surroundings—shock icing through her when she caught sight of Will and Gracie just a dozen yards away, Gracie pressed against the wall and Will's arms around her as they kissed passionately.

For a second Ellen could only blink, stunned by the scene; she'd known Will was protective of Gracie, but she hadn't fully appreciated how much she interested him, no matter what spark they'd seemed to share on the dance floor.

Quickly, feeling embarrassed for their sakes as well as her own, she was about to turn to go back into the hotel, when Will caught her eye.

Ellen ignored his surprised gaze as she pushed her way back into the hotel, barely aware of the impressive lobby around her—the fireplace of Italian marble, the crystal chandeliers, the luxurious draperies and the plush carpets. From the open doors of the Cocoanut Grove, she saw the sea of bodies, heard the loud music, and she turned away, unsure where to go, what to do. Then she saw Emmett coming out of the club, and he met her gaze with a bleary one of his own.

"I'm heading home," he told her. "No point in staying when I'm not enjoying myself."

"I'm thinking of retiring myself," Ellen replied. Although how could she, when she needed Will to drive her back to Pasadena? And what about Gracie? "Do you know if it's possible to call a taxi?"

"A taxi?" Emmett blinked at her. "Don't bother. I'll drive you."

"But it's so far—"

"It's not as if I've got anything better to do. And don't worry, I'm tired, but I'm stone-cold sober. It's been lemonade all the way, after all."

"I know," Ellen said with a small smile. "If you're sure it's no trouble, then I would be very grateful to you for taking me." And yet what about Gracie? Surely she couldn't just leave her here, and yet neither, Ellen suspected, could she compel her to go.

"Ellen." Will's voice, low and commanding, cut across her words and she fell silent, turning to see him walking toward her, his arm around Gracie.

"Will." She glanced at Gracie, whose cheek was pressed against Will's shoulder, her eyes fluttering closed. "Is Gracie all right?"

"She's fine." Will hesitated, giving Emmett a sharp glance before he said in a low voice, "But I need to take care of her."

"I've just arranged our transport home," Ellen replied, glancing in concern at Gracie, who had slumped even further against Will.

"Mr. Hughes is willing to drive us. I think we should leave immediately."

"I want to stay with Will." Gracie's voice was slurred as she opened her eyes to stare blearily but defiantly at Ellen. "I'm going to stay with him."

"Gracie—"

"I'll take care of her, Ellen," Will said quietly. "I promise. You don't need to worry about her."

Ellen pressed her lips together. She trusted Will, of course she did, but she hated being put in this position. "I'm responsible for her—"

"No, you aren't," Gracie returned, her voice rising. "And you never have been. Go home, Ellen. I'm staying with Will."

His arm tightened around her as he continued to look steadily at Ellen. "You don't need to worry, I promise. I'll bring her safely home."

Ellen nodded, her throat too tight to speak. She felt a tumult of emotions—anger and hurt and worry, and above it all, exhaustion. "Very well," she finally managed, and, pulling her wrap more tightly around her shoulders, she turned away from them both.

Just a few minutes later, she was in the passenger's seat of Emmett's Rolls-Royce as he drove down Pasadena Avenue, leaving the city behind, the Arroyo Seco canyon falling away on their left, rocky and barren under a silver spill of moonlight.

"I think I will go home," Emmett mused after they'd driven for a quarter of an hour, and the lights of the city had disappeared behind them. "I wanted to stay for the opening of *The Lady and the Brute*, but I don't see much point, really. I've had enough of it all."

"Oh, Emmett," Ellen said sadly, although she was inclined to agree with him—for his sake as well as her own. He didn't belong in Hollywood, and neither did she. She wanted to go home as well, she realized. She wanted to be in her own house; she wanted to be in Lucas's arms. She wanted to stop wondering and worrying and simply enjoy each precious day with her family. But it was only late March; there might still be snow in New York. For Jamie's sake, she couldn't leave yet. But she wanted to.

For the first time, Ellen realized she was counting the days until she could put California behind her.

CHAPTER SIXTEEN

Ellen scanned the letter that had come in the morning's post and then put it down, her eyes narrowed against the dazzling morning sunlight. It was the Monday after the party at the Cocoanut Grove; Rosie was at school, and Jamie with Eduardo, helping him with one of the little chores around the house. If he was lucky, Eduardo would let him hammer a nail, which Ellen knew would be an unbelievable thrill. Gracie had not yet risen from bed.

On Friday night, Ellen had heard her stumble into the house sometime after dawn; she'd rolled over in bed, dragging the pillow over her head as Gracie clunked upstairs in her high heels, and bumbled around noisily in the bathroom before finally going to bed —just as Jamie and Rosie were waking up.

She'd slept nearly all day Saturday, and while Ellen was brimming with questions about how her evening had ended, she chose not to ask a single one when Gracie finally came downstairs at five o'clock in the evening, still in her dressing gown and smelling of cigarettes.

"Are you terribly angry with me?" she'd asked Ellen as she flung herself into a chair. Rosie and Jamie had been outside in the garden, and Ellen had lifted her gaze from them playing in the yard with a red rubber ball to regard Gracie with a weary acceptance.

"I'm not angry," she'd said, and realized she meant it. "Why should I be?"

"Jealous, then?" Gracie had suggested frankly, a spark in her eyes even as she sprawled back lazily.

"You mean because of Will?" Ellen had shaken her head firmly. "I'm not jealous, Gracie. Why should I be? I'm married."

"So?" Gracie had fished for her cigarettes in the pocket of her dressing gown. "What does that have to do with the price of eggs? Will is your friend. Now he's mine." She'd given Ellen a rather cool stare. "What do you think of that?"

"I don't have any real opinions about it," Ellen had answered after a moment. "I hope neither of you gets hurt, I suppose."

"You suppose?" Gracie had let out a hollow laugh and Ellen leaned forward.

"Will told me he thinks your... careless manner is some sort of façade. A way to cover how much you're... you're hurting."

Gracie had stilled, her cigarette halfway to her lips, an arrested look on her face. "Oh, does he?" she'd asked after a moment, and Ellen hadn't been able to tell a thing from her tone.

"Is that true?" she'd pressed, and Gracie had lit her cigarette without replying. Ellen had tried a different tack. "Will you see him again?"

Gracie had shrugged. "Maybe."

Ellen had reached one hand out toward Gracie, but when her cousin didn't move she had let it fall to her side. "Gracie, is there anything I can do? Any way I can help you?"

Gracie had raised her thin, arched eyebrows. "You think I need help?"

"I don't know." Ellen had paused, feeling her way through the words, the emotions that were churning across Gracie's face even as she remained completely still, doing her best to look unmoved, indifferent. Ellen still saw something dark underneath. "Maybe."

"Well, I don't." Gracie's voice had turned hard. "Thanks very much, anyway." She'd stubbed out her cigarette and risen from the table. That, it seemed, was the end of their conversation.

The rest of the weekend passed uneventfully enough, although Ellen still felt dispirited about what she hadn't been able to say. Gracie spent all of Sunday away from the bungalow, while Ellen took the children to church and then lazed by the pool all afternoon while they splashed and played.

When Gracie returned in the evening, she'd avoided them all, heading straight up to her room, and Ellen decided not to ask any questions, as much as she wanted to. She had no idea how to help Gracie, but more and more she was coming to believe she *did* need help. Her reckless lifestyle was, Ellen feared, no more than a symptom of her deep unhappiness. Had her broken engagement with Fred broken her heart, as well? Or was there something else? Something more? And how, Ellen wondered rather despondently, could she find out?

Now it was Monday morning, and with no answers to her concerns about Gracie, she had something else to think about. The letter in front of her had come as a complete—and unexpectedly welcome—surprise. Yet how to respond?

She mused over the dilemma as she poured herself more coffee, and Gracie came onto the patio, dressed in a smart white blouse and dark skirt, her hair neatly brushed and pinned, her face freshly scrubbed and devoid of any makeup. She looked, Ellen thought, as much of an island girl as she ever had.

"Good morning." Ellen gave her what she hoped was a welcoming smile, although in truth she never knew how to handle Gracie in all of her varied moods. What role was she playing today? "Would you like some coffee?"

"Yes, please. I'll get another cup."

Gracie went to the kitchen and returned with another cup and saucer. Ellen duly poured, and they sat in sunshine for a few moments, sipping in silence.

"I'm going to be good today," Gracie finally said, and Ellen raised her eyebrows.

"Today?" she repeated, and Gracie burst out laughing.

"I suppose I should start small. One day at a time. Otherwise I'll fall at the first hurdle, won't I?"

"And what does being good entail?" Ellen asked, genuinely curious, and also a bit amused. "I suppose that's the meaning of your so very sensible ensemble?"

"Do you like it?" Gracie looked down at herself in smiling approval. "I picked out the staidest outfit I possibly could."

"Why?" Ellen asked. "Why do you—as you say—need to be good?" It seemed an odd choice of words.

For a second, Gracie's laughing mask dropped and she gazed down at her coffee, her lashes fanning her pale cheeks as she rotated the cup between her small, neat hands. "For Will," she said in a low voice. "I want to be good for him."

"I imagine," Ellen answered slowly, "that Will wants you to be yourself."

"He may think he does, but he doesn't," Gracie replied in a hard voice, her gaze still lowered. "Trust me, I know."

"Gracie... are you talking about Will—or Fred?"

She shrugged. "All men are the same, aren't they?"

"I certainly don't think so." Ellen hesitated, having no idea how to handle this conversation, yet longing, more than anything, to say the right words. "Where did you and Will go, on Friday night? Did you stay at the party?"

"We drove to the Arroyo Seco and watched the sun rise." Gracie's voice sounded faraway as she leaned back in her chair, her gaze distant. "It was beautiful, Ellen—the most amazing light, all pinks and oranges and reds flooding the canyon, setting it on fire. I'd never seen anything like it before. An island sunrise has nothing on it. I felt as if I were watching fireworks, as if the world was being reborn and I got to see it happen."

Ellen pictured it, Will and Gracie in his car, his arm around her perhaps, as the sun rose fiery in the sky. "And Sunday?" she asked after a moment.

"Will took me to the pier at Santa Monica. We went dancing

in the La Monica Ballroom—it can hold five thousand people!—and took a turn on the Whirlwind Dipper. I laughed ever so much. My head was absolutely spinning. He even won me a teddy bear at the coconut shy. And we sat on a bench and watched the sun set over the ocean..." Gracie let out a long, soft sigh. "If I could have stayed sitting there on that bench forever, I would have."

"It sounds like a lovely day," Ellen replied. She felt an ache of sadness for Gracie, although she wasn't sure why. It had all sounded marvelous.

"It was," Gracie replied quietly, fiercely. "It *was*."

"And now? You're dressed like a librarian as if this will impress him?" Ellen couldn't help but sound gently skeptical. She didn't think Will was the sort of man who wanted a woman to be staid.

"Reassure him, perhaps." Gracie's eyes lit up again, and she looked as light-hearted as ever. "Have I overdone it, do you think? I'm even wearing sensible shoes." She held out one slender foot for inspection; the block heel and thick strap were more like Ellen's shoes than Gracie's.

"Perhaps you've overdone it just a bit." Ellen smiled, and Gracie threw back her head and laughed.

"Well, you know I can't do anything by halves."

"Too true. But I do think Will likes you for who you are, and not some pretend schoolmarm."

Gracie's fingers twitched restlessly on her cup. "Maybe," she said, but she didn't sound convinced.

"Perhaps you need to ask him, then. Or at least let him see you for who you are."

"I already have, too much probably." Gracie looked away. "I want to show him I can be something else. Something more."

"I think Will already knows that, Gracie. If you can trust him..." She trailed off, because Gracie and Will barely knew each other. Should she really be telling Gracie to trust him?

"Well, we'll see what happens," Gracie said after a moment, her tone deliberately airy. "I won't bore him, anyway, that's for sure."

Ellen had no doubts about that. She hesitated, and then said, "Gracie, I'm thinking of taking a short trip, out to Claremont." She gestured to the letter lying on the table. "I've been invited to tour Scripps College—it's a college for women that was started a few years ago. One of the trustees, Eleanor Toll, has seen my painting *Starlit Sea*, and when she heard through the headmistress of Rosie's school that I was in the area, she made the invitation."

"Goodness!" Gracie sat back, impressed. "Aren't you the dark horse."

"Nothing dark about it," Ellen replied wryly, although her heart was flipping in her chest at the thought of having a little adventure on her own. "Maria and Eduardo have agreed to look after Jamie and Rosie while I'm gone, so you won't be inconvenienced. I'll only be away one night."

"Inconvenienced!" To Ellen's surprise, Gracie looked genuinely hurt. "Is that what you think I'd be? I only came to California to help you look after your children, after all!"

"Yes, but..." Ellen hesitated, unsure how to articulate how she felt without offending Gracie even more. In the two months since they'd been in Pasadena, her cousin had involved herself less and less with the goings-on of their little household, and in retrospect Ellen realized it had been something of a relief.

"Don't you trust me?" Gracie demanded.

"You've seemed busy—"

"I've finished filming. I haven't a care in the world." A dangerous glitter had entered Gracie's eyes and her lips trembled. "I've nothing to do but watch your precious kiddos, if you'll *let* me."

"Of course I'll let you." What else could she say? And she did trust Gracie, really. She could be so much fun, and the children adored her. It was only when she got in one of her moods... which, she wouldn't, Ellen told herself, now that she was trying to be *good*. "Maria and Eduardo will be here, of course," she couldn't help but add. "To help."

. . .

Two days later, after tight hugs and heartfelt goodbyes with both Rosie and Jamie, Ellen took the Pacific Electric Railway Red Car to Pomona, and then changed to another train to Claremont. The scrubby brush and sandy soil of the landscape passed in a blur under a bright blue sky as the train chundered eastward, and Ellen finally disembarked at Claremont.

Founded only forty years ago by the Pacific Land Improvement Company, a subsidiary of the Santa Fe Railway her father had worked for many years ago, Claremont had become something of an educational center when a consortium of colleges, including Scripps, had decided to make it their base. Now with its elegant sprawl of Spanish-style buildings, red-roofed and climbing with ivy, it looked a truly gracious and genteel city.

"Mrs. Lyman?" A fiftyish woman with a round, friendly face and flyaway gray hair stepped forward. "I'm Eleanor Toll."

"Oh!" Ellen had not expected the trustee to meet her herself immediately off the train. She put one hand to her dusty straw hat with a self-conscious smile. "Yes, that's me. I'm very pleased to meet you."

"And I you! Come this way—I've brought my own motor. I'm sure you'll be dying for a cool drink and a chance to wash off the travel dust."

Ellen followed Eleanor to a waiting car, surprised when the older lady slid behind the wheel.

"I learned how to drive several years ago," she informed her with a smile. "So convenient! And women really can do anything these days. That's what Scripps College is all about."

"Indeed," Ellen murmured. She felt a pulse of energy, excitement, and she resolved that she would learn to drive when she returned to New York. Or maybe even to Bungalow Heaven— Eduardo might be willing to teach her. What a surprise it would be for Lucas, to see she could drive! Ellen smiled to think of it.

Within just a few minutes, Eleanor had driven them to Scripps College's beautiful campus, with its Spanish-style stucco buildings with wide verandahs looking out over a verdant quad.

"A residence hall was the first building we put up," Eleanor told her as she parked in front of one of the buildings. "I helped design it myself. We wanted our students to feel at home—each hall has its own living room, dining room, library, and courtyard, with single rooms for the students. We've put up a new hall every year since we started, in 1926. We're going to be building a library next—Ella Denison has agreed to fund it. Now, let me show you your room." Impulsively, she grasped Ellen's hand. "I'm so glad you're here."

"As am I," Ellen replied. She still felt bemused by the invitation; surely she was no one important? And yet Eleanor Toll, who, she learned later that evening at dinner, was tipped to serve in Congress, seemed to think she was.

Ellen spent the afternoon drinking iced tea on the verandah of the residence hall where she was staying and learning more about the college. Then, as the heat faded from the day, she was given a tour of all the buildings, as well as the plots where future buildings, including the anticipated library and even a swimming pool, would be built. Afternoon tea in Seal Court was, apparently, a Scripps tradition, including the rule of only having two cookies each, which Ellen gamely obeyed.

Eleanor had arranged a dinner in the evening for Ellen and some of the faculty and trustees of the college, including the president Ernest Jaqua and one of the founding trustees, Margaret Fowler. Ellen was tongue-tied in such elegant, erudite company, and yet she found herself listening with rapt attention as the conversation flew around her.

"Women must learn the arts! Civilization is founded on culture, not expediency."

"The point of education is not to know, but to *think*."

"Women are the bedrock and future of society. Do not argue the point, Ernest, even if you are a man."

It was heady to listen to such conversations, even if she wasn't daring enough to take part in them. Ellen spooned her cream of tomato soup and sipped lemonade while Margaret Fowler and

Ernest Jaqua continued to debate the finer points of a female education.

"And of course there must be art," Eleanor announced when the dessert was brought in—an impressive pineapple upside-down cake. "Scripps must have a professor of art, and a studio for drawing and painting. We are planning an exhibition of lady artists."

"How exciting," Ellen said, and an expectant silence fell on the table, while she looked around rather blankly.

"We were thinking of you, my dear," Eleanor told her almost gently, while Ellen continued to stare. "To contribute to our exhibition of women artists. I believe Miss Ramsey mentioned it to you?"

"Yes," Ellen replied after a moment, "but I didn't think she was serious."

"She was, and so am I," Eleanor returned with a smile. "Why shouldn't we be?"

Ellen thought of the sketchbook she'd used several times in the last few weeks; she'd even packed it in her case to come here. "I must confess I have not practiced art seriously for many years—"

"Your painting *Starlit Sea* remains incomparable," Eleanor cut across her, firm now. "I saw it myself, in The Metropolitan."

"That was a long time ago..." Ellen protested. She felt both astonished and embarrassed, almost wondering if they were playing a joke on her. They couldn't possibly want her to contribute her little sketches in a prominent exhibition! She'd barely done more than scribble in *years*.

"As I recall, you were once due to take up a position at the prestigious Glasgow School of Art," Eleanor continued. "It was mentioned in your biography at the museum."

"Before the war," Ellen affirmed. "Over fifteen years ago." Before she'd decided to return to Amherst Island instead, a decision she had not regretted since.

. . .

By the time Ellen had retired to her dormitory room, replete from the delicious meal and her mind still spinning, she was exhausted and yet also strangely energized. She sat by the window overlooking the college's quad washed in moonlight, and imagined her sketches hanging in the museum. Perhaps she and Lucas could come for the opening... Eleanor had said there would be a party. They could bring Jamie back for another bout of hot, dry air; perhaps they could even travel, go all the way to San Francisco...

The possibilities were tantalizing, and they made her realize just how quiet and strained the last few years had been in many ways, watching the children, worrying over Jamie, losing a part of herself without even realizing.

Impulsively, Ellen reached for her sketchbook and started drawing the moonlit scene outside—the buildings cloaked in darkness, the looming shapes of trees and flowers. A world of possibility, only just beginning to be illuminated.

As she drew, she felt something loosen in herself, and fly free... she did not necessarily want to travel to San Francisco, or even have her sketches exhibited at Scripps, honor though that would be. But she did, she realized, want to make some changes in her life. What those would be she didn't yet know, but the possibility of it—for once—excited her more than it scared her.

Change could be good, she told herself as she laid down her pencil and gazed out at the moonlit night, the college buildings looking peaceful in the dark. It could be exciting. In less than a month she'd be returning to New York, to her and Lucas's life together. She still wasn't entirely sure how that would look, or even how Lucas would greet her return, but with a new determination firing through her spirit, she was resolved to move forward, to love her husband and her family and build and protect their life together. And, she thought as she drew the curtain across the window, she was going to learn how to drive.

CHAPTER SEVENTEEN

As soon as Eduardo picked her up at the train station in Pasadena two days later, Ellen knew something was wrong. His usually smiling face looked grave, his olive skin possessing a slightly grayish cast.

"Eduardo...?" she asked, already panicked.

"I'm so sorry, Mrs. Lyman—"

Ellen pressed one hand to her now-thundering heart. "Is it Jamie?"

"No, no," Eduardo said quickly, shaking his head. "It's neither of the children. They've been as good as gold, and as cheerful as crickets."

Ellen sagged a little as Eduardo took her valise. "Then..."

"It's Miss McCafferty," he confessed. "She went out last night and she hasn't yet returned."

"Hasn't returned!" Ellen's stomach dipped with genuine fear. It was already the afternoon. Goodness only knew what Gracie might have got up to, or what danger she could have found herself in. "Do you know where she was going?"

"No, Mrs. Lyman. She didn't say. Just ran out, laughing in her bright way." He gave her a miserable look, full of guilt. "We should have asked, I know. My poor Maria has been beside herself. We didn't know who to telephone... we called the college, but you'd already left."

"I see." Ellen took a deep breath to steady herself. "I suppose the first person to ask is Mr. Turner. He's a particular friend." Eduardo nodded, still looking both worried and guilty, and Ellen laid a hand on his arm. "This isn't your fault, Eduardo, nor Maria's. You mustn't blame yourselves."

A streak of anger went through Ellen, as she thought of Gracie's recklessness. She'd promised to look after Rosie and Jamie, and then she'd just gone? Even if she'd known Maria and Eduardo would help, it had been a selfish act... or a desperate one?

Perhaps she was really the one to blame, Ellen thought wretchedly. She'd known Gracie was vulnerable, despite her bright ways, her laughing determination to be *good*. Ellen had sensed her fragility—and yet she'd still gone traipsing off to Claremont, because she'd been so desperate to have an adventure of her own. How could she have been so thoughtless, so careless? Practically as reckless as Gracie herself...

Ellen's stomach was churning with nerves as Eduardo drove in silence back to the bungalow. The house was quiet as Ellen came inside, although at the sound of the door opening, Jamie came running from the kitchen.

"Mama!"

"Hello, darling." Ellen put her arms around him as he burrowed his head into her stomach, as energetic as ever. "What have you been up to?"

"Maria and I have been making bis—bis—"

"*Biscochitos*," Maria filled in as she came into the hall to greet them. She was smiling, but her eyes looked troubled. "A cookie from Mexico, very sweet."

"They smell delicious." Over the top of Jamie's head, she met Maria's worried gaze and gave her a reassuring smile. "Now, I want to hear about everything you've done while I was away, but first I must wash off this dust and make a telephone call."

"Is it about Gracie?" Jamie asked seriously. "She didn't come back last night. Rosie was worried for her, before she went to school."

Ellen's heart ached to think of her daughter worried—and Gracie somewhere unknown, doing goodness knew what. "I'm sure she's with friends, Jamie," she told her son. "You don't need to trouble yourself."

"I'm not troubled," Jamie declared, puffing out his chest, and Ellen managed a smile.

"That's very good to hear." She kissed his cheek and then she went upstairs to wash the traveling dust from her hands and face before she set out to find Gracie.

Her cousin was sure to be fine, she told herself as she tidied her hair. In the mirror, she saw her own pale, unhappy reflection, and knew she didn't really believe what she was telling herself. She'd heard the horror stories about Hollywood, recalled how Will had said starlets had been chewed up and spit out. She'd known all of that, and yet she'd still left Gracie alone. If something had happened to her, Ellen knew she would never forgive herself.

Back downstairs, she dialed Will's number that he'd written on his card, listened to it ring several times before the operator informed her there was no reply and she should call later. Ellen was disconnected before she could so much as make a reply.

"I'm afraid I need to go out," she told Maria. Jamie was leaning over the table, his hands and shirt covered in flour. "Will you be all right minding him for a little longer? And collecting Rosie from school?"

"Of course, Mrs. Lyman." Maria's round face creased in a worried smile as Jamie reached for a sack of sugar. "Of course."

Ellen grabbed her hat and coat before walking quickly towards the center of town, and the Caltech campus, looking for Gracie along the way. She wished she had a better idea of where Will could be; wandering around Caltech's buildings was hardly a fool-proof way to find him, but what choice did she have? She had no idea where Gracie was. She could only hope Will might know how to find her, or even know where she was.

As she approached the campus, she began to search the faces of the students walking and chatting along the sidewalk, hoping to see Will. She'd run into him by chance once before, after all, but today she could not catch sight of his straw boater, his smiling face, as much as she longed to.

Finally, in desperation, she approached a serious-looking student. "Excuse me," she called, her voice cracking in her urgency, "but do you know where Professor Turner might be? He is a professor of physics—"

The student looked surprised to be so accosted, but after recovering his composure, he nodded towards a Spanish-style building up ahead. "I imagine he'd be in the lab."

"Thank you," Ellen called back over her shoulder as she headed toward the laboratory. *Please let Will be there. Please let him know where Gracie is...*

As she slipped through the front doors, she was stopped by an officious-looking attendant. "Excuse me, miss, but only students and professors are allowed in the laboratory! You must leave immediately—"

"I'm looking for Professor Turner," Ellen cut across him, doing her best to sound imperious. "It is a matter of great urgency. Can you please find him for me, at once?"

The man looked as if he wanted to object, but after a second's pause he nodded reluctantly. "I shall see if I can locate him."

Ellen paced the foyer as she waited for the man to return. A minute passed, and then another. *Where could Gracie be?* Ellen's nails bit into her palms. Out all night... having told no one where she was going... she *had* to find her.

She heard footsteps, and whirled around. "*Will*."

He was wearing a white lab coat over his usual poplin suit, his eyebrows knitted together in concern. "Ellen, what on earth has happened? Lewis told me it was urgent—" He reached for her hands, taking them in his own.

"It's Gracie. She went out last night and she hasn't returned."

Will's face paled beneath his tan. "I was hoping you might know where she is. Was she... was she with you?"

"No." He shook his head. "I don't know where..." A pause as he slipped his hands from hers to rake them through his hair. "The truth is, we argued the day before last."

Ellen's heart sank. If they'd argued, who knew what mood Gracie might have been in? "Argued?" she asked. "About what?"

"About Gracie having notions of what I expect from her. How I expect her to be." His lips tightened and his eyes flashed. "She seemed to think I'd finish with her if she didn't toe some imaginary line, but that isn't it at all."

"She said something similar to me," Ellen replied shakily. "Oh, where could she have gone?"

"I don't know, but I'll start looking."

"Where—"

"What about that movie producer she hung around?"

"Emmett Hughes?" Ellen frowned. "Maybe, but he seemed as if he wanted to quit Hollywood altogether. He was staying at the Beverly Hills Hotel—"

"Then let's go there," Will interjected. "I'll get my hat and coat."

Just a few minutes later, they were in Will's car, heading down Pasadena Avenue towards Los Angeles. The sky above was bright blue, the sun glinting off the desert canyons, the world rushing past in a blur of scrub and sand.

Will's hands flexed on the wheel of his Ford Roadster as he stared straight ahead, his expression set. "I shouldn't have argued with her," he said after a moment, his voice low. "I told you I knew she was struggling, and yet I still let her pick a fight with me." He let out a weary sigh as he shook his head. "She thinks she's more trouble than she's worth, but she isn't."

"You love her," Ellen stated, only partly making it a question.

Will blew out a breath. "I don't know. I barely know her, really.

But I recognize in her something I see in myself, and that draws me to her, I suppose."

"You told me you were both broken souls."

"We are."

"Still, Will, for you?" Ellen asked gently. "Because of the war?"

He gave a jerky shrug, his gaze narrowed on the road. "Some things you never get over."

Ellen nodded slowly, accepting, even as her heart ached. "And Gracie?" she asked eventually. "Did she tell you what was troubling her?"

"No, but I know it's something. It's like... a burden she carries. Invisible, but always there, bowing her down. I know, because I feel the same."

"I've been suspecting that something happened, as well," Ellen admitted, "but I have no idea what. I've asked her about Fred—" She stopped abruptly before asking cautiously, "Has she... has she told you about him?"

"A little."

"She insists she's not bothered by him breaking off the engagement, but..." Ellen shrugged helplessly. "She seems so bitter about it, still."

"Well, wouldn't you be, if your lovely Lucas had just walked away?" There was an edge to Will's voice that made her jerk back a little. "With no explanation, no excuse? Just that he's decided he doesn't want to get married, after all, after you'd begun planning the wedding?"

"Is that what she told you happened with Fred?"

"More or less."

"She told me it was a relief when he ended it." Ellen stared out the window, her mind circling endlessly. "What do you suppose she meant?"

"I don't know."

Ellen gave a sigh that was half frustration, half despair. "We have to find her."

Will's hands tightened on the steering wheel. "I know."

They didn't talk much after that, until Will pulled up to the Beverly Hills Hotel. Ellen hadn't been there since Emmett had taken them to lunch and Gracie had got drunk. She'd been so alarmed by the events of that afternoon, but now she feared much worse.

Will strode into the elegant lobby of the hotel with Ellen close behind. He asked at the desk for Emmett, and his manner must have been commanding enough, for the concierge quickly stammered out that Mr. Hughes was by the pool. Seconds later, they were wending their way through a sea of tables and loungers, looking for Emmett.

"Ellen!" He lurched up from the lounger where he'd been reading the *Los Angeles Times*, dressed casually in a linen button-down shirt and khaki trousers. The paper fell to the ground as he ran a hand through his hair. "What on earth are you doing here?"

"We're looking for Gracie," Ellen said bluntly. "Do you know where she could be?"

"Be?" Emmett looked flummoxed. "I haven't seen Gracie since that wretched party at the Cocoanut Grove." He glanced at Will, his expression hardening a little. "I thought you might know where she is."

"No, I don't," Will said shortly. "So you haven't seen her at all? She went out last night and hasn't returned."

Emmett glanced uncertainly at Ellen. "Well... you know how she can be. Maybe she's sleeping it off somewhere."

"She's a young woman alone," Ellen reminded him, her tone turning a bit sharp. "We're worried for her, Emmett."

"Understandable, of course." Emmett looked abashed. "And I am too, naturally. You must let me know when you find her. I'm... I'm sorry I can't help you."

Back outside, they got silently into Will's Roadster, both of them despondent.

"I don't even know where to look," Ellen confessed. "She could be anywhere."

"Did you know any of her friends?"

Ellen shook her head. "Only Emmett."

"What about the other actors in the movie?"

"I only know the names of the big stars, and I doubt they care about Gracie. Rowland Lee told me Mary Astor was annoyed with her, for stealing her scenes without even trying."

Will heaved a long, heavy sigh. "I feel so damned useless."

"I... I don't think she would have done something truly reckless," Ellen offered hesitantly. "She can act so devil-may-care, I know, but at heart Gracie is still an island girl, like me." As she said the words, Ellen realized she believed them. "She pushes people's buttons, tests their boundaries... but only a little."

Will was silent for a moment, his jaw tight as he looked straight ahead at the line of palm trees fringing the hotel's parking lot, their green fronds swaying in the breeze. "When we argued, it was as if she was trying to push me away. Testing me, to see what I'd do. If I'd reject her somehow."

"I can believe that. Sometimes I felt she was doing the same to me."

"And yet I still let myself get angry." He shook his head, his face drawn in harsh lines of self-recrimination. "This is my fault."

"Will, you can't blame yourself," Ellen insisted shakily. "Heaven knows I started to, for going to Claremont, but Gracie's a grown woman. She's responsible for her own actions. And if there is something that's been torturing her, well, she's not going to recover from it if we don't let her face up to whatever she has to, rather than taking the blame ourselves." She took a deep breath. "Let's think about this sensibly. Maybe she hasn't gone out to some party or club. Maybe she went somewhere else—somewhere she liked."

Will made an impatient noise. "What do you mean?"

Ellen racked her brain trying to think of places where Gracie might have gone. "She said you went up to Arroyo Seco to watch the sun rise..."

"I doubt she's wandering among the canyons in this heat. I hope she isn't, at any rate."

"What about the Santa Monica Pier? She said you had a lovely day there, dancing and going on some fairground ride."

Will hunched one shoulder. "So?"

"So, maybe she went back there, where she'd been happy." Ellen knew she sounded desperate, but she couldn't think of anything else. "Why don't we go there and see if we can find her?"

"At the Santa Monica Pier? It's enormous." Will sounded disbelieving, but then he shrugged his assent and started the car. "I guess I don't have any better ideas."

It was a journey of ten miles from the hotel to the pier, and they rode the whole way in mute misery, both of them lost in their thoughts about Gracie. Ellen thought of all the times she'd been impatient, frustrated, annoyed, even angry. It was true Gracie could be incredibly exasperating, and yet... she should have been more patient. More understanding. Especially if there had been something that had been torturing Gracie all along, making her act out, as Will seemed to think.

Ellen knew there was no real point in recriminating herself, just as she'd told Will, and yet she couldn't keep from doing it. What if something had happened to Gracie? What if she was in trouble or danger... *or worse?*

Finally they arrived at the pier, which was busy with day-trippers, even on a weekday. The sound of laughter and delighted screams, as well as the screech and grind of wheels and motors, came from the Pleasure Pier amusement rides, including a large carousel with hand-painted horses and the Blue Streak Racer roller coaster. The air smelled of the briny ocean and roasted peanuts.

They walked slowly up and down the crowded promenade, ducking into shops and arcades, peering between the carefree daytrippers, looking for Gracie's slight form.

After half an hour, Will shook his head. "Even if she is here, we'll never find her," he said despairingly. "This is a ridiculous wild goose chase."

Ellen suspected he was right, but she still felt they had to try. It wasn't as if they had any other leads. "Let's keep looking."

Slowly and painstakingly, they continued to comb through the crowds on the pier as best as they could, ducking into the enormous ballroom, checking every huckster's stall or cheap café. Ellen's feet ached and her head was starting to throb under the heat of the sun. She feared Will was right and this was nothing more than a wild goose chase; they would never find Gracie.

"I think you were right," she told Will after they'd been searching the pier for over an hour, in vain with all the surging crowds. "She's not here. I just don't know where she could be." Her stomach hollowed out at the thought. What if Gracie was in danger?

"Nor do I." He let out a groan of frustration. "I don't know where to go next. I can't even think—" He stopped abruptly and they both turned as they saw one of the street sweepers causing a commotion a little way down the pier.

"You've been here all day, stinking of drink," the man complained as he pulled at a woman's arm. She'd been curled up on a bench, barely visible behind the strolling crowds, but now she stumbled off it, falling hard onto her knees. "Sleep it off some-where else, my girl! This is a place for decent families, not the likes of you."

Ellen grabbed Will's arm. "Will—"

"Gracie," he confirmed tersely, and started forward. "That's quite enough manhandling," he told the sweeper in a commanding voice. "I know this woman. I'll take care of her now."

Gracie looked at him blearily. "Will," she whispered, and then she collapsed into his arms.

CHAPTER EIGHTEEN

Ellen watched as Will scooped Gracie tenderly up in his arms. The crowd parted, many whispering and pointing, as he strode back up the pier toward the parking lot, Gracie nestled against him. Hurrying to keep up with him, Ellen followed.

He laid Gracie in the backseat, covering her with a blanket he'd had in the trunk, before getting into the driver's seat. "Thank God we found her," he said. "Let's take her home."

Ellen glanced back at Gracie, who had already fallen asleep. Her hair was a bird's nest around her face, and her dress was dirty and stained. She was missing one high heel, and she reeked of alcohol, cigarette smoke and sweat. What on earth had she been up to? Ellen shuddered to think, and yet they'd found her, thank goodness. She could only be glad of that.

"Let me go in first," she told Will when they reached Bungalow Heaven. "I don't want the children to see her like this. I'll take them outside and you can bring her upstairs." Once she would have flushed in mortification to think of suggesting such a thing—an unmarried gentleman taking a young lady up to her bedroom! Now she was simply thankful there was a solution.

"All right," Will said, and in the backseat Gracie stirred.

"You came," she told Will, her voice slurred. "You shouldn't have."

"Of course I came," Will replied, his voice rough with emotion.

Gracie closed her eyes as Ellen hurried into the house.

"Mama!" Jamie cried, running toward her as she opened the door to the bungalow. "Did you find Gracie?"

She wrapped him into a quick, tight hug. "Yes, we did, darling."

She glanced at Maria, who understood at once and, clapping her hands, said, "Come on, *bambina*s. We need oranges. I want to make an orange custard for dessert tonight."

"But I want to see Gracie," Jamie protested, while Rosie looked anxiously at Ellen.

"What's happened, Mama? I thought you were going to pick me up from school today."

"Everything's all right," Ellen reassured her. "You don't need to worry about a thing. But Gracie's a bit poorly, and we need to get her settled in bed without any fuss. You can see her later, after she's had a sleep."

Rosie's eyes were wide. "Poorly? Is she ill like Jamie?"

"No, nothing like that." Quickly, Ellen caressed her head, and then Jamie's, grateful for them, healthy and whole right in front of her. "You're not to worry. She'll be right as rain soon enough, especially once she's had some of Maria's orange custard."

Maria shepherded them out then, and Ellen let out a sigh of exhausted relief.

Within a few minutes, Will had carried Gracie upstairs and settled her in bed. "I'll let you take care of her for now," he told Ellen once they were back downstairs. "And I'll visit her when she's feeling better."

"She'll want to talk to you—"

"Maybe," Will replied grimly. "Although I'm not so sure. But I'll certainly visit, because I want to talk to her." He gave her a tired smile, and Ellen's heart ached for him.

"Thank you, Will. For everything."

He nodded. "I would have done just about anything..." he began, and then stopped. "I should go."

With Will gone and the children still outside with Maria, Ellen headed upstairs to Gracie. She was lying in bed, looking disheveled, but her eyes were open, her gaze dull as she looked at Ellen.

"Have you come to scold me?"

"Not at all," Ellen replied, trying to pitch her tone somewhere between brisk and gentle. "I've come to help you bathe, actually, because you smell awful."

Gracie sniffed her armpit experimentally. "You're right, I do."

"Let me run you a bath."

With a shrug and a sigh, Gracie leaned back against the pillows. "You can if you want to."

Ellen ran the bath and laid out towels, doing her best to remain cheerful and efficient. She felt her nurse's experience during the war kick in, and she realized she was treating Gracie the way she'd treated soldiers who had come to the field hospital at Royaumont Abbey—as someone wounded in desperate need of care and not pity. Gracie might not have any visible wounds or scars like those soldiers had had, but in her own way, Ellen thought she was similarly damaged. But why? And what did it mean for the future—for Gracie's and for Will's, since he cared for her so much?

When the bath was full, she went to fetch Gracie, who hadn't moved from the bed. "Come on, now. Your bath is ready."

Gracie closed her eyes. "I can't."

"You can't what? Get off the bed? Into the bath?" Ellen put her hands on her hips, her head cocked, her manner determinedly practical.

"Do any of it." A tear slipped from Gracie's eye and trickled down her cheek. "I can't, Ellen," she whispered, her voice breaking. "I can't pretend anymore that I'm having the most *fabulous* time."

"Then don't," Ellen said simply. "Because I'll be honest with you, you haven't done all that good a job of pretending. I know

Rowland Lee said you're a natural, but you've got to try a *little* harder than that to convince me, Gracie McCafferty."

She raised her eyebrows and Gracie let out a huff of surprised laughter. "How dare you, Ellen Lyman," she returned without any heat, "give me a taste of my own medicine."

"Perhaps that's exactly what you need," Ellen replied briskly. "Now, you'd best get a wiggle on before the bath water goes cold."

With a small smile, Gracie rose from the bed and, taking her arm as if she were an invalid, Ellen helped her into the bath. She left her to wash in privacy while she went to check on the children, who were trooping into the kitchen with their arms full of oranges.

"Look at you!" Ellen exclaimed. "I've never seen so many."

"Maria's going to make orange custard," Jamie said excitedly, "and she said we could help."

"Aren't you lucky."

Rosie tugged on Ellen's sleeve. "Is Gracie all right?"

"Yes, darling," Ellen assured her. "She's absolutely fine."

While the children helped Maria to make the promised custard, Ellen went back upstairs to make sure Gracie was fine, never mind absolutely. The bathroom was awfully quiet, without even the sound of a splash, and with trepidation making her heart beat a little harder, Ellen knocked on the door.

Silence.

She hesitated, wondering if she should be so bold as to go in, when she heard Gracie say with a sigh, "Come in if you want."

Cautiously, Ellen opened the door of the bathroom. Gracie was sitting in the tub, her knees drawn up to her chest, her back, bony and bare, to Ellen.

"I haven't drowned myself, if that's what you're worried about," she said.

Ellen choked on a gasp of shocked dismay.

"I wasn't worried," she said, closing the door behind her. "At least, not really." She hesitated, then asked gently, "Shall I wash your back for you?"

Gracie was silent for a moment and then she whispered, "Yes, please."

Ellen wrung out a washcloth and scrubbed the bar of soap over it while Gracie waited, still and silent, her head bent. She began to move the washcloth over Gracie's back in slow circles, the only sound the drip of the cloth into the bath.

"You remind me of my mother," Gracie said after a moment. "Bathing me when I was little. I always forgot to wash behind my ears."

"I can believe that."

Gracie gave her a soft sigh. "I miss her."

Ellen smiled to think of her dear Aunt Rose, getting older as they all were, but still so warm and beloved, her faded blue eyes crinkling in humor and lit by kindness. "When did you see her last?"

"A while ago." Gracie was silent, her arms tightening around her knees. "Over a year."

"It must be hard to get up to Gananoque, I suppose."

"It wasn't that."

Gracie fell silent, and Ellen stilled, the cloth in her hand, as she considered how to reply, sensing Gracie was struggling to say more. Then Gracie spoke first.

"I'm sorry," she whispered. Her head was still bent so Ellen couldn't see her face. "I'm so sorry," she said again, and then she let out a choking sound that had Ellen flinging aside the cloth so she could put her hand on Gracie's shoulder.

"Gracie—"

"The bath water is cold. I think I'm going to get out." With water sluicing off her, Gracie rose in one fluid movement that had Ellen quickly averting her eyes as she handed her a towel. Gracie wrapped herself up tightly. "Goodness, but it's easy to shock you, Ellen. And yet I could shock you even more." She sounded despairing rather than daring.

"I'm sure you could," Ellen managed lightly. "But don't stand there dripping."

With a faint, sorrowful smile, Gracie knotted the towel and then walked into the bedroom, closing the door behind her. Ellen went back downstairs.

She spent the next few hours with the children, and then helping Maria with dinner. She thought Gracie could use the privacy, or perhaps just the rest. When the table was set, she went back upstairs to call her to dinner, and saw she was fast asleep in bed, one hand curled up by her head like a child's. Ellen let her sleep.

It wasn't until Rosie and Jamie were both asleep themselves that Ellen checked on Gracie again, and saw she was sitting up in bed in her darkened bedroom, the lamp on her bedside table casting a warm pool of light. She'd slept on her hair while it was wet and it had dried in wavy tangles that she hadn't bothered to brush away from her face, giving her even more of a vulnerable, child-like air.

Ellen paused in the doorway. "You're awake."

Gracie didn't reply.

"Would you like some dinner? Maria made up a plate for you. I could warm it."

"I'm not hungry."

"When was the last time you ate?"

Gracie leaned her head back against the bed. "I had caviar and lobster mousse at The Cocoanut Grove."

"That's where you went last night?"

"Among other places. Café Montmartre, the Embassy Club... I can't remember them all."

Ellen took a step into the room and closed the door softly behind her. "Who were you with?"

Gracie shrugged. "A bunch of good-time gals and young swells I'd met while filming. They were all having the *grandest* time." She sighed heavily and closed her eyes.

"And how did you end up going from there to the Santa Monica pier the next day?" Ellen asked gently.

"We drank and danced till the money ran out, and then we

drove to the pier for a laugh... I can't remember it exactly, but there were a few of us. They all stumbled home and I stayed, because I was happy there, just a few days ago, and I wanted to feel that again, even if I knew I couldn't."

"Oh, Gracie." Ellen sat on the edge of the bed. "Will cares for you, you know."

Gracie said nothing.

"Do you care for him?"

She turned her head away, her eyes still closed.

"Gracie..." Ellen hesitated, longing as ever to reach out to her, yet not knowing what words would prove to be the key that would unlock her cousin's closely kept secrets. "What happened? Will called you a... a broken soul and I've felt that, too. It's like you're running from something but you'll never get far enough away."

"I won't."

Ellen took a deep breath. "You said you'd shock me, but you won't. Well, that is, I may be surprised, but I won't be... I won't judge you."

Gracie opened her eyes to give her one of her old, laughing looks, or almost. "That's rather brave of you, Ellen, considering you have no idea what I might say."

"Well." Ellen bowed her head, abashed. "I suppose I should say I'd try."

Gracie was silent for a long moment, restlessly picking at the fringe of her bedcover.

Ellen waited, hoping, praying... and then Gracie finally spoke.

"I came to New York because I wanted to have an adventure. I wanted to work and prove I was smart and fall in love. And I did all three." She let out a soft, weary sigh. "I met Fred at a party. A petting party—do you know about those?"

"I'm afraid I don't."

"Well, it's a party where you get to kiss all the boys." A small smile flirted with her mouth and then disappeared. "See, I've already shocked you. Really, they're quite tame—it's just a chance to see who you like. And I liked Fred, and he liked me."

"I see," Ellen said, doing her best not to sound censorious. A petting party! She'd never heard of such a thing, and she was glad of it.

"We started stepping out—dancing at the Stork Club, concerts at the Savoy... Fred knew how to have a good time. He was funny and charming, too, even if he was a little fast. Even I could see that. He was generous, too—he bought all those frocks of mine, was always splashing money about. Mother wouldn't have liked him, though. Good thing she never met him, I suppose."

She lapsed into silence, still picking at the fringe, while Ellen waited. Finally, when it seemed as if Gracie wasn't going to say anything more, she asked gently, "What happened, Gracie? Why did he break it off?"

"Because I got in the family way." Gracie's lips twisted as she lifted her head to give Ellen a look full of both pain and defiance. "I was going to have a baby. There. Now, I've really shocked you, haven't I?"

"You've surprised me," Ellen admitted carefully. She was doing her best not to show just how surprised she was—of course she knew girls got "in trouble," but even knowing her wild ways, she hadn't expected such a thing of Gracie. She'd always thought, beneath that laughing recklessness, Gracie possessed a certain childish innocence—had she been wrong? She must have been.

"Fred didn't want to know. He was furious—wanted me to get rid of it, even, but I wasn't about to do that. He broke it off with me completely." Her lips trembled and she pressed them together. "You hear stories about how dangerous doing such a thing is... and in any case, I knew I couldn't. It was our baby. *My* baby." She bowed her head, and Ellen's heart ached at the throb of grief she heard in Gracie's voice.

"So you were expecting," she said slowly. "Is that why you left your job? And stayed away? To hide the fact?" It was all starting to make a sorrowful sort of sense.

Gracie nodded, her head still bowed. "I hid it as long as I could—those sack dresses do hide a bump! But one of the girls at the law firm was able to tell and she ratted me out when I was nearly six months gone. I suppose I shouldn't really complain—Fred had given me enough money to keep me afloat for a while."

"But what..." Ellen's head spun. "What were you going to do? What *did* you do, once you had the baby?" Because there had to be a baby, surely? A child with Gracie's snapping eyes and dark curls? "You couldn't have managed forever, hiding that way—"

"I didn't have to." Gracie sniffed. "I was going to give it up. I had written to a maternity home in Nyack—they said they'd take me. I didn't know what else to do—I didn't have enough money to stay where I was, and I couldn't let my family know. I didn't want to."

"Your family would have stood by you, Gracie. We would have." She swallowed, her throat turning tight at the thought of all Gracie endured alone. "You could have come to us—"

"No." Gracie shook her head, the movement decisive. "I couldn't bring that shame onto them, or you. The maternity home seemed as good an option as any—they let you stay there till you have the baby and then someone takes it away. They go to good families, they said." A pleading, yearning note entered her voice. "I thought I was doing the right thing. I really did." A shudder went through her. "But it was horrible there. The matron kept telling us how *morally bankrupt* we were. How unfit to be mothers. Fallen women, she called us. One girl in there was only fifteen. I don't think she even realized what had happened to get her in the family way. She was so confused."

Ellen shook her head, her heart aching. "The poor thing."

Gracie nodded miserably. "It was awful, *awful*. We had to clean the whole place every day—scrub the floors on our hands and knees, and some of the girls were as big as houses! There were a few kindly nurses, it's true, but not nearly enough." She let out a deep sigh. "But then, after just a few weeks, I started having pains... it was too early, far too early. They wouldn't take me to the hospital, said I'd just have to manage on my own." She shivered, wrapping her arms around herself as the terrible memory assailed her. "I thought I was going to die. I *wanted* to die. Alone in that bed, feeling as if I were about to be split in half... and then my baby was born—what a tiny, wee thing! He was so pale, I could almost see through his skin. He'd been born two months early, but he just looked small. He was dead—never even took a breath, but there was nothing wrong with him. Not a single thing."

"Oh, Gracie." Ellen's eyes filled with tears.

"They wouldn't even let me hold him. I barely got to see him— they whisked him away that quick, bundled him up like... like he was rubbish. They said it was better he was dead." Her voice broke. "*Better!* How could they, Ellen? How could they?" A sob escaped her, and then another, and she bent forward, her head clasped in her arms as she wept openly.

"Oh, Gracie, *Gracie*." Ellen put her arms around her as Gracie continued to weep, the sobs coming from deep within her body. "You poor thing," she murmured as she stroked her tangled hair. "You poor, poor thing, going through so much. Keeping it all secret. How hard that must have been for you, my darling."

"I didn't know what else to do," Gracie said, still choking on her sobs. "I left the home after just a few days—they said they didn't have any beds for women who weren't expecting. I felt so weak, so *ill*..."

Ellen's arms tightened around her. "Where did you go?" she asked, wishing Gracie had felt she could have come to them. They could have sheltered her, cared for her, helped her to grieve and heal. Instead she'd had to stumble along, making her own way, feeling so alone and afraid, never telling anyone.

"I bunked with a girl I knew. I wanted to go back to the way I was, before it happened. I told myself I could, if I just pretended hard enough. I had the dresses, the jewelry, the perfume. Fred had given it all to me. I could still be the life of the party, and it would make me forget." Her voice choked. "But it never did, no matter how hard I tried, no matter how much I wanted it to. And I couldn't find a decent job, without a reference. I'd left the last place in disgrace, you see. To tell you the truth, if you hadn't asked me to come to California, I don't know what I would have done. I was running out of money and Elsie, the girl I was staying with, wanted me gone. I had nothing to my name but a few pretty dresses."

"It was Providence that had me ask you," Ellen said. "I only wish I'd known all this before." She thought of how prim and priggish she'd been, pursing her lips at every little thing Gracie had done, when she'd been acting out of her grief and pain, feeling so desperate and alone.

"Would you have let me come, if you'd known? I'm a fallen woman, after all. A bad example for Rosie."

"Rosie adores you," Ellen replied firmly. "And while it is true I wouldn't tell her, at only seven years old, everything you've told me, that doesn't mean you're a bad example. She could do well to be more like you—spirited and fun—instead of so serious like me." Ellen lapsed into silence. "This is what you've been afraid to tell Will, isn't it?"

Gracie eased back from her embrace, wrapping her arms around her knees. "Can you blame me?"

"Will is a very understanding man, Gracie. You should give him a chance."

Gracie shook her head. "Men are understanding until it affects them. Then their compassion suddenly disappears."

"Will is different."

Gracie lifted her chin, a hard look in her eyes. "Well, I'm not willing to take the chance. Anyway, it doesn't matter. We're leaving here in less than a month and I'll never see him again." She pressed her lips together, her expression both resigned and determined. "It's better that way, I'm sure."

CHAPTER NINETEEN

The next few weeks passed in an almost dreamlike haze. Ellen's world had shrunk to the bungalow, ferrying Rosie to school, entertaining Jamie—and taking care of Gracie. It had taken her a long time to realize how broken Gracie's soul really was, and now she longed to help to mend it. She treated Gracie gently, almost like an invalid, fetching her cups of tea and blankets for the occasionally chilly breeze. They sat by the pool and watched Jamie swim and sometimes spoke of the weather, or the news in the paper, or nothing at all. Sometimes Ellen sketched—the pool, the orange trees, Gracie looking pensive; she was considering a set of drawings about their time in Pasadena to submit to the exhibition at Scripps College, a prospect which excited and worried her in equal measure.

Still, it was peaceful simply to sit and let time do its work, for this new Gracie was both battered and quiet, resilient yet weak. Ellen wished they'd come to this moment sooner, so Gracie could have spent these months in California recuperating rather than running away from the grief she was now finally letting herself feel.

Still, at least they had these weeks, quiet as they were, to sit together, to chat or simply be. Ellen hoped it would be enough.

The day after Gracie's revelation, Will had come to visit her. She'd received him in the sitting room, while Ellen had kept the children away, and he'd left after only fifteen minutes, his hat jammed low on his head as he strode out of the house without so much as a word to Ellen.

"I told him it was over," Gracie had explained flatly after he'd gone. "It really is better this way. There's no future for us, Ellen."

There might have been, Ellen had wanted to say, but didn't. Gracie had made her decision, and it was clear she wasn't going to go back on it. It wasn't her place to tell her otherwise, and yet she felt sorry for both Gracie and Will, broken in their own, different ways. Were they too damaged to be with one another, or could they have helped each other to heal? She didn't know, but Gracie seemed determined.

As the weeks passed, the time to set their departure date loomed closer. Although she hadn't really discussed with Lucas when to return, Ellen felt three months was surely long enough, and the weather in California was becoming uncomfortably hot while, according to Lucas's last letter, spring had finally burst upon New York after such a hard winter.

"Shall I book your tickets?" he asked when Ellen telephoned him one balmy evening, the children still in the pool even though it was after supper. "It will be lovely to be all together again, won't it?"

"It will," Ellen agreed, although she couldn't help but be reminded that Lucas had not called or written very much in the last month; at the start of this telephone call, he'd been full of apologies about how busy he'd become. "Will you be very busy this summer?" she asked. "I thought perhaps we could rent a house in the Hamptons from June. I think being by the sea would be good for Jamie. I've never liked him being in the city in the summer, with the bad air, and I don't want to lose the progress we've made here."

"I think that's a capital idea." Lucas paused. "I couldn't come for the whole summer, of course, but perhaps a week or two in August..."

A week out of three months. Last summer, they'd spent the entire month of August together—days on the beach or pottering about South Hampton, afternoons playing tennis or collecting seashells. Ellen told herself not to mind; she was the one who had suggested the Hamptons, after all. There had been dinner parties, too, which Ellen hadn't particularly enjoyed; Lucas courted that sort of life more than she did.

"Only a week?" she asked, even as she tried to tell herself that if she wanted to see more of Lucas, she should be content to stay in the city—except she knew, with his work hours, she wouldn't see much more of him at all, and the city was so hot and dirty in the summer months, the dank, humid air breeding all manner of disease.

"Ellen..."

"I know, I know, I'm sorry." She sighed. "I don't like to think of being apart for even longer."

"We said three to six months at the start, didn't we?" Lucas said, ever practical, which somehow stung. Six was twice as many as three. "Perhaps I could come for two weeks," he added placatingly, as if he hadn't just said "a week or two" a few minutes earlier.

Ellen took a deep breath, determined to be as practical as he was. Arguing over the telephone was not the way she wanted their marriage to go on. "Very well," she said as briskly as she could. "Two weeks would be lovely. Will has mentioned his parents have a cottage on their estate that is free for the summer—I thought we could go there. I don't want anything grand."

"As you like." Had a slightly diffident note come into his voice? Surely he wasn't still worried about Will's interest in her? Admittedly, she hadn't told him about Gracie's abbreviated romance with Will. "I thought we'd bring Gracie, as well," Ellen continued. "She could help with the children and she'd be at a loose end, back in the city. She hasn't any other plans." She hadn't told Lucas about Gracie's poor lost baby, either, and wouldn't, at least not until she could tell him in person. It was hardly the sort of news to impart over a crackling telephone line.

"That sounds like a practical plan," Lucas agreed. "I'll rest easier knowing you're not having to manage alone."

And so it was settled, as simply as that. Lucas booked their tickets for the middle of May, and Will made the arrangements for them to take over the cottage on the Turner estate, one of the grand properties in East Hampton, although he assured Ellen the cottage itself was modest and small, just as she wanted.

"You won't be rattling around some massive mausoleum, I promise you. It's no more than three little bedrooms, a kitchen and sitting room and a porch out back, with a view of the sea. That's all."

"It sounds perfect," she told him with a smile.

They'd been in touch several times over the last month and on each occasion, Will had inquired about Gracie, although in the sort of tone one might use to ask after an elderly aunt or a distant acquaintance. Ellen suspected he was hurting far more than he let on, but it was so clearly a taboo subject she had not yet dared to broach it.

"So how have you found your time in California, in the end?" he asked just a week before they were scheduled to leave on *The Chief*, from Pasadena to Chicago, and then *The 20th Century Limited* to New York, just as before. They were having a coffee in a diner around the corner from Caltech while an unexpected rain spattered the windows and turned them steamy.

"It's been strange," Ellen admitted. "And a whirlwind, but there have been peaceful times, as well. I certainly won't forget any of it in a hurry." She gave him a wry smile.

"And do you think you'll come back? Next winter, perhaps?"

"I hope not to," Ellen replied frankly. "I don't think it's good for the children to be going to and fro every year, although Rosie has loved being at Westridge. She's come out of her shell a bit, which I'm very glad of. But I want us to be back together in New York, as a family. I just hope and pray Jamie's lungs are strong enough now."

"He seems quite the sturdy little fellow."

"He has grown stronger since coming to California. It must be all the sunshine." She smiled and then they both lapsed into silence. "I'll miss you, Will."

He smiled back, the twist of his lips bittersweet. "And I, you."

"And Gracie?" Ellen finally dared to ask gently. "Will you miss her?"

"You know I will." He looked away, his expression hardening, the smile slipping from his face. "Not that it matters."

Ellen could say nothing to that. Gracie's secret was not hers to tell. Her heart ached for both of them, but she knew there was nothing she could do.

As the time of their departure approached, Ellen found herself accosted by poignant memories—lazy afternoons by the pool, drinking Maria's freshly squeezed orange juice, going to that strange play with Gracie when they'd first arrived... Rosie starting school and Jamie growing stronger... her adventure to Scripps College, the determination to make a better life for her and Lucas back in New York.

She recalled attending The Cocoanut Grove and feeling entirely out of her element... Jamie's little hand in hers as they walked along the sunny street... Gracie's wild antics and also her irrepressible sense of fun... it had been a tumultuous few months, and yet at its center was a newfound peace. When she returned to New York, Ellen vowed, she would make things better with Lucas. She would try harder, and perhaps he would too. She would make sure of it. Life would be better for both of them. At least she had, she acknowledged ruefully, learned to drive in these last few weeks, although she hadn't tried to go out without Eduardo, despite his cheerful encouragement. Still, that was something. She could change. Anyone could.

. . .

And then, with it seeming strangely sudden, it was time to leave. Rosie watched as Ellen packed their cases, folding clothes, laughing at the things they'd brought that they'd never worn.

"Three sweaters! And with it so warm here. We really had no idea back in New York, did we?" She smiled at her daughter. "Will you miss it here, Rosie?"

"Yes, I've liked Westridge, but I want to see Daddy." Rosie's tone turned wistful. "Will he be glad to see us?"

"Of course he will!" Ellen gave her a brief, tight hug. "How can you doubt it? He'll be so excited, Rosie, I know it."

Yet the doubts she saw lingering in her daughter's eyes made Ellen doubly determined to speak to Lucas honestly when she returned.

The last few days before they left were a flurry of goodbyes—Rosie had tea and cake at school, with all the parents invited and a party atmosphere, girls rushing about, laughing and playing. Rosie wasn't the only girl returning east for the summer; just as Mary Lowther Ranney had said, many families came to Pasadena for the winter.

Emmett Hughes came to say goodbye one afternoon, taking them all for one last spin in his Rolls-Royce, thrilling Jamie with a ride in his precious Phantom.

"I've decided to give Hollywood one more whirl," he told Ellen and Gracie with a jaunty grin as Rosie and Jamie pressed their noses to the window and watched the world blur by. "I can't leave it after just one picture. Rowland Lee's making a Western with Gary Cooper—*A Man From Wyoming*. It sounds like just my sort of thing."

"I wish you much success," Ellen told him sincerely. She'd developed a fondness for the young producer over the course of the last few months.

"What about you, Gracie?" he asked. "You've had enough of your name in lights? You're going back east without a care in the world?"

Gracie gave a wan smile. She'd been rather listless since her hazy evening and painful confession, often spending hours staring out a window or simply into space, summoning a smile when necessary, but not always easily. "I don't think I've got the stomach for it," she told Emmett. "But like Ellen, I wish you success."

Emmett smiled at her, the curve of his lips rueful and a little sad. Ellen had always suspected he'd been more than half in love with Gracie but had known he'd never had a chance. "Thank you, Gracie," he said, and they drove on.

The night before they were due to leave on the train, Maria made a Mexican feast—*chiles en nogada*, *sopa de lima*, *enmolada* and *pozole*, with fried ice cream for dessert. They all ate till they could burst, and then sat out by the pool, watching the sun set over the orange trees in vivid streaks of crimson and tangerine, savoring every last moment.

In these last few days, much to Ellen's relief, Gracie had roused herself more than she had in weeks, eating and laughing, her old spark coming back, but with a different, deeper fire. The wild recklessness had been replaced by something stronger and more abiding, although it still seemed fragile, needing to be nurtured and protected.

They had not talked about the future, and Ellen decided there was no need to, with the promise of a summer in the Hamptons stretching before them, and its long, lazy days of rumination and possibility. Come September, she hoped the world would look very different for all of them—Jamie with a strong, healthy chest; Rosie blossoming in school; she and Lucas united and together, and Gracie finding her own way, wherever it led her. Yes, Ellen hoped, the autumn of 1929 would be the wonderful beginning of new kinds of lives for them all.

CHAPTER TWENTY

"Last stop, New York City, Grand Central Station!"

Ellen and Gracie exchanged looks of both trepidation and excitement as Rosie and Jamie scrambled about in their seats. It had taken nearly four days to travel from Pasadena to New York. Recalling their journey to California just three and a half months ago, Ellen felt as if it had been a lifetime. This trip had certainly been different, with none of the tension she'd felt between her and Gracie. There had been a poignant, bittersweet melancholy to the journey as they'd said goodbye to California, but as the train had traveled eastward, the sweet sorrow of parting had been replaced by an excitement to return to life as it once had been—and to Lucas.

"Do you think Daddy will be waiting at the station?" Rosie asked, peering out the window as the train pulled into the station, the platform sliding by, with a long, low hiss of exhaust.

"I'm sure he will be." She'd telephoned Lucas from Chicago, and he'd promised to meet them at Grand Central. Surely he wouldn't forget?

Gracie gave her a reassuring smile as she met her gaze. "He'll be there," she said quietly, and Ellen smiled back. She'd insisted that Gracie stay with them upon their return to New York, before they headed to the Hamptons in a few weeks' time.

"Haven't you had enough of me?" Gracie had asked when Ellen had made the suggestion, during their first night on *The Chief*.

"I haven't, and where else would you go? I won't even discuss it, Gracie. You must make your home with us."

Gracie had smiled rather tremulously as she'd blinked back tears. "You're too kind to me, Ellen."

"I haven't been kind enough," Ellen had returned frankly. "When I think how priggish I must have seemed to you at the beginning!"

"I was trying to shock you."

"Even so—"

"I might shock you still," Gracie had added, that old light returning to her eyes. "I haven't completely reformed, you know. I doubt I ever will."

"Good," Ellen had said, and meant it. She didn't want Gracie to lose that irreverent, effervescent sense of herself. She hoped time would restore it and put it in its proper place.

Now, as the train came to a stop, they stood up and began to gather their things. One of the Pullman porters would collect their cases, so they had only their hats and handbags to worry about, as well as a tin airplane that Eduardo had given Jamie and which he'd been playing with for the whole trip, but now, much to his panic, couldn't seem to find.

"Where is it—where is it—"

"It's here, you scamp," Gracie said, fetching the little plane from beneath her seat. "Best hold onto it now!"

Ellen's heart was beating strangely hard as they made their way down the train's corridor and out onto the platform. As she stepped from the train, she breathed in the smell of the city—coal smoke and engine oil, dirt and dust and roasted peanuts, a smell like no other. A city like no other. She felt a rush of gladness, as well as a little apprehension, that she was back.

"Ellen!"

And there he was, her own dear Lucas, striding down the platform in his suit and overcoat, his fedora on his head. Before she could open her mouth to greet him in reply, he'd pulled her into a tight embrace, kissing her soundly on the mouth, while Rosie and Jamie both squealed in delight, tackling his legs, and Gracie simply smiled.

After several wonderful, endless moments, Ellen pulled away breathlessly. "You did miss me," she exclaimed, and Lucas's expression turned fondly stern.

"Of course I did. Terribly. And as for you two—" He hoisted Jamie up on one hip and Rosie on the other, while Ellen did her best not to flutter about in panic that such antics were too much for Jamie. It was easier now, she realized, not to fuss.

She met Gracie's laughing gaze and smiled.

"We have so much to tell you, Daddy," Rosie said as they started walking down the platform.

"I can't wait to hear it all," Lucas assured her. "The car is waiting. Let's find your porter and we'll be away home sooner than you can blink, and then you can tell me everything!"

It was so very strange to be back in the tall, elegant brownstone that was her home, Ellen reflected as she changed from her traveling clothes to join Lucas downstairs for supper. The children were in bed, having regaled him with their tales of California for several hours, and Gracie had, rather quietly, retired to one of their guestrooms, claiming she was too tired to join them for dinner. Lucas had been unfazed at her staying, but Ellen had yet to explain to him that it wasn't simply for the night, but indefinitely.

Now she glanced in the mirror, running a hand through her short, wavy bob. Lucas hadn't remarked upon it, which made her wonder if he liked it. Now that they were alone, without the exuberance of the children to keep them from talking properly, how would they be with one another? The tension she'd felt during the phone calls, as well as the weeks and even months before she'd gone to California, weighed heavily on her.

I want things to be different now, she thought. *I want to be different*. But could she dare to be? There was only one way to find out. Taking a deep breath, she headed downstairs.

Lucas was in the living room, sipping a sherry as she came into the room.

"Don't you look a picture! I opened our last bottle of Domecq in celebration of your return."

"I didn't realize we had any left," Ellen replied as he handed her a glass.

"Just the one bottle. But they're saying Prohibition won't go on forever, so I live in hope." He raised his glass, clinking it with hers. "To happy returns, Ellen," he said tenderly, "and to us."

"Hear, hear," Ellen murmured, and drank. She felt strangely nervous, her gaze flitting away from Lucas's even though she wanted to look at him, to drink him in at long last. How she'd missed him, and yet as familiar as he looked, right then he felt a little bit like a stranger.

"I love your hair," Lucas told her. "It suits you wonderfully."

"I suppose you weren't surprised, since I'd written about it in my letters."

"It was still a shock to see, but not a bad one. I'm glad you tried something new. Expanded your horizons." He paused. "I'd begun to worry that you'd felt stuck here, with the children, hardly ever getting out."

"I still had the children in California," Ellen reminded, meaning to tease, but Lucas looked at her seriously, his blue eyes as unblinking as Rosie's.

"Yes, you did, but I think you know what I mean. Life can become stale, flat. I was afraid it had become that way for you."

"Is that why you'd been so eager for me to go?"

Lucas frowned. "In part, I suppose, although I don't know that I would say I was eager. Are you annoyed?"

"No." She hesitated, trying to sort through her feelings, which seemed as if they were in a hopeless tangle, despite her determination to be different. "Why did you think that? That my life had become... stale?"

He gave a little shrug. "You seemed less animated, I suppose. Less... happy in yourself."

"I was worried about Jamie."

"I know. I don't mean just that."

She was silent for a moment, and Lucas took a step toward her, one hand held out in appeal.

"I don't mean it unkindly. Anything I felt was out of concern and love for you."

She nodded, accepting yet still disconcerted. "I know. But why didn't you tell me before?"

"I don't know that I could have put it into words before now. And things seemed... tense between us." He searched her face, looking for answers, and yet Ellen didn't know herself what they were. "That was partly my fault, I know. More than partly. I work too hard. I still do. I know that."

"I think you were right," she said slowly, feeling her way through the words. "I did feel a bit flat, without realizing it, perhaps." She smiled faintly. "You've always known me better than I've known myself, Lucas Lyman."

"And I'm glad for it." His expression eased, relief flickering across his familiar features. "I really have missed you, you know."

"I believe you." And yet, as they went into the dining room for supper, Ellen couldn't shake the feeling that things weren't as easy or assured between them as she would have liked. Everything felt slightly stilted, and Lucas, despite his honesty, seemed distracted.

When the telephone rang in the middle of the meal, and Eva came in to say it was a Mr. Taylor from Westinghouse, Lucas gave her an apologetic glance before rising from his seat.

"I'm sorry, but I really must take that. It's bound to be urgent."

Ellen nodded without replying. She toyed with the heavy sterling-silver fork, snatches of Lucas's conversation audible from the hall. "With the market the way it is, you should make a convertible bond... no, no, nobody's going to buy it at this rate.... I'm telling you, the market is only going up." A few more murmurs that Ellen couldn't hear, and then Lucas hung up the telephone.

"I apologize for that," he told her as he came back into the dining room. "A client needed some advice on investments."

"Do you really think the market is only going to go up?" Ellen asked, and Lucas raised his eyebrows.

"Why shouldn't it?"

"It can't go up forever, surely?" She couldn't help but think of what Will had said.

"No, but it will level off, most likely within the year." He sat back down, putting his napkin on his lap. "I didn't think you concerned yourself with such things."

"Do you not want me to?" she asked quietly.

"No, it's not that at all, I just don't want you to worry." He smiled and reached for his fork. "I know things can seem volatile, but the Federal Reserve has it well in hand. I'm not worried, and you shouldn't be, either."

Ellen knew she didn't know enough about the stock market to make any further remarks. "I'm sure you're right."

"Tell me more about California, then."

Ellen hesitated and then said impulsively, "I've learned how to drive."

Lucas beamed. "Have you, indeed!"

"Eduardo taught me. He was very patient. By the end, I was able to drive all the way to Los Angeles and back. I'm thinking I might get my license." Driving licenses had only become mandatory in New York a few years ago and now required the driver to take an exam, a prospect which made Ellen nervous.

"I'm very impressed."

"Well, we'll see. It would be helpful, I suppose, when we're in the Hamptons, to have a car."

"Yes, I should think so."

Why, Ellen wondered, did everything feel so awkward?

Lucas must have been wondering the same thing, for he cocked his head and said quietly, "It is a bit odd, isn't it, to be back together, after so much time?"

A lump formed in Ellen's throat as she nodded. "I don't want it to be this way."

"Nor do I. It can't be helped, I suppose. We've gotten used to life apart. It will fade. We can make sure of it."

"But I'm going away again in a few weeks." She suddenly wished she wasn't, even though she knew it was the right thing to do—for Jamie, for Gracie.

"I promise I'll come in August," Lucas told her. "I don't want to be apart any more than you do. And things will settle down with work—"

"When?" Ellen asked on a huff of sad laughter. She felt as if Lucas had been making that promise since they'd moved to New York four years ago. First it had been that he'd needed to prove himself on the job, then that he wanted to make partner. Then the stock market had started soaring and companies began clamoring for legal advice, and things had only become busier. She was starting to wonder if it would ever end, if Lucas would ever get tired of pursuing the glittering prize of his ambition, whatever it was. She wasn't sure she knew.

"Soon," he told her with a wry smile. "I told you things are going to level off. It will be calmer then. Right now, everyone is trying to get in on the ground floor, and we're already soaring upwards. Once we get to the top, it'll be fine."

"And you really don't think things will come tumbling down again?" It seemed to her as obvious as the laws of nature themselves; what went up had to come down.

"There might be a bit of a slump," Lucas allowed. "In fact, I'm quite sure there will be. But we're prepared for that. I promise you, you don't need to worry."

"I'm not worrying," Ellen said, even though she was.

"You can't fool me." Lucas rose from the table, even though they hadn't finished their main course, one hand outstretched to her. "Enough of this awful, stilted talk. We've been apart from each other too long, and I want to hold you in my arms. Let's go to bed."

Ellen blushed as she rose from the table and took his hand. His fingers slid across hers, tightening, reassuring. Yes, their talk had been a bit stilted, but she knew she loved him as much as ever, and he her. Surely that was all that mattered, she thought as, smiling tenderly, Lucas led her upstairs.

The next few weeks were a flurry of activity as Ellen prepared for their summer holiday in the Hamptons. Rosie and Jamie had both grown out of all of their clothes after three months in the California sunshine, and Ellen was determined to make good on her promise to buy a few more fashionable dresses for herself. She offered to buy some new things for Gracie, but her cousin just laughed and shook her head.

"I have far too many fashionable dresses already, and I have enough sensible clothes to see me through the summer. After that, who knows?"

Although Gracie seemed at peace, Ellen still sensed a melancholy from her that worried her, and which she suspected was caused by Will, or rather, his absence. No letters had come from California, and none had been sent. Ellen feared Gracie had well and truly burned those bridges, for better or for worse. She occupied herself well enough with helping with the children and the house, but Ellen suspected she still longed for a life of her own. A love of her own.

Two weeks after her arrival back in New York, Ellen worked up the courage to take her driving exam—and passed, returning home brandishing her license triumphantly. It was decided they would take the train to East Hampton and then hire a car for the summer.

"Perhaps I'll learn to drive," Gracie said with some her old spark. "It's galling to think you've learned first, Ellen Lyman!"

· · ·

"Gracie seems more like her old self," Lucas remarked when he and Ellen were getting ready for bed, one evening a few days before she was due to depart. "She was quite quiet upon your return. Was there an abandoned romance in California?"

"Something like that," Ellen admitted. She felt reluctant to share Gracie's various heartaches without her express permission, although she didn't like keeping secrets from Lucas.

"What will she do after the Hamptons? Look for another job, or try to find a husband? She's a lovely girl."

"She is," Ellen agreed.

"She could head back up north, I suppose? Rose would love to have her nearby, I should think."

"I can't see her returning to Canada just now," Ellen replied after a pause. "But I don't know what she'll do."

"You know she's welcome here as long as she likes," Lucas told her as he took her into his arms.

Ellen rested her cheek against his chest, savoring the solid strength of him. Things had started to feel more natural between them again, and she was sorry to have to be leaving again so quickly. "I know," she said quietly. "We'll see what happens." She really had no idea what Gracie would do come September. It seemed very far away, yet in reality it was only a few months.

Just a few days later, they were alighting from the train onto the platform in East Hampton, the briny breeze rolling off the ocean as they collected the car and the porter brought their bags and piled them in the trunk. The village itself was tranquil, little changed from the days when it had been a farming and fishing colony in the 1700s, save for a few more shops.

Nearby, however, five huge Mediterranean-style estates had been built for businessmen from Cincinnati and New York, nicknamed the Devon Colony. A little further afield in Montauk, the businessman Carl Fisher was in the process of building a new resort on nine thousand acres, including a school, two churches, tennis courts, a bathing pavilion, a casino and a yacht club. Ellen was glad that their little summer home would be away from all the hubbub. Tucked in a corner of the impressive Turner estate, it was just as quaint and cozy as Will had promised—a small, shingled cottage with a porch overlooking the beach and the sea, and out of view of any other buildings.

Before Ellen had even put on the handbrake, having successfully navigated down bumpy roads from the station to the cottage, the children were scrambling out of the car, eager to explore the cottage and the beach, Jamie as unstoppable as ever, much to Ellen's quiet delight.

"Oh, Ellen, it's perfect," Gracie exclaimed as she got out of the car. "Such a dear little place."

"It will be very quiet," Ellen warned, and Gracie gave a soft laugh.

"I don't mind quiet, at least for a little while. And if we want to kick up our heels, I'm sure we could get invited to some party or other." Her teasing smile reassured Ellen that she had no intention of doing any such thing, or at least not much of one.

Even so, Ellen couldn't keep from giving a little shudder. "No, thank you." Summers in the Hamptons were now, more than ever, the playground of the spoilt rich; the parties to be had there were understandably notorious, although not as wild as those on Long Island's Gold Coast, where artists and actors rented houses and partied the night away in deep debauchery. Ellen was more than glad to be away from it all.

It didn't take long to set up their temporary home; the cottage was well-equipped, and while Ellen made supper, Gracie took the children for their first dip in the sea, and Ellen watched from the cottage, smiling to see Jamie dive into the water, when once she would have been fretting, determined to keep him safe and warm. She was thankful for his progress—and for hers. Exhausted by all the activity, both children were in bed by seven o'clock, and she and Gracie watched the stars come out from the front porch, the only sound the gentle shooshing of the ocean.

"This really is perfect," Gracie remarked as she drew her cardigan more closely around her. "Although there is a chill in the air, isn't there? I suppose it's not quite summer yet."

"Come July we'll all be wilting, I'm sure," Ellen replied with a laugh. "I like it like this. It reminds me of home."

"You mean the island?"

Ellen nodded, a sudden lump forming in her throat. She still missed Amherst Island, even all these years later.

"I miss it, too," Gracie said quietly, even though Ellen hadn't spoken out loud. "I couldn't get away from it fast enough when I was younger, of course, but now? Part of me wishes I could go back, but I know I can't."

Ellen did not argue the point. There was little opportunity for work on the island, and as much as Gracie might hanker after a quieter life now, the island was a poky place for a young woman alone, especially for one with Gracie's exuberant nature.

"You can never go back anywhere really, can you?" Gracie mused. "At least not back to the way things were, even if you return to the place."

Ellen glanced at her in cautious curiosity. "Gracie... are you talking about Will?"

She sighed, a long, low release of pent-up breath. "I suppose I am."

"You miss him?"

Gracie was silent for a long moment, and Ellen could barely see her face in the darkness, the only light coming from the scattering of stars. When she finally spoke, her voice filled with the ache of regret. "I don't just miss him, Ellen," Gracie told her as she gazed out at the moon-washed sea. "I still love him."

CHAPTER TWENTY-ONE

The days and then the weeks slipped by in a hazy languor of sun and sea, long walks on the beach collecting sea glass or bits of driftwood, nights playing cards or checkers or simply sitting on the porch, watching the endless, changing tides. The house had no telephone, which suited Ellen just as well, but she wrote Lucas regularly, and was heartened by his replies, brief as they were.

Occasionally, they made use of the Turners' tennis court, and once, at the start of the summer season, they were invited into the grand house itself, for afternoon tea with Will's mother.

Ellen had never met the matriarch of his impressive family before, and she was every bit as intimidated as Gracie as they took their seats on wicker chairs on a screened-in porch the size of a tennis court, and a maid in a black dress and frilly apron brought out a tray of freshly made macaroons and a pitcher of sweet iced tea. Rosie and Jamie had been taken in hand by another maid, and shepherded to the nursery.

"Will has spoken so fondly of you both," Elizabeth Turner remarked as she poured their tea. She was an elegantly coiffed woman in her sixties, with delicate bone structure and blue eyes as vivid and sharp as her son's, but without, Ellen suspected, the same wry humor. "And your time in California."

Having no idea just how much Will had revealed, Ellen murmured something innocuous, while Gracie remained silent, and, she saw, looked stricken. When, a few weeks earlier, Gracie had confessed that she still loved Will, Ellen had urged her to be in touch, but Gracie had staunchly refused.

"There's no point," she'd told her. "After all this time."

"It's only been a few weeks—"

"I don't mean just that. I'm over here, he's there..." Gracie had sighed. "And it isn't as if he's been in touch, is it?"

"You told him not to," Ellen had reminded her.

"The thing is," Gracie had said, her voice hitching a little, "I couldn't bear it if I told him everything, and then he rejected me." She'd looked away from Ellen, to hide her face. "I couldn't *bear* it, Ellen. I'm only just starting to feel myself again... I can't go back to the way I was before. I'd... I'd lose myself completely, and I can't risk that. I simply can't."

"But what if he doesn't?" Ellen had asked gently. "Surely that's a risk worth taking?"

But Gracie had just shaken her head.

Now, as they listened to Will's mother chat about the summer season in the Hamptons, the tennis and croquet matches, the yacht club's parties, the end-of-summer ball, Ellen knew from Gracie's expression she was realizing in a whole new way how unsuited she and Will truly were. She was a simple girl from the country, turned would-be flapper, and Will was, incontrovertibly, the heir to an estate and empire. It had been less obvious out in California, its distance from this social set a great equalizer, but it was all too apparent now.

"If I needed any more convincing that we don't belong together, that was it," Gracie stated rather glumly as they walked along the top of the dunes, back toward their cottage, the children racing ahead. "I think I actually forgot the kind of money Will came from, the kind of status. Why on earth would he have anything to do with me?"

"Because he loves you too?" Ellen suggested with a smile in her voice, but Gracie shook her head.

"You don't know that."

"You're twisting yourself up into knots thinking about him," Ellen told her. "Why not just write?"

"I told you..."

Ellen sighed. "I know you did."

Yet a few weeks later, as she sat at the little desk in her bedroom and gazed out at the white-ruffled sea, the sun sinking toward it in a blaze of pinks and oranges, Ellen wondered if it was far too invasive for her to write Will... and mention Gracie. She didn't want to interfere, and yet... she sort of did. The more she'd considered it, the more she'd begun to feel that Will and Gracie could be right together, if they were both willing to take a risk. And if all she managed was a little nudge...

And so, after writing several paragraphs describing how Jamie had taken to swimming and Rosie to tennis, and how she herself had got very adept at driving the car and playing card games with Gracie, Ellen added, *On which note, someone here is missing you quite a lot. More, perhaps, than you think.*

"Ellen?" Gracie called, her voice floating upstairs. "We were going to walk into town. I promised Rosie and Jamie an egg cream each."

"Coming," Ellen called. She was dismayed to see her hands tremble as she folded up the letter. Was it wrong of her, to say as much as she had? And yet it had been so little. Still, it was interfering of a sort, and Ellen had a feeling that Gracie would be furious if she knew she'd implied that she was missing Will. Furious, but maybe grateful, too...?

Quickly, Ellen put the letter into an envelope and wrote Will's address on the front. She'd post it in town, after they'd been to the soda fountain for the promised egg creams.

Sure enough, as they were strolling down East Hampton's

pleasant main street, with its quaint, shingled shops and houses, Ellen took the opportunity to nip into the post office and post the letter to Will, along with one to Lucas and another to her Aunt Rose, whom she tried to write as regularly as she could. Perhaps nothing would come of it, she thought as she gave Gracie a quick, distracted smile on the way out. *Or perhaps something would.*

Another lazy week slid past, as the promised heat arrived, scorching the grass brown and causing the children, and even Ellen and Gracie, to run into the ocean several times a day, just to cool off. The breezes off the Sound were welcome, and Ellen delighted to see both Rosie and Jamie turning tanned under the sun; Jamie hadn't coughed once all summer, which both relieved and thrilled her.

"I still worry about when we return to New York," Ellen confessed to Gracie one afternoon as they lay on the beach and watched the children play in the surf, as happy as larks. "When the weather turns cold and damp. The cough rattles right through him then."

"But he's older now," Gracie reminded her. "And sturdier. Just look at him!" She nodded toward Jamie leaping through the waves, as brown as a nut. "I think those lungs of his have gotten stronger."

"I certainly hope so," Ellen replied with both a sigh and a smile. It had been so lovely not to worry for a little while; to watch Jamie run and play like any other little boy. She didn't want to lose that, for Jamie or for herself.

They went into town for the fourth of July fireworks and parade, smiling at the sight of a little girl dressed as Lady Liberty in flouncy red, white and blue, with Jamie letting out shouts of joy as the fireworks exploded overhead in a blaze of rainbows and sparks. Later, they built a bonfire of driftwood on the beach, sitting around it until it turned to embers, and the wind off the sea grew chilly. The children had fallen asleep right there in the sand, and so Gracie hefted Jamie and Ellen Rosie, staggering across the beach to the cottage to flop them into bed.

Another week, and the weather grew hotter and finally broke with a terrific thunderstorm one evening, the sky lit up with forks of lightning, the sea churning and crashing on the shore, the branches of the trees battering against the roof of their little cottage.

"Mama, when will it stop?" Rosie asked, curling into her as they sat on the sofa in the living room, rain streaming down the rattling window panes.

"Don't be frightened, Rosie," Gracie exclaimed, as she jumped up from the sofa. Ellen watched in bemusement as she threw open the door and stood there, letting the wind blow over her, the rain spattering against her skirt. "Thunderstorms are wonderful, really. 'Thy wind, thy wide gray skies!'" she quoted. "'Here such a passion is as stretcheth me apart.'"

"Is that Millay?" Ellen asked, laughing.

"Yes, 'God's World'." Gracie flung her arms out as she lifted her face to the pouring heavens. "'My soul is all but out of me, let fall no burning leaf, prithee, let no bird call.'"

"What does that mean?" Rosie asked, wrinkling her nose, distracted for a moment from the booms and crashes.

"The world is too beautiful," Gracie said as she dropped her arms. "Almost too beautiful to stand." She sighed, her moment of joy dropping like a mask, and Ellen's heart twisted with sympathy. She'd been secretly hoping that Will might have written Gracie after receiving her own letter, but so far there had been nothing.

Rosie looked nonplussed by Gracie's explanation, and Ellen put her arms around her. "Close the door, Gracie," she pleaded with a little laugh. "Or you'll get us all soaked."

"You haven't any romance in your soul," Gracie complained with a teasing look, and then, as she started to close the door, she stopped suddenly.

"What is it—" Ellen began, as Gracie frowned and peered into the rain-misted distance.

"Someone's coming toward our house," Gracie said, her eyes narrowed against the slanting rain. "A man. In this weather! He must be positively *soaked*."

Ellen rose from the sofa as Rosie and Jamie hurried to the door and peered out.

"Who is it?" Jamie asked anxiously. "Is it someone we know?"

"I don't know…"

Rosie squinted at the approaching figure. "How silly, he's taking off his hat, even though it's raining!" She sounded both thrilled and scandalized.

Gracie, Ellen saw, was looking transfixed, tremulous, incredulous and wondering. Realization flickered through her.

"Gracie…" she breathed.

"It's Will," Gracie said softly. "He's here."

And so he was—dressed in his usual poplin suit and soaked to the skin, smiling uncertainly, with eyes only for Gracie.

She let out a laugh that sounded near to a sob as he reached her. "Why are you here?"

"Because I wanted to see you."

"Will…" Gracie looked at him helplessly, and Ellen decided this was a good time to gather the children.

"Rosie, Jamie," she said briskly, "it's time for bed. Upstairs for stories, please."

"But Will's come—" Jamie protested, looking outraged. "And I want to talk to him!"

"I think he's going to stay for a while," she told him. "There will be plenty of time later to catch up with Will, don't worry." Then, with an encouraging smile for Gracie and a fleeting one for Will, she gathered her children and hurried upstairs.

It took all of Ellen's willpower not to strain her ears to listen to the murmured conversation from downstairs as Rosie and Jamie got grumpily into their pajamas. It was a small cottage, and words floated up anyway, even without her trying to eavesdrop.

"But why…" Will's voice, low and insistent.

A choked sob from Gracie, and then more low murmuring from Will, then silence.

Ellen opened a storybook and began to read. "Once upon a time there was a little boy who lived deep in the woods…"

More murmurings. A sound almost like a laugh. Ellen continued to read.

After three stories, both Rosie and Jamie were looking sleepy, and the thunderstorm had quieted down to no more than a misting drizzle. Ellen tucked them both into bed, kissing their foreheads in turn before they said their prayers. She closed the door softly behind her and stood hesitantly at the top of the stairs. She didn't want to interrupt Gracie and Will's conversation, but she felt as if she were skulking about on the stairs. What to do? Where to go?

"It's all right," Gracie called after a few uncertain moments. "You can come down, Ellen."

Ellen couldn't tell anything from her tone except that she sounded wrung out. She tiptoed down the stairs, feeling apprehensive, and then felt a great rush of relief at the sight of Will and Gracie sitting together on the sofa, his arm around her.

"Oh," she said, and smiled foolishly.

"Yes, oh," Gracie agreed. She laughed, but the sound was wobbly. "I've told Will everything." Her eyes filled with tears. "He's been so understanding."

"And you've been so brave," Will replied, drawing her closer to him. "I only wish you'd told me sooner, and we could have avoided this whole awful muddle."

"Yes, I should have," Gracie agreed, sniffing. "I should have been braver still."

"Well, you've sorted it out now," Ellen said firmly, determined not to let them waste a moment more on pointless recriminations. "And isn't it wonderful!"

Even so, she was longing for details; although Will had had his arm around Gracie, she couldn't tell if they'd simply sorted out their differences or he was halfway to a proposal, and she couldn't ask. Despite her curiosity, they spent the rest of the evening chatting about far more inconsequential matters; Gracie and Ellen regaled Will with stories of their time in the Hamptons, including plenty of tales about Rosie and Jamie, and how Ellen was managing the car.

"Are you staying up at the big house?" she asked, when it had grown late and he was making to leave.

"Yes, for now." He glanced at Gracie. "I've taken the rest of the summer off, but after that..." He let the words trail away, brimming with both uncertainty and hope. After that, who knew. Who knew, indeed.

Gracie just smiled and nodded, saying and promising nothing.

"Well?" Ellen asked when Will had gone up to the big house for the night.

Gracie gave one of her old, catlike smiles. "Well, what?" she asked as she switched off the lamp, plunging the little sitting room into moonlit darkness.

"Oh, Gracie! You know what I'm asking. Is it all sorted? Are you... are you together, truly?" After an hour of chitchat, she longed for more details.

"Well, we're not married," Gracie replied, giving her hair a playful toss. "Not yet, anyway."

Ellen couldn't keep from giving a little squeal. "I'm so happy for you!"

Gracie embraced her briefly. "I know you are. You've been such a good friend to me, Ellen, even when I've been really rather horrible."

"I've been just as horrible, if in a different way," Ellen replied. "I'm just so glad you've sorted things out between you."

Gracie let out a heartfelt sigh. "So am I." She paused to give Ellen another squeeze before stepping back. "Will said you wrote him."

"Oh, well..." Ellen blushed, hoping Gracie wouldn't be cross, all things considered.

"Thank you," she said. "For being brave enough to do that."

"Ha! Nosy and interfering, more like," Ellen replied with a grimace.

"That too!" Gracie laughed, a peal of pure joy. "Oh Ellen, I really am so happy. Happier than I've been in such a long while. It feels so strange and so wonderful."

Tears stung Ellen's eyes as she gave Gracie another impulsive hug. "And I'm so happy for you, Gracie," she said. "Truly."

The rest of July passed in a lovely, leisurely haze of days on the beach or wandering through East Hampton, flying kites on the dunes or playing tennis on the Turners' court. Will had promised to stay through July and August, and Ellen reveled in seeing him and Gracie together, gently, tenderly learning to love one another, teasing and laughing and holding hands.

She'd continued to write Lucas every few days, to keep him updated; she'd expected some response to Will and Gracie's new romance, but the letters Lucas wrote back were all too brief, a few lines that could just as well have been written by a passing acquaintance on the back of a postcard. *Miss you all! Take a dip in the ocean for me!* Ellen tried not to mind, but her sense of unease deepened as July sank into August and Lucas did not write with a date when he would be arriving for his promised two weeks' vacation with his family.

"I miss Daddy," Rosie told her, climbing into her lap like a much smaller child, one evening when the night air had turned chilly, already a hint of autumn in the August air.

"I miss him too," Ellen said, putting her arms around her daughter and giving a squeeze. "Shall we telephone him tomorrow? We can walk into East Hampton and use the telephone there."

"Why not use the one in the big house?" Will suggested. He was sitting in a rocking chair on the porch, the cuffs of his trousers rolled up, for he and Gracie had been clamming; they'd eaten them fresh for dinner.

"It's such an expense..." Ellen began, to which Will gently scoffed.

"Not at all! It's hardly worth the hassle of venturing all the way into town and mucking about with a handful of nickels and dimes. My parents will be pleased to offer you such hospitality."

Ellen had seen Elizabeth Turner out and about over the last six weeks, and while she'd given a friendly wave, she hadn't been any more forthcoming. Ellen had no idea just how much the Turners welcomed their stay in their guest cottage, or would welcome their son and heir's budding romance with a girl most certainly not from their set, which, as far as she knew, neither Will nor Gracie had yet informed them about.

"Very well," she said finally, because she really did want to speak with Lucas. "Thank you."

The next afternoon, Will himself answered the door when Ellen and Rosie ventured up to the big house, feeling nervous among all the crystal and marble, the antiques and oil paintings. The telephone had its own room off the magnificent entrance hall, with a comfortable chair, table, and of course, a telephone. She sat down, her heart starting to pound hard, not because of her rarefied surroundings, but because of the task in front of her. Rosie leaned against her side.

"Aren't you going to call Daddy?"

"Yes." Ellen gave her daughter a quick smile. "Yes, of course."

She didn't know why she was so nervous. She had a curdling sensation in her stomach, her hand slippery on the receiver as she reached for it and began to dial. Was it just silliness, or something deeper and ill-founded? A premonition, perhaps, because of Lucas's silence these last few weeks...

For, sure enough, when the call went through and Lucas answered the telephone, Ellen could tell he sounded harassed before she'd so much as spoken a word. She put her arm around Rosie.

"Lucas, it's Ellen."

"Ellen, my dear!" His tone was too jovial; underneath it, Ellen heard exhaustion, perhaps even irritation. "How are you? Nothing is wrong, I hope?"

"No, nothing's wrong. Rosie's here to say hello."

"Rosie!" Lucas exclaimed, and Ellen handed the receiver to her daughter, heartened by their eager exchange, Rosie detailing all their little adventures while Lucas listened attentively. A few minutes later, Rosie handed the telephone back to Ellen and she took it, smiling and beckoning Rosie to go out in the hall where Will was waiting to play a game of checkers while Ellen spoke privately to Lucas.

"You're well?" Lucas said after a moment, and Ellen answered cautiously,

"I'm telephoning because it's already August and I was hoping you could tell me when you're coming to stay. The children are so looking forward to seeing you, and I am, as well."

A terrible, telling silence ensued, only a few seconds but long enough for Ellen's stomach to start to feel leaden.

"Lucas..."

"I'm sorry, Ellen, but I can't." His voice was heavy, his tone final.

"Can't?" she repeated numbly.

"I can't come to see you and the children. The city's manic right now, everyone's on edge. I told you things were going to level off, but our clients are getting worried about a slump... it's simply not the time to hare off to the Hamptons as if I hadn't a care in the world." He sounded hassled but also quite firm. "I really am sorry."

"You mean... you can't come at all?" She realized, even in her nervous fears, she hadn't been expecting his response to be this drastic. "Surely at least for a weekend...?"

"I'm sorry, but I simply can't."

"But we've been apart for two months already," Ellen burst out. "And three months before that, Lucas—"

He let out an impatient sigh. "That wasn't my choice, Ellen—"

"What!" Were they actually arguing? "You were certainly supportive of our trips."

"For Jamie's sake, yes."

"And mine, you said—"

"Yes. *Yes.*" Another sigh, this one full of aggravation. "You're right, of course, and I don't mean to sound accusing. But things have changed here, I simply can't just run off." He let out a sound close to a groan. "I'm sorry, Ellen, but there's nothing I can do. My hands are as good as tied."

No, they aren't, Ellen thought with a sudden spurt of bitterness. He hardly had a gun held to his head. He'd chosen this—all of it. His ambition and desire for status had brought them to New York, brought them to this moment. Ellen hadn't wanted any of it, and she felt that truth keenly now.

"Ellen, say something," Lucas pleaded, a break in his voice. "I hate feeling as if I'm at odds with you about anything. I truly am sorry—"

"Are you?" Ellen asked quietly. "Because I've been hearing these apologies of yours for months now, Lucas. For years." Her voice throbbed with pent-up emotion, with hurt she couldn't bear to feel. "I just want us to be a family together. I don't care about having a big house or going to parties—"

"And what about having the opportunity to take Jamie to California and help his lungs?" Lucas's voice had turned briefly, uncharacteristically hard. "That wouldn't have been possible without my work, which you now seem to find rather easy to disdain."

"I don't disdain it," Ellen protested. Tears pricked her eyes and she blinked them back. "I just want us to be together."

"As do I," Lucas replied. "But if you choose to be in the Hamptons, it simply isn't possible now."

So it was her fault. Ellen swallowed past the hot lump of misery that had formed in her throat. "Then I suppose there is nothing more to say," she replied, doing her best not to cry, and then, because she couldn't bear to hear anymore, she quietly put down the receiver to end the call.

CHAPTER TWENTY-TWO

The weather turned dank and gray in August, which suited Ellen's mood. Her easy, lazy joy in June and July had given way to something bleak and despairing; she no longer wanted to be in the Hamptons, but neither did she wish to return to the city, and whatever remained for her there. She'd neither written nor telephoned Lucas again, although she'd started and then torn up more letters than she cared to remember. The trouble was, she had no idea what to say to him. What he'd be willing to hear. Lucas hadn't written either, and she wondered if he even noticed the silence between them. Perhaps it came to him as a relief.

Rosie had been desolate when Ellen had had to tell her that her father wasn't coming after all; she'd run outside and sat on the beach by herself, her skinny knees huddled to her chest, her head bowed. Ellen's heart had ached with both guilt and sorrow. Jamie had been even more heartbreakingly stoic, shrugging aside Ellen's words and insisting he didn't care if Lucas came or not.

"Maybe I shouldn't have come here at all," Ellen had told Gracie in despair. "As lovely a time as it's been, it's driving Lucas apart from me as well as the children. I hate that."

"You being in the Hamptons is not driving you apart," Gracie had replied as quick as a flash, with her usual spirit. "It's his work.

If you'd stayed in the city, you would have seen him hardly any more than you are now—and it most likely would have been even more frustrating!"

"That's what I told myself," Ellen had agreed, "but I'm starting to doubt it now. Perhaps we should go back early... What are your plans, Gracie, when we return to the city?"

On this point, Gracie had been evasive. "I'll have to wait and see," she'd murmured, but Ellen knew what she was really waiting for was Will. They'd been spending nearly every moment together since he'd come to the Hamptons, but he hadn't introduced Gracie to his family as anything more than a friend, and although Ellen was quite sure he was not someone to play a woman false, she began to wonder if even he knew what his feelings were, considering how quickly the romance with Gracie had sprung up.

One rainy afternoon in the middle of the month, when they all walked into the village to visit the library, she decided to ask him outright.

"What are your intentions, Will, when it comes to Gracie?"

They were walking a little way behind Gracie, who held Rosie and Jamie by the hand.

Will glanced at Ellen, first startled and then bemused. "Are you the right person to be asking me that?"

"Who else will?" Ellen demanded baldly. "You of all people know how fragile she is—"

"She's stronger than you think."

"She is," Ellen agreed, "but she's been through a lot and I want to protect to her."

Will's eyes flared. "So do I."

"Then why haven't you introduced her to your family?" Ellen spoke gently. "The fact that you haven't makes Gracie doubt what you intend."

He frowned, a look of unease coming into his eyes. "Has she said as much?"

"No, she's playing at being as carefree as ever, but I still believe it to be a worry. She's waiting to find out what her future holds, and whether you're a part of it. That's a lot for a young woman to bear."

"Of course I'm a part of it!" Will sighed as he raked his hand through his rain-dampened hair. "But I want to spare her my family for as long as possible. My mother won't be pleased—I know that already, full well. She has always had aspirations of me marrying some society girl. My father probably won't care all that much. But my family isn't like yours, Ellen—"

"My family?" Ellen raised her eyebrows. "My father hared off to New Mexico practically the very minute we arrived in this country, and my mother died when I was ten—"

"I mean your island family."

"We've been scattered to the four corners of the world, or near enough," Ellen reminded him. "I know what you mean, Will, but all families have their troubles. The longer you keep Gracie some secret, the more it seems as if you're ashamed of her."

"I'm not ashamed of her!"

"I *know*." Ellen laid a hand on his arm. "But don't you see what I mean? Your mother will wonder. Gracie will wonder." She paused. "Are you going to ask her to marry you?"

"Yes." Will's lack of hesitation made her smile.

"Then introduce her, for heaven's sake! Gracie can handle them. What she needs is your unwavering support and love. With that, she can take on anything or anyone, I'm sure."

"She has that," Will said in a low voice. "She always will."

"Good, then make it official," Ellen told him in her brisk nurse's voice. "Introduce her to your parents not just as a passing acquaintance or friend, but someone important. The woman you love, and never mind what your mother thinks!"

Will invited Gracie to dinner at the big house the very next week. Gracie begged Ellen to help her "look respectable"—laughingly, Ellen teased how their roles were reversed, and now she was the one primping and styling while she kept Gracie from looking in the mirror.

"You need to be yourself," she advised. "There's no point trying to pull the wool over their eyes, making them think you're some boring bluenose like me."

"You're not boring!" Gracie cried. "I never should have said such a thing."

"Oh, I am," Ellen replied amiably as she gave her a quick hug. "But I don't mind. Still, as long as you cover your knees and don't drench yourself in perfume, you should pass muster."

"Cover my knees!" Gracie hooted. "What an old maid I'll seem, and yet one who has snagged their son." She turned her anxious gaze on Ellen. "What if they hate me? I wouldn't blame them if they did."

"Well, you should! They of all people should know you're just what Will needs—someone fun and full of life, but also who understands what it means to suffer. You're perfect together, Gracie, you really are. And if Will's parents can't see that, well, who cares?"

Gracie let out a tremulous laugh. "I never thought I'd hear you say such a thing, Mrs. Grundy!"

Ellen gave her as stern a Mrs. Grundy look as she could, although, in truth, she still wasn't entirely sure what a Mrs. Grundy was. "Well, you just did," she said.

Thankfully, the dinner went off without too much of a hitch—in fact, Gracie told Ellen later, "I think his parents were relieved he's finally set his cap at someone. They want him to provide an heir at long last." She blushed pink. "Not to put too fine a point on it, of course! He is getting on in age, after all. I think they'd have been pleased if he was marrying the parlormaid."

"But he isn't, he's chosen you," Ellen answered with a laugh. "And it's about time too, considering his grand old age." Will was, in fact, the same age as she was.

"What about you, Ellen?" Gracie's expression turned serious. "Have you heard from Lucas?"

Ellen's smile dropped as she shook her head. "Not a word, and I haven't offered one, either. It's been complete silence since that awful telephone call." She bit her lip. "I'm trying not to think of it, to tell you the truth."

"Things will be better when you return to New York and talk properly," Gracie insisted. "No one can have a real conversation on a telephone."

"Perhaps," Ellen replied, but she had her own leaden-hearted doubts. The weeks of silence had stretched endlessly for her, filled with self-recrimination and worry that she'd done her best to hide both from the children and Gracie, and even herself. If she just didn't think of Lucas, it didn't hurt so much, but what sort of state of affairs was that?

By the beginning of September, it was time to pack up and head back to the city. Ellen dashed Lucas a quick note, letting him know when their train would arrive, and told herself not to mind when she received no reply. If he didn't meet them, they could take a taxi, it was as simple as that. As for what sort of greeting she'd have when she got home... well, that was something else not to think about.

"I'll miss this little house," Gracie said mournfully as they brought their cases out to the car, and Rosie and Jamie ran to the beach to say goodbye to the ocean. "I've loved it so."

"So have I," Ellen agreed. Even with the uncertainty and tension between her and Lucas, she'd savored her days at the beach, the time spent with Rosie and Jamie, Gracie and Will. June and July would always be a sweet, sun-soaked memory.

Will was accompanying them back to the city, and intended to take the train to California in the next few weeks. Ellen secretly hoped there might be a significant announcement to be made before then, and she suspected Gracie was waiting, as well, although she hadn't said as much.

"Time to go," she called to the children brightly. "We don't want to miss the train!"

Lucas wasn't at the station. Ellen lifted her chin and did her best not to act as if she minded, when in fact she felt sorely grieved—and afraid. They'd been gone for nearly three months. How could he have failed to meet them after all this time? Was he sending a message, or had he simply forgotten?

"Never mind," she told the children as breezily as she could. "What a surprise Daddy will have, when he sees us all at home! And it's always fun to take a taxi, isn't it?"

Gracie shot her a quick, sympathetic look and Ellen did her best to smile back even though she felt as if she were breaking apart inside.

Eva met them at the door as they returned to the townhouse on Ninety-Third Street. It felt empty inside in a way Ellen couldn't articulate, stuffy and stale despite the comforting scents of lavender and lemon polish, which made sense when Eva told her that Mr. Lyman had hardly been home at all.

"He's been very busy with work, Mrs. Lyman," she told her as she took their coats. "Sometimes he's even slept at the office! We've barely glimpsed hide or hair of him, to tell you the truth."

"I see," Ellen replied, and left it at that.

Lucas didn't return until after suppertime; the children had eaten in the kitchen and were up having their bath with Gracie supervising when the front door opened and Ellen came into the hall.

"You made it back safely," Lucas said. He sounded exhausted and he looked haggard, his tie askew, his hair ruffled.

"Yes, we did." Ellen regarded him for a moment, her hurt and anger warring with concern and compassion. "Lucas, what's going on?" she asked. "You look as if a breath could blow you over. Have you slept at all?"

Wearily, he took his hat from his head and hung it on the stand. "Roger Babson announced a crash is coming, and when it does it will be terrific. That was his word—terrific!" He shook his head, his shoulders slumped as if they had the weight of the whole city on them.

"And?" Ellen asked when it seemed as if he wouldn't say anything more.

"Well, what do you think happened, when one of America's most significant entrepreneurs says something like that? Everyone began to panic. The market slumped—Babson's Break, they're calling it, and hopefully it will only last a little while. But in the meantime our clients are going crazy." He shook his head again as he drove his hand through his hair. "I feel as if I haven't stopped for weeks, not even to catch my breath. I've barely slept, barely eaten—"

Ellen was silent for a moment, absorbing this news. "Why didn't you tell me this before?"

"I tried—"

Was that what he'd been getting at, on the telephone? She'd been focused only on her disappointment, the children's sorrow. She shook her head, not wanting to argue, not now. "And what if this 'Babson's Break' lasts longer? What if it's more than a slump?"

Lucas stilled for a second, his face averted from hers. "It can't be," he said flatly. "It simply can't."

"But what if it is?" Ellen pressed. It wasn't like Lucas to avoid the practical—he was usually so level-headed, so eminently sensible, yet right now there was something almost savage in his tone, something terribly bleak in his face. "Lucas..."

"There's no point dreading the worst," he told her with an approximation of his old joviality. "It's most certainly just a small slump. Plenty of investors are saying that it's good to have a break— the market will correct itself, and there will be even more buying opportunities."

"But what if—"

"Ellen!" His voice was sharp enough to make her fall silent. "It won't," he said in a quieter yet no less firm tone. "Whatever you're worrying about, it won't happen."

She stared at him, struck by the strangeness of his manner, the distance that had so clearly sprung up between them, yawning even wider than before. Except, of course, it hadn't sprung up; it had been there, a tiny crack that now suddenly felt like an endless chasm, an abyss.

As he started into his study, she couldn't keep from saying, "Don't you want to see the children?"

Lucas barely glanced over his shoulder. "Aren't they in bed?"

"No, not yet. They've been waiting for you." Ellen's voice shook and she strove to steady it, even though she felt like bursting into tears, although perhaps she was too shocked and empty for that. "They want to see you, Lucas. They've missed you terribly."

"I'll go up in a minute, then," Lucas said. "After I've seen to some business."

He closed the study door with Ellen still standing there in the hall; he hadn't even hugged or kissed her hello.

As the weeks passed, Ellen tried her best to ignore the distance that continued to yawn between her and Lucas. Although he'd been attentive to the children when he'd seen them, giving them hugs and kisses and listening to their news, he'd immersed himself in work right after and as August drifted into September, he'd still barely said a word to her.

She threw herself into getting Jamie and Rosie both ready for school; Jamie would be starting kindergarten, and was very excited by the change. Even though the weather had turned damp, his cough had not yet returned, for which Ellen was very glad.

Yet as she went about the city, taking the children to Macy's on Herald Square for shoes, and to the menagerie in Central Park for a treat, Ellen couldn't help but notice how frantic everything seemed, as if everyone in the city was on the edge of hysteria or collapse, or even both. The taxis seemed to screech a little louder, people walk a little faster; even the simple act of buying shoes had been tinged with a desperation Ellen didn't understand, the sales assistant fumbling with the shoes, his fingers nearly trembling. It was as if everyone knew something bad was going to happen, as if they were all on the precipice, holding their breath, waiting, hoping... Everyone, she thought, but Lucas.

For all of September he worked so much, Ellen barely saw him at all. He left before she'd breakfasted in the morning and came home when she was already in bed. When she tried to talk to him about it, he brushed her off, insisting that this really was just a little slump—Babson's Break, stretching on longer than anyone had anticipated, but when it was over, he could relax. They would spend time together, he would see the children, all the old promises.

The stock market, Ellen read in the newspapers in mid-September, had peaked on the third of the month, and had been going steadily downward since. When she remarked as much to Lucas, he dismissed her at once.

"It will level off, I tell you! This is the greatest city in the world, with the brightest future ahead of it. Why, just this year plans were made to build the tallest skyscraper in the world, on Thirty-Fourth Street. They'll start it next year. Nothing will stop this city, this great country, Ellen. Nothing." He spoke so firmly, she wondered if he was trying to convince himself.

Jamie and Rosie started school the second week of September, the leaves on the trees began to turn color, and, if anything, Lucas worked even harder. In the same week, Will proposed to Gracie in Central Park; they decided on a small ceremony there in New York before they would travel out together to California for the start of the semester at Caltech.

"You don't want a big island wedding?" Ellen asked a bit sadly. "With all your family there, everyone celebrating?"

"Part of me does," Gracie admitted, "but the bigger part of me wants to begin life with Will as soon as possible. And his mother would have six fits to have an island wedding—what a rustic thing that would be! No, it's better this way. Lots of people have quick ceremonies these days. Really, it's practically the rage. And the truth is, I just want to be married."

Ellen was happy for both of them, but she knew she would miss Gracie's company terribly. Lucas, at least, was able to spare time off work to see them married at St James' Church on Seventy-First Street; Will's parents were in attendance, as well as Ellen and Lucas and the children, and that was all. Ellen couldn't help but be a little saddened that Gracie had not invited Aunt Rose or any of her siblings, but she understood the rush. Life was short, Gracie and Will had both learned that much already, and they wanted to make the most of the time they had together.

Gracie made a beautiful bride, more radiant than ever; she wore a simple, fitted dress of ivory satin with lace sleeves and buttons all the way down the back, a short veil resting on her curls. Tears came to Ellen's eyes as Lucas walked her down the aisle, and Will looked as if he were bursting with both pride and joy.

They had a quiet luncheon afterwards at the Stanhope Hotel, and then, two days later, Ellen saw them off on the *20th Century Limited* for a transcontinental honeymoon, before they started life together back in Pasadena.

"Will has rented the sweetest little place, just around the corner from ours in Bungalow Heaven," Gracie told her. "I'm going to do it up myself, all nice and proper. Can you see me sewing curtains? I'm an island girl at heart, I guess, after all."

"You'll have to say hello to Maria and Eduardo for me," Ellen told her. "And write as often as you can." She would miss Gracie, she realized. Despite their rocky start, she loved her like a sister now, and she knew Gracie felt the same.

"Of course I'll write, you ninny," Gracie said as she hugged her tightly. "Just about every week! You're the best friend I've ever had, Ellen."

"Oh, Gracie." Ellen sniffed back her tears. "And you're mine, as well." Their time in the Hamptons and here in the city had only strengthened their bond.

She hugged Will and kissed his cheek, and she stayed on the platform waving until the train had left the station in a plume of smoke.

With a sigh, Ellen finally turned back into the station, fighting a sense similar to homesickness at the loss of Gracie. She'd been her near constant companion for the better part of a year, and even with their ups and downs, she already missed her.

As she waited for a taxi outside the station, she glanced at the newspaper headlines written on hoardings with a frisson of unease. *London Stock Mark Crashes due to Fraud!* Would that affect them here in New York? she wondered. It seemed so far away, and yet if it could happen there...

She had no answer on the matter from Lucas, for, once again, he stayed at the office until after she was in bed; the evening passed quietly without Gracie's company, and Ellen ended up writing a letter to her cousin Caro and another to Aunt Rose. She felt a pang of longing for the island, for the life she'd once had there. It seemed a thousand years ago, when she'd been sitting on the porch of the McCafferty farmhouse on Jasper Lane, shelling peas and watching the sun set. How simple life had been! How easy... and yet, of course, it hadn't been easy at all, with their money troubles and Peter's shell shock, and a host of other concerns, besides.

Still, she missed it, missed the white-ruffled blue-green waters of Lake Ontario, the yellow-tinged birches fringing the shore, the well-trodden path that had once separated the McCafferty and Lyman farms, although it was all one holding now. Everything, Ellen acknowledged, had changed. Everything always did, no matter how much she might try to resist; really, it was just a matter of time.

· · ·

"Why don't we see Daddy anymore?" Rosie asked matter-of-factly one evening when Ellen was putting her to bed. She was sitting up, her knees draw to her chest, giving Ellen her disconcertingly unblinking stare.

"He's very busy, just now, as you know," Ellen replied, as she had every other time Rosie had asked in the last few weeks. "But things will get better, you'll see."

But they didn't seem to get any better, at least to her. Whenever she scanned the newspapers, the headlines seemed both desperate and dire, lurching from terror to relief with dizzying speed. *Panic Seizes City as Scare Orders Halt Ticker... Bear Market Liquidating? Panic Ended, Banks Assure. Boom Will Run Into 1930!* another paper promised, but to Ellen it seemed worryingly rash. And yet she longed, just as she had when Will had first warned her, to believe it would all be all right, that it was just a matter of time until things settled down, until life became normal again—for the world, for the city, for them.

And really, she told herself as practically as she could, if there *was* a crash, what would it matter to them? Surely they wouldn't be affected too badly, not like the big corporations gambling millions, losing fortunes. Perhaps it would even be good for them; Lucas would finally work less. It wasn't as if they needed more money, and this heightened sense of both expectation and fear would finally subside.

As autumn encroached and Jamie's cough did not return, Ellen allowed herself to be convinced that it would all turn out all right. The headlines had become cheery again, insisting, by mid-October, that brokerage houses were "optimistic about recovery." Lucas was still working flat out, but he seemed a bit more cheerful. Ellen had stopped asking about work and when he'd made it home for supper one evening, they'd talked about the children, and Ellen had read him her latest letter from Gracie.

"An entire paragraph on the curtains she's sewn," Lucas said with a laugh. "I never would have thought it!"

"And another paragraph on how she's thinking of assisting Will in his laboratory," Ellen reminded him. "Gracie has always been smart as a whip. She sounds so happy." She laid the letter on the table next to her plate. "I think they both are."

"That's a honeymoon for you, I suppose," Lucas replied lightly, and Ellen wished she could say something of the strain she still felt between them, the silence on so many matters she was struggling to keep. But Lucas had turned back to his meal, and the moment, like so many others, had passed without a word of true understanding between them.

Then, on the twenty-fourth of October, the market finally fell, but did not crash, and within a few days, newspapers and officials alike were assuring everyone that the worst was really over, and "real bargains" could be bought.

"It seems as if it has levelled off," Ellen ventured cautiously to Lucas one evening, and he smiled and nodded and then, to her pleased surprise, swept her up into his arms.

"I really think it has! I'm so sorry, darling, that I've been so terribly preoccupied these last few months. I've been horrible, I know I have. It's just been because of the strain, but it's over now, I really think it is. Can you ever forgive me?"

Ellen let out a wobbly laugh. "Oh Lucas…"

"I wish I could have come to the Hamptons. I know that hurt you, that I didn't. Perhaps I should have gone anyway, but it really did seem so fraught at the time—"

"I just want—"

"Us to be together. I know. It's what I want, as well. I've been frantic about work, too frantic. I do realize that." He kissed her tenderly. "It's all going to be better now, I promise."

Ellen put her arms around him, filled with a relief so deep and heartfelt she could have wept. "I know it is," she said, and as he kissed her again, she believed it utterly.

For a day or two, it felt as if it truly was. Lucas came home from work early with a brand new kite, and took the children to the park to fly it. At supper, he was cheerful, so much like his old, easy self, that Ellen felt as if she'd flown back in time, as if all her cares had blown away on the wind like so much chaff. The next morning, he walked them to school himself before going to work; Ellen went about the house humming. She wrote a letter to Gracie telling her how things had changed, how everything was so much better now. *The worst is over,* she wrote, *and I'm so very glad.*

When she walked out to post it, she saw a man rushing to buy a newspaper from the boy on the corner. A frisson of unease went through her, like a shiver of premonition. Slowly, she walked over to the boy hawking papers and bought a copy, scanning the headlines.

Bingham Accuses Senators of Plot to Besmirch Him; Senators Renew Demand on Hoover for Tariff Stand; Europe is Disturbed by American Action on Occupation Debt. Nothing much to concern herself about, she thought with something like relief... and then she saw it. *Stock Prices Slump $14,000,000,000 in Nation-Wide Stampede to Unload.*

Her stomach swooped as she scanned the article. Despite the shocking amount of money that had been lost, the article was strangely, determinedly upbeat, insisting that bankers would support the market and once again it would all be all right, just as it had been before.

Ellen looked up from the paper and glanced around the usual quiet street; people were hurrying toward the subway station on Eighty-Sixth Street, faces drawn in concern or even panic. Were they going downtown, to the Stock Exchange, to see for themselves? Quickly, the paper tucked under one arm, Ellen strode back home.

That evening, Lucas assured her it was fine. "The bankers saved the day, thank goodness. This is nothing more than what we were expecting," he insisted, although only a few days ago he'd told her the worst was over. "It's happened, and now we can move on. The banks have put two hundred and forty million into the stock market. It's all going to be fine."

But according to the paper, the stock market had lost fourteen billion, a number that boggled Ellen's mind as she recalled all the zeroes on the front page. She couldn't get her head around it, and neither could she be reassured by Lucas's breezy manner.

The next day, when she went to buy the newspaper after taking Rosie and Jamie to school, the headline was worse. *Stocks Collapse, Bankers Optimistic, To Continue Aid.*

She couldn't ask Lucas about any of it, for he was back to working from dawn till dusk, or more, but as the days passed, Ellen could see for herself that things were not improving. The market continued to slide, and people were turning desperate. She watched in horror when, coming home from collecting Rosie and Jamie from school one day, she saw furniture being piled up outside the brownstone just a few down from theirs.

"What's happening?" Rosie asked, anxious as ever. "Are they moving?"

"Evicted," a passing pedestrian told them grimly. "They lost it all."

"Never mind, children," Ellen said quickly. "Let's go home. It's so chilly out." Shaken by the sight, she shepherded Rosie and Jamie into their own house, taking comfort in its reality, its solidity —the smell of lemon polish, the sound of Maisy in the kitchen. Then she saw that the door to Lucas's study was open, when he always kept it firmly closed, not wanting the children to disturb his papers.

Slowly, almost tiptoeing, she went to the doorway, stopping at the sight of Lucas at his desk, his head in his hands. Papers were everywhere, as if blown by the wind; drawers upended, and a crystal ashtray lay on the floor, smashed.

"Lucas..." Ellen's heart dropped as she stared at him; he didn't even look up, his hands driven through his hair, his head bowed.

Despite the increasing panic in the city as the stocks continued to slide, Lucas had assured her it was all in order. Now, as her children came over to clutch her hands and stare silently at their father, she knew it couldn't be. "Lucas," she said again, this time like a plea.

"I'm sorry," Lucas said in a low voice. "I'm so sorry, Ellen. Rosie. Jamie." He looked up at them in bleary despair, his eyes filling with tears while they all stared at him in stupefied horror. "I've lost it," he said. "I've lost it all."

CHAPTER TWENTY-THREE

"Tell me what happened," Ellen said wearily. "Tell me from the beginning."

It was nearing midnight; after discovering Lucas looking so despairing, she'd done her best to take control of the situation. She'd fed Rosie and Jamie in the kitchen, read them stories, and put them to bed hours ago now, doing her best to reassure them that everything was all right, before she'd tidied up Lucas's study and then gone into the sitting room, determined to find out what had really happened.

Lucas had been steadily working through his supply of medicinal brandy, and was now, she feared, quite drunk, although the look he gave her was sober enough.

"What does it matter?" he asked wearily. "The end result is the same. It's all gone. We're ruined."

A shiver of apprehension ran through her like a chill, and Ellen did her best to shake it off. He couldn't mean that, not truly. "Lucas, you're not telling me what you really mean."

"I'm not *telling* you?" He looked up, and she saw a shocking flash of rage spark in his bloodshot eyes. "How much more clearly can I tell you, Ellen? It's—all—gone." He spoke as if she were a toddler who was hard of hearing. "There's nothing left. Nothing."

Ellen took a deep, steadying breath and then let it out slowly. She glanced around the sitting room, taking comfort once more in the solidity of things she'd taken for granted—the heavy drapes at the window, the brass andirons by the fireplace, the matching set of leather club chairs, in one of which Lucas was slumped. All of it was real, reassuring—the very fact that they were sitting in this room, having this conversation, meant they weren't *ruined*. They couldn't be.

"What do you mean, nothing left?" she asked, adopting her best practical tone— Nurse Ellen coming to the fore. "There has to be something."

"Well, there isn't."

"Lucas!" She felt exasperated, as if he were a truculent child. "You know that can't be true. You have your position, we have this house—"

He shook his head. "No."

Ellen stilled, a new, icy sensation tricking through her. "What do you mean, no?"

"I lost my job today. Fired for doing exactly as I was told."

"You... you've been fired?" Ellen repeated numbly.

"In a word, yes." He looked up at her with a humorless smile. "I was tasked with issuing securities for one of the big banks. They asked me, as a Canadian, to set up a shell company in Toronto. I did it, and it turns out they wanted to use it to hide their profits from the taxman. I could have guessed that, of course, but I was told not to inquire." His lips twisted bitterly. "Now, with this crash, the government is investigating everything, and I'm the scapegoat who has to go."

Ellen shook her head slowly, hardly able to believe what he was telling her. "And... the house?" she asked faintly.

"I remortgaged it last year, to make some investments. Investments that are, as it happens, worth nothing now." His lips curved again, his smile bleaker still. "So the bank owns this house more than we do, Ellen. I suspect they'll come calling one day soon, just as they have for our neighbors."

"But..." She found she couldn't speak. She could barely breathe. She doubled over, trying to breathe deeply, as her mind spun and panic iced her veins. They'd lost the house... his job... and presumably all their money.

"So, you see," Lucas continued, watching her unemotionally, "we really are ruined. We've nothing to our names but the clothes on our backs." He threw one arm out to encompass the room, the house. "Even the furnishings and things will have to be sold, to cover our debts."

"What about Eva and Maisy?"

"I told them this morning I couldn't pay them anymore. I said they were welcome to stay if they wanted to, as long as we had the house. Cook's going to go to live with her sister in New Jersey. Eva's already gone to her mother's, in the Bronx."

"Oh... oh, dear heaven." She hadn't even said goodbye to Eva. Lucas said nothing as Ellen stared into space, trying to make sense of this awful new world they'd just been plunged into. "We can rent something, surely," she said after a moment. "An apartment downtown, where it's cheaper..."

"What for? I haven't got a job, and no one in this city will hire me now that my name is as good as Mudd."

"But..." She put her hands up to her head as if to steady herself. It was so very hard to think. "Where will you go?"

Lucas shrugged. "I suppose we can wait and see. I still have the stocks... I haven't let go of them, not yet. If they rise again... we might be all right."

"The *stocks?*" Ellen stared at him in disbelief. "After all this, you're still hoping on the stocks?"

Lucas shrugged, the twist of his shoulders a despairing gesture of defeat. "What else can I do?"

The next few weeks passed in a dreamlike blur. Life went on in a strangely normal way and yet it was also utterly odd and surreal. Rosie and Jamie continued to go to school; the fees had been paid through Christmas, at least. Ellen learned to make do without the servants, she realized, somewhat to her shame, she'd become dependent on. It had been years since she'd had to do the laundry, or make every meal herself, and yet she was determined to rise to the challenge. She was a Springburn lass, after all. Hauling water, scrubbing clothes, inspecting old vegetables for bruises—all of this was familiar to her, and she felt herself falling into a rhythm she remembered from her childhood. Darning Rosie's stockings, letting down hems, making a shin of beef last for a week... there was something pleasing about it, satisfying in a soul-deep sort of way. This was who she really was, at heart. She found she didn't mind the menial work, the counting pennies, making things last, whether it was a pair of shoes or a casserole made to stretch with a few more potatoes. She liked being busy, even as Lucas spent the days reading the papers or simply staring into space, marking time, staying silent, impossible to reach.

As the stocks began to climb again in December, he lost a little of his apathetic despair. He arranged to have some of their furniture sold, choosing things the children wouldn't miss too much, to pay some of their debts, and made arrangements with the bank to hold off on repossession for a few more months. Ellen wasn't sure what promises he had made, but they were holding onto their old life by a thread, at least for now—yet how long could any of it possibly last?

Amidst the odd normality of their lives were scenes of terrible devastation. When Ellen took the children Christmas shopping in December, having hoarded some pennies to buy a few small presents, they were all struck silent by the breadline snaking down Broadway for five or six blocks, men and women looking haggard and cold in raggedy overcoats, gaunt faces etched with hunger and despair.

Jamie tugged on the sleeve of Ellen's coat. "What are they waiting for?"

"Food," she answered bleakly. Breadlines and soup kitchens had become normal up and down America, supported by the Red

Cross or the government, and, in Chicago, even by the notorious gangster Al Capone, offering free food for the homeless and the hungry, the despairing and the destitute.

After a quiet Christmas, Rosie and Jamie had to be withdrawn from their private schools, and Ellen took them to the public Lillie Devereaux Blake School on Eighty-Fifth Street, to enroll them for the new term. It seemed an absurdly small price to pay, considering everything else that was going on—so many houses empty, furniture carted away to be sold, windows broken and doors boarded up in their once-gracious neighborhood.

In Central Park, shanty towns or "Hoovervilles" had sprung up for those who had lost their homes, a sea of houses made out of bits of wood and corrugated iron, or even just cardboard boxes. At night, from her bedroom window, Ellen could see the fires blazing in oilcans, sometimes hear the faint strains of a harmonica or a banjo from the groups of men who had turned the park into an apartment block for those who had nowhere else to go.

At least their family still had a roof over their heads, food in the pantry, even if it was less than ever before. The children had shoes; they could go to school.

"The children seemed nice there," Ellen told Lucas when she returned from taking them for their first day. He was sitting in his study, scanning the paper's help wanted ads, which, she supposed, was better than what he was usually doing—reading the headlines, hoping the stock prices would continue to climb.

"I'm glad," he said with a weary sort of acceptance. "It's considered to be a very good school. I don't know why we didn't send them there in the first place."

Because you wanted them to go to private schools, Ellen thought, but didn't say. "Is there anything in the help wanted?" she asked, trying to sound bright.

"No." He tossed the paper aside. "No one's hiring for the kind of work I'm trained to do. Maybe when the market picks up a bit more..." For once, he could not inject the usual desperate optimism into his voice.

"What about another sort of job?"

He looked at her blankly. "What else can I do?"

"There must be lots of laborer jobs," Ellen said. "There's buildings going up all over the city." Mainly, she knew, to provide work for desperate men, but surely Lucas was one of those?

He grimaced slightly. "You want me to be a builder?"

"You grew up on a farm, Lucas," she reminded him. "And a job is a job."

He hesitated, considering, then shook his head. "For every menial job going, there's a hundred men desperate to fill it, and the only thing I'm qualified to do, I can't, at least not in this town. I'll never be hired again, even if I want to be." He sighed. "I might as well accept that my career is finished."

"We could leave New York," Ellen suggested after a moment.

Lucas looked up at her in surprise. "Leave the city?" He sounded as if the possibility had never even occurred to him.

"Why should we stay? Our family isn't here. Your work isn't here. It's expensive and dirty and there are too many people who are desperate for jobs."

"That's everywhere in this country, Ellen."

"If that's so, then I'd rather live somewhere I like, where the air is clean and the sky is big and I can breathe and think."

Lucas frowned, his eyes narrowing. "What are you saying?"

She took a deep breath, let it out slowly. This had not come to her suddenly; she knew it wasn't a whim. It had been growing inside her for months, maybe even years. "I want to return to the island."

"What!" He was incredulous, almost scathing. "Amherst Island?"

"Is there any other island in the world?" Ellen teased, smiling faintly.

Lucas shook his head, more out of instinct than outright

refusal, or at least Ellen hoped so. "There's nothing left for us there, Ellen. It's not the same place it once was."

"I know that." She'd realized it afresh when they'd rented a cottage for the summer, six years ago. She supposed it would have changed even more now. "But Caro and Jack are there, and their children. There are other people we know, as well. Old friends."

"Whom we haven't spoken to since we left," Lucas replied. "But that's beside the point. What would we do there? Where would we live? If I can't get a job here in the biggest city in the world, do you honestly think I could get one on a poky little island where there are most likely no jobs at all?"

"I don't know," Ellen admitted. "But we can't stay here, Lucas, unless you find work, or I do. The bank will take the house one day —you know they will." Something like hurt flashed across his face, and determinedly she kept going. "I'm not saying it to be cruel, but the stocks won't rise enough to keep this house, or our old way of life. I don't even mind—I really don't. I'd move to a small apart-ment, do whatever it takes, if it felt right. But it *doesn't* feel right, Lucas, and it hasn't for a long time. You say there's nothing for us on the island, but I don't believe there's anything for us here."

Lucas stared at her for a long time, his expression forbiddingly blank. Finally he spoke. "I'm not ready to give up yet," he said, and picked up the newspaper once again.

CHAPTER TWENTY-FOUR

MAY 1930

The ferry to Amherst Island was a little steamer, now, piloted by a weathered-looking man in a flat cap and overalls. Captain Jonah, who'd piloted the old ferry in the days of her youth, had died in his bed several years ago, or so a woman, holding several chickens in a crate on her lap, told Ellen as she boarded the boat, Rosie and Jamie's hands clutched in hers. Lucas followed behind her, as taciturn as he'd been for months, since it had become all too abundantly clear that they could not stay in New York.

First it had been the house. The brief pickup of the stock market that had caused everyone's hopes to desperately rise had ended in March, and since then there had been a steady, continuous decline. The bank had come before the end of the month, and they'd suffered the shame of seeing their furniture carted out, packing up their pitifully few belongings as they left the grand home that had been theirs for just over two years.

Lucas had managed to secure several rooms in a boarding house on Broadway; Ellen had collected the children from school, explaining it all as best as she could without alarming them, as if it were all such a grand adventure, a lovely lark. Jamie seemed to take it in that spirit, but Rosie had been silent and pinched, and when Ellen had woken up in the night, because the resident in the room next to theirs had started a blazing argument with his wife, she saw Rosie lying in bed, staring straight ahead, her pale face looking as if it were made of marble.

Lucas vowed they wouldn't spend another night in that place, with its smell of cabbage and drains, the broken beer bottles in the hall and the shouting next door. He managed to find an apartment in Harlem, a tiny one bedroom with a gas ring for a kitchen, the toilet and pump both outside. At least it was clean and the neighbors were friendly. Rosie and Jamie were able to continue at their school, and Ellen did her best to make the apartment as cozy a home as she could.

They lived there for four weeks, Lucas picking up day jobs when he could, whether it was hauling bricks for the newly started Empire State Building, or delivering messages for the types of men he used to work for. He stayed jovial for the children's sake, but to Ellen he barely spoke. When she tried to encourage him, he simply turned away, as if he couldn't bear her praise. Although they lay side by side in a bed barely wide enough for one, they hardly touched.

Each day had enough trouble of its own, Ellen told herself, and she did her best to soldier through, not thinking too much about the future, or when Lucas would come back to himself—to her. It was hard enough to scrounge up food for three meals a day, and make sure the children were washed and dressed for school. There wasn't enough money for stamps, for which she was glad, because she couldn't bear to let anyone know how drastically they'd fallen, although, as far as she knew, everyone else was struggling, as well. She'd been able to pick up the post from their old address, at least, to learn everyone's news; Gracie had written that while Will's job was secure, his parents had lost most of their money. The big house in the Hamptons had had to be sold. Ellen's other cousin Sarah's husband had lost his job; while her old friend Louisa wrote that the bank Jed Lyman worked for had closed, and he'd turned back to farming. Louisa's parents' savings had all been in stocks, just like so many other people's, and they had moved in with them until they could get back on their feet.

So when Gracie's sister Caro wrote from Amherst Island, telling her the Ellises' place a little bit down the road toward Emerald was empty, Ellen took it as a sign. Just two days later they were threatened with eviction from their apartment for not paying the rent, Lucas looking grimmer than ever.

"Maybe if I try down at the docks," he'd said, running a grimy hand through his hair. There were new lines carved into his face, new strands of gray in his hair. Ellen couldn't bear to see him look so weary, so defeated.

"Lucas, what are we doing?" she'd cried. "Caro has written to say the Ellises' place is freed up, because they've gone to try their luck in Toronto. The bank isn't interested in selling it; we could live there for a paltry sum. Caro said they could even rustle up a few sticks of furniture for us. You could farm their holding while you think about what to do next—that's something you know how to do. If we go now, there will be time to plant."

"I'm not a farmer," Lucas had replied, his voice caught between a growl and a cry. "I never have been."

"You're not a lawyer, either," Ellen had reminded him gently. "Not now. There's nothing for us here. I'd suggest we go somewhere else—Chicago or even out to California, but it's the same the whole country over, isn't it? At least on the island we have friends, family, a house to live in."

"No one's moving to the country, Ellen," Lucas had stated flatly, "because there's no work. It's the cities that—"

"But we're in a city, and we have nothing," she'd cried in desperation. "Why would we stay? At least on the island we could grow some food, make ends meet, and the air would be good for Jamie." Since moving to the small apartment with its poor heating and draughty windows, he'd started coughing again, if only a little. "For Jamie's sake, Lucas, if not for mine."

And so he'd agreed, reluctantly, even sullenly, knowing he had no choice. They'd sold Ellen's engagement ring to pay for the train fare; she hadn't even minded, had given it up gladly, but Lucas's face had looked as if it had been set in stone.

Now they were here, the breeze off the lake chilly even though it was May, the pale blue sky buffeted by gray clouds, the island an emerald smudge in the distance, lifting Ellen's heart, buoying her hopes, despite all the exhaustion and strain.

Home. It would always be home.

She turned to Lucas, longing for him to share in the joyful possibility of the moment, but his expression was shuttered, and when she caught his eye, he pretended she hadn't and looked away.

The island's main village, Stella, was just the same, Ellen thought, as when she'd come before—at twelve, for the first time; at twenty-seven, after the war, and all the times in between, when she'd been so excited to finally return to the island she loved and knew so well.

"Nothing's changed at all," she exclaimed, while the children looked bemused and Lucas said nothing. "It's exactly as it was." At last, she thought with a smile, something hadn't changed. Admittedly, the village's few buildings were weathered and old, the sleepy street of packed dirt looking forgotten in the drowsiness of a late afternoon, but still. She'd been happiest here, of all the times in her life. They could be happy here again. She would make sure of it.

"There's Jack," she said, nodding towards the dilapidated wagon led by a single weary horse that was coming down the street, driven by Caro's husband, Jack, a war veteran who had suffered from terrible burns, so half of his face looked like a lumpen piece of clay.

Ellen had warned the children, matter-of-factly, about his injuries, as they hadn't seen him since they were small and she didn't want them to be shocked, but Rosie still looked pale-faced, while Jamie clearly wanted to ask a dozen questions about how it had happened and whether it hurt.

"It's so good to see you, Jack," Ellen said as she embraced him. "Thank you for coming to fetch us."

He nodded awkwardly, always a man of few words. "Caro's been getting the Ellis place ready for you all. I think it'll look pretty cozy."

Lucas shook his hand, half-mumbling his thanks, not meeting his eye. Ellen did her best to suppress the sharp pang of irritation she felt at his unfriendly behavior. It was so very unlike him, a man who had always been cheerful, affable, easy-going. When would he recover that old equanimity? Surely here on the island, where they'd once fallen in love and first been so happy. She prayed it would be so.

Caro was all brisk practicality when Jack pulled the wagon up to the little clapboard farmhouse and they all tumbled out.

"Dinner first," she announced, placing a freshly baked loaf of bread, a golden lump of butter, and several thick-cut slices of ham on the table. Ellen couldn't remember when she'd last seen so much food. "Then we'll take you over to the Ellises' place." She gave Ellen a quick, hard hug. "It's so good to see you." She glanced at Lucas, who was still standing in the doorway, with a smile. "To see you both. And these little ones!" She patted Jamie's head and then Rosie's cheek. "I haven't seen your little boy since he was a baby. You're the spit of your father, aren't you? And you, your mother, Rosie."

Soon enough, they were all seated around the wooden table— Caro and Jack, their five children, and Ellen and Lucas with their two. It was crowded, but there was food enough for everyone, and Ellen realized she was famished. She was glad to see the children tuck in heartily, although she worried that Caro would be emptying their pantry for their sakes.

Caro, meanwhile, filled them in on all the news of Ellen's cousins. "So Sarah and her husband have moved to Toronto. He's found a job there, in a prison of all things! Working as a guard.

Pays pretty well, it seems. They stayed with Peter until they found an apartment. Peter's doing all right too, I think. Dominion Bank has kept afloat, if only just. And Andrew's still got work out west. I wonder if he'll ever come back."

"And what about your mother?" Ellen asked, thinking of her beloved Aunt Rose. "Has she gone with them?"

Caro shook her head. "She went at first, to help them settle, but she can't abide the big city, and in any case there isn't enough room. Another mouth to feed and all that."

Ellen's heart turned over. "So what will she do?"

"She's coming back here," Caro stated. "Train gets in to Ogdensburg tomorrow, and Jack'll meet the ferry." Her face set into determined lines. "She'll always have a place with us."

"Oh, Aunt Rose!" Ellen exclaimed. "I'll be so happy to see her. It's been far too long."

Caro nodded somberly. "It has been far too long, for all of us."

After their supper, Caro walked them over to the Ellises' farmhouse, while Jack took their bags in the wagon. The sun was setting, the sky lit up with vivid streaks of pink and orange, the trees just coming in bud. Ellen paused to touch a new cherry blossom, still tightly furled and pink, a promise in the making.

"I'd forgotten just how much I love it here," she said softly. "I thought I hadn't, but I had."

Caro smiled tolerantly. "You always were an island girl," she said. "More than any of us, I think, never mind that you weren't born here."

"What do you think, Rosie?" Ellen asked, turning to her daughter with a smile; she'd been very quiet all afternoon, eating her meal in wary silence, while the other children had been boisterous, Jamie joining in. "Do you think you'll be an island girl?"

"I don't know," Rosie said quietly, and Caro let out a huff of laughter.

"You remind me of your mother, when she was just a bit older than you. All eyes and hair you were, Ellen, and scared of cows. Do you remember that?"

"I'm scared of cows," Rosie admitted in a small voice, and Caro gave her the same tolerant look she'd given Ellen.

"Proper city folk you've all become! Well, we'll soon get it out of you. Your Uncle Jack will take you to see our cows, Rosie. That'll cure you of any old fears. Our milch cow Daisy has the softest nose, you can imagine. You might as well be touching velvet."

"Mama has a velvet dress," Rosie said shyly. She darted an uncertain look at Ellen. "At least she did."

Caro exchanged a brief look of understanding sympathy with Ellen before nodding. "Well, it must have been pretty soft, I'd say," she said, touching Rosie's head lightly. "Look, here we are."

The Ellises' farmhouse was similar to Caro and Jack's in style, made of clapboard, with two front rooms and a kitchen downstairs, and three small bedrooms above. Although Caro had done her best to scare up some furniture—an old horsehair sofa for the living room, a rickety table for the kitchen—it was a far cry from the cozy home she'd made for her own family. The cabbage rose wallpaper in the living room was coming off in shreds in places, and there were water stains on the ceiling. The bathroom was outside, the pump by the kitchen door. Still, Ellen told herself, it was better than the apartment they'd lived in for nearly a month, and it was on the island. *Her* island. They would manage.

Jack came up with the wagon, and after hauling their suitcases inside, he and Lucas went out to inspect the barn, which looked to Ellen as if it were halfway to falling down. The children went to explore the garden, which was overgrown with weeds, but looked to be big enough for a vegetable patch and space to play besides.

"I can hardly believe I'm here," Ellen said dazedly. "Are you sure no one else wants it?"

"This place?" Caro let out a laugh as she glanced around the kitchen, with its bare pine shelves and the coal stove that had to be at least twenty years old. There wasn't even an icebox. "I should think not. Just about half the houses on the island are empty right now, and the rest of us are just trying to hold on. It hasn't been easy for farmers, you know, any more than bankers or lawyers or those fancy fat cats in the city. Most of us invested the same as you did, putting all our pennies into General Electric or Ma Bell. We didn't invest, because we didn't have enough put by!" Caro let out a laugh. "That was a mercy, I suppose."

"It's been dreadful for everyone, hasn't it?" Ellen said. She rested her hand on the back of a wooden chair. "I'm so grateful, Caro, that we're able to stay here. And that the bank's willing to accept our token rent."

Caro shrugged. "What else can they do, with so many places empty? At least you'll take care of it, make the land yield again. You just might be able to scratch a living, if there's a good harvest."

"We weren't even doing that, back in the city," Ellen admitted on a sigh. Her gaze moved to the window, the weathered barn visible in the distance.

"Give him some time," Caro advised, and Ellen turned to her, startled.

"What—"

"I know you're worried about Lucas. It's hard on the men. They're meant to be the breadwinners, supporting their families, bringing food to the table. When they can't..." She shrugged. "They feel like failures."

"But he knows I don't think like that," Ellen protested, even as a tiny, treacherous voice whispered inside her, *Don't you? Just a little?*

Caro shrugged. "It doesn't much matter what you think, if it's what *they* think. Lucas looks like a man who has been beaten down. He wants to feel useful, important. Give him time and he will."

Ellen nodded slowly, accepting Caro's plain speaking. She'd always been the bluntest of the McCafferty tribe, hardworking and practical, so different from Gracie's spirited playfulness. Ellen was grateful for her good advice, and she longed for it to be true, for now, more than ever, she hoped that the island could be the making of them—and yet still feared it might be their destruction, if Lucas didn't take to farming, if the harvest was bad… if they couldn't find their way back to each other again, even here, in the place she loved best.

CHAPTER TWENTY-FIVE

Weeks passed and the sun shone, the children ran in and out of the house, barefoot, brown, happy, and wild, while Ellen did her best to make the worn little farmhouse a home, and Lucas tended to the land.

It was amazing how industrious you could be, she thought, when you didn't have two nickels to rub together. She scraped the wallpaper from the living room and painted the walls with a tin of white paint she'd found in a shed; she made curtains from some old dresses, as well as patchwork quilts for all their beds. There had been enough money left over after their train fare to buy some food staples, and more importantly, a milch cow and some chickens. The fall in wheat prices had left Lucas with little choice but to plant potatoes; but they'd had a good crop, so at least they wouldn't go hungry.

"Now is not the time to be a farmer," he'd told her grimly, during one of their first nights in the little farmhouse. "Wheat prices have crashed along with everything else, and the government's farm relief is only for the big outfits out west, the kind where your cousin Andrew now works. They don't care about the little man, and I'm the littlest of all."

"We have enough money to tide us over for the summer," Ellen had replied equably. "And we'll have food."

"And what about clothes?" Lucas had demanded. "Or shoes? Or if, God forbid, one of us gets sick? We haven't a dime for any of that, Ellen." He'd shaken his head, misery drawing his features downward. "Don't you see what a mess we're in?"

"It's a mess I've been in for a good part of my life," Ellen had replied steadily. "And you, as well, Lucas. Money was always short when we were children. Few farmers ever had more than a few dollars to their name. It was all tied up in the land."

"We don't even own this land—"

"But we can farm it," Ellen had said firmly. "We can survive."

Now, as she set a loaf of bread to rise, she glanced out the kitchen window at the barn whose roof Lucas been trying to repair for most of the morning, to little avail, judging from the occasional shout or curse that came from that direction. He'd been grimly working every day since they'd arrived, tilling the fields, repairing the barn, milking the cow, seeming to enjoy none of it.

He was here on sufferance, Ellen acknowledged with a pang of anxiety. If he could have had his old job back, his old life, he would, and in a heartbeat—and yet she was realizing, with more and more conviction, that she wouldn't.

She didn't particularly like being poor, but she loved being back on her island. She'd spent hours walking its meadows and woods, its rocky shores and golden stretches of beach, reacquainting herself with every precious inch, greeting the houses and barns, even the trees and rocks, as if they were all old friends, which they *were*.

There was the rocky point she'd taken guests to when her aunt had helped her briefly run Jasper Lane as a holiday destination; there were the sun-dappled woods she'd wandered through, lost in daydreams. A field of daisies, a copse of birches, the smooth, flat rock jutting over the lake waters... she remembered and loved it all.

Having her Aunt Rose here had made it all the more poignant;

Ellen had walked over to Caro's when Jack came back from Stella with Rose next to him in the wagon.

"*Ellen!*" she'd exclaimed, and they'd both wept as they'd held each other in their arms. Aunt Rose looked older—her skin a bit more papery, her eyes a bit more faded—and yet wonderfully the same. Her arms were wiry and strong as they embraced her. "Isn't it good to be back on our dear island?" she'd stated with a laugh. "Doesn't it feel right?"

And, both laughing and weeping, Ellen had to admit it did.

After they'd been back on the island for a week, she'd taken Jamie and Rosie to the one-room schoolhouse she and Lucas had both attended as children. Emptier now than it had been before, thanks to the exodus to the cities, Miss Browning, the teacher, was glad for two new pupils. Jamie and Rosie were at first bemused and then enchanted by the very different education they were getting than in the four-story brick building on Eighty-Fifth Street.

They'd been happily settled there for several weeks now, while she'd continued to make the house their home, planting a vegetable garden, reacquainting herself with island life, spending time with Rose and Caro. Every day she felt more at home, and yet she feared Lucas continued to resist.

Another shout came from the barn, and then the clatter of a hammer being hurled. Ellen bit her lip as she turned away from the window. A few minutes later, Lucas strode into the house, hurling himself down at the table as he kicked its leg with one booted foot.

"Damned barn. It would be easier to tear the whole thing down and start again, not that I want to." He raked a hand through his hair as he scowled.

"What's the trouble?" Ellen asked as mildly as she could. Anger radiated from Lucas like rays of lightning.

"What isn't the trouble? The wood is rotted, the beams aren't stable, the tin is warped..." He shook his head and then burst out bitterly, "And I'm no good at this. I never have been."

"Lucas, you were—"

"Raised on a farm. Yes, I *know*. But I left, didn't I? I *wanted* to leave. I never meant to be a farmer. I'm good with numbers, with facts and figures, not with hammer and nails, tractor and plow. You knew that when you married me." He spat it like an accusation.

"We all have to adjust—"

"Adjust to what? Eking out a miserable living from this poor soil? Living like sharecroppers, hand to mouth, for the rest of our lives?"

She met his gaze steadily, even though inside she trembled. "If that's what we have to do, then yes."

"But I don't want to!" The words came out in a near roar. "If we moved to Chicago or Los Angeles, I might be able to get another position. Or even Toronto, Kingston..." He shook his head in helpless rage. "I'm not a farmer, Ellen. I never will be."

Because you don't want to try. Ellen bit down on the words, on the frustration she felt at having to bear months of his surly intransigence. He was hurting, she reminded herself, just as Caro had told her. "Lucas," she tried again. "I know it's difficult, but we haven't any choice now, do we? If we can just see ourselves through the summer..."

"And then what? A hard winter where we all turn to skin and bone? If Jamie's cough comes back, there will be nothing we can do. *Nothing.* You might appreciate the money I made a bit more then."

"I always appreciated it," she said quietly. "But it's gone. And whether you like it or not, you have to be a farmer now, at least for a little while. At least until something else comes up."

His expression hardened, his mouth twisting bitterly. "If you wanted a farmer so much, maybe you should have married Jed, after all."

She reared back, stung, and then found herself saying in a hard voice, "He didn't ask me, did he?"

Lucas glared at her while Ellen stared back, miserable and defiant, and then he slammed out of the house hard enough to rattle the window panes. Ellen watched from the kitchen window, her whole body trembling, as he stalked through the fields glinting in the noonday sun, and then was swallowed up by the woods that fringed the shore.

She let out a gasping sob and then clapped her hand to her mouth, desperate not to break down. Even in all the difficulties they'd faced over the last few months, the tension they'd endured through their separation and silence over the summer, they'd never fought like that. Lucas had looked at her as if she were a stranger... and she'd looked at him likewise.

What if it had been a terrible, terrible mistake to come back to the island? Just because it was the stuff of Ellen's dreams didn't make it the right place for Lucas. Right now it felt like the worst thing they could have done. And yet what had been the alternative? Starving in some miserable, rat-infested slum in the city?

Oh God, she prayed silently as she stared out over the empty fields, *what should I do? How can I help him?*

She waited for an answer, as if God Himself would speak from the heavens. All she heard was silence, and then the sweet trill of a robin, its innocent chirping the sound of renewal, of hope.

Slowly, Ellen opened the kitchen door and walked through the newly planted garden, the plowed field beyond, and then the long golden-green grass that brushed against her legs to the shadowy wood. She breathed in the cool, damp air as she kept going, driven by instinct rather than knowledge.

She emerged from the woods to the rocky shoreline, the Bay of Quinte sparkling in the distance, the waves lapping at the shore. Lucas sat on a piece of driftwood, his head in his hands, his shoulders slumped. He looked, Ellen thought, like someone who had fallen down and couldn't remember to get up. And really, wasn't that exactly what he was?

The day was sunny and bright, and a tiny butterfly bumbled happily by his downturned head, the world around him so achingly beautiful while he was caught up in the desperate throes of his own grief.

A line of poetry by Edna St. Vincent Millay, who Gracie had once quoted, ran through Ellen's head:

All the things we ever knew
Will be ashes in that hour,
Mark the transient butterfly,
How he hangs upon the flower.

All Lucas had known, all he'd valued and taken pride in, had been utterly destroyed. For the first time Ellen was able to see—to *feel*—how utterly grief-stricken he had to be. He was mourning his job, his home, his life, in a way that she'd never had to. Yes, she'd found it hard, even devastating, to move from their stately home to a poky apartment; to count pennies and darn socks and peel moldy old potatoes. And yet she'd also relished the challenge; it had made her feel strong, and all the while it had been making Lucas feel so very weak. She understood that in this moment more than she ever had before, even when Lucas had told her he'd lost it all, or Caro had said how hard it was on the men.

Slowly, picking her way through the strewn rocks, she walked toward her husband.

She knew he heard her coming by the stiffening of his shoulders, but he didn't lift his head.

Ellen had no idea what to say, how to bridge this chasm that now yawned between them. She prayed for the words, the wisdom.

And then she heard herself saying, "If you want to leave the island, I will."

Lucas didn't reply for a long moment. "You love it here," he said at last. He sounded hopeless.

"I love you more," Ellen replied steadily. "And I always will."

Lucas let out a choking sound, and she dropped to her knees next to him, heedless of the rocks beneath her as she put her arms around him.

"Lucas, oh Lucas, all I want is us to be happy together. The children, too."

"They like it here, too, by the looks of it."

"They'll like it *anywhere*, as long as you're there."

"They were happy enough in California without me," he replied flatly. "Maybe it would be better if—"

"No." Ellen's arms tightened around him. "No. They missed you in California. They want to be with you. They need you, Lucas, just as I do."

He sighed, shaking his head, seeming as intransigent as ever, and then, to Ellen's surprise, he let out a sob. His shoulders shook as she kept her arms wrapped around him and held on—and he wept.

"Lucas..." she murmured as he pressed his fist to his forehead and the tears continued to fall, the sobs shaking his whole body. "*Lucas.*"

"I'm sorry," he gasped out after several endless, heart-rending minutes. "Oh Ellen, I'm so sorry." She realized it was the first time he'd said those words since the end of October, the end of their lives as they'd known them. "It's all my fault. Everything..." Another choking sob as he ran his sleeve along his eyes. "I got so caught up in it all. It was so exciting, and I felt so powerful... like the king of the world." He glanced at her with wet eyes, his face full of self-recrimination. "I always felt as if I were in Jed's shadow and for once I wasn't."

"Jed's shadow?" Ellen exclaimed, surprised despite the words he'd hurled at her in the kitchen. "Lucas, I think he always believed he was in yours." Growing up, Lucas had always been seen as the smarter one, the one who went to university, who did something important and secret during the war, who made a name for himself in Toronto, while Jed had stayed on the island and farmed, at least until Louisa had returned and he'd agreed to move to Vermont with her. "Why did you feel that way?"

He shrugged, giving a raggedy sigh. "Where should I start? Because Jed knew how to farm while I knew books, I suppose. Pa was never one for book learning—that was Mother's domain. When she died..." He fell silent for a moment. "Jed stayed while I went to university; Jed fought properly, had a missing arm to show for it, while I did something I couldn't even talk about and came back without a scratch. Even worse, I left for the bright lights of the city while Jed stayed, faithful and true, and worked the farm." He gave her a sorrowfully knowing look. "Even you thought that, Ellen, back in the day."

"Only because I was so stupid!" she exclaimed. "If I'd had any sense at all, I would have realized you were sending money back to help your family." And had been doing without notice or acclaim for over a year before Ellen had discovered the truth. She could hardly believe that her misapprehension still stung him, all these years later, and yet she saw that it did. "Lucas, you were never in Jed's shadow, not in my eyes."

"Wasn't I?" he asked sadly, and she couldn't help but stiffen, for while they'd both always known she'd believed herself in love with Jed first, they'd never truly talked about it and Ellen hadn't thought it really mattered.

"No, you weren't," she said fiercely. "*Ever.* What I felt for Jed all those years ago... why, I was no more than a child! It was puppy love, girlish infatuation, nothing more. Nothing like what I feel for you." She pressed her cheek against his shoulder. "You must believe me."

"I do believe you," he said tiredly. "And maybe these are all just excuses. It was my pride—my recklessness—my failure that got us into this mess. It doesn't really matter the reason."

"It was the failure of the stock market," Ellen reminded him. "You did not single-handedly cause the economic collapse of the entire world."

"If I hadn't invested so much money—"

"Would it really have made much difference? You lost your job because you obeyed your superiors. We would have lost our house anyway. Everyone's lost money, Lucas. So many have lost their houses, and more besides. We're the lucky ones, really." She was silent for a moment, struggling to put into words how she felt. "Maybe you were a bit reckless," she conceded slowly. "And I daresay your head was turned by ambition. I felt that even before any doom and gloom about the stocks began. But what of it? We all have our foibles, our failures, our mistakes and regrets. I know I do. And I wouldn't be much of a wife if I loved you when you were rich but not when you were poor, or more when you were successful and flying high than when you'd fallen low." Another pause as she gathered her words, her courage. She felt Lucas listening keenly, even though he didn't speak. "And you wouldn't be much of a husband, if you didn't learn from those mistakes and failures, as we all must do. Yes, we've fallen low, we've fallen hard. But we're still here, we can get up again. Together, as I've always wanted."

Another silence; she waited for him to speak, but when he didn't, she went ahead anyway. "If we have to leave the island, then we can leave the island. If you want to move to Chicago or Los Angeles, we can do that, too. Heaven knows I feel as if I've been around the world twice already! I don't mind having a bit more of an adventure. Because the world changes and we have to change with it, at least a little. But whatever we do, let's do it together. Talking it through and making plans and sharing dreams. That's what I want, Lucas. That's what I've always wanted with you. I love you," she finished, her voice choking a little on the words.

Still Lucas didn't reply, and Ellen's heart gave an unpleasant little flip. Had anything she said made any difference at all? Then he turned his head, pressing his cheek against her hand, his eyes closed. A tear slipped silently down his cheek, and with one hand he fumbled for her other, lacing his fingers tightly through hers. Ellen let out a sound that was half laugh, half sob, as she sank to the ground, pressed against him. It was going to be all right, she realized. It was going to be hard, yes, she was quite sure about that, but it was going to be all right.

CHAPTER TWENTY-SIX

"Ellen, come quick!"

Ellen turned from the stove where she'd been stirring a great big pot of bubbling, boiling raspberry jam. Caro stood in the doorway, one hand pressed to her side as she gasped for air. She must have run all the way from her house; it was a good half-mile.

"Caro, what's happened?"

"It's little Tommy Edwards. He was playing with my Jackie and he fell out of a tree. I'm pretty sure his arm is broken."

"Broken!" Ellen stared at her in dismay. "But what can I do about it?"

"You're a nurse, aren't you? You've set a bone before, I reckon."

Briefly, Ellen's mind flashed back to her days at Royaumont during the war, and then at the field hospital on the front, Villers-Cotterêts. Yes, she'd set a bone, but only when a doctor hadn't been available, and she'd had to do it. "It's been years," she protested. "I wouldn't know how now, I'm sure. I've forgotten—"

"There's no doctor on the island," Caro said grimly. "And there hasn't been since December. Dr. Evans just upped and left, because no one had any money to pay him. You're the next best thing, Ellen."

"Surely not!" They'd been on the island for two months now,

and Ellen's medical services had never been needed. She hadn't even known the doctor had gone, although considering how many others had, she wasn't surprised.

"I'm telling you, you are," Caro said in exasperation. "Now are you going to come or aren't you?"

With little choice, Ellen took the pot of bubbling jam off the stove, hoping it wouldn't set before she could put it into jars, and hurried after Caro, back towards the Wilson farmhouse, racking her brains to remember just how to set a bone.

Tommy Edwards was sat at Caro's kitchen table, sweaty and pale-faced as he cradled his arm which Ellen could see right away was indeed broken. To her relief and some surprise, she found her old nurse's training kicking in, and a calm settled over her.

"Well, then," she said briskly. "Let's see about your arm." Fortunately, Ellen could see it was a clean fracture, and after washing her hands and telling poor Tommy to be brave, she was able to align the bones and then bandage it tightly, splinting it with a piece of wood Caro had found for the purpose. "It'll be no more climbing trees for you, at least for a little while. Six weeks with the splint on," she told Tommy's mother, who had shown up just as Ellen had been bandaging his arm, "and change the bandages every three days. If you need me to do it, I can."

Tommy's mother nodded gratefully, and then took him off with a scolding and a clip on the ear.

Ellen turned to Caro with a laugh. "I imagine he's regretting his treetop adventure now, never mind the broken arm!"

"You were good at that," Caro told her seriously. "Better than Dr. Evans, if I'm to tell the truth. He was always a bit gruff."

"I'm glad I was able to help."

"And you could help some more. We don't have a doctor but we could make do with a nurse."

"What!" Ellen shook her head, shocked and instantly dismissive. "You can't mean me, surely—"

"I do mean you," Caro stated baldly. "Why shouldn't I?"

Ellen stared at her, incredulous. "I didn't even complete my training."

Caro shrugged, unmoved. "You did four years in wartime. I'd say that beats any traditional hospital training you might have missed."

"But... surely people want a proper doctor?"

"They'll take what they can get. If you put out your shingle, you'd have patients. Now, they couldn't pay you, of course, not properly. A chicken here, a string of trout there, a can of nails... it would be that kind of thing."

Ellen let out a skeptical laugh. "I can't believe you're saying this!"

Caro thrust out her chin. "Why not? 'Make do and mend' and all that. You're here, and I don't see a trained doctor anywhere nearby."

"Perhaps, but..."

"You *are* going to stay on the island, aren't you?"

Ellen was silent for a moment, considering. The last two months had been hard, just as she'd expected, but they'd been good, too. In many ways they'd been wonderful. A few days after she'd confronted Lucas on the beach, Jack Wilson had shown up with a handful of island farmers and they'd all gone to work together on the roof of the barn. Lucas had been both grateful and humbled by all the help, and a few days later he'd gone to the Taylors' farm to help with the plowing. That was the sort of place the island was, and always had been.

Lucas had in fact returned from the Taylors' with a newly formed determination of his own. "So many of the farmers around here have been overlooked," he'd told her, his forehead furrowed with distress. "The government forgets about them in favor of the big, commercial outfits, and the banks who took their hard-earned money for investments no longer care. They need a voice. Someone to represent them, speak for them, both to business and parliament. Frank Taylor lost all his money to an investment that went bust, and the bank won't even talk to him. It's not right."

Ellen's heart had leapt even as she'd kept her voice casual. "And do you think you might be that voice?"

Lucas had looked shocked by the suggestion, but then thoughtful. "I have the training," he'd admitted grudgingly. "But there's no money in it, of course."

"I don't care about that," Ellen had replied, and she meant it. Somehow they'd get by, just like all the other islanders who had chosen to stay. Neighbors who helped out, scraping a living, making do with secondhand or not at all, whatever it took, she knew they could manage... if they stayed.

Lucas had agreed to give it the summer, but Ellen had no idea what the autumn would bring. A year ago she'd been so sure their future in New York would be bright and shining; she could never have predicted what had come to pass. Now she recognized her ignorance, but what she did know was that now, more than ever, she wanted to stay... and now, more than ever, she'd be willing to leave.

It was a strange tension, the push and pull of desire and loyalty, and yet in the midst of it, as Lucas had planted potatoes and corn and Ellen had weeded the garden and picked raspberries, she'd felt at peace. They were making a life here, even if it was only a temporary one.

"Well?" Caro demanded now, startling Ellen out of her thoughts.

"Caro, I need to think about it," she protested with a little laugh. "And I'll need to talk to Lucas, of course."

"Well, I'll make some inquiries on your behalf. We can see if you can have Dr. Evans' premises in Stella—his office is empty, and I think he left some equipment, as well. There will be a parish meeting. We can discuss it then."

"Goodness," Ellen said faintly. She could still hardly believe Caro was serious, and yet she felt a surprising tug of interest, even longing. To be useful again, and in such a way...

· · ·

Ellen kept thinking about the proposition as the summer days stretched out, long and golden. She, Rosie, and Jamie picked raspberries until their fingers were stained red, and Ellen made batch after batch of jam as well as several pies bursting with fruit. The garden was bursting with vegetables—fat, red tomatoes, zucchinis nearly the size of baseball bats, yellow and green beans dangling from their leafy plants, an abundance from the earth.

Ellen canned as much as she could, and they ate from the bounty every night, supplemented by potatoes from the field, and the occasional bit of meat Lucas was able to procure.

She'd also started sketching again; it seemed a long time ago she'd done her Pasadena sketches which had been included in the Scripps College exhibition, although she'd never got to see it. Now she enjoyed capturing the little moments of island life that she'd always hold dear—the sun setting over the lake, the children running through the long grass. Life lived simply and to the full.

For it *was* a good life, if, to some, a seemingly meager one. Come winter, if they stayed, she knew it would be hard. The little farmhouse would be freezing, and food would surely become scarce. She didn't think she was deluding herself on that score, but she still wanted to stay. But did Lucas? She had yet to ask him, wanting to give him time to think, to adjust, to decide... and to let him remember that he loved the island just about as much as he did.

In August, Lucas received a letter from the newly elected MP for Prince Edward—Lennox, John Aaron Weese. Lucas had written to him about the farmers' plight soon after the general election in late July, and Weese had written back with encouraging alacrity.

"He's concerned about the farmers of smallholdings," he told Ellen after he'd read the letter, a spark of excitement in his eyes that she hadn't seen in a long while. "He asked me to meet him in Kingston to discuss what can be done for them in terms of legal aid."

"Oh, Lucas!" Ellen was thrilled on his behalf. "What do you think he will say?"

"I don't know, frankly," he replied. "He might just shake my hand and tell me there's nothing to be done. That's how politicians often are, all they want is a nice photo in the newspaper. But if he's different, perhaps he'll actually want to *do* something. I certainly hope so, for all our sakes."

"So do I," Ellen replied fervently. And especially for Lucas's sake, for she thought this might be just the sort of boost he needed.

She saw him off to the ferry the second week of August, kissing his cheek and grateful for the new spring in his step.

"When will Daddy come back, Mama?" Rosie asked, a wrinkle in her brow. Both she and Jamie had reveled in Lucas's increased attention and care over the last few months, along with the freedom island life had given them.

Ellen swept her up in a hug. "Oh, very soon, my darling, very soon! In just a few days, in fact."

She stopped by the post office in Stella on the way back home to pick up any mail, pleased to see letters from both Gracie and Sarah. Humming under her breath, she walked along Front Road with Rosie at her side. It was three miles back to the farmhouse, but after several months of island living, neither mother nor daughter thought much of such a walk, especially on such a sunny day, with a fresh breeze blowing off the lake.

As they walked, Rosie slipped her hand in hers. "We won't have to leave here, will we?" she asked, a note in her voice that was both pleading and hopeful.

Ellen stopped walking to gaze down tenderly at her daughter's anxious face. "Do you like it here on the island, Rosie?" she asked.

"Yes, oh yes, better than anywhere. And so does Jamie, I know. He told me."

Ellen smiled at that. Her son finally had the freedom he craved, spending most of his days exploring the island with his Wilson cousins as well as other island children, getting into all sorts of scrapes any self-respecting almost-seven-year-old would want, but at least suffering no broken bones—so far. And to think her daughter, only eight years old, had experienced so much—the highs and lows of life in New York, living all the way out in California and even briefly appearing in a movie, and now the simple island life that she, like Ellen herself, preferred.

"So do I," she told Rosie conspiratorially. "But as to whether we'll stay..." She thought of Lucas traveling to Kingston, the unvoiced hopes and possibility of a position in law. Would it make a difference? Would it make him want to stay? She hoped so. She was starting to believe it might. "We'll see, Rosie. We'll see."

Two days later, while Ellen was sitting in the kitchen, rereading Gracie's letter for the third time, Lucas popped his head through the back doorway.

"What are you smiling about?" he asked as, startled, Ellen put a hand to her heart.

"Gracie's letter. I didn't expect you back till evening!"

"I took an earlier train. I found I wanted to be back here, somehow." He pulled her up from the table and into his arms, kissing her thoroughly before Ellen pulled back, laughing.

"I like the sound of that," she told him.

"Walk with me?" Lucas asked, his laughing look dropping as he turned serious, and Ellen's heart did a painful little flip-flop. He clearly had something to tell her, but what was it? The children were up at Caro's, as they often were, so all Ellen had to do was take off her apron and hang it on the hook by the door before she headed outside with Lucas.

The sun was shining, the birch leaves tinged with yellow even though it was only mid-August. Autumn was already on the wing, but the air as they walked towards the shore was sun-kissed and balmy.

"Well?" Ellen asked after they'd strolled in silence for a few moments. "Are you going to tell me what happened in Kingston?"

"Do you remember when we wandered along the shore to Kerr Bay, all those years ago?" Lucas asked as he swung her hand in his.

"Yes, of course I do," Ellen answered. She'd told him about the offer she'd had to move to New York to take up a position as an art teacher, and he'd encouraged her to accept, even though she'd been reluctant. He'd confessed the feelings of inadequacy he'd felt compared to Jed—something she'd forgotten, in all the intervening years, but had cause to remember more recently. When he'd said goodbye, smiling and squeezing her hands, she'd felt a loss, and she hadn't understood why.

The seeds of their lives had been planted on that afternoon, Ellen thought, or perhaps even before, and they'd come to fruition over the years, played out in a motley variety of scenes. And yet here they were, walking the north shore once again, the wind blowing over them as Lucas looked for a smooth, flat stone to skip.

"I was so in love with you," he told her with a smile. "It just about tore me in two back then to wish you well and encourage you to move to New York."

"And I thought you were giving me a push!"

"I'd determined to act as your friend, and only your friend."

"Which is why I felt so disappointed, when you said goodbye. I just didn't realize it at the time."

"I'm glad you did realize it, eventually," Lucas told her. He paused, his gaze once again on the lake. "I told you then about how I felt about being compared to Jed, although, as I recall, I tried to make light of it."

"I don't think I ever realized how sorely it tried you," Ellen said quietly. "I'm sorry for that."

He shook his head, squinting as he looked out over the bay. "So much has happened since then. We've come so far, and yet here we are, right back where we started."

Ellen caught her breath, and then let it out slowly. "And is that a good thing?" she asked cautiously. "Or a bad one?"

"I don't always know," Lucas admitted. "I had such dreams,

once. It's hard to let them go." He skipped a stone, and they both watched it leap nimbly over the water—one, two, three times.

"It is hard," Ellen agreed. "Even if you make new ones."

Lucas nodded slowly. She waited, knowing not to rush. Not to press. "John Aaron Weese offered me a job," he told her after a moment. "It wouldn't pay much, and it would only be part-time. It's to set up a legal charitable society for farmers in eastern Ontario, with an office in Kingston." His mouth twisted, but his eyes were full of wry humor. "A far cry from being partner of one of New York's best law firms."

"That's not a bad thing," Ellen said quietly.

"No," Lucas agreed, his voice just as quiet. "It's not."

They were both silent for a long moment as they gazed out at the lake, its placid surface burnished by the sun, like a golden mirror. "Caro has offered me a job as well," Ellen said finally. "If you can call it that. There's no doctor on the island and she's said I can set out my shingle as a nurse. Take over Dr. Evans' office in Stella, even."

Lucas's eyes widened. "Caro said this...?"

"She speaks for the islanders. They're going to hold a parish meeting and discuss it, so it's yet to be officially approved, but I suspect that's only a matter of time, as long as I'm willing. And, of course," she added quickly, "it won't last forever. A doctor will come at some point, when there's the money or the need."

"Or not," Lucas said soberly. "The world is changing. Small communities like this one might not last forever, especially as people move to the city for jobs."

Ellen nodded, knowing she could not resist the pull of the tides of time and fortune, even though part of her still wanted to. She was learning, at least a little, in that way. "But it's here now," she said. "And so are we." She paused. "Aren't we?"

Lucas took her hands in his. "You want to stay."

"Yes." Ellen spoke firmly as she searched his face. "But do you?"

He squeezed her hands as he let out a sigh. "I admit, it's been hard, and I'm sure you've known that. I haven't been the easiest man to live with, and for that I'm truly sorry."

"Lucas..."

"But the island is in my blood, if not as much as yours, then almost. And I want to do something with my life, something that helps people. What I did in New York wasn't that. I can see that now. It was about money and power."

"Well, we don't have either of those now," Ellen replied with a smile. She didn't mind, but Lucas knew that already.

"We don't," Lucas agreed, "and at this rate, we probably never will again. That's not nothing, you know—there are opportunities I would have wanted for Rosie, for Jamie, that I won't be able to give them now."

"But look at you, an island boy made good," Ellen replied. "It's possible, Lucas. Just about anything is."

"Maybe." He was silent, still holding her hands. As he looked at her, Ellen felt her heart lighten. Was he saying he wanted to stay...?

"Gracie wrote that she's expecting," she told him. "And Will has accepted a position at Queen's, in Kingston. Gracie wants to be close to Aunt Rose when she has her baby. Can you believe it? Such wonderful news, and it would be good to have more family nearby, if we did stay on the island."

"It would," Lucas agreed. He spoke soberly, but there was a glint in his eyes that made Ellen burst out,

"*Lucas!*"

He gathered her up in his arms, his cheek pressed to hers. "Shall we stay, my island girl?" he asked softly. "Stay here to make what fortune we can, and help those who need it?"

Ellen wrapped her arms around him. "Yes," she agreed fervently. "Yes, we shall."

"It might not be easy."

"I don't care."

He eased back to look down at her face. "Won't you miss our old life?" he asked quietly. "If just a little bit?"

"A little bit," Ellen allowed, for she could not deny that. "But I would still rather be here."

"So would I," Lucas said slowly. "And I do mean that, actually."

She smiled, relief and joy bursting in her heart. "I know you do."

She took her hand in his as they both gazed out at the lake, the sun sending its long, golden beams slanting over the water. A loon swooped down low over the lake, followed by another, and then rose in a graceful, dark vee of wings.

"A pair," Ellen exclaimed. "Isn't that considered good luck?"

"It is now," Lucas replied with a soft laugh, and her heart felt as if it were full to overflowing. As she looked out over the shimmering water, the sun sinking towards the horizon, Ellen knew there was nowhere else she'd rather be, standing here on the shore, hand in hand with the man she'd always loved.

It was all so perfectly peaceful, so heartrendingly beautiful, that she found it hard to imagine the breadlines and Hoovervilles that had sprung up over America, or worse yet, the specter of war that Will still insisted loomed, a shadow on the horizon that she couldn't bear to think about.

No, here on their island, there was only peace and beauty, hope and joy, and most of all, love, deep and abiding and true. All the things they'd fought for, and all they'd found.

With her hand in his, Ellen turned to walk back toward the farmhouse, and the new life they were making together, on the island they'd never truly left behind.

A LETTER FROM KATE

Dear reader,

I want to say a huge thank you for choosing to read *The Island We Left Behind*. If you enjoyed it, and want to keep up to date with all my latest releases, just sign up at the following link. Your email address will never be shared and you can unsubscribe at any time.

www.bookouture.com/kate-hewitt

I really thought my Amherst Island series was finished with the last book in the original trilogy, *Return to the Island*. But then I found myself thinking about what might have happened next, for Ellen and Lucas, as well as for Will Turner, and so this story was born! It's been so fun to continue Ellen's story through the years.

I hope you loved *The Island We Left Behind* and if you did I would be very grateful if you could write a review. I'd love to hear what you think, and it makes such a difference helping new readers to discover one of my books for the first time.

I love hearing from my readers—you can get in touch on my Facebook page, through Twitter, Goodreads or my website.

Thanks,

Kate

KEEP IN TOUCH WITH KATE

www.kate-hewitt.com

 facebook.com/KateHewittAuthor

twitter.com/author_kate

ACKNOWLEDGEMENTS

As with any book, I must first thank my fabulous editor, Isobel, who offers me such wonderful editorial support and encouragement. It is a true thrill that she has enjoyed Ellen's story as much as I have! I'd also like to thank the tireless team at Bookouture—Kim, Noelle, Sarah, Alex, and Mel in marketing and publicity; Alex, Saidah, Rhianna, Alba, Radhika, and Laura with editorial and audio; Richard and Peta with translations; and Debbie who designed such fabulous covers for the whole series.

Finally, I'd like to thank my mom, who gave me a love of Ellen's island life, although not on an actual island! I was fortunate enough to spend my childhood summers in the Canadian wilderness near Amherst Island—picking raspberries, swimming in the lake, and enjoying the brilliant sunsets and the lonely calls of the whippoorwill. My parents created a very special place in our family cottage, with many happy memories there that have inspired this story, and I will be forever grateful for them. I love you, Mom!

BOOKS BY KATE HEWITT

STANDALONE NOVELS
My Daughter's Mistake
Beyond the Olive Grove
The Edelweiss Sisters
The Girl from Berlin
When You Were Mine
Into the Darkest Day
A Hope for Emily
No Time to Say Goodbye
Not My Daughter
The Secrets We Keep
A Mother's Goodbye

The Other Mother
And Then He Fell
Rainy Day Sisters
Now and Then Friends
A Mother like Mine

AMHERST ISLAND SERIES
The Orphan's Island
Dreams of the Island
Return to the Island
The Island We Left Behind